MAGIC TREE HOUSE®

AFTERNOON ON THE AMAZON

MARY POPE OSBORNE'S
MAGIC TREE HOUSE®
AFTERNOON ON THE AMAZON

THE GRAPHIC NOVEL

ADAPTED BY
JENNY LAIRD

WITH ART BY
KELLY & NICHOLE MATTHEWS

A STEPPING STONE BOOK™
RANDOM HOUSE 🏠 NEW YORK

Text adapted by Jenny Laird

Visit us on the Web!

rhcbooks.com

MagicTreeHouse.com

Educators and librarians, for a variety of teaching tools, visit us at RHTeachersLibrarians.com

Library of Congress Cataloging-in-Publication Data is available upon request.
ISBN 978-0-593-48882-9 (pbk.) — ISBN 978-0-593-48883-6 (hardcover) —
ISBN 978-0-593-48884-3 (lib. bdg.) — ISBN 978-0-593-48885-0 (ebook)

The artists used Clip Studio Paint to create the illustrations for this book.

The text of this book is set in 13-point Cartoonist Hand Regular.

MANUFACTURED IN CHINA

10 9 8 7 6 5 4 3 2 1

First Graphic Novel Edition

This book has been officially leveled by using the F&P Text Level Gradient™ Leveling System.

For Troy Vidal, a great reader
—M.P.O.

For Will Osborne, faithful friend and protector of all
the world's creatures
—J.L.

For Tonka and Puma
—K.M. & N.M.

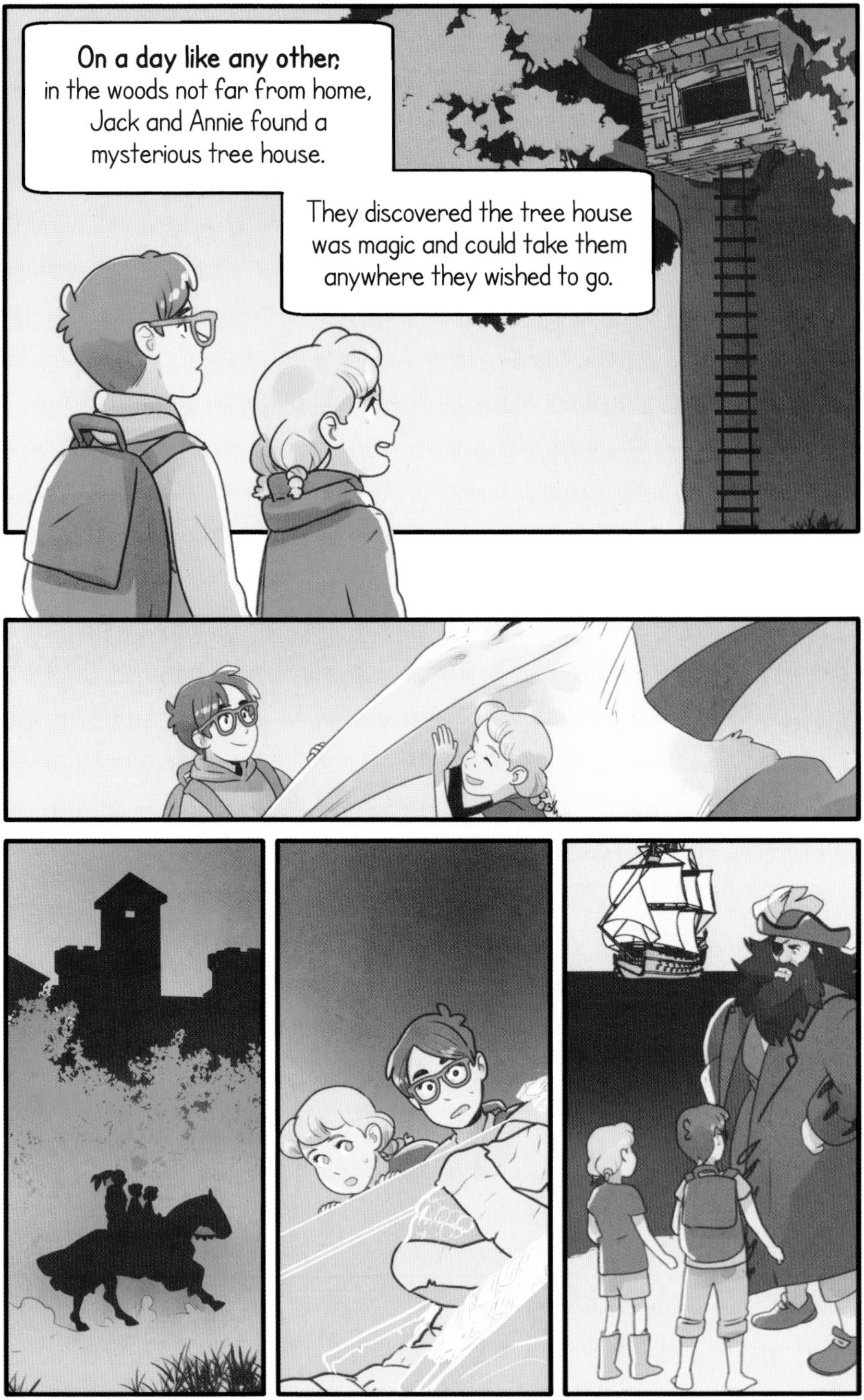
On a day like any other, in the woods not far from home, Jack and Annie found a mysterious tree house.
They discovered the tree house was magic and could take them anywhere they wished to go.

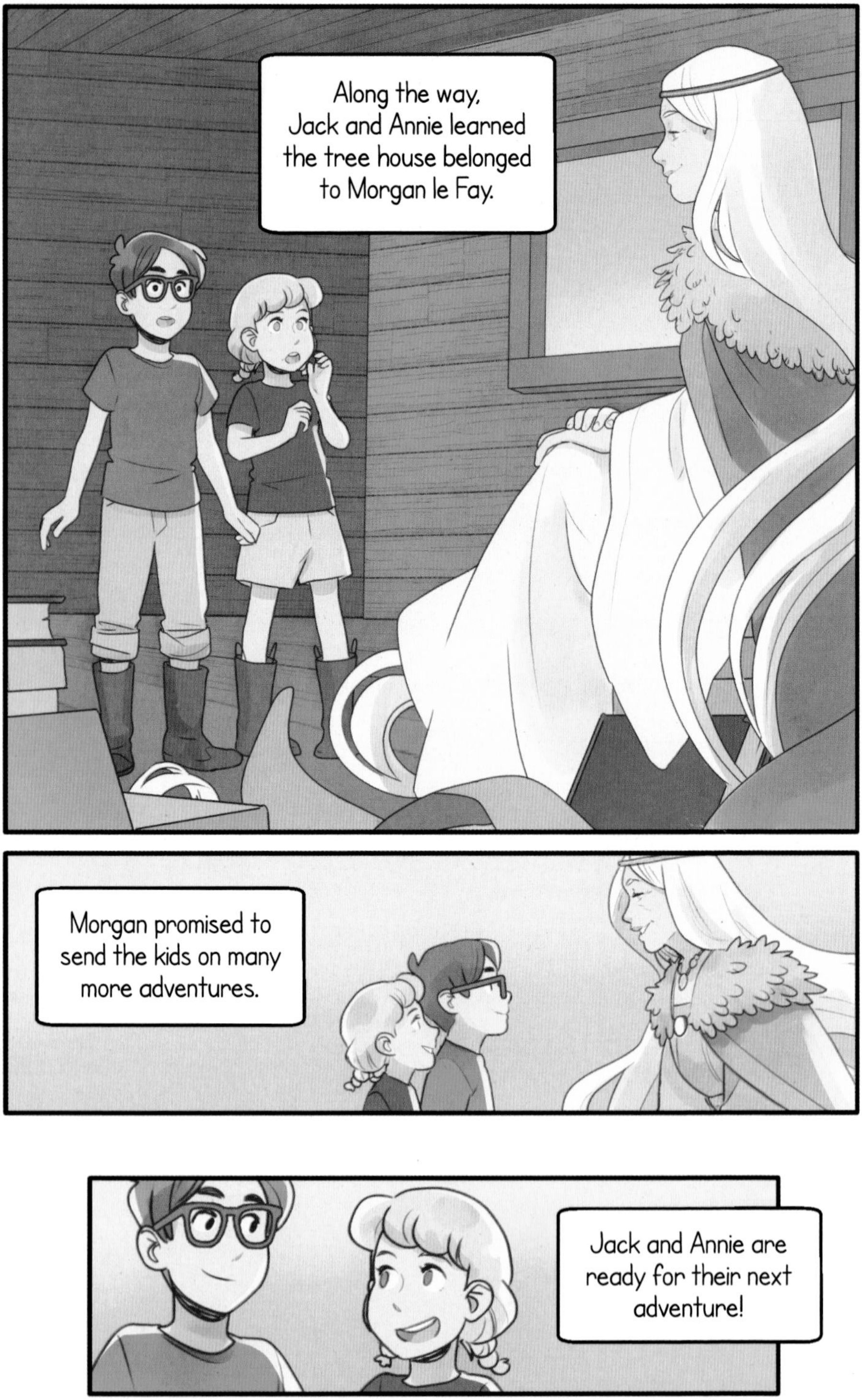
Along the way, Jack and Annie learned the tree house belonged to Morgan le Fay.
Morgan promised to send the kids on many more adventures.
Jack and Annie are ready for their next adventure!

CHAPTER ONE
Where's Peanut?

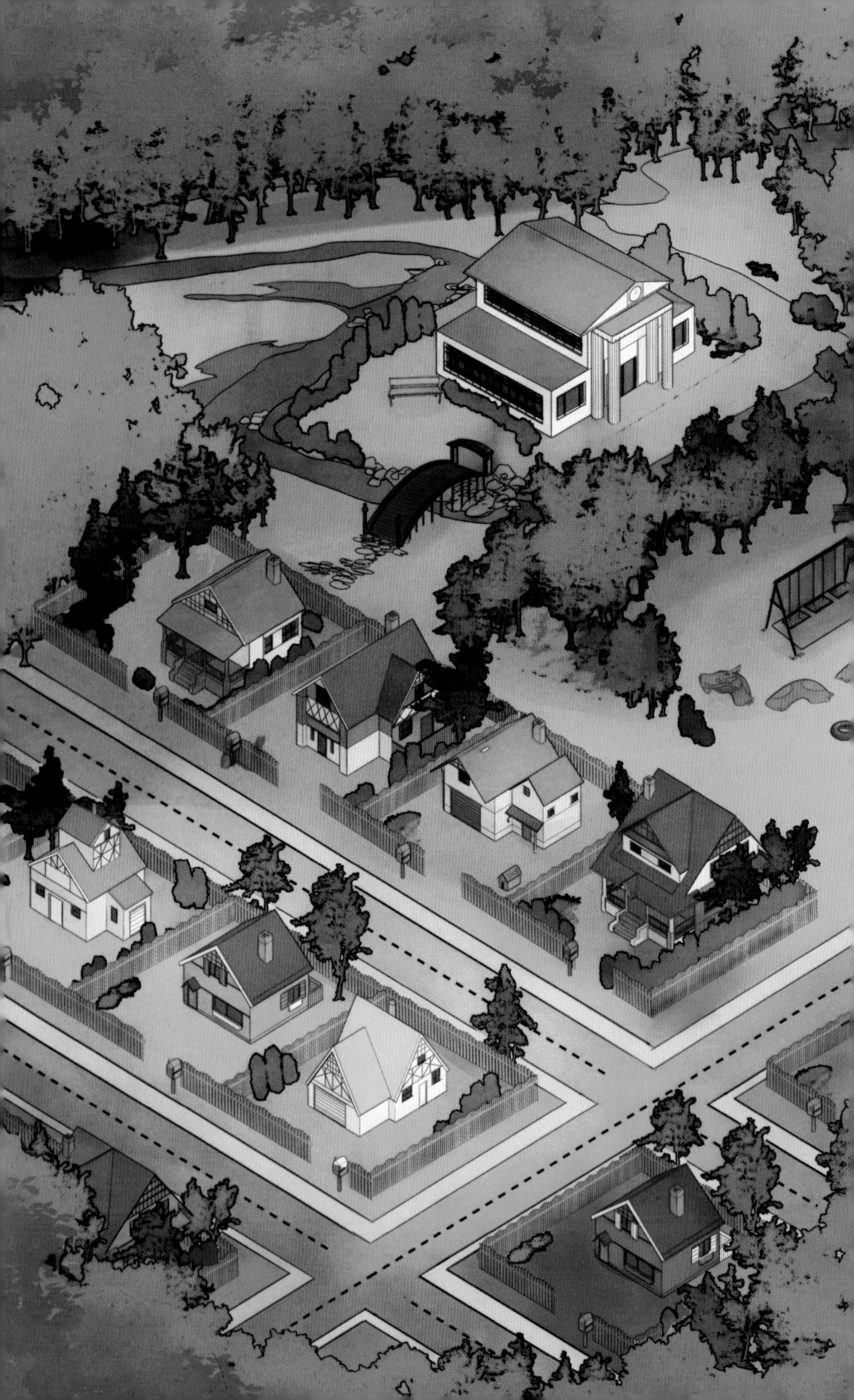

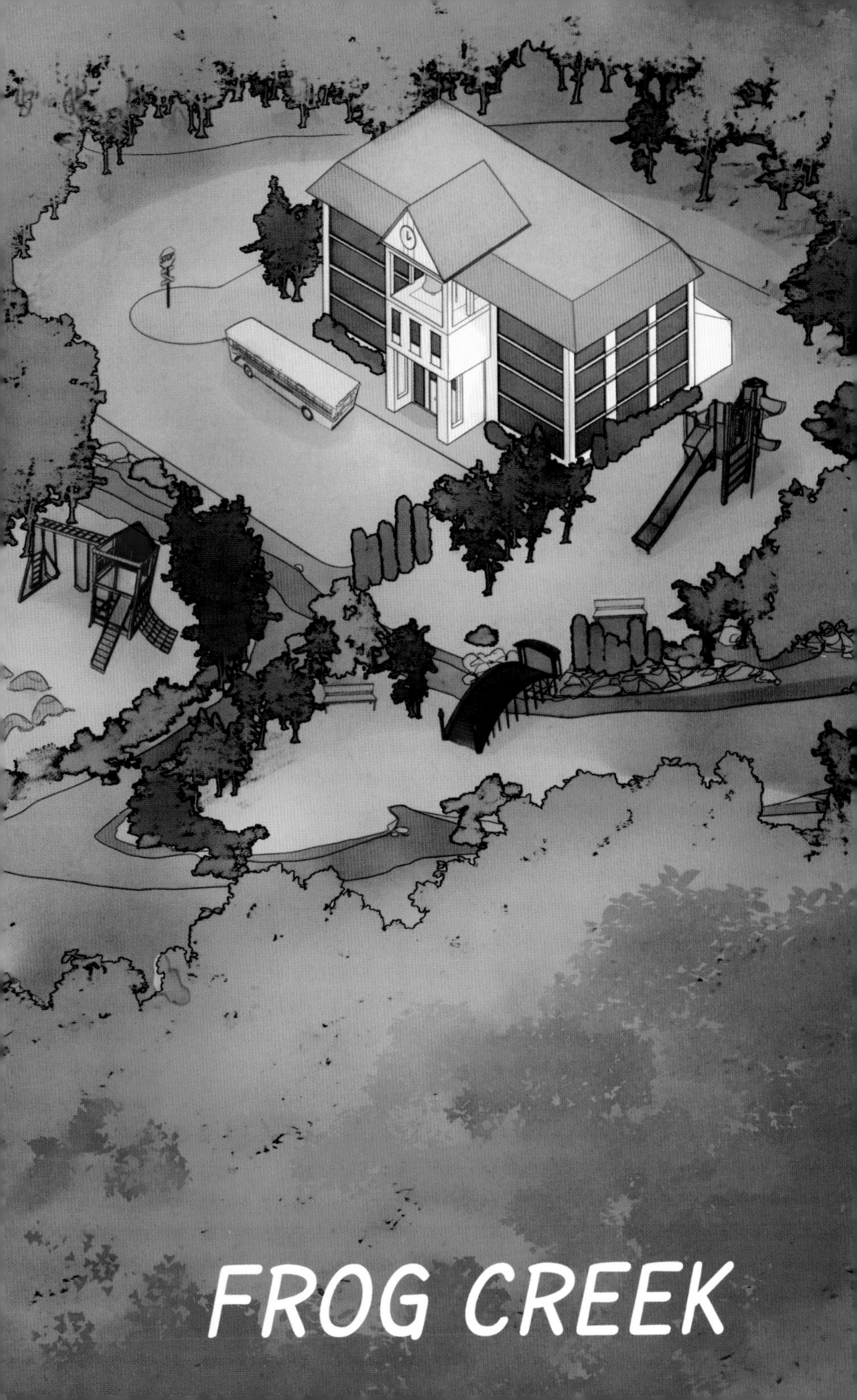
STOP
FROG CREEK

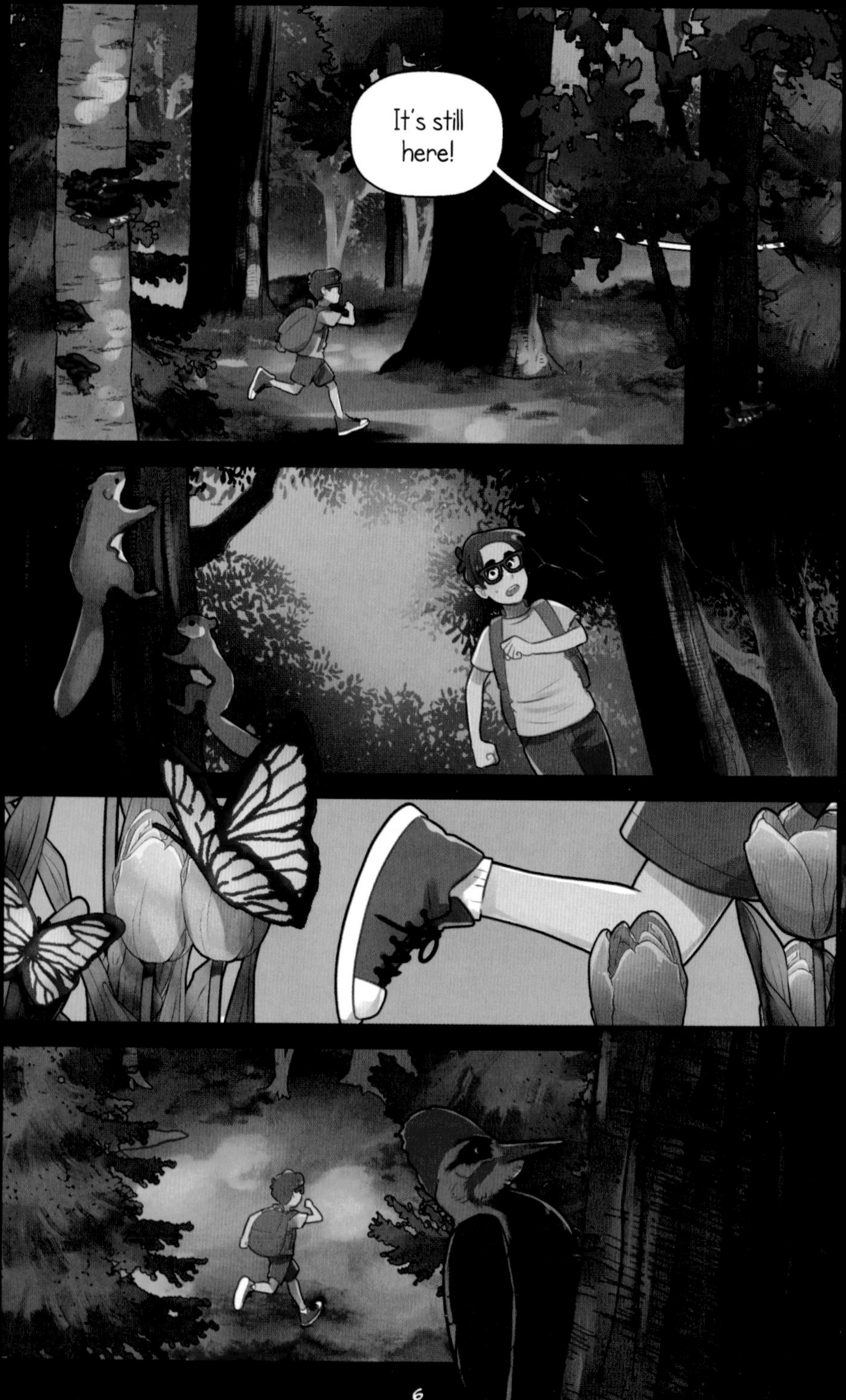
It's still here!

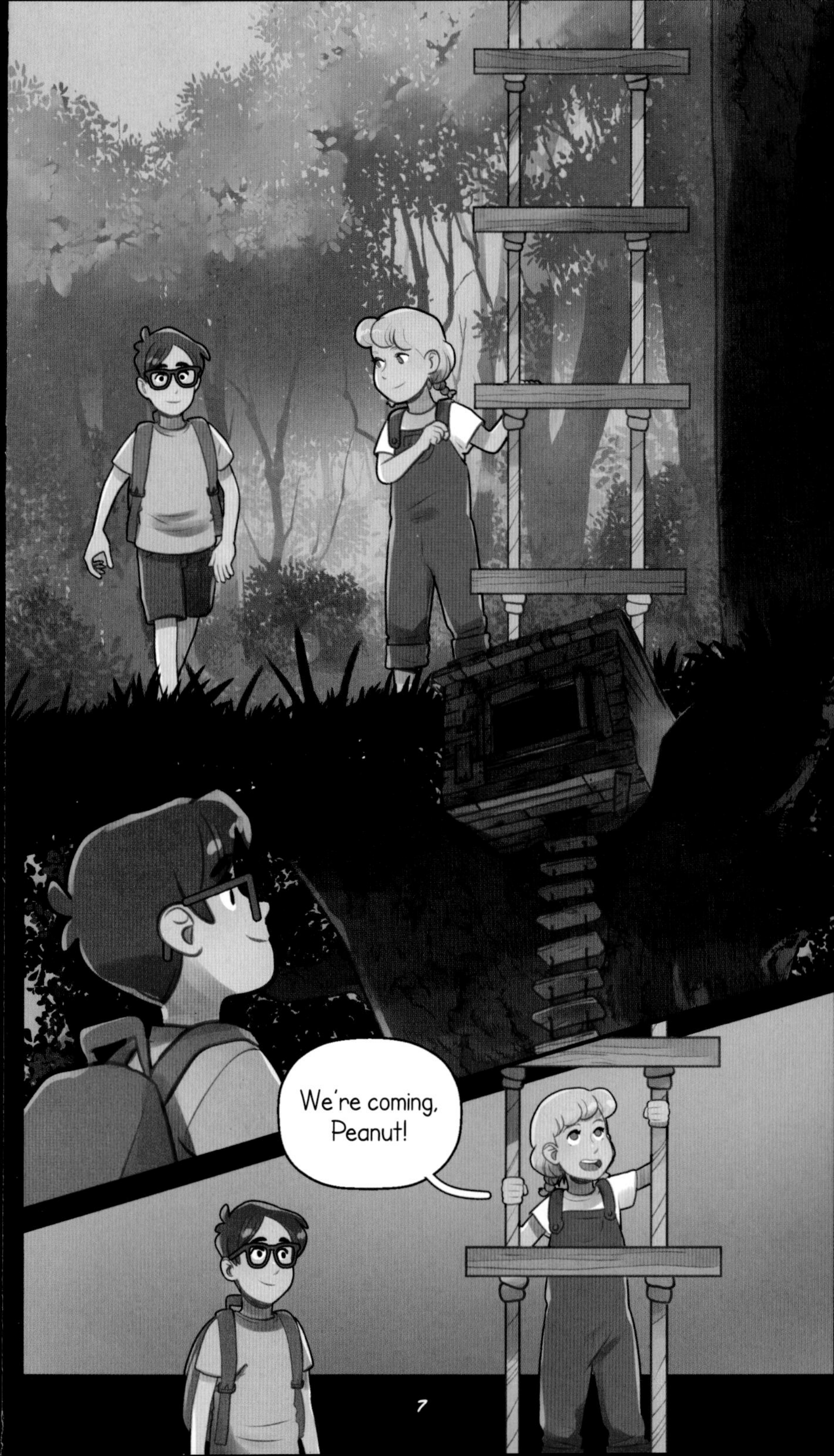
We're coming, Peanut!

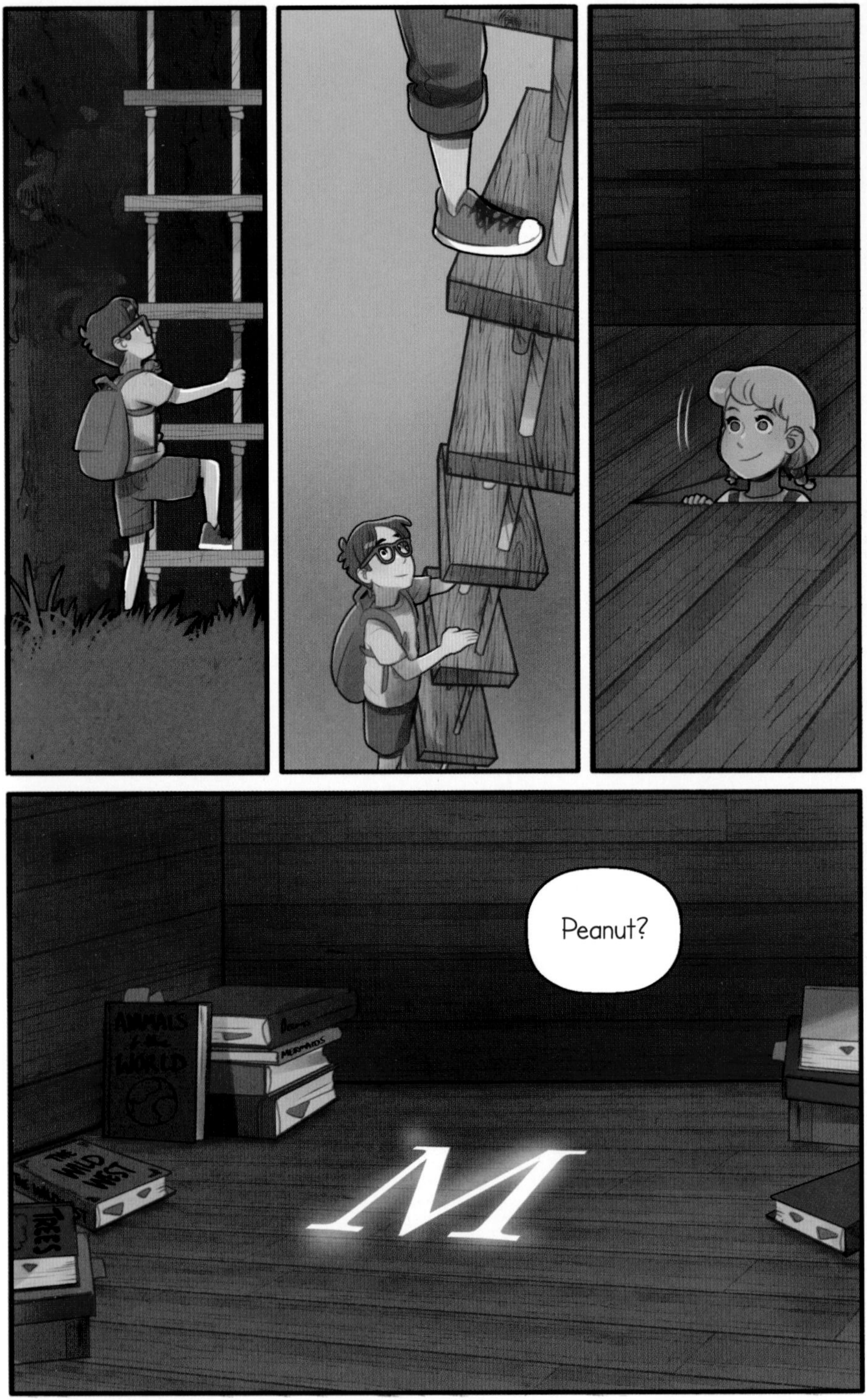
ANIMALS
WORLD
MERMAIDS
Peanut?
TREES
M

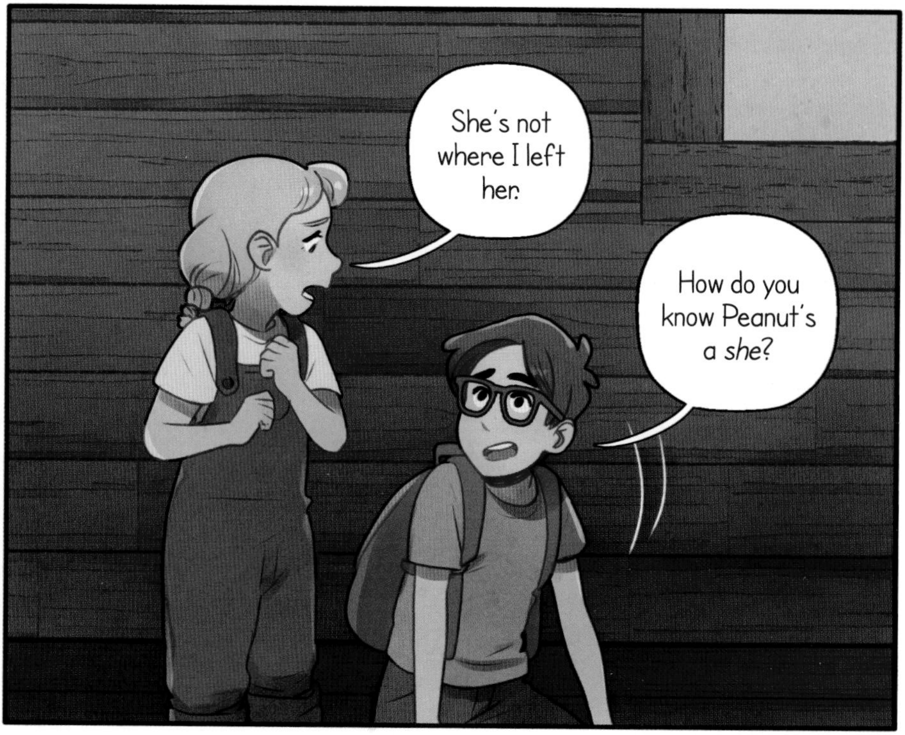
She's not where I left her.
How do you know Peanut's a *she*?

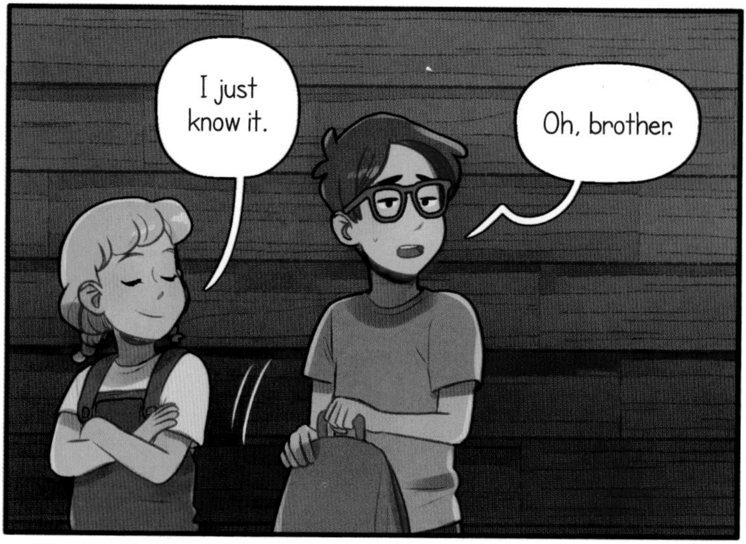
I just know it.
Oh, brother.

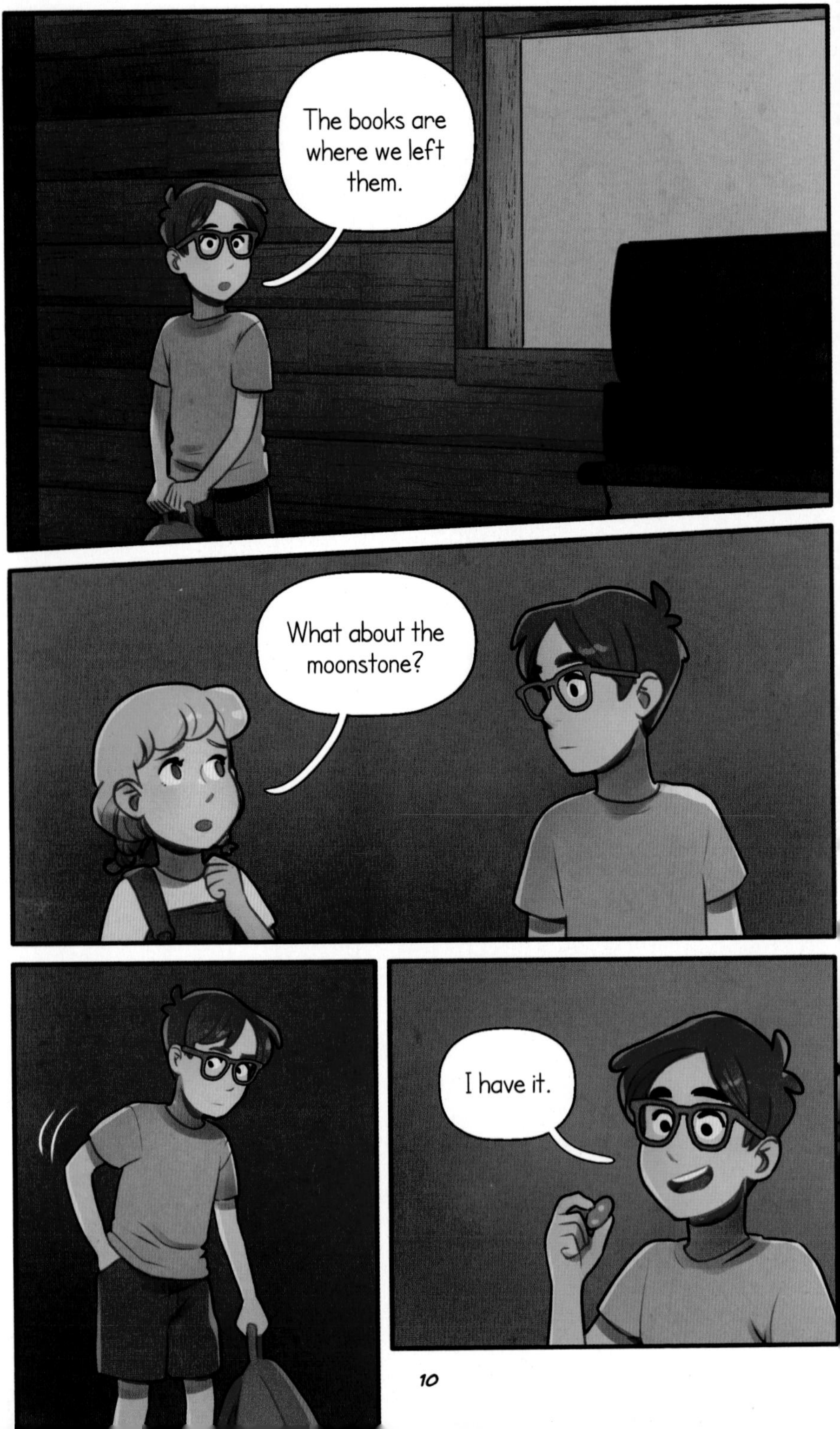
The books are where we left them.
What about the moonstone?
I have it.

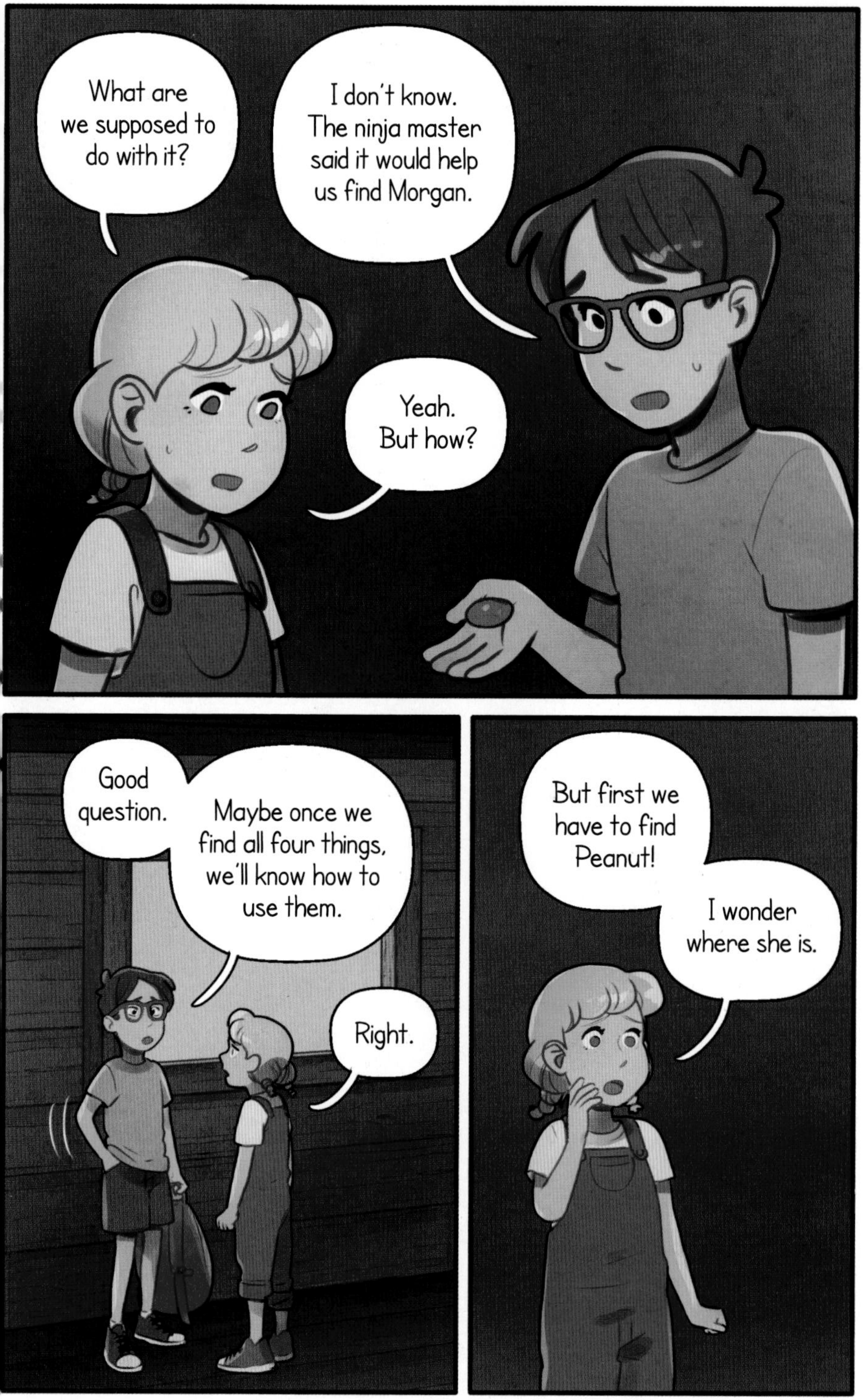
What are we supposed to do with it?
I don't know. The ninja master said it would help us find Morgan.
Yeah. But how?
Good question.
Maybe once we find all four things, we'll know how to use them.
Right.
But first we have to find Peanut!
I wonder where she is.

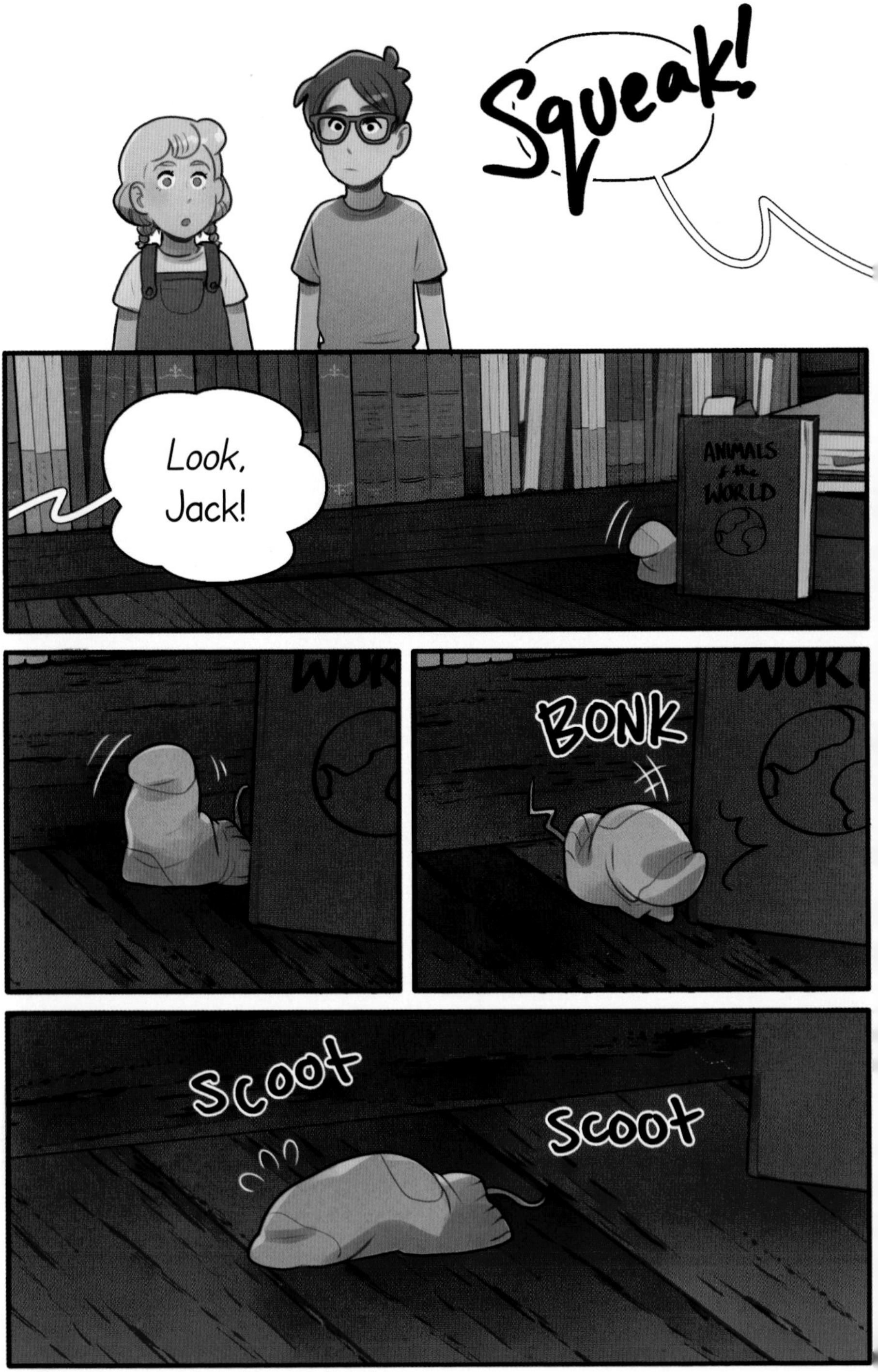
Squeak!
Look, Jack!
ANIMALS of the WORLD
BONK
Scoot
Scoot

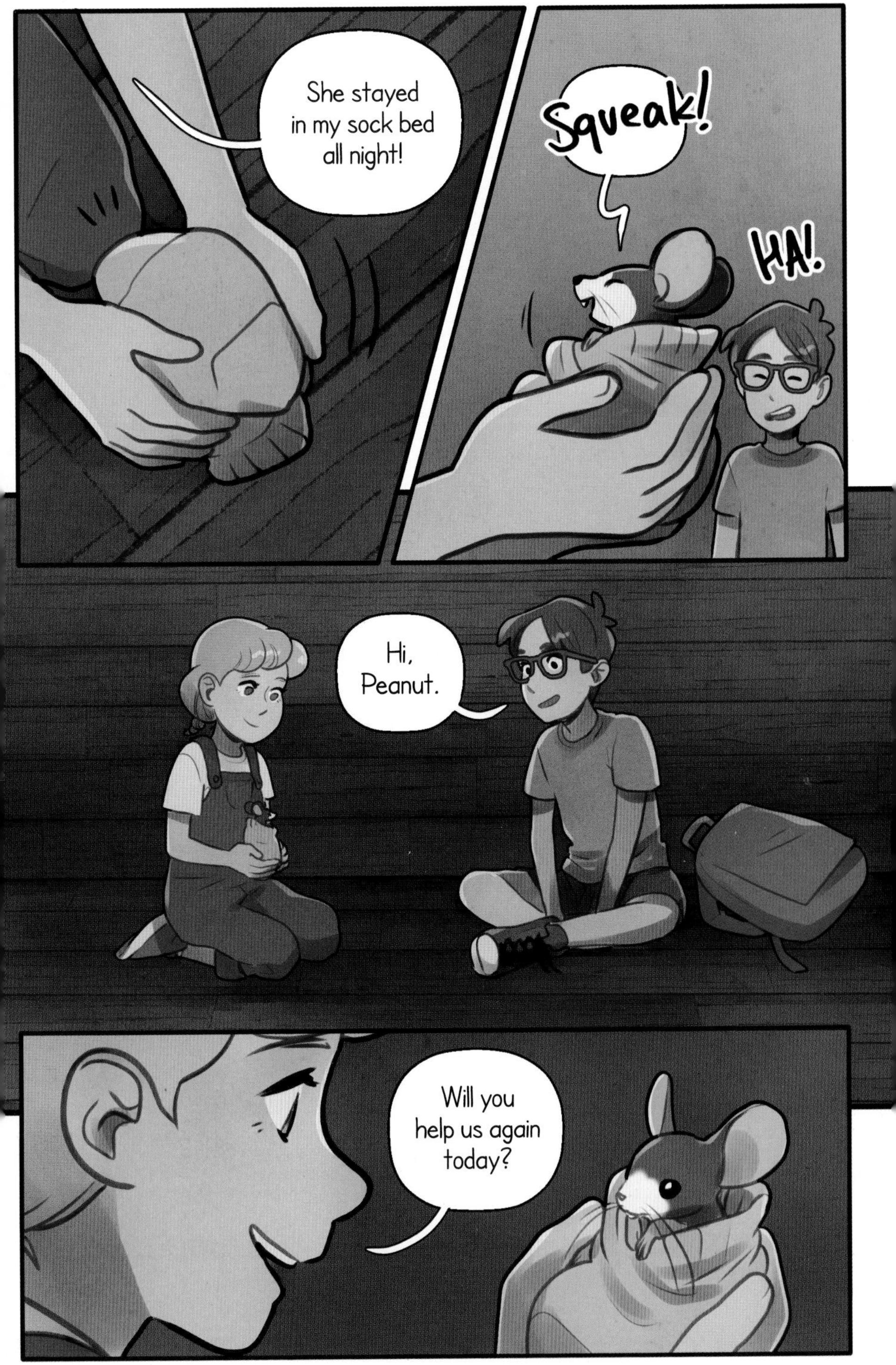
She stayed in my sock bed all night!
Squeak!
HA!
Hi, Peanut.
Will you help us again today?

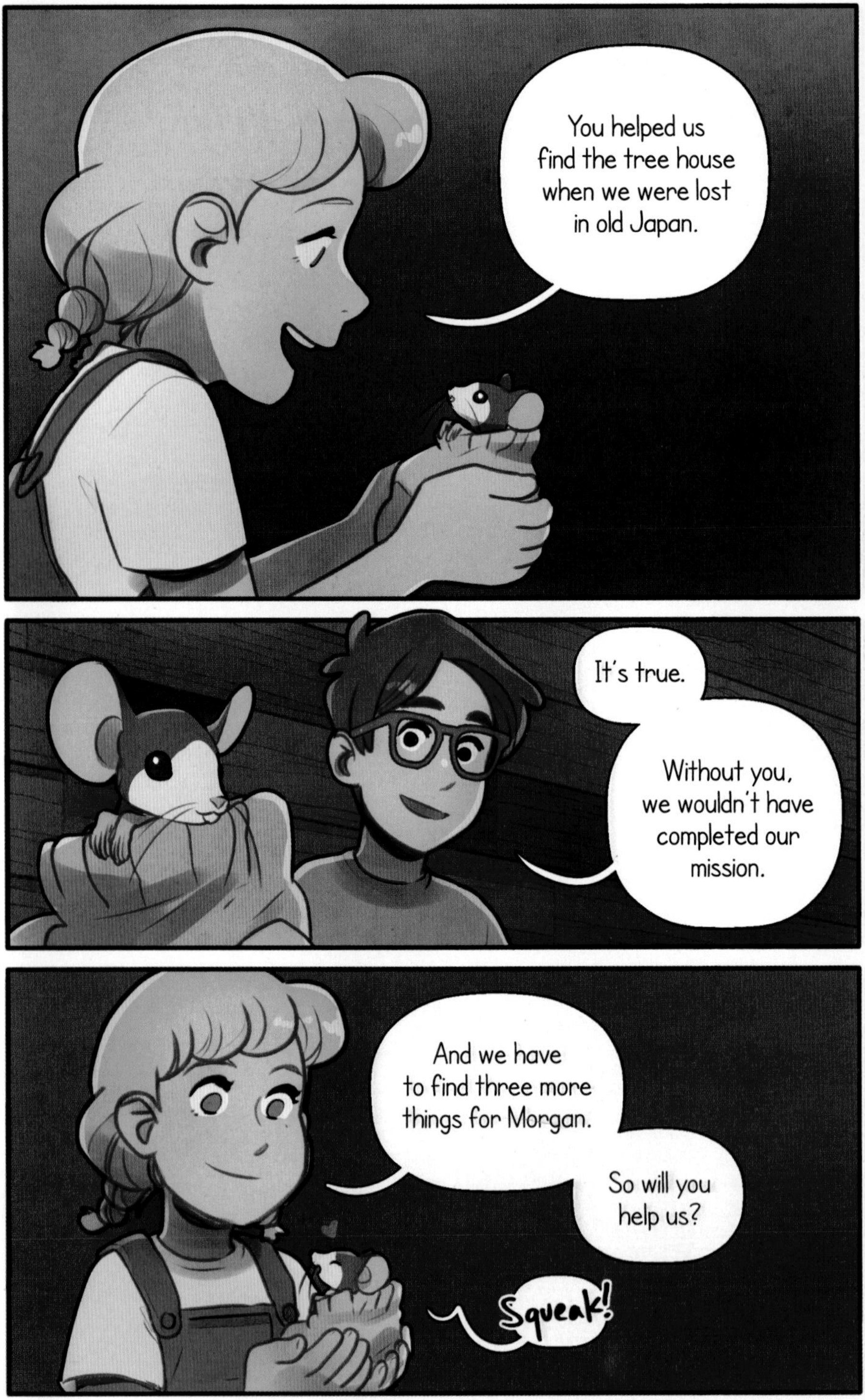
You helped us find the tree house when we were lost in old Japan.
It's true.
Without you, we wouldn't have completed our mission.
And we have to find three more things for Morgan.
So will you help us?
Squeak!

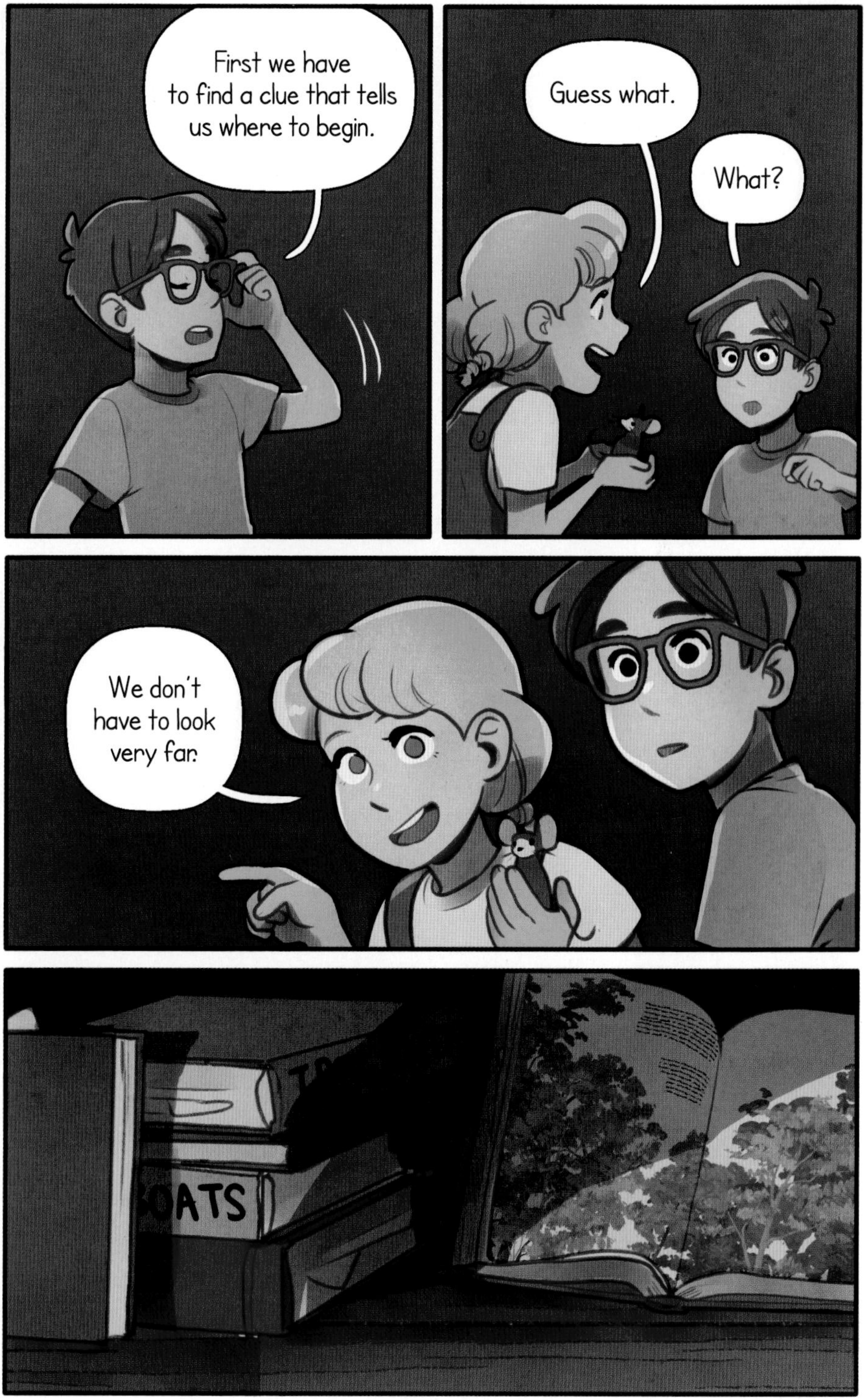
First we have to find a clue that tells us where to begin.
Guess what.
What?
We don't have to look very far.

CHAPTER TWO
Big Bugs

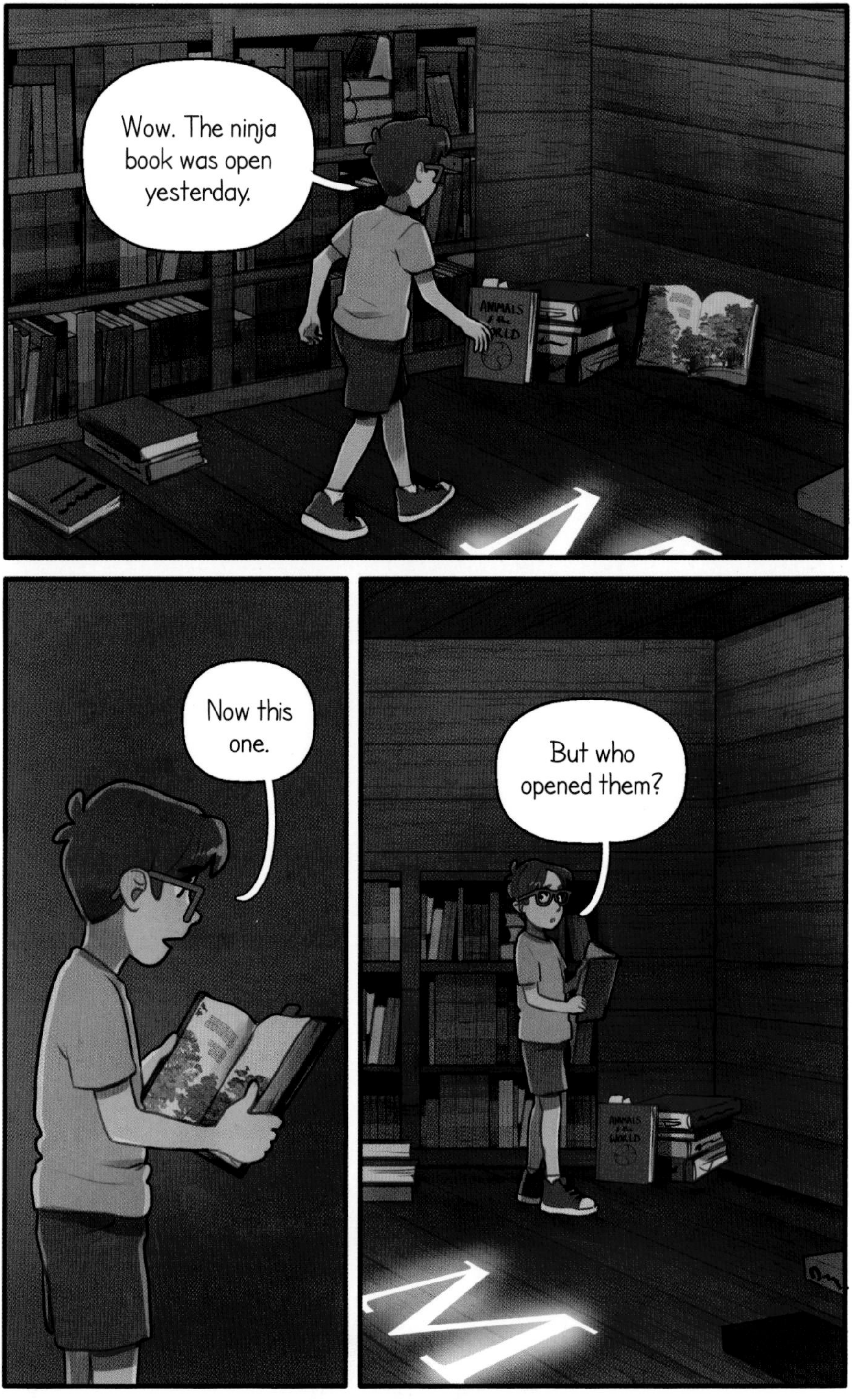
Wow. The ninja book was open yesterday.
ANIMALS of the WORLD
Now this one.
But who opened them?
ANIMALS of the WORLD

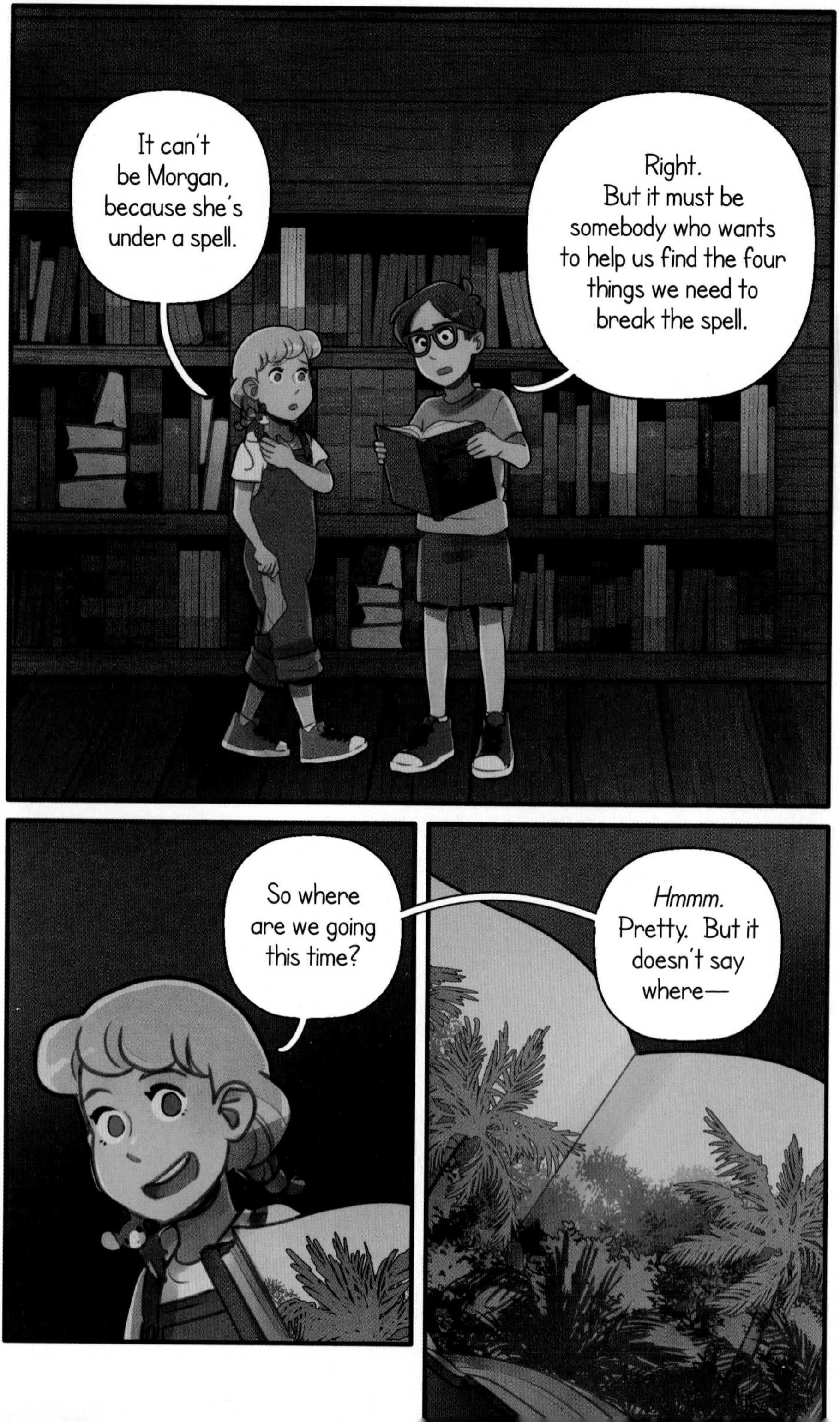
It can't be Morgan, because she's under a spell.
Right. But it must be somebody who wants to help us find the four things we need to break the spell.
So where are we going this time?
Hmmm. Pretty. But it doesn't say where—

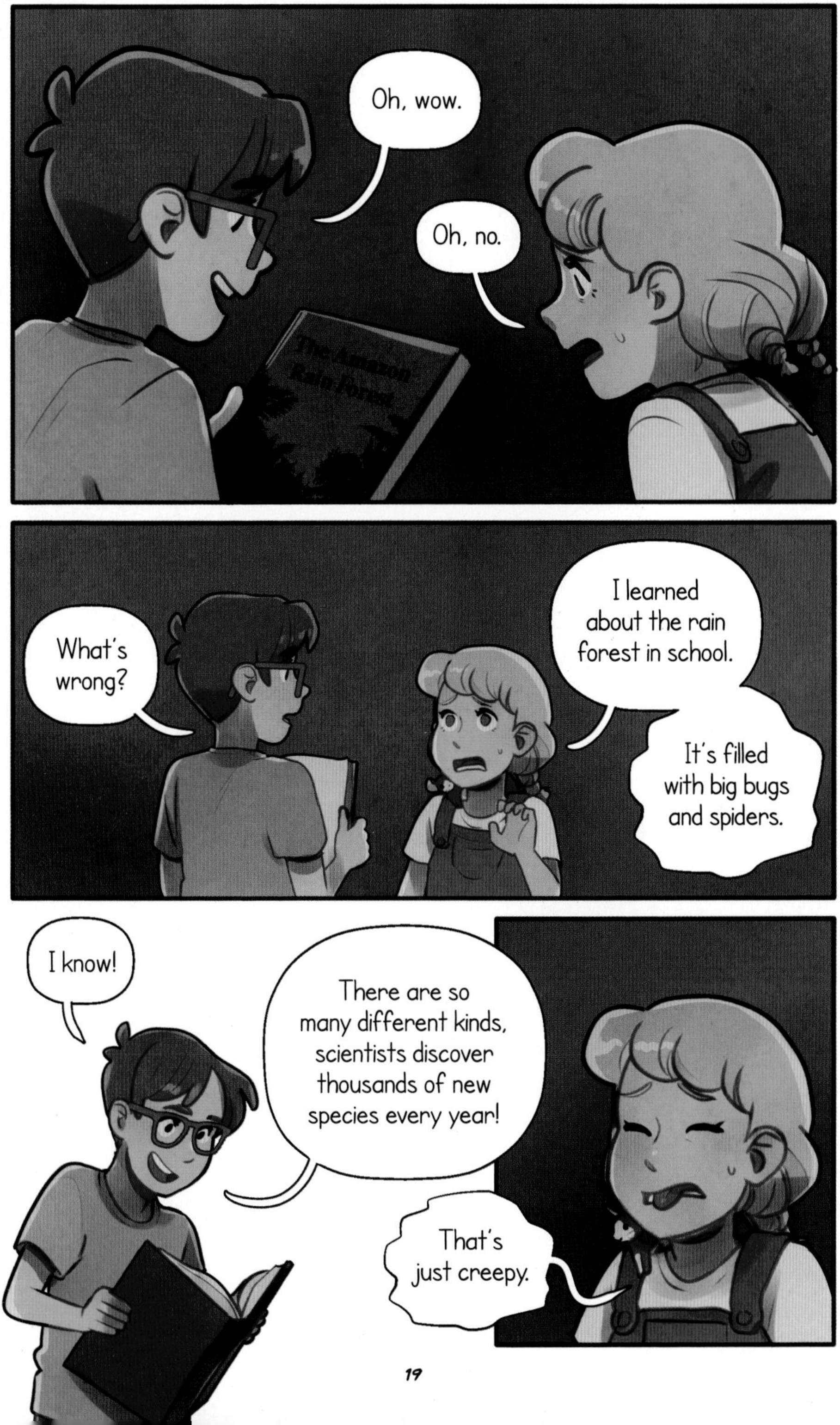
Oh, wow.
Oh, no.
The Amazon Rain Forest
What's wrong?
I learned about the rain forest in school.
It's filled with big bugs and spiders.
I know!
There are so many different kinds, scientists discover thousands of new species every year!
That's just creepy.

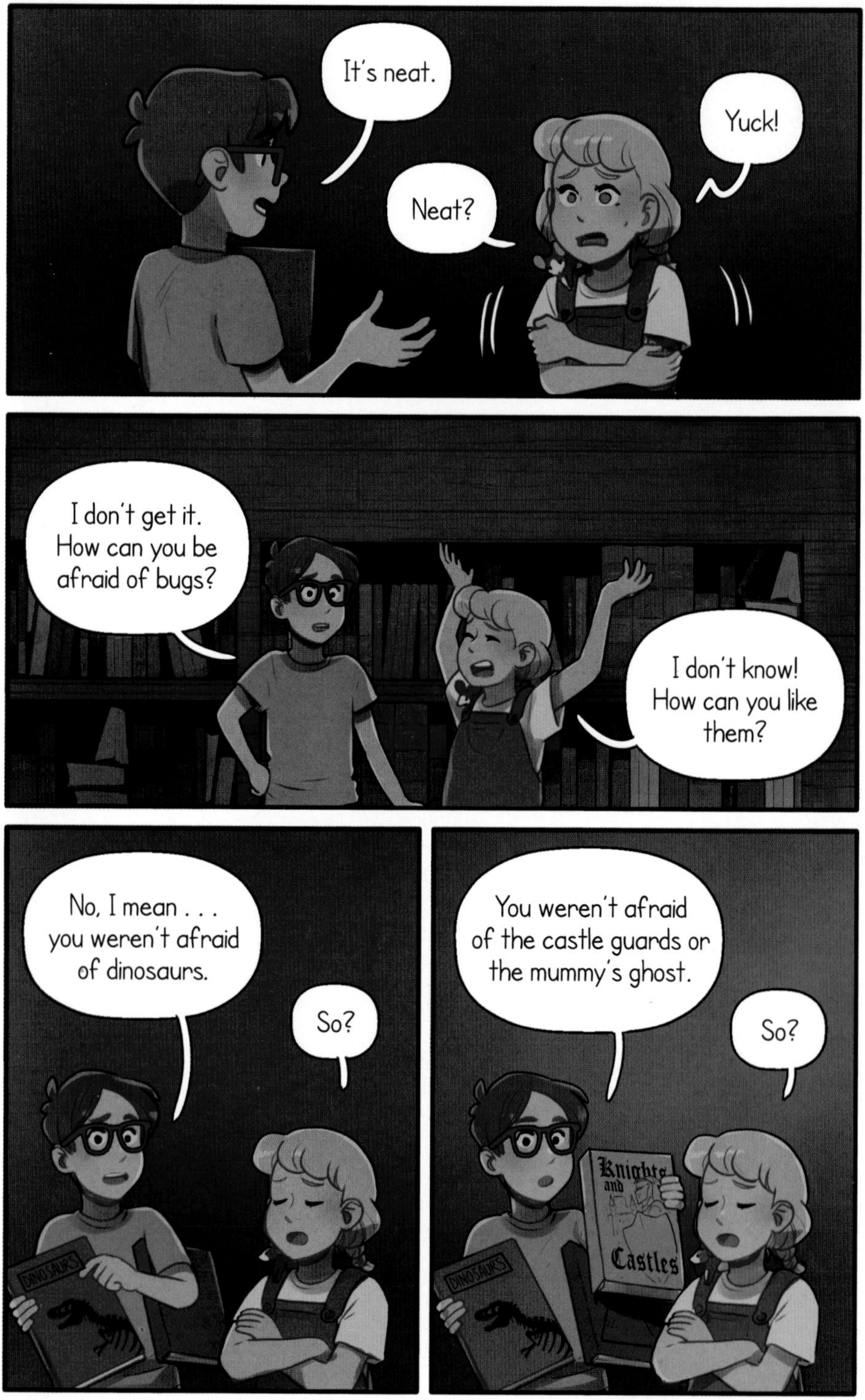
It's neat.
Neat?
Yuck!
I don't get it. How can you be afraid of bugs?
I don't know! How can you like them?
No, I mean . . . you weren't afraid of dinosaurs.
So?
DINOSAURS
You weren't afraid of the castle guards or the mummy's ghost.
So?
DINOSAURS
Knights and Castles

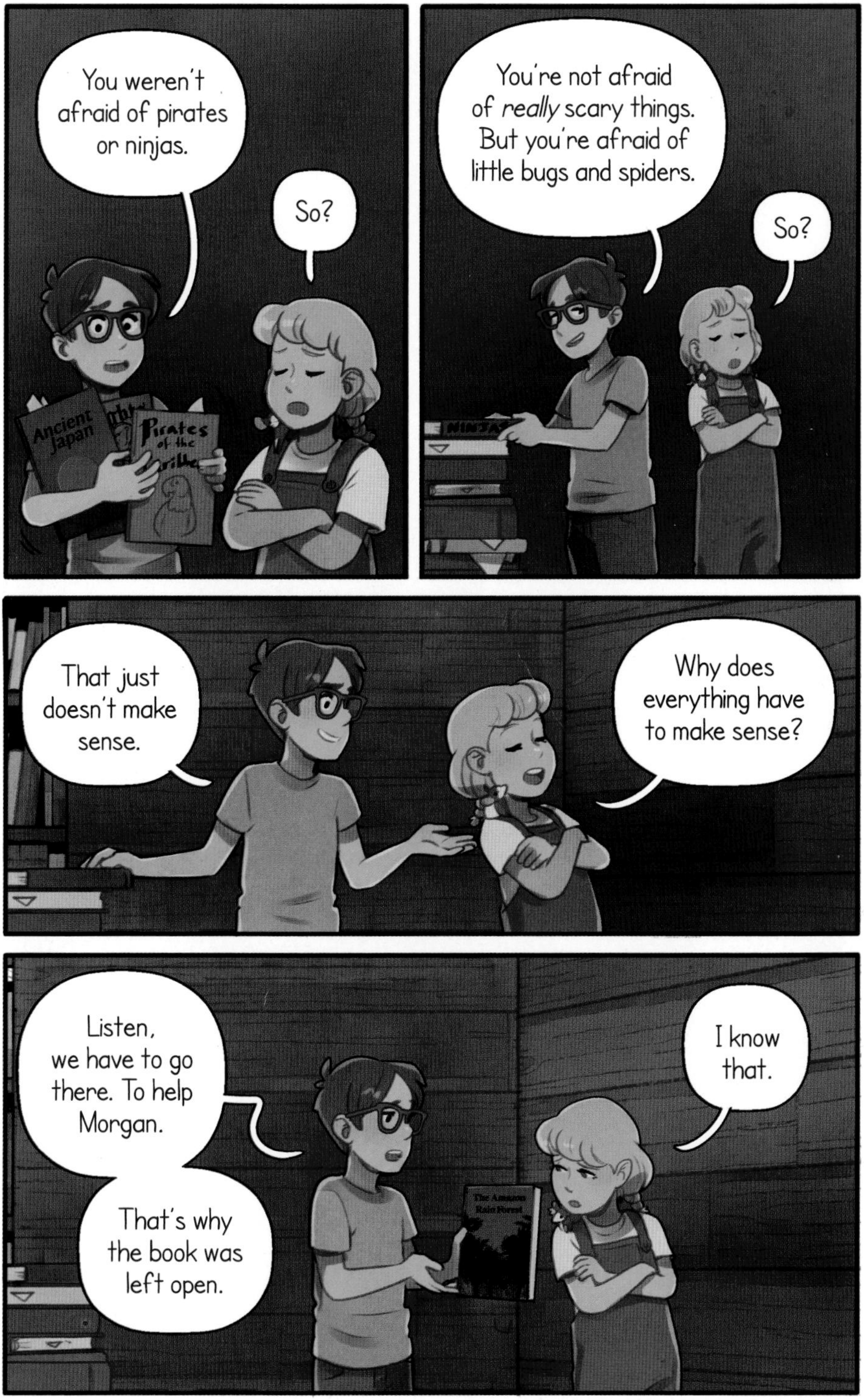
You weren't afraid of pirates or ninjas.
So?
Ancient Japan
You're not afraid of *really* scary things. But you're afraid of little bugs and spiders.
So?
That just doesn't make sense.
Why does everything have to make sense?
Listen, we have to go there. To help Morgan.
That's why the book was left open.
I know that.

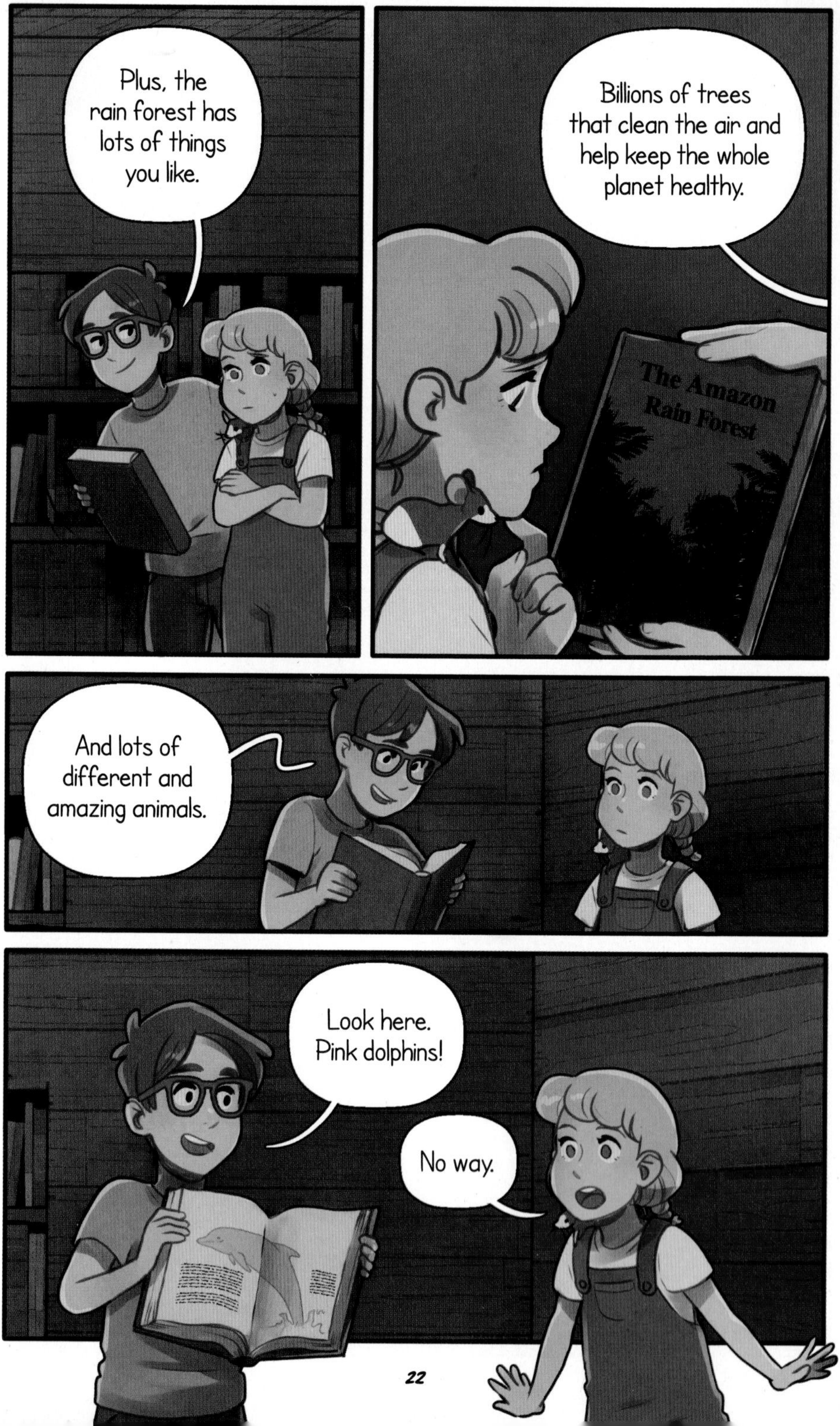
Plus, the rain forest has lots of things you like.
Billions of trees that clean the air and help keep the whole planet healthy.
The Amazon Rain Forest
And lots of different and amazing animals.
Look here. Pink dolphins!
No way.

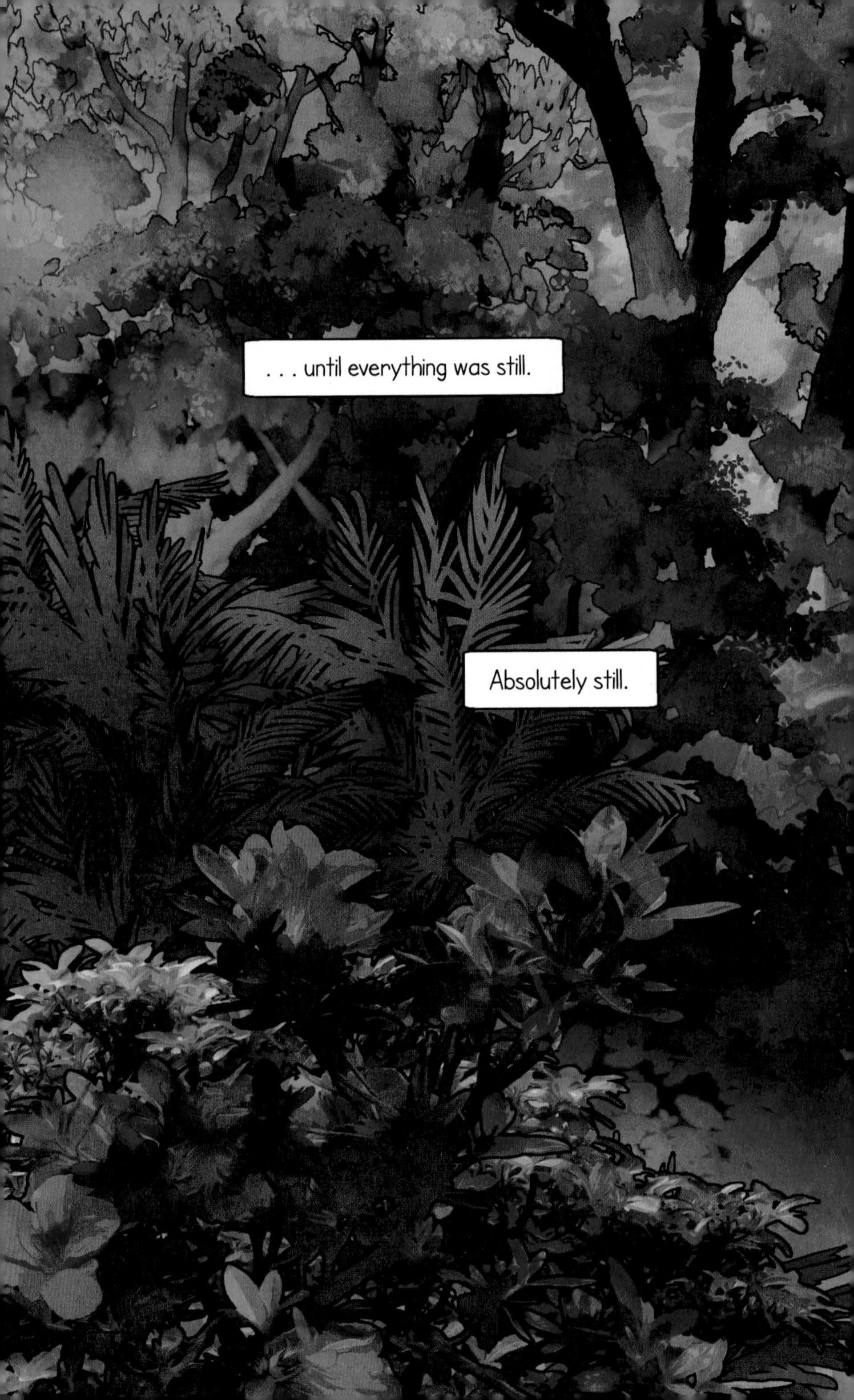
. . . until everything was still.
Absolutely still.

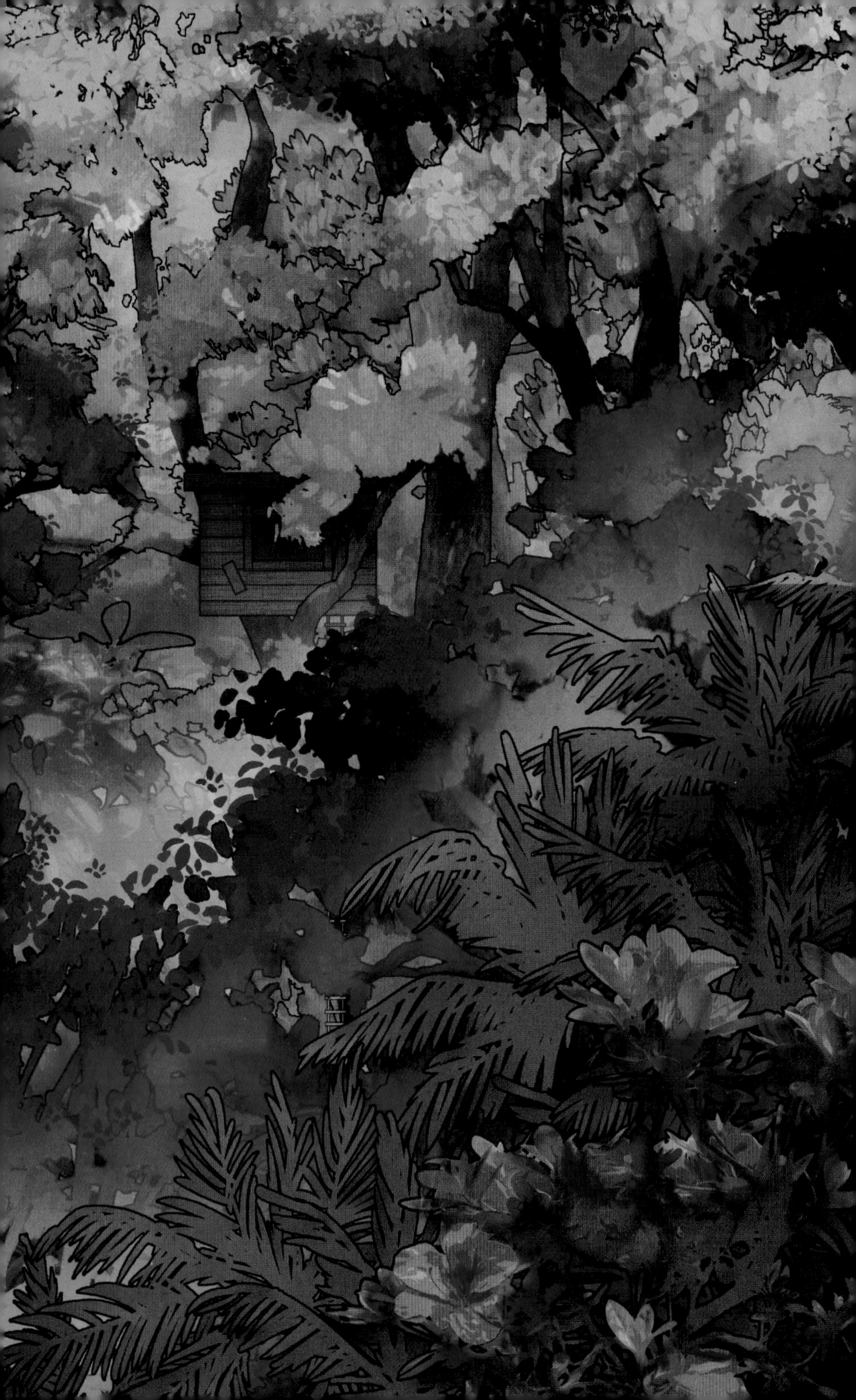

The book says the rain forest is in four layers.

The top layer is called the emergent layer.

What does that mean?

I don't know. Let me read.

This is called the forest canopy and can be over 150 feet in the air.

Thick treetops make up the next layer

Below that is the understory. Then the forest floor.

Cool. Let's go!

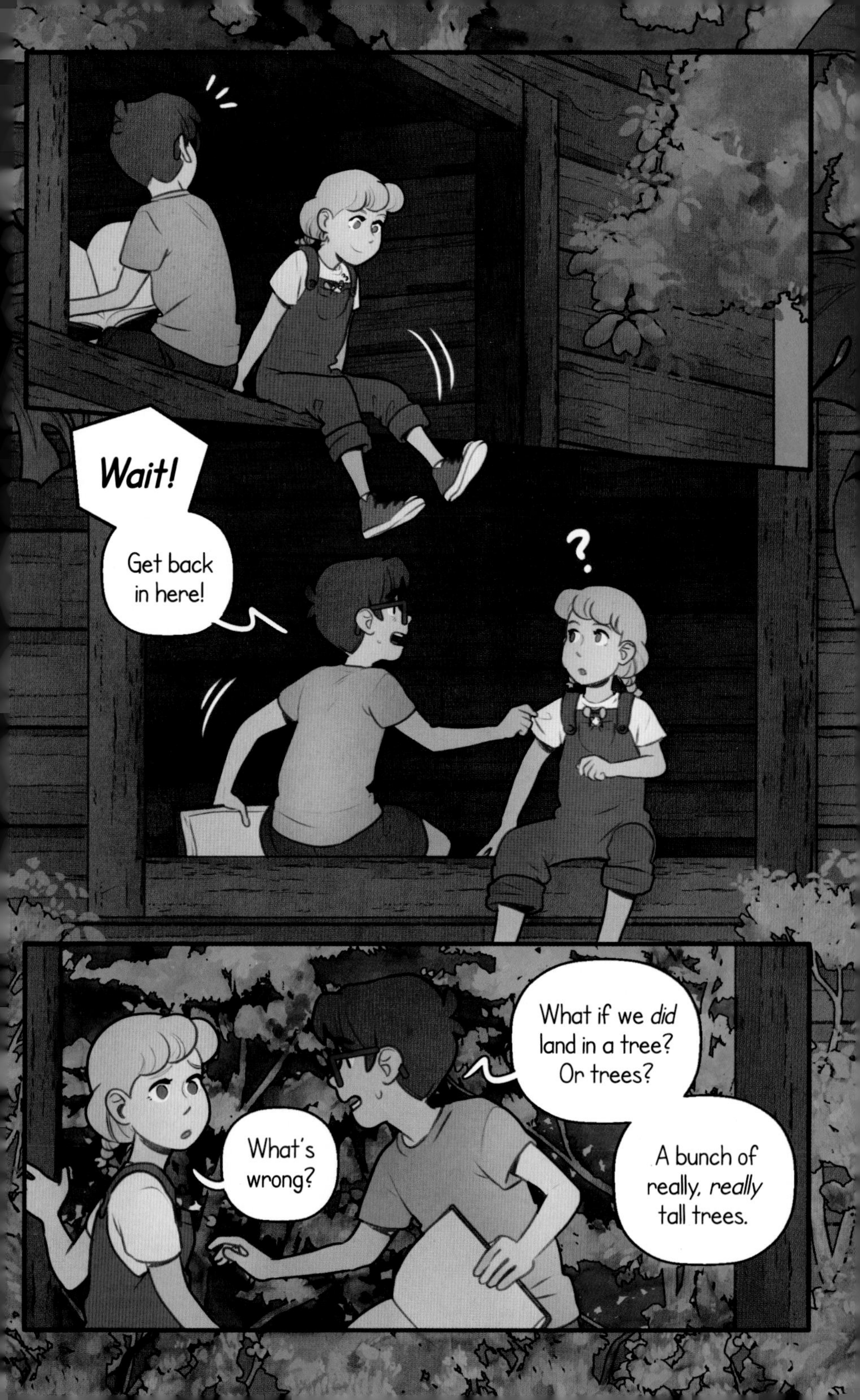
Wait!
Get back in here!
?
What if we *did* land in a tree? Or trees?
What's wrong?
A bunch of really, *really* tall trees.

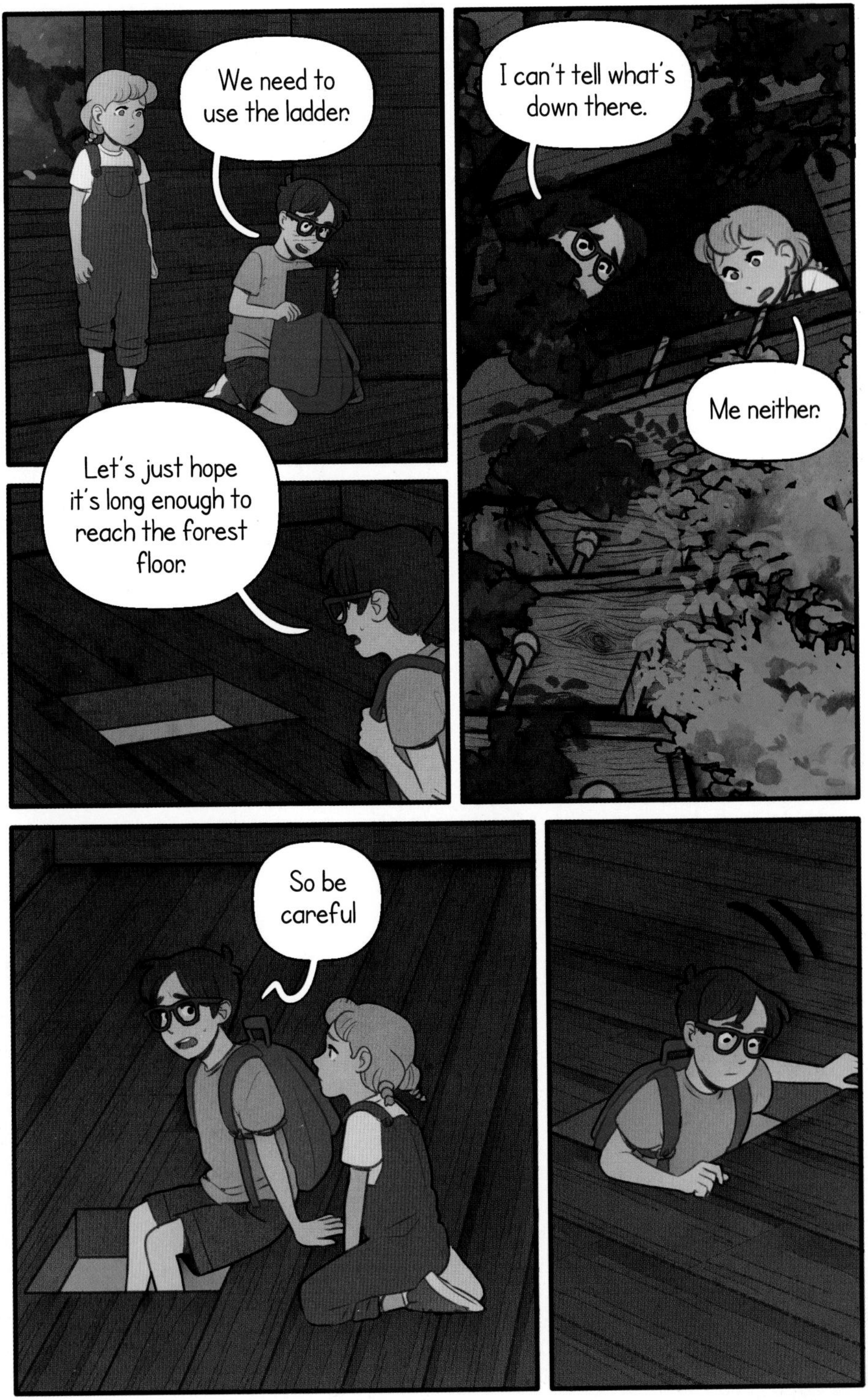
We need to use the ladder.
I can't tell what's down there.
Me neither.
Let's just hope it's long enough to reach the forest floor.
So be careful

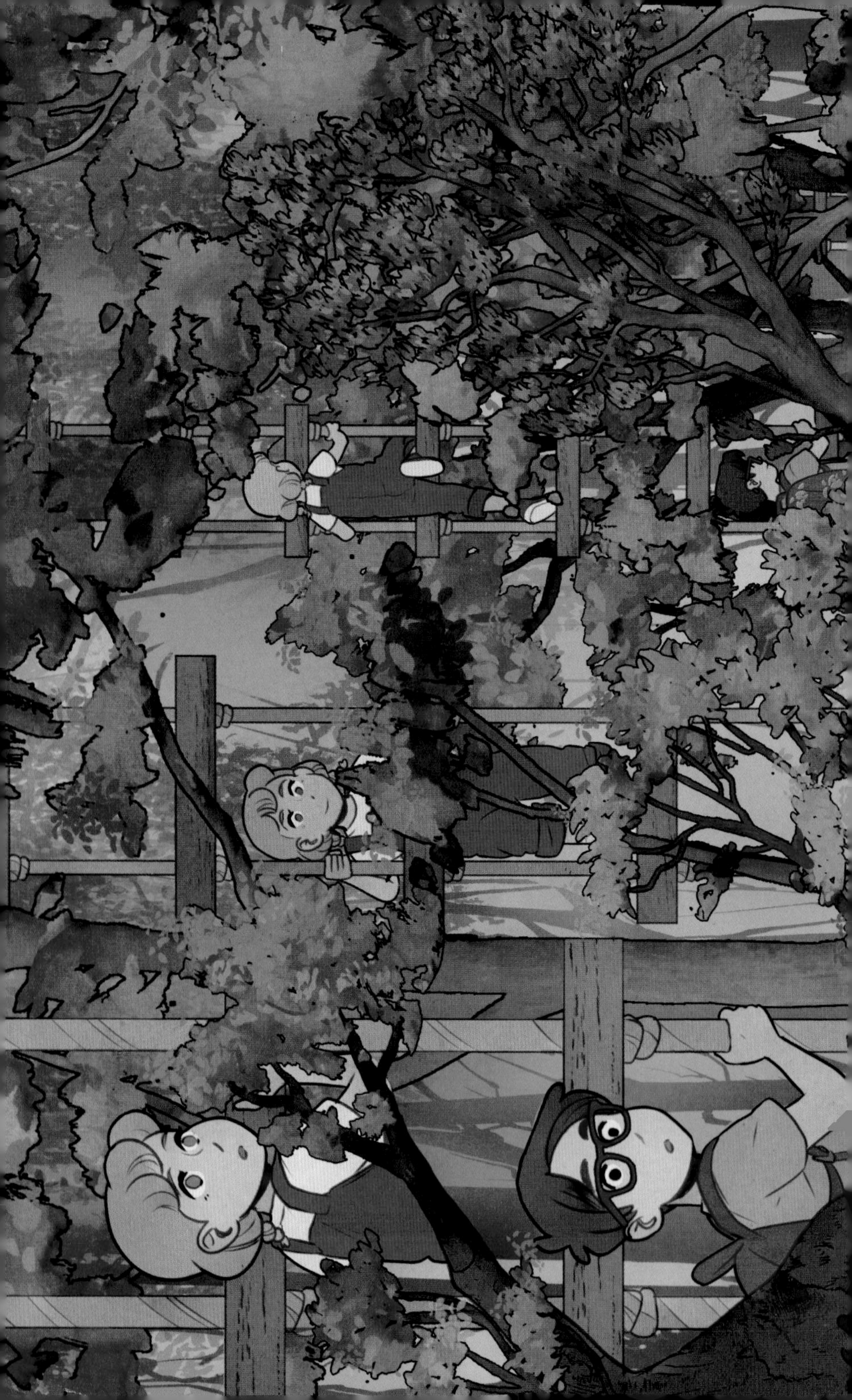

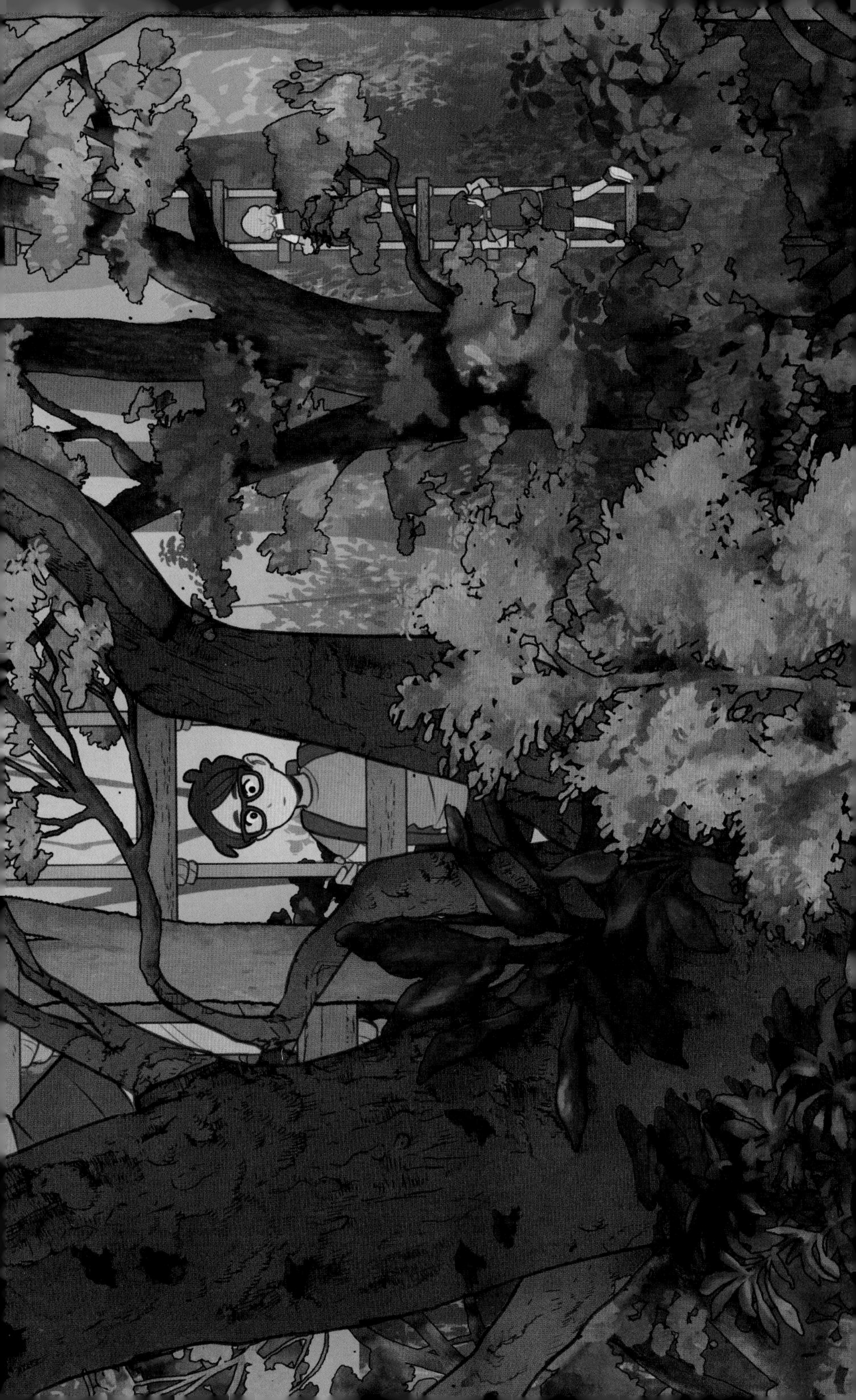

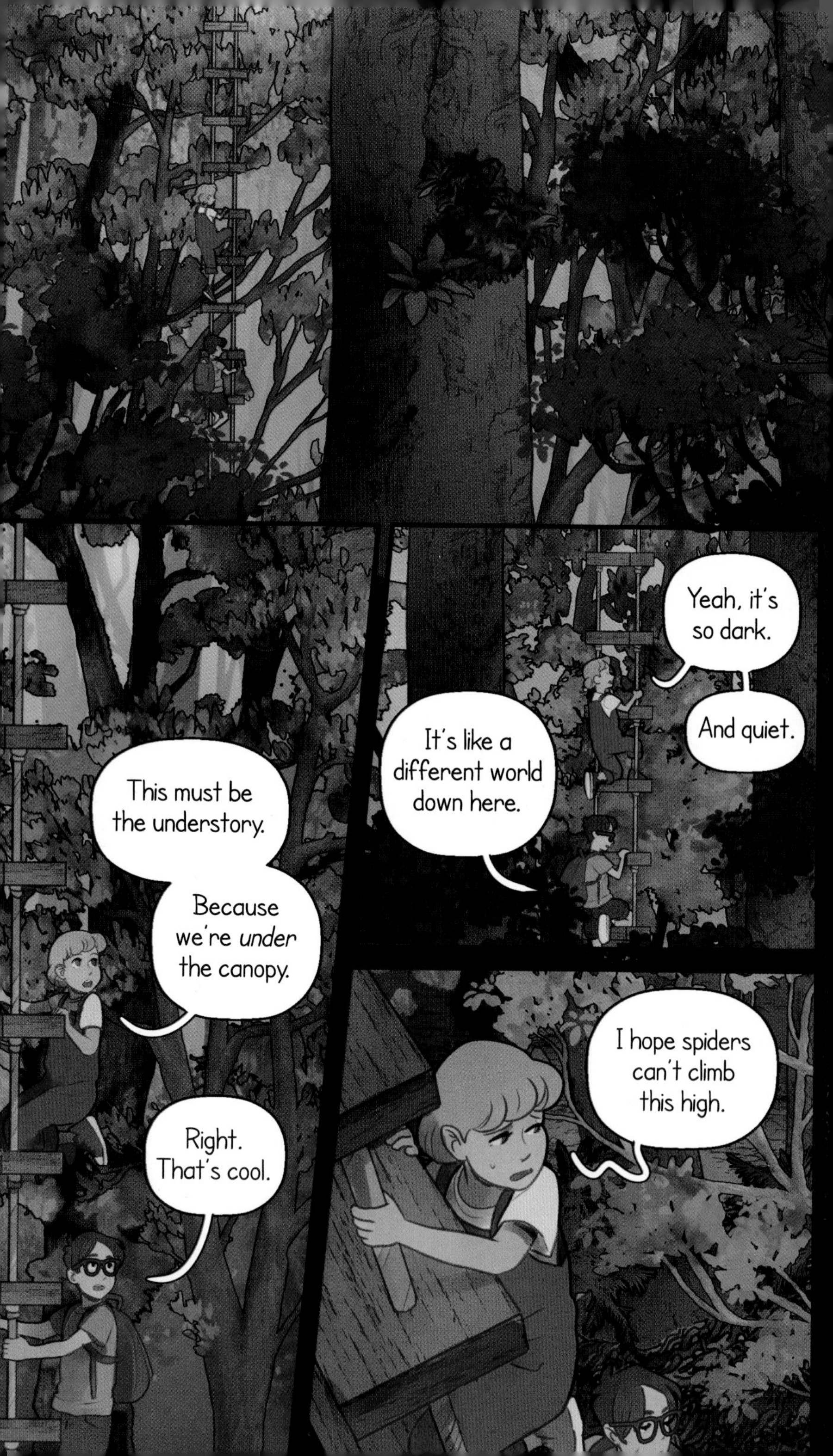
This must be the understory.
Because we're *under* the canopy.
Right. That's cool.
It's like a different world down here.
Yeah, it's so dark.
And quiet.
I hope spiders can't climb this high.

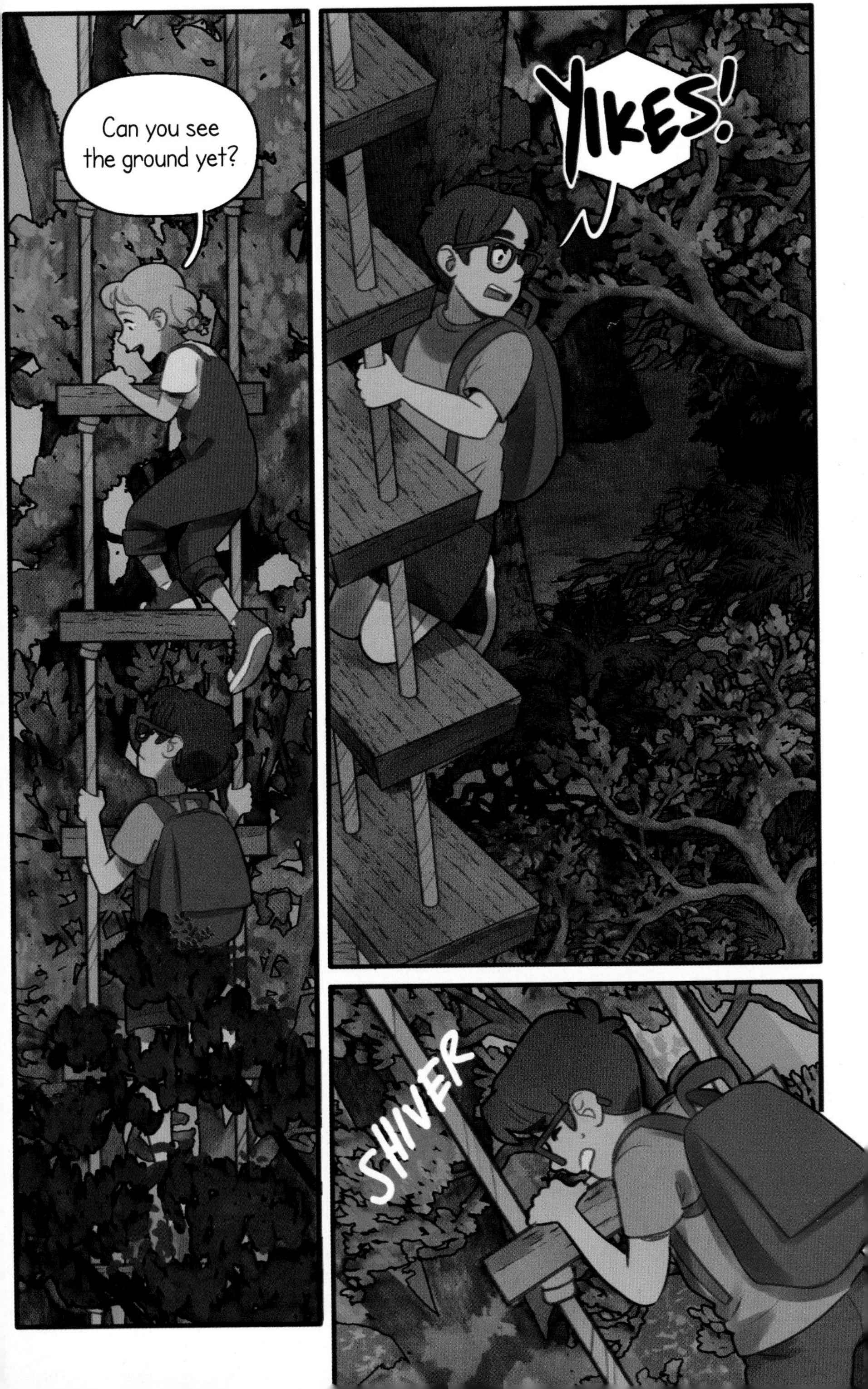
Can you see the ground yet?
YIKES!
SHIVER

CHAPTER THREE
Millions of Them!

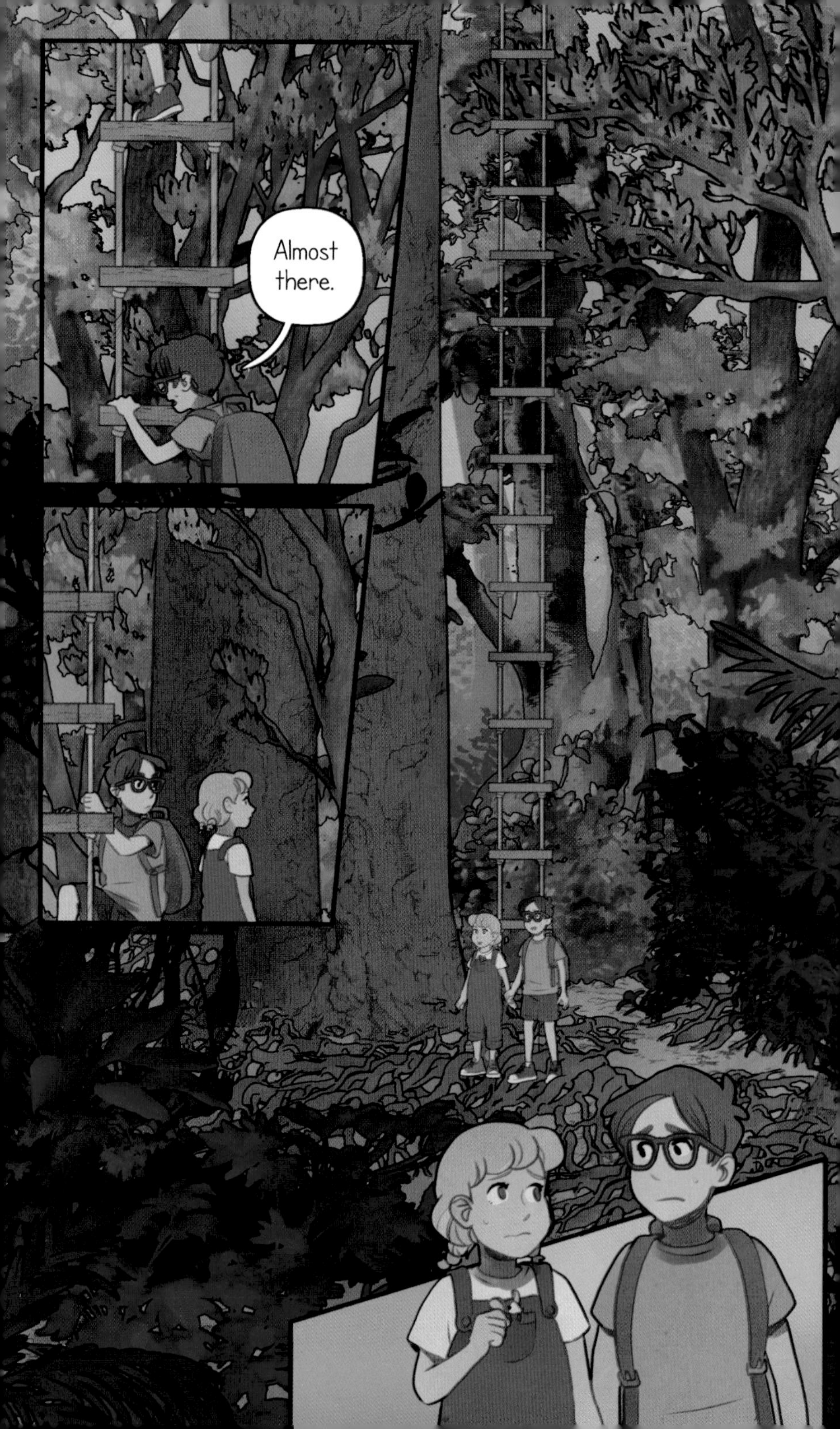
Almost there.

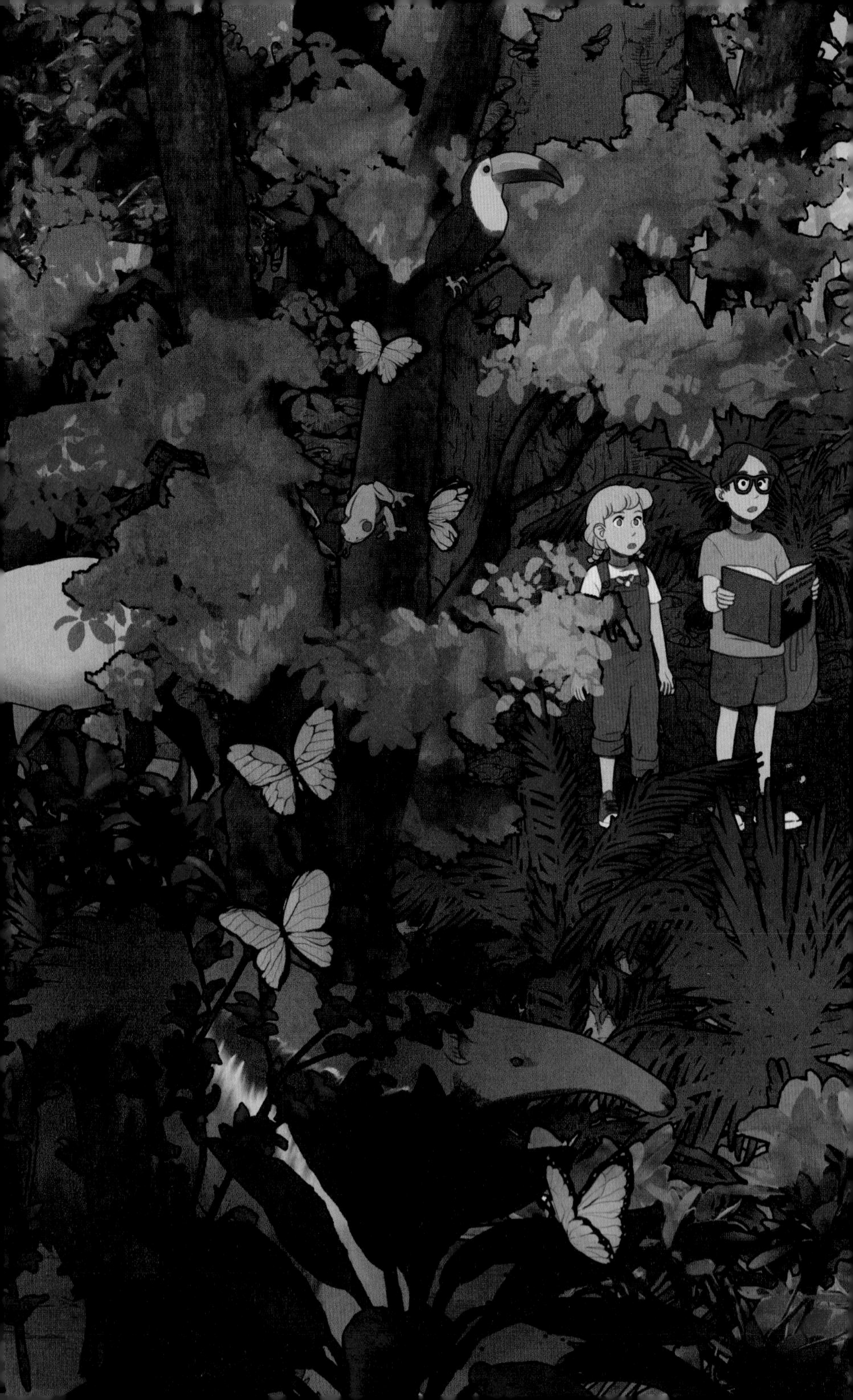

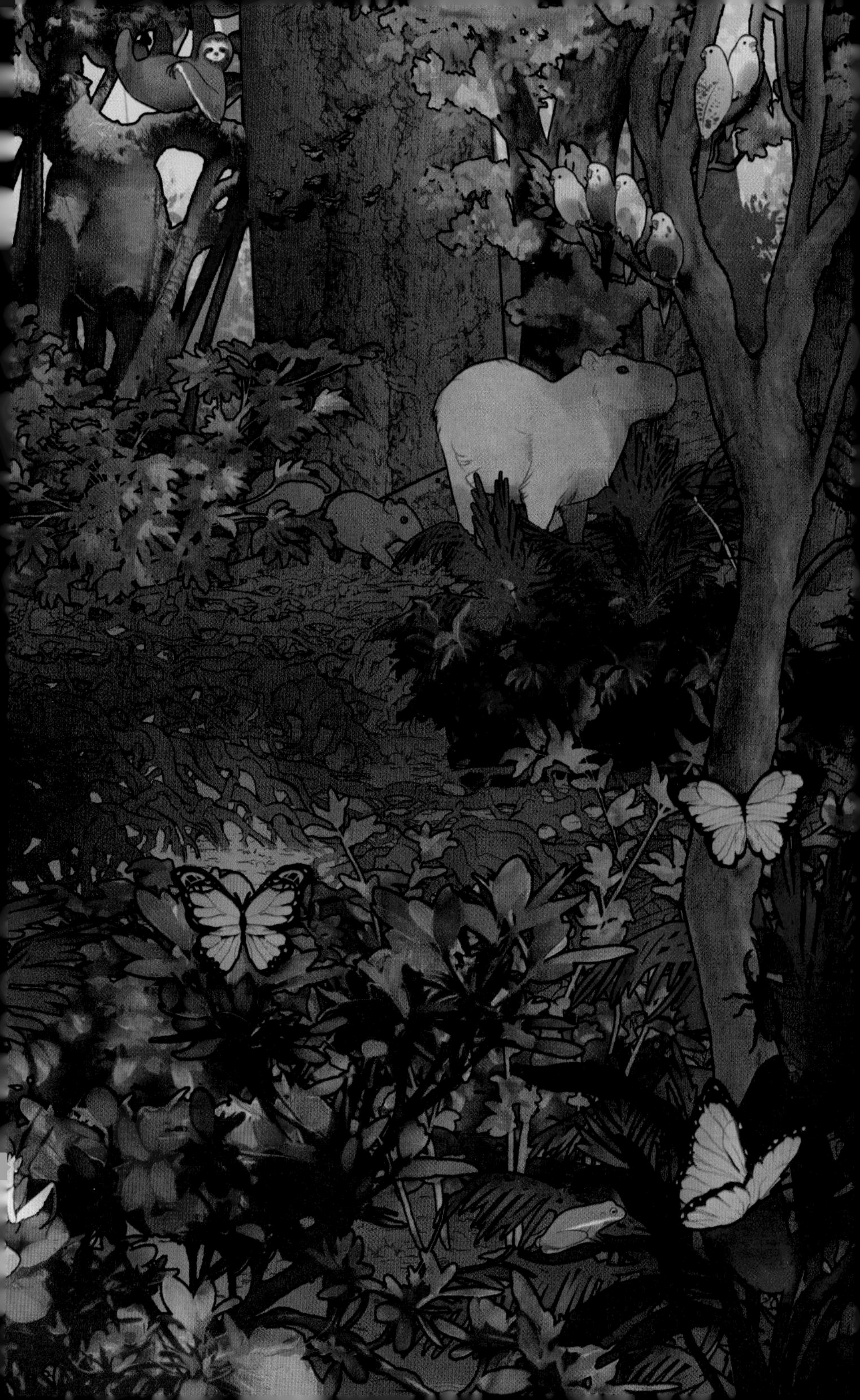

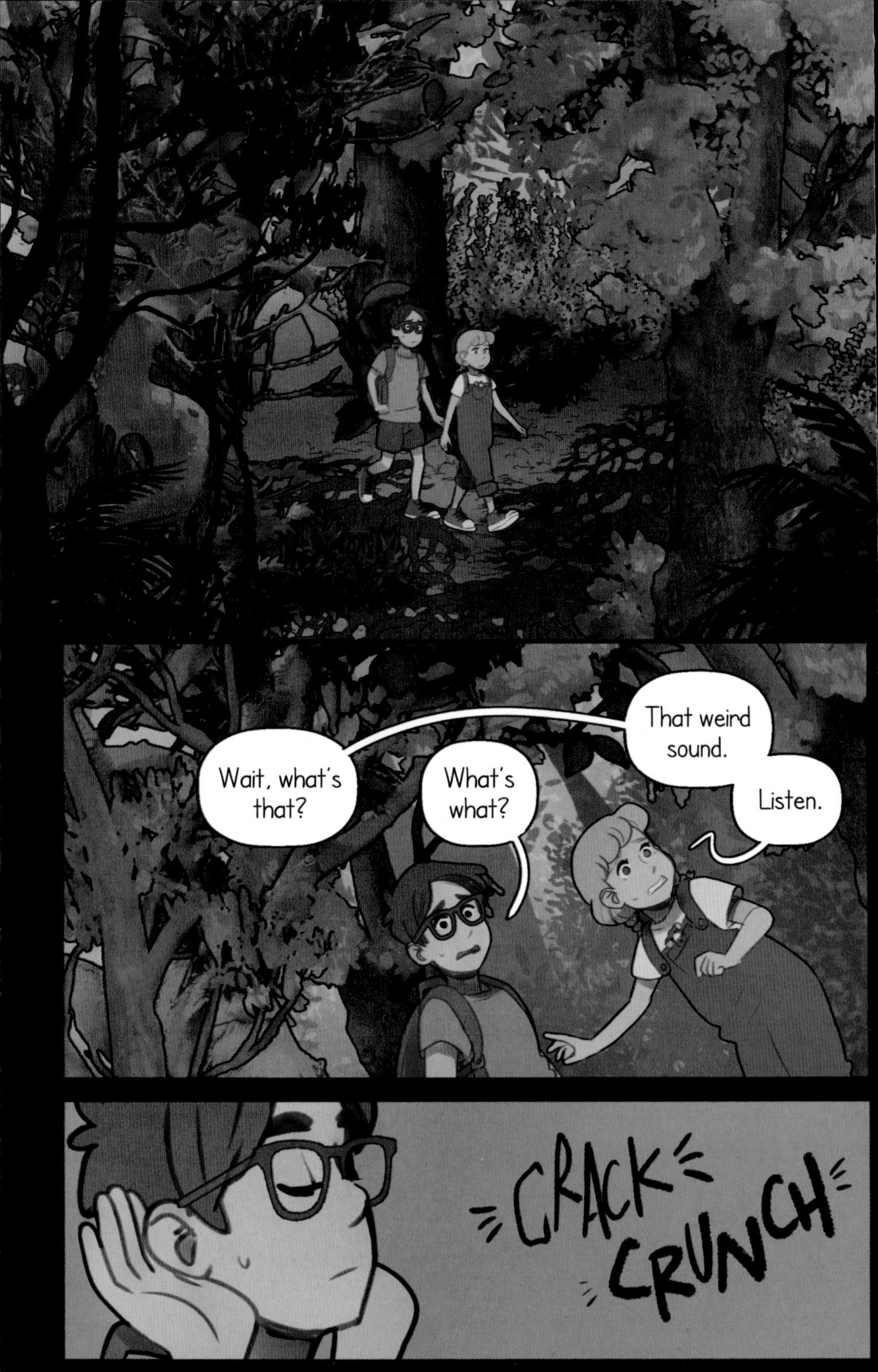
Wait, what's that?
What's what?
That weird sound.
Listen.
CRACK
CRUNCH

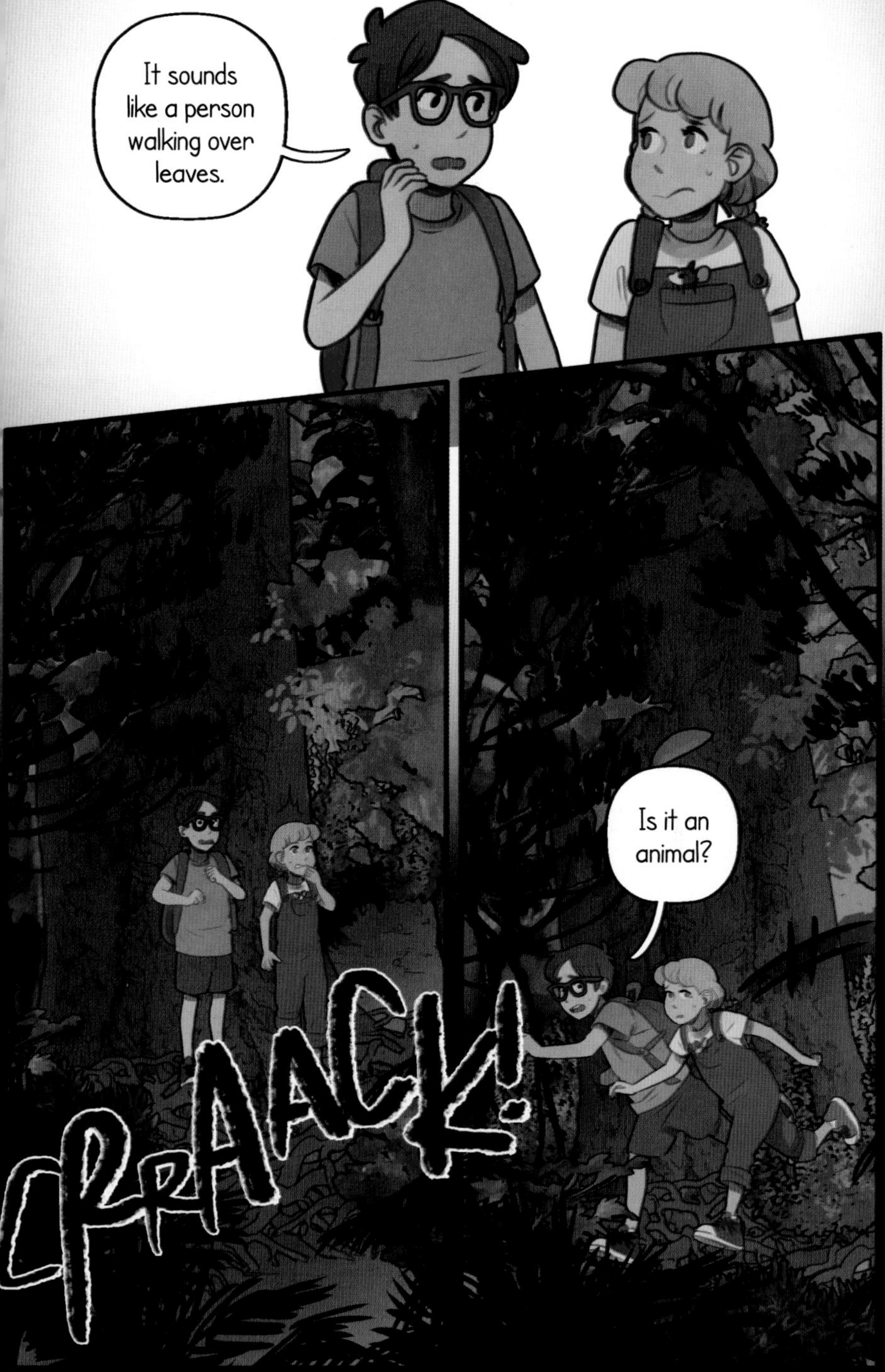
It sounds like a person walking over leaves.
CRRAACK!
Is it an animal?

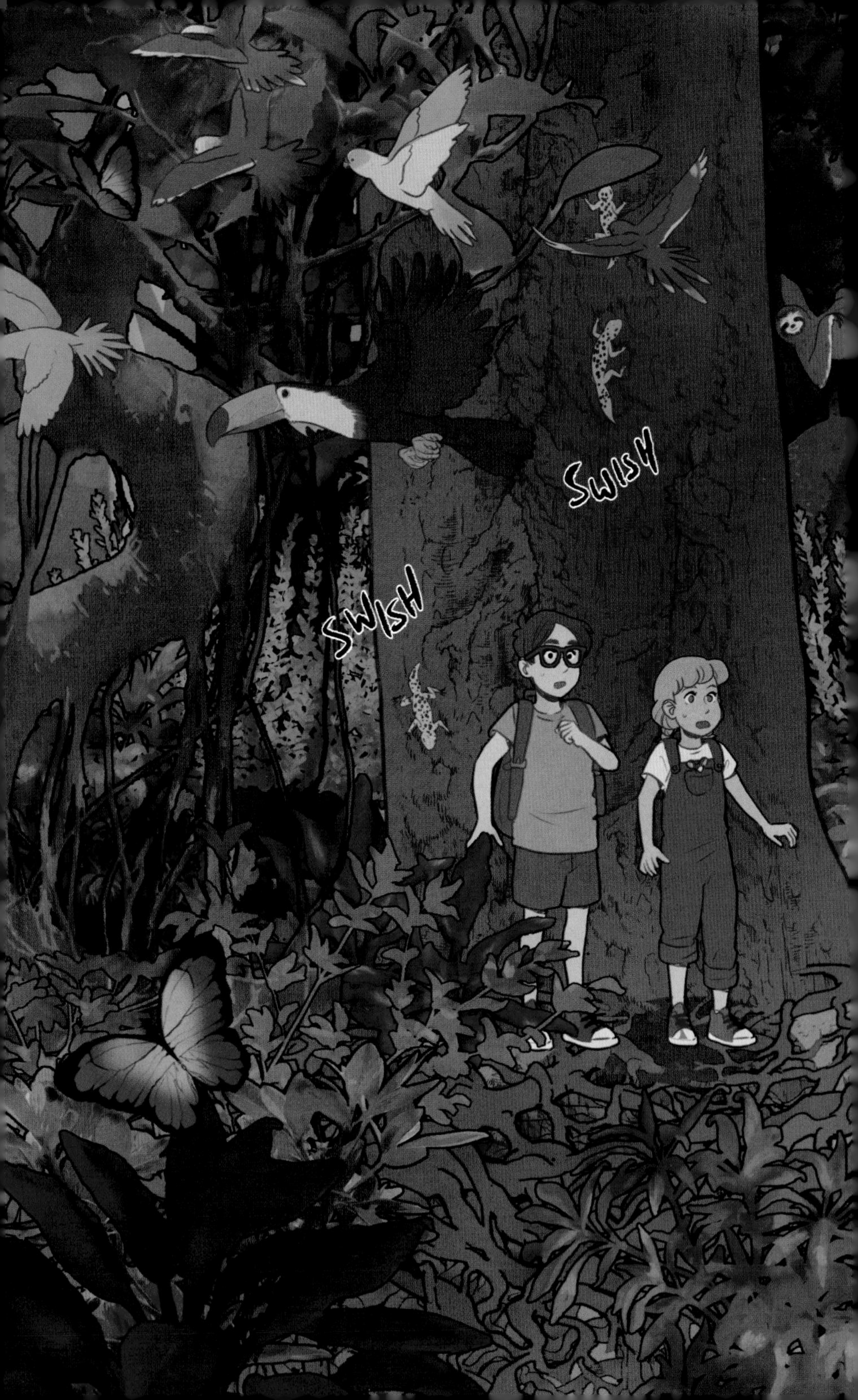
SWISH
SWISH

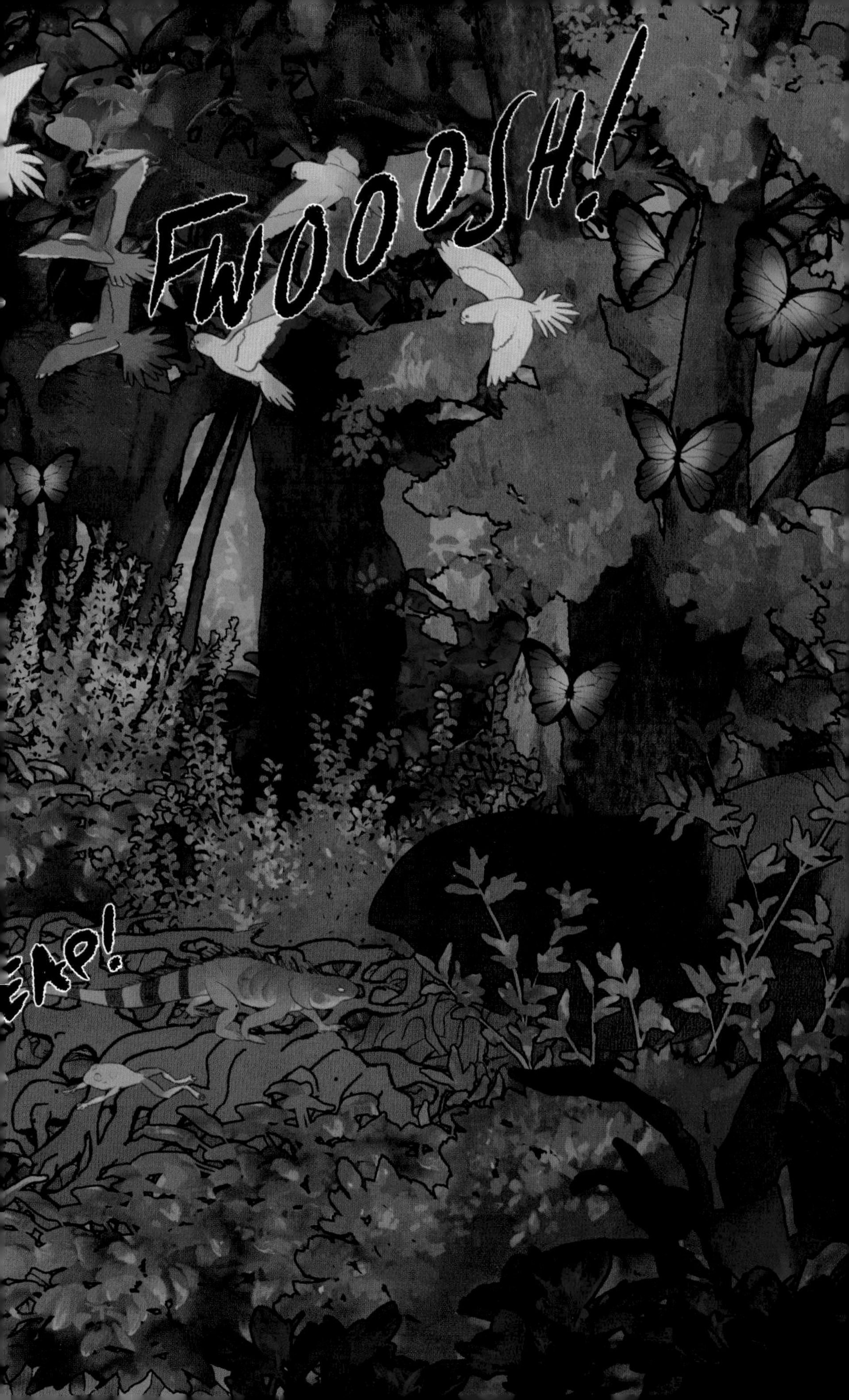
FWOOOSH!
EAP!

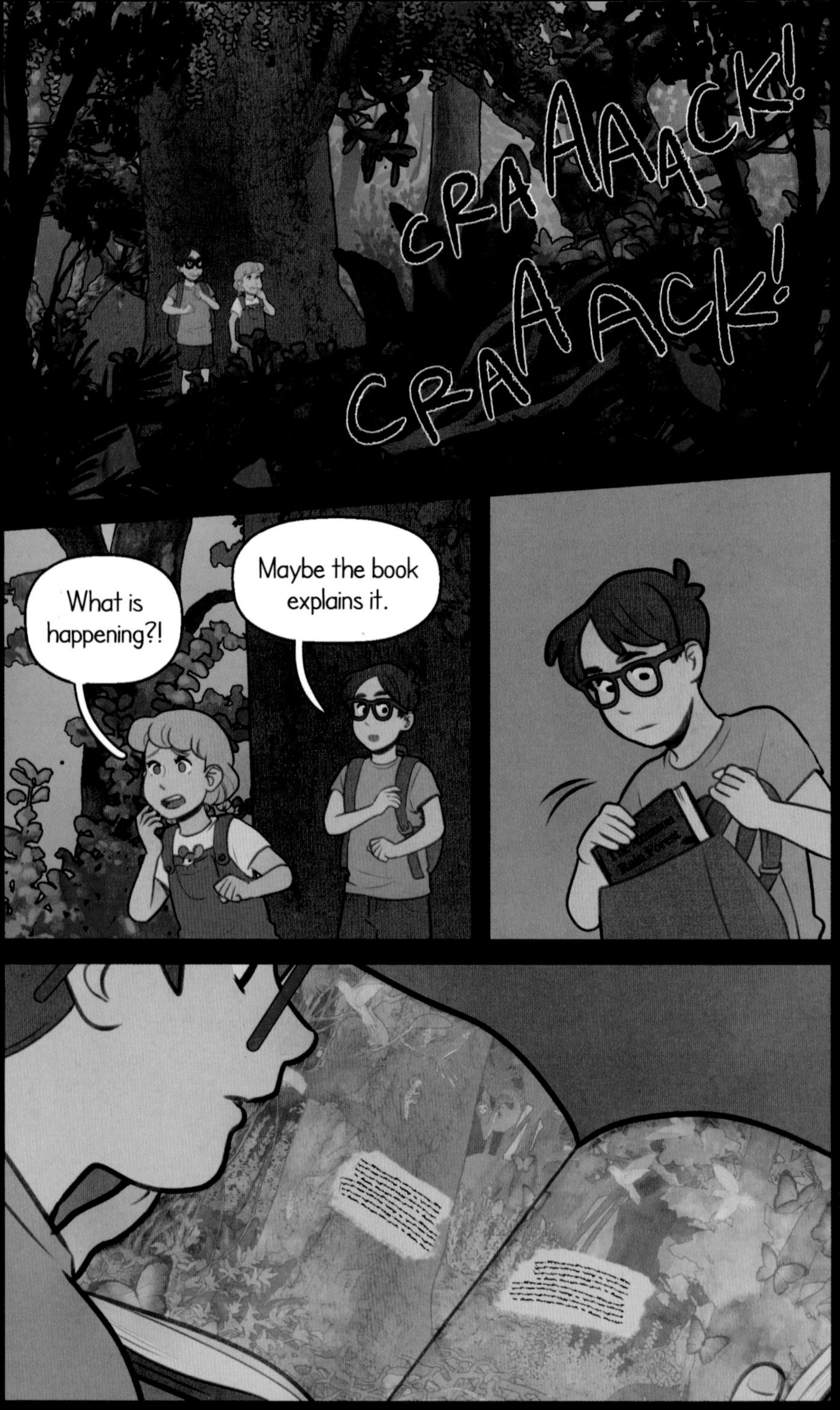
CRAAACK!
CRAAACK!
What is happening?!
Maybe the book explains it.

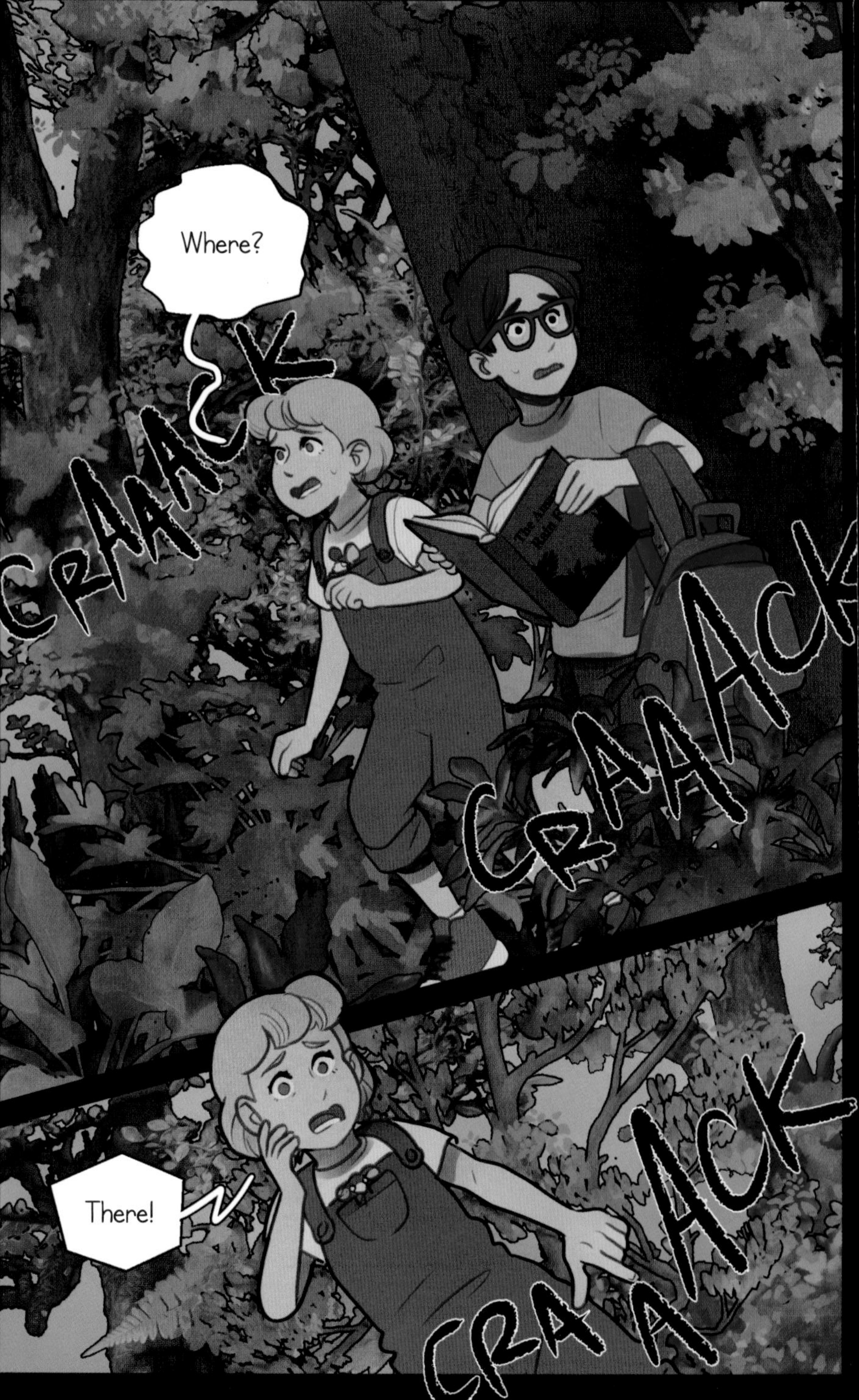
Where?
CRAAACK
CRAAACK
There!
CRAAACK

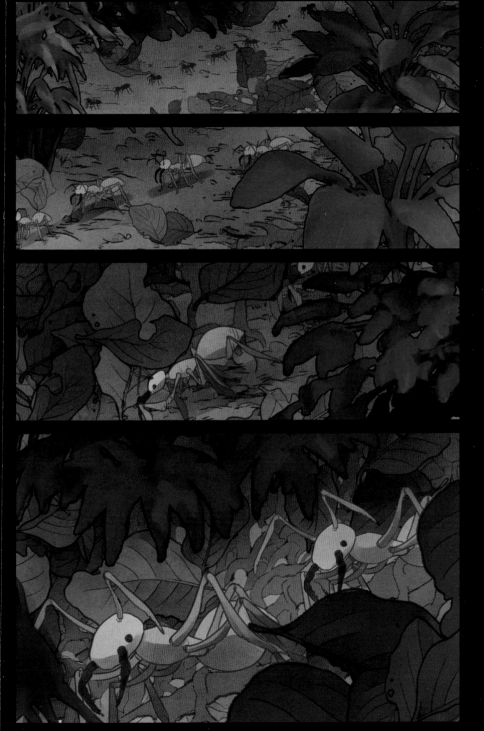

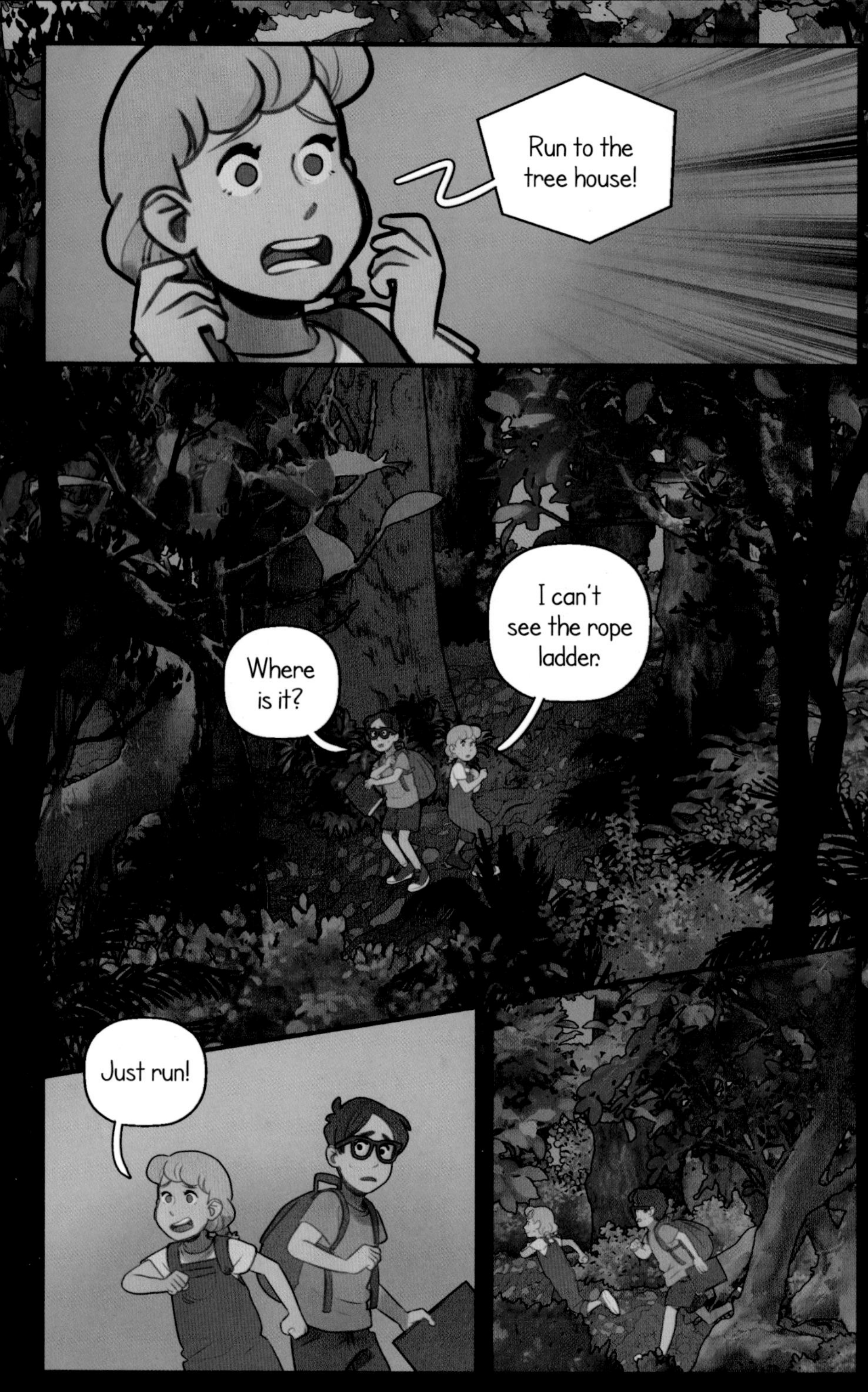
Run to the tree house!
Where is it?
I can't see the rope ladder.
Just run!

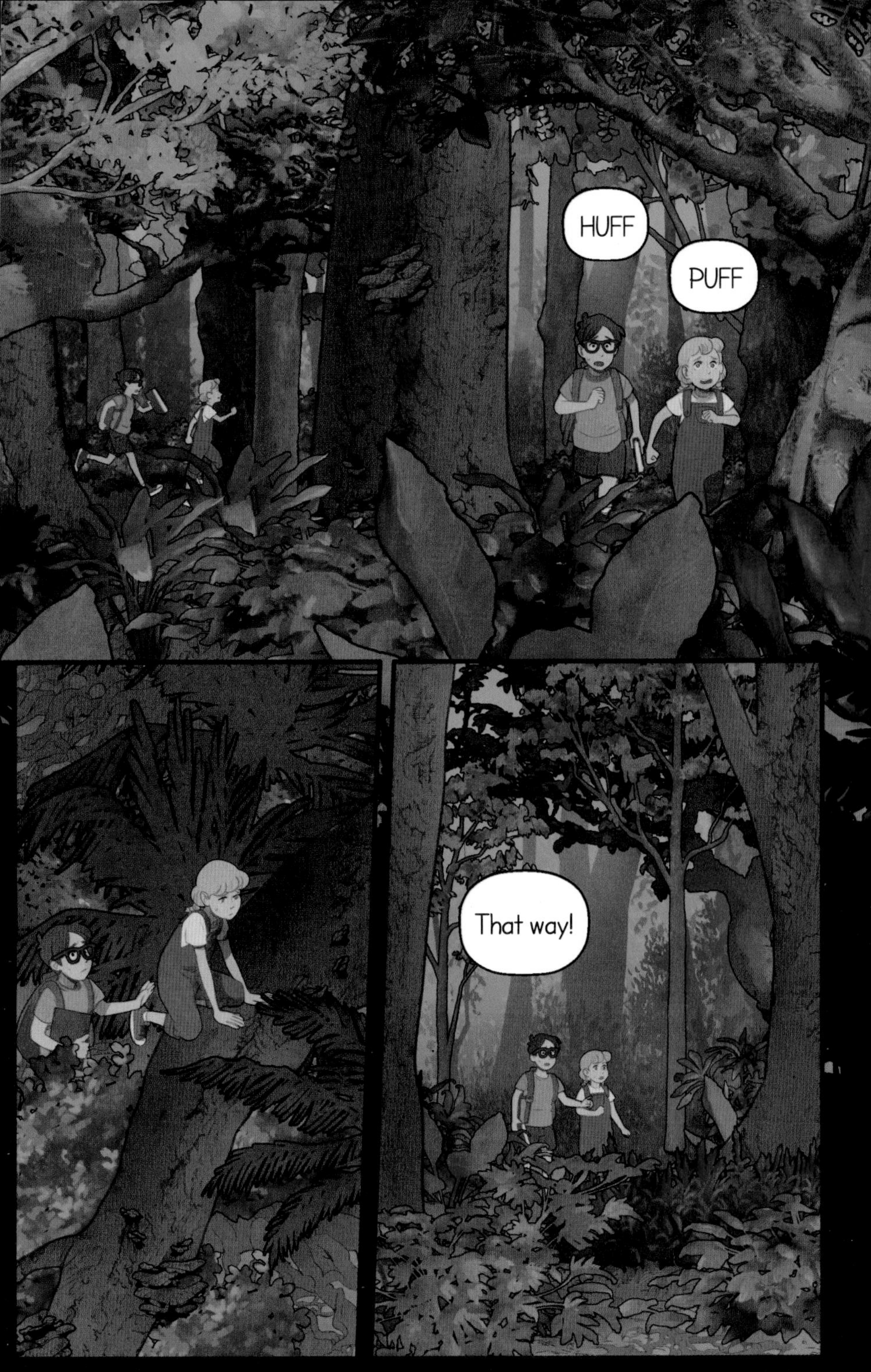
HUFF
PUFF
That way!

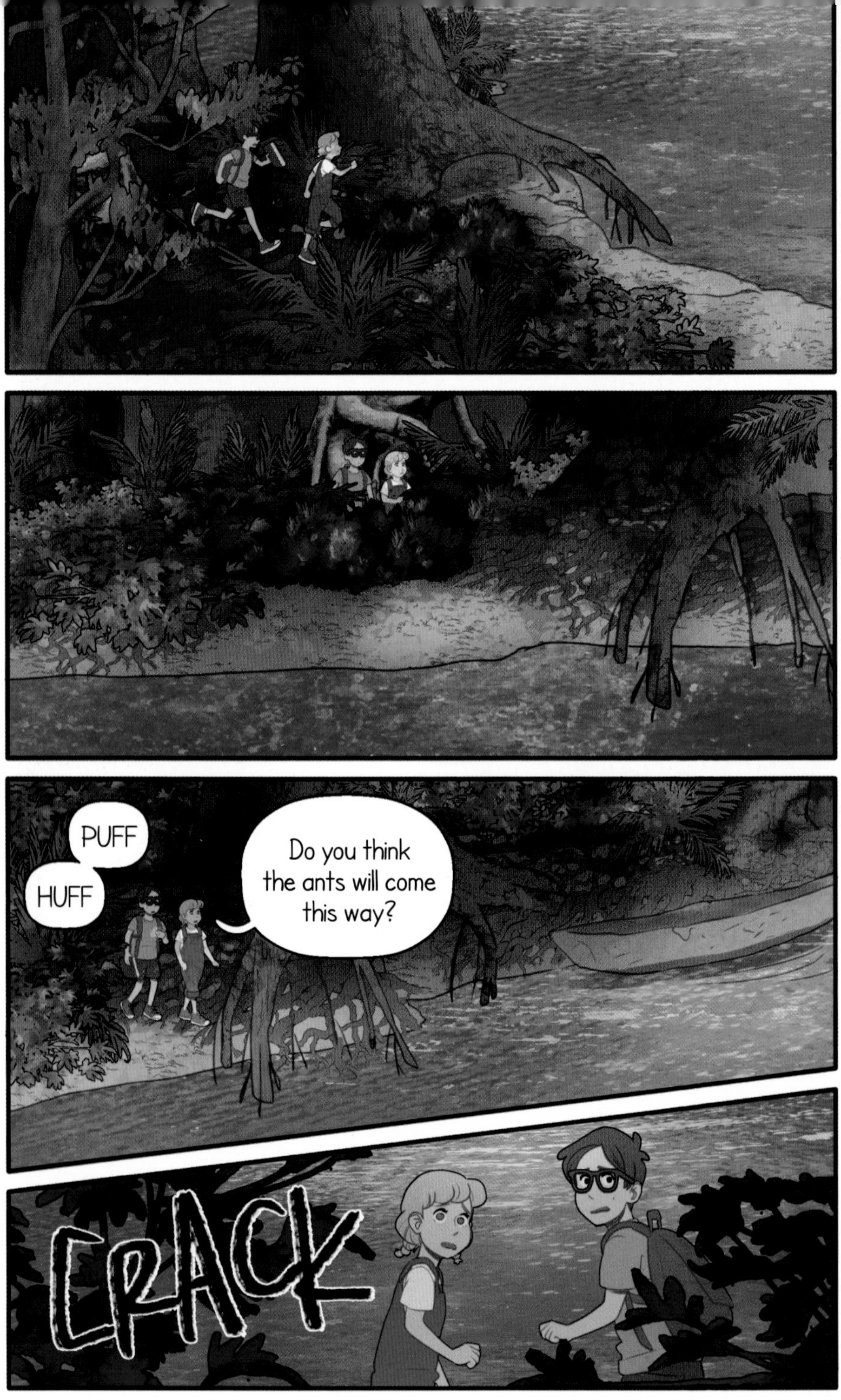
PUFF
HUFF
Do you think the ants will come this way?
CRACK

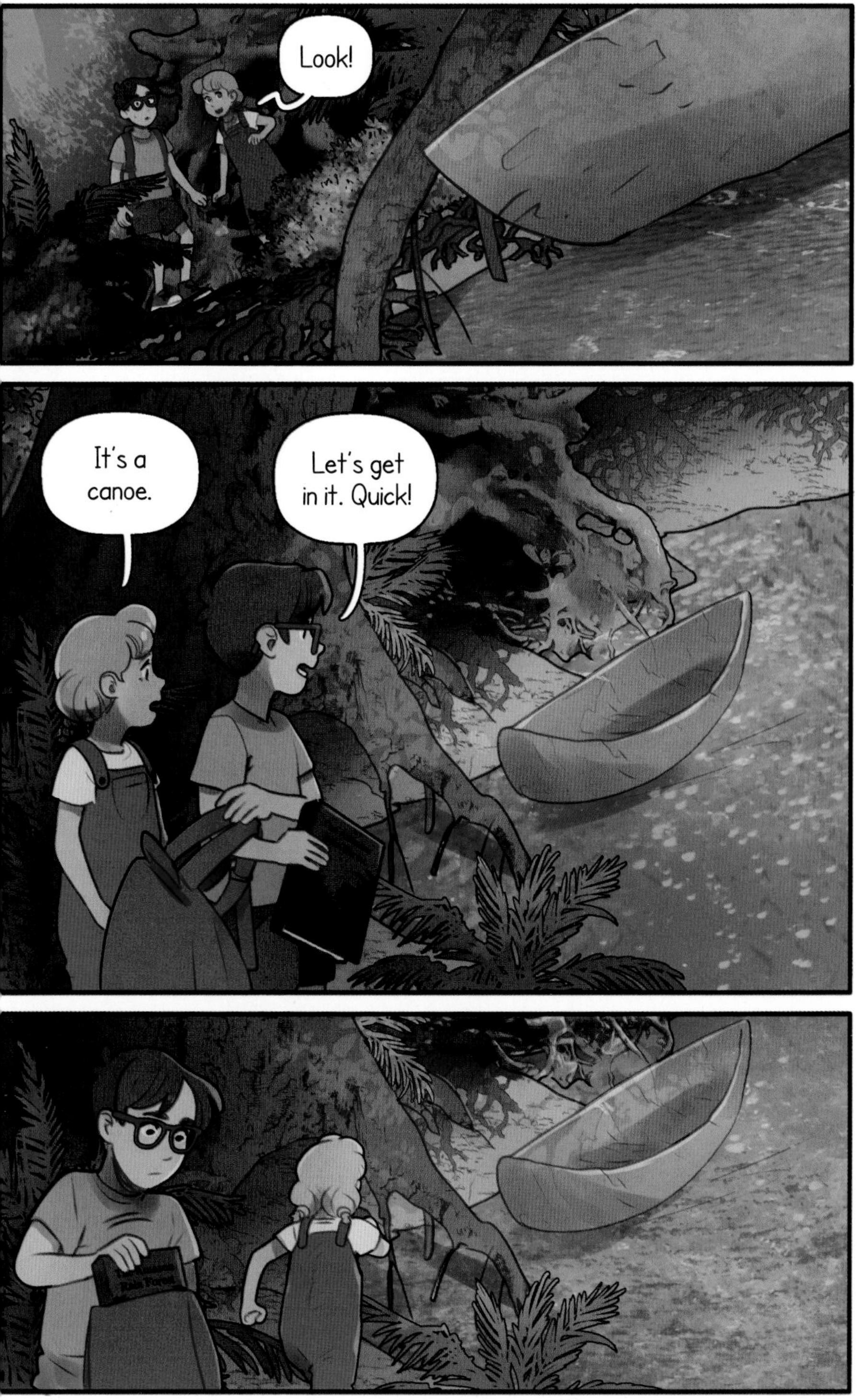
Look!
It's a canoe.
Let's get in it. Quick!

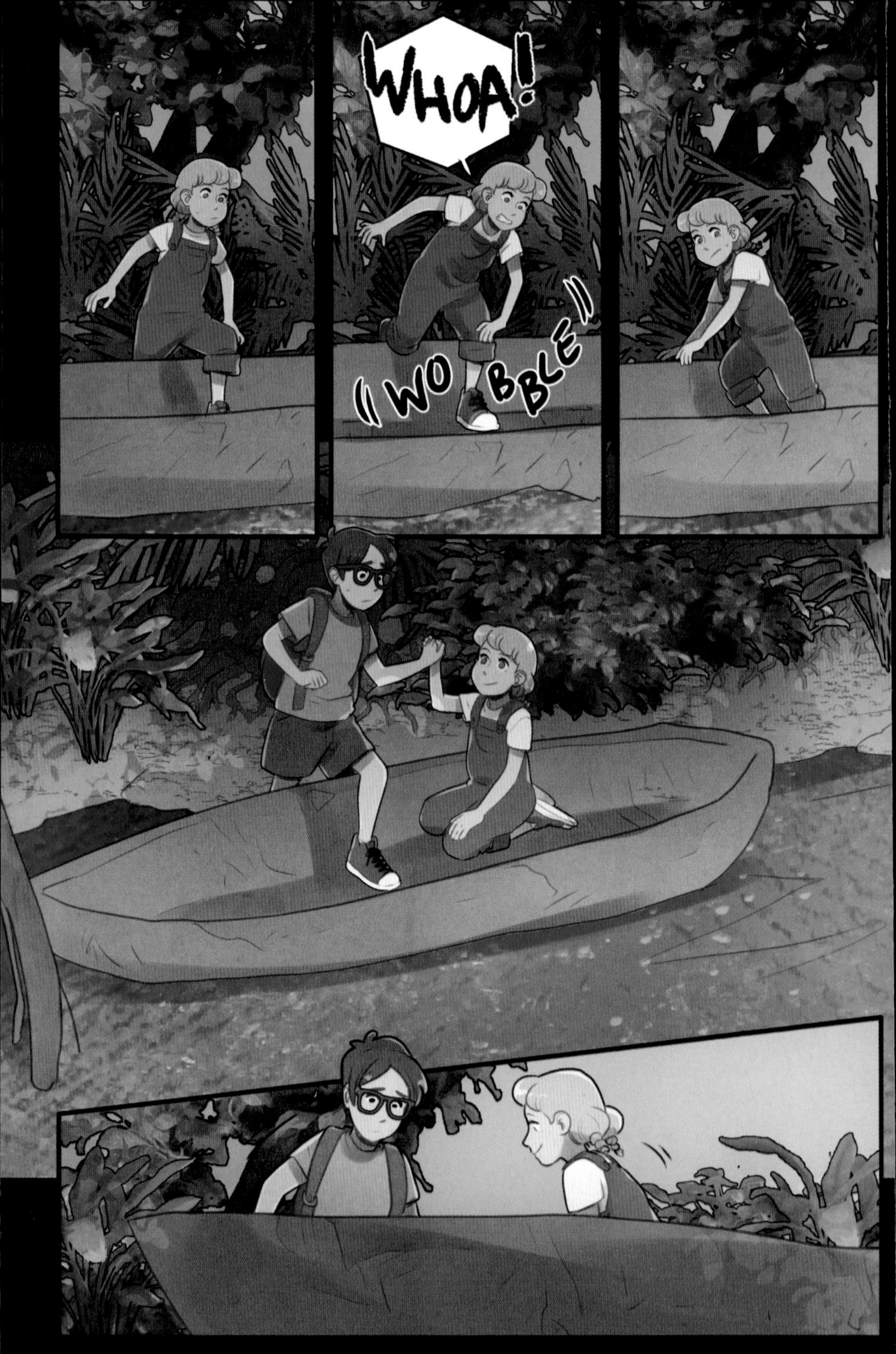
WHOA!
WOBBLE

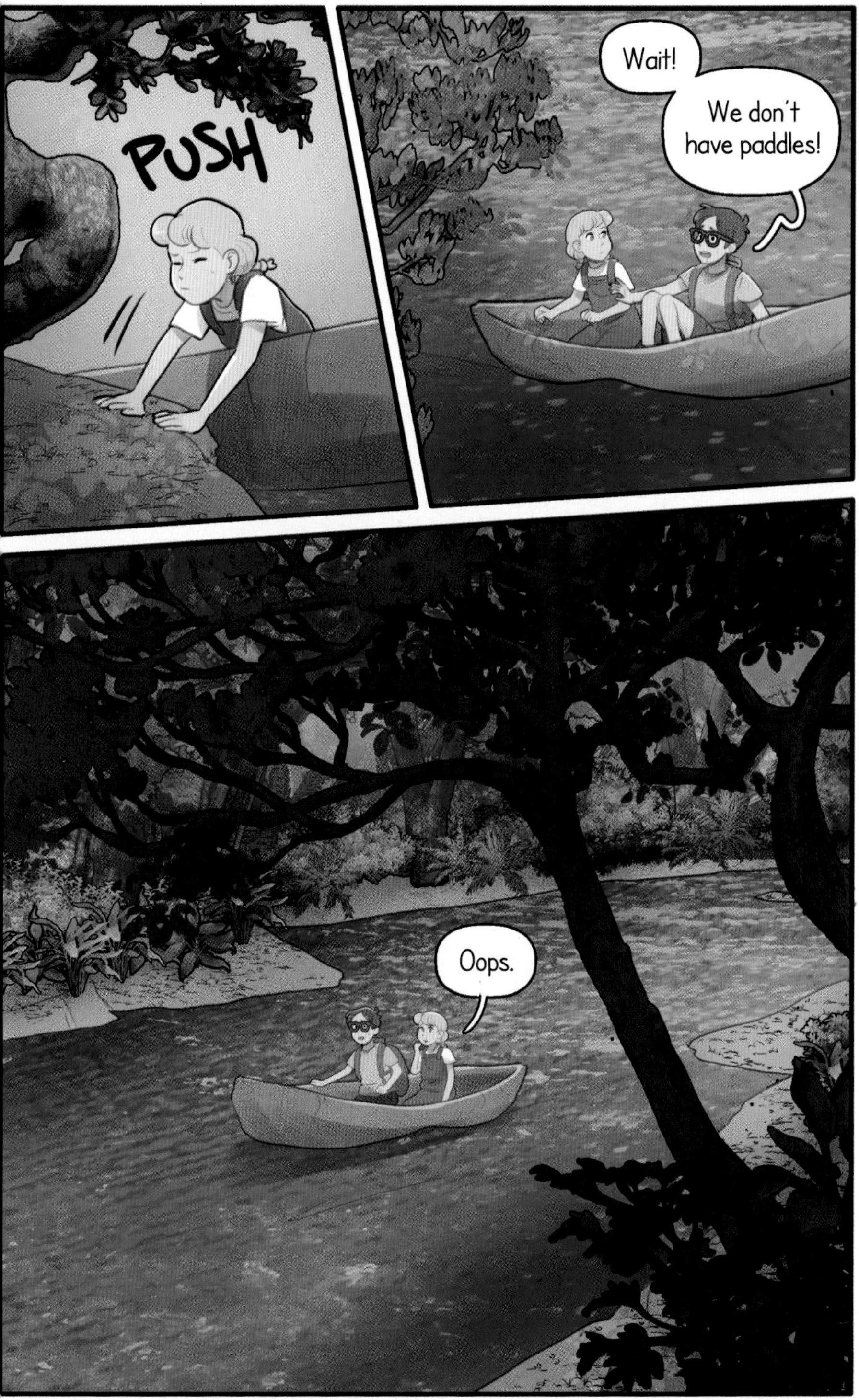
PUSH
Wait!
We don't have paddles!
Oops.

CHAPTER FOUR
Pretty Fish

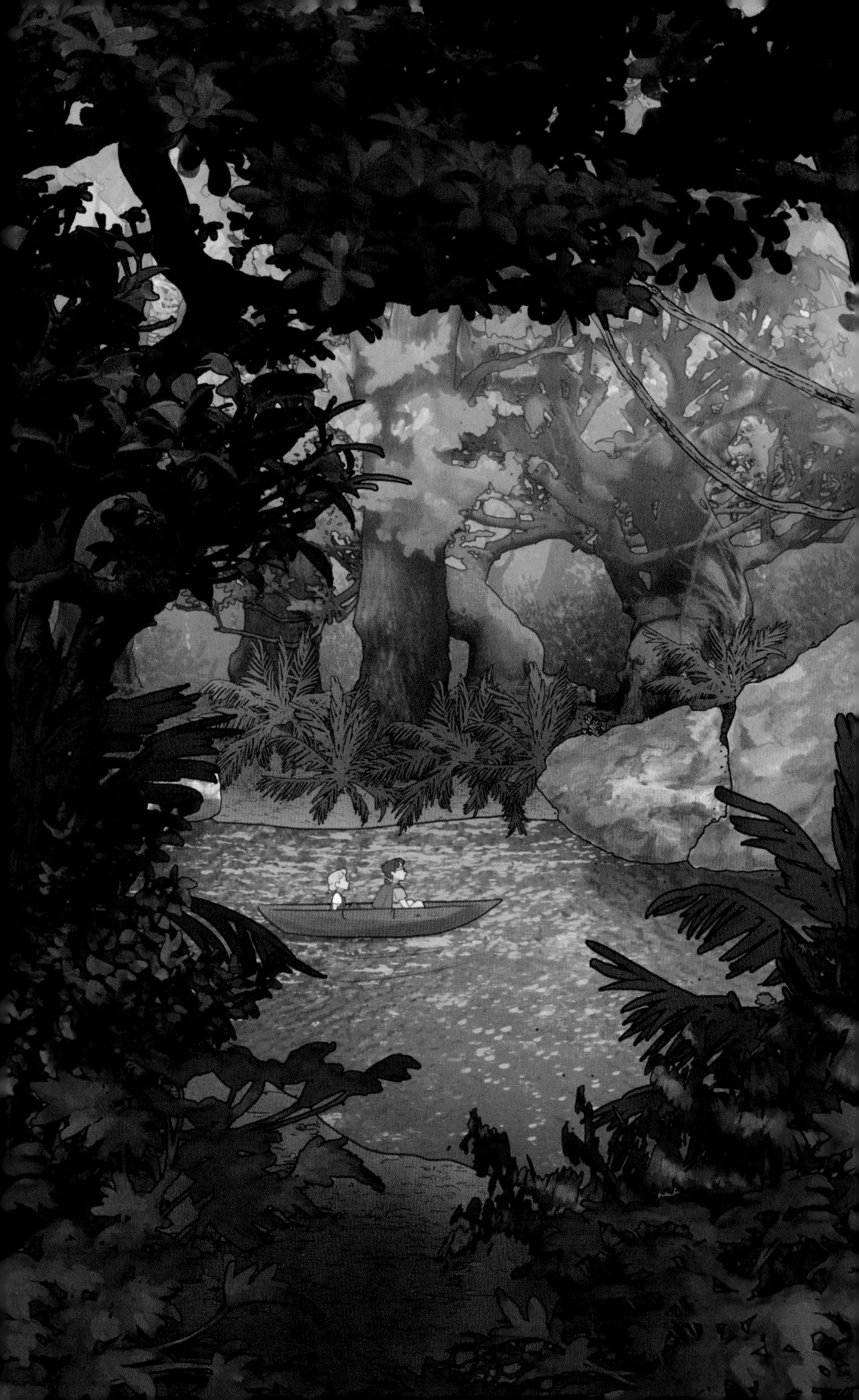

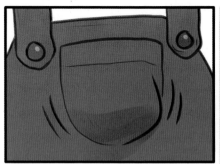

SQUEAK!

It's okay, Peanut. The ants can't get us in the river.

We're safe.

Maybe safe from the ants.

But where is this canoe going?

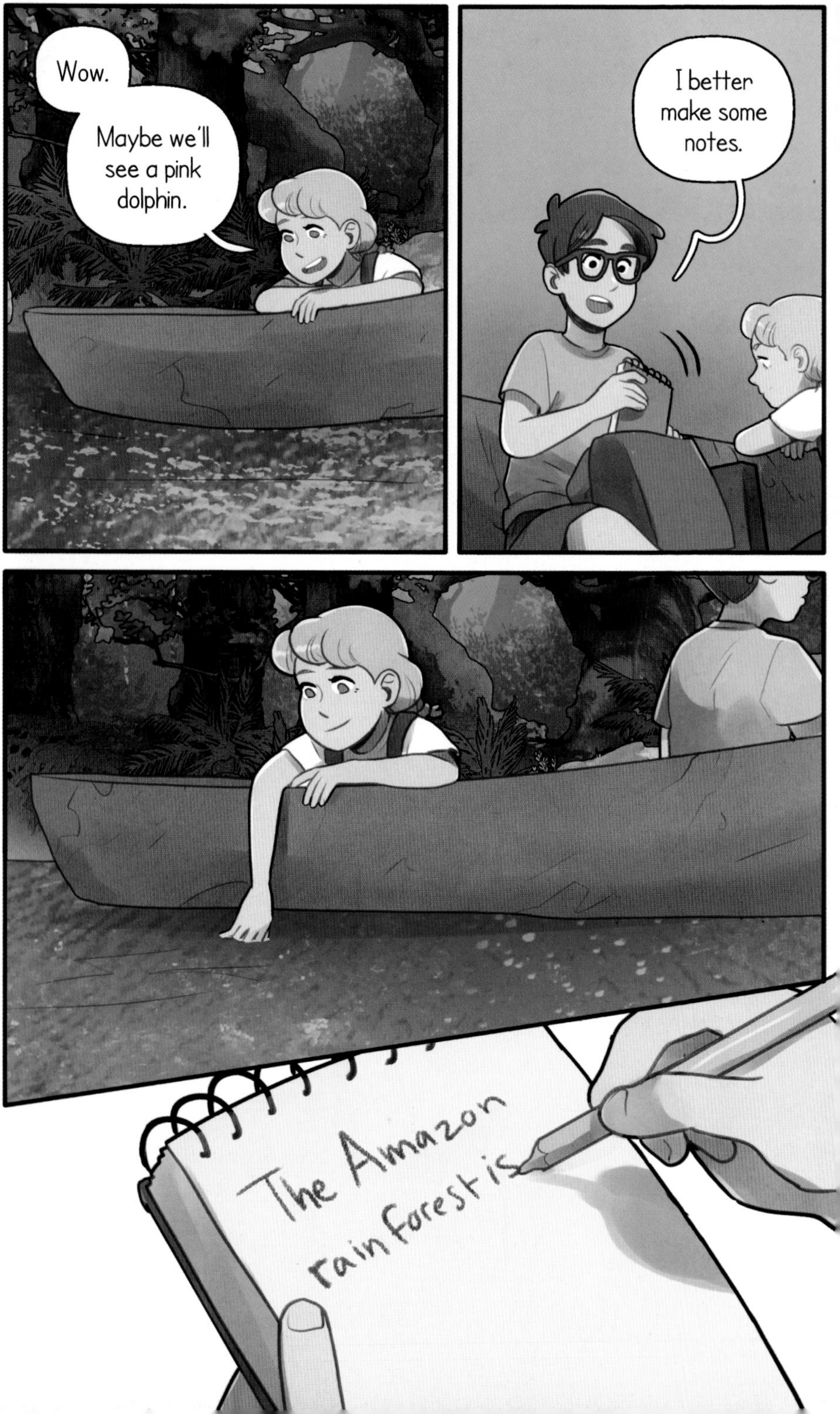

Wow.
Maybe we'll see a pink dolphin.
I better make some notes.
The Amazon rainforest is

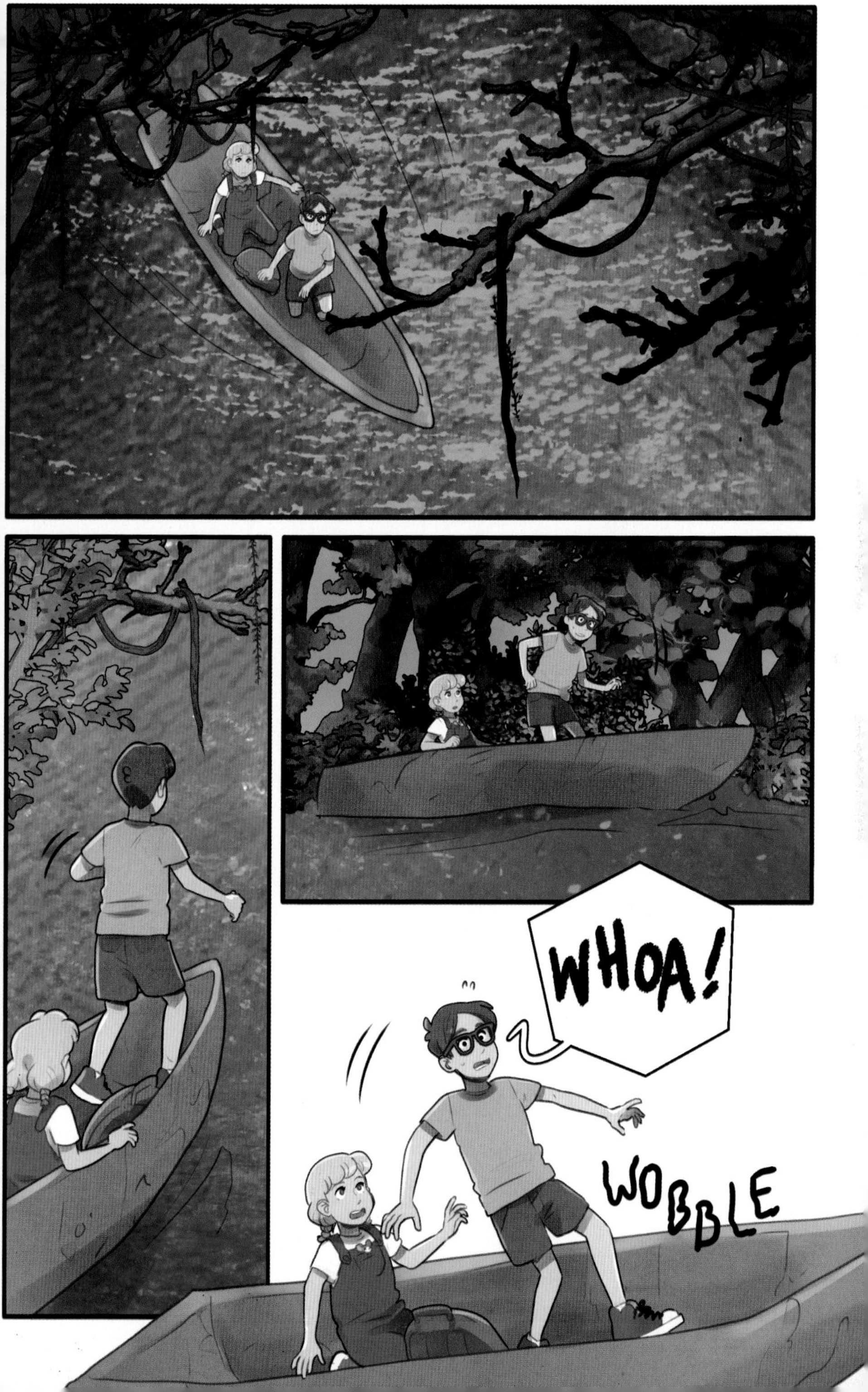
WHOA!
WOBBLE

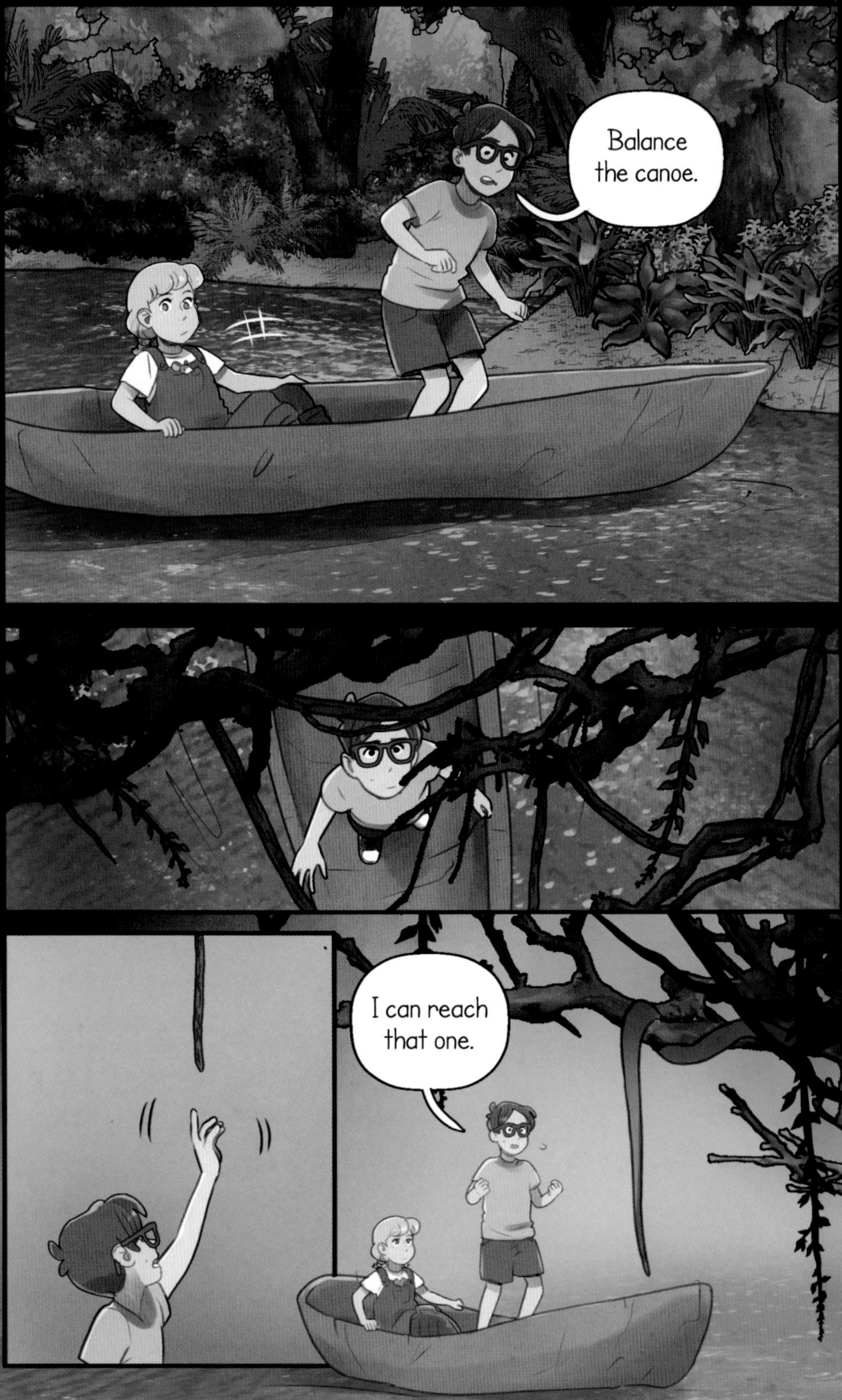
Balance the canoe.
I can reach that one.

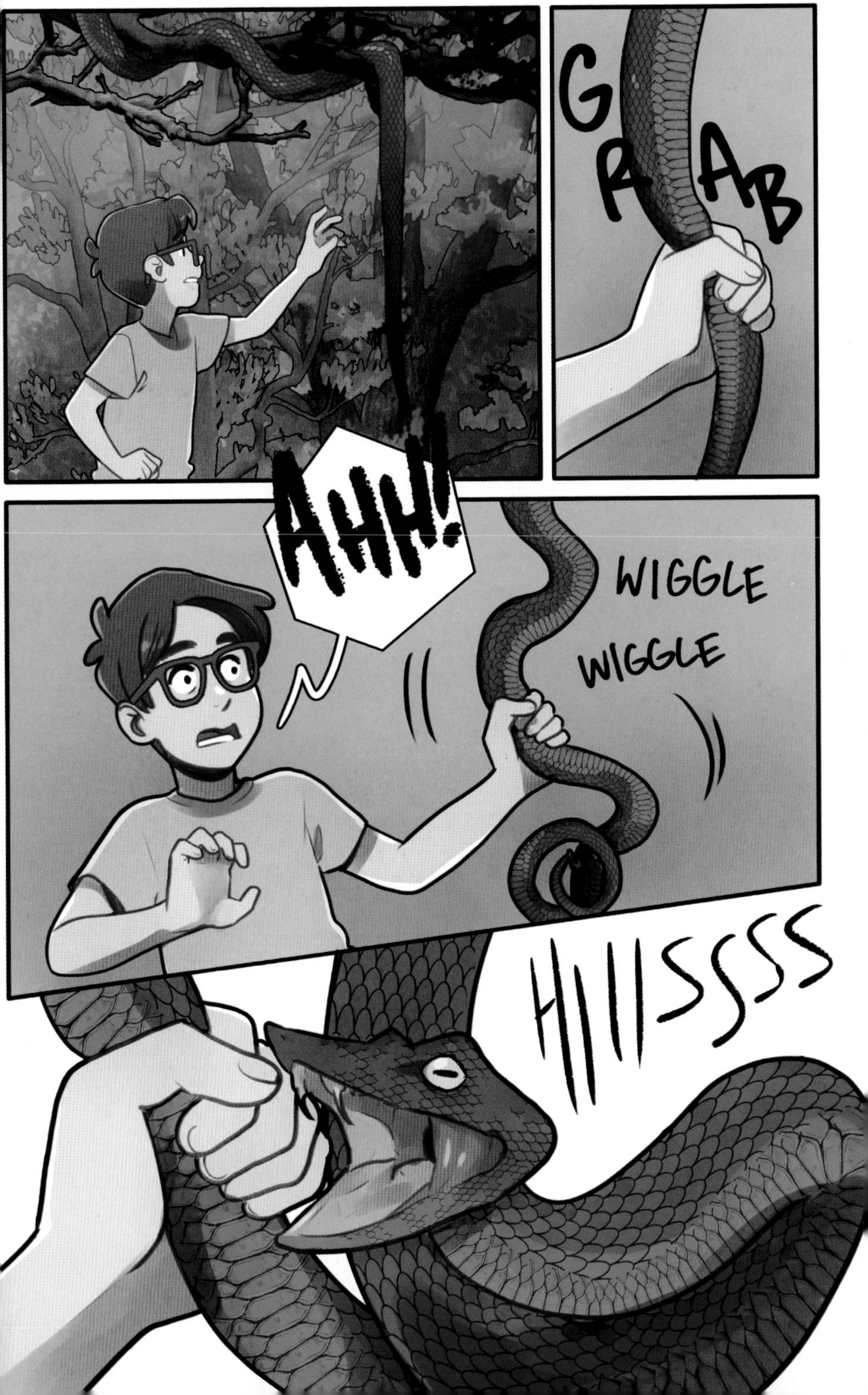
GRAB
AHH!
WIGGLE
WIGGLE
HHHSSSS

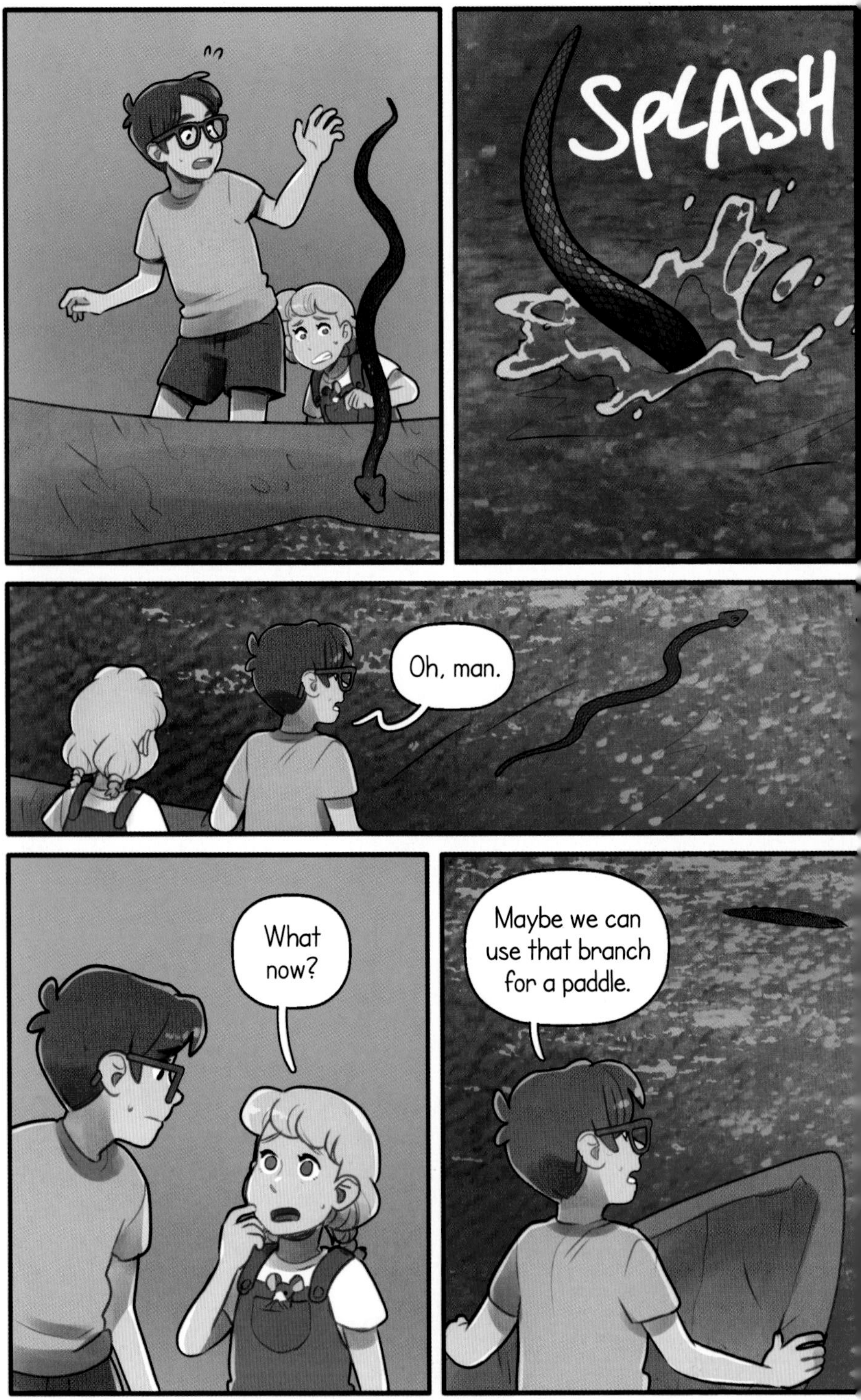
SPLASH
Oh, man.
What now?
Maybe we can use that branch for a paddle.

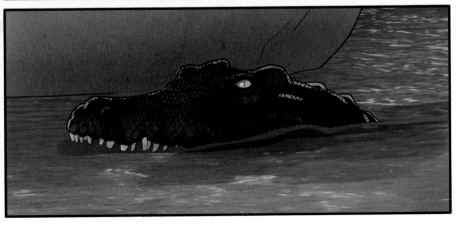

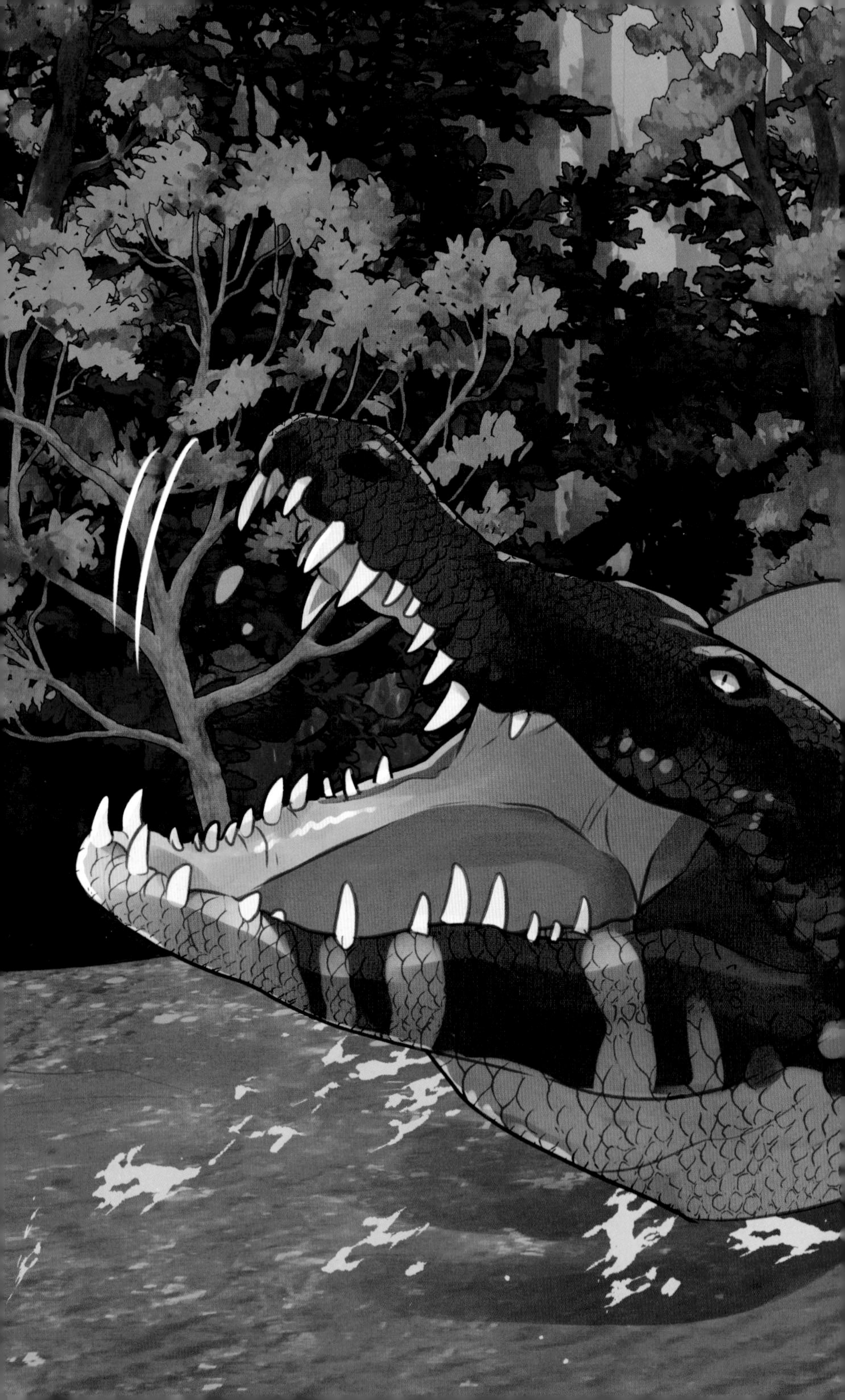

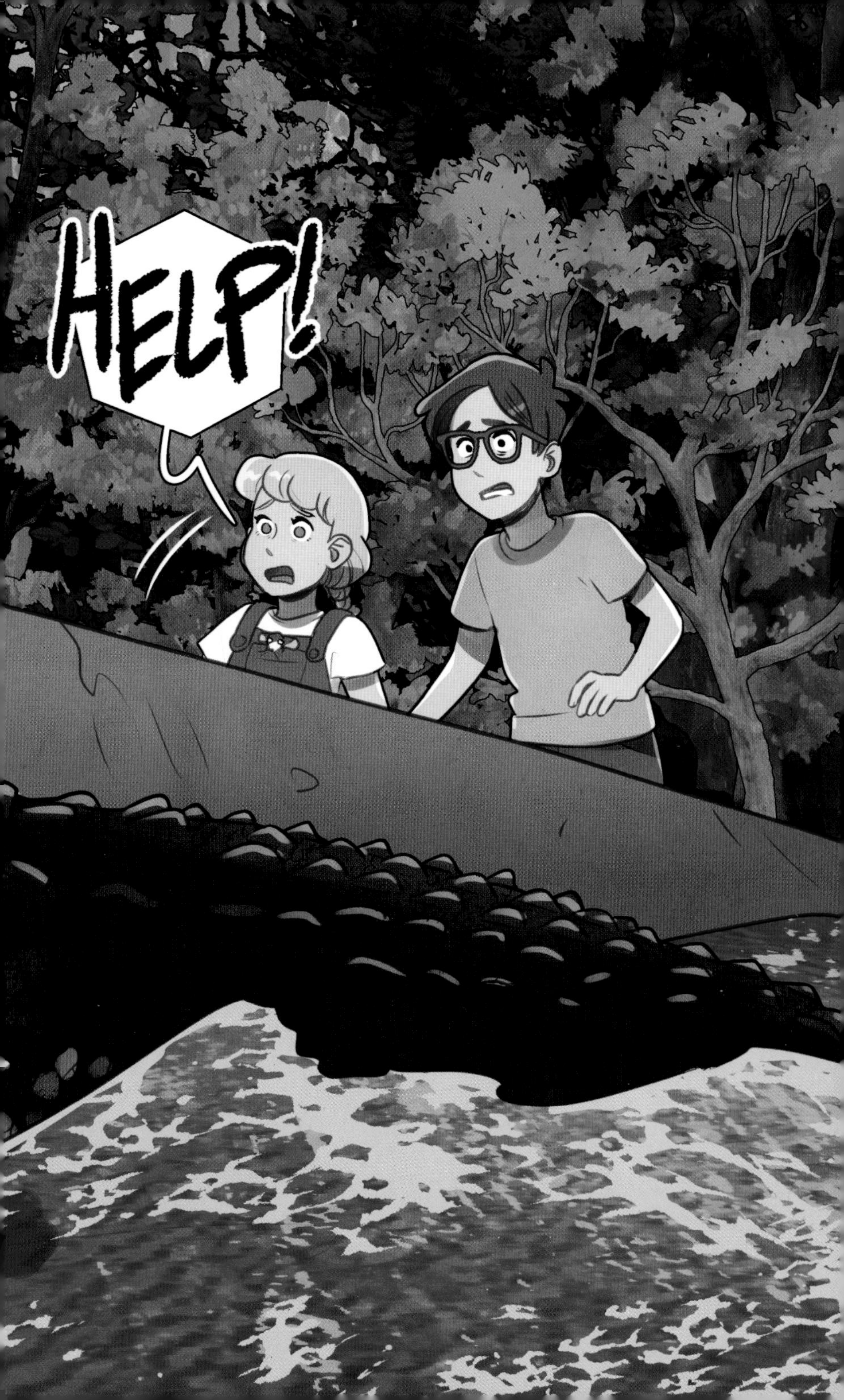
HELP!

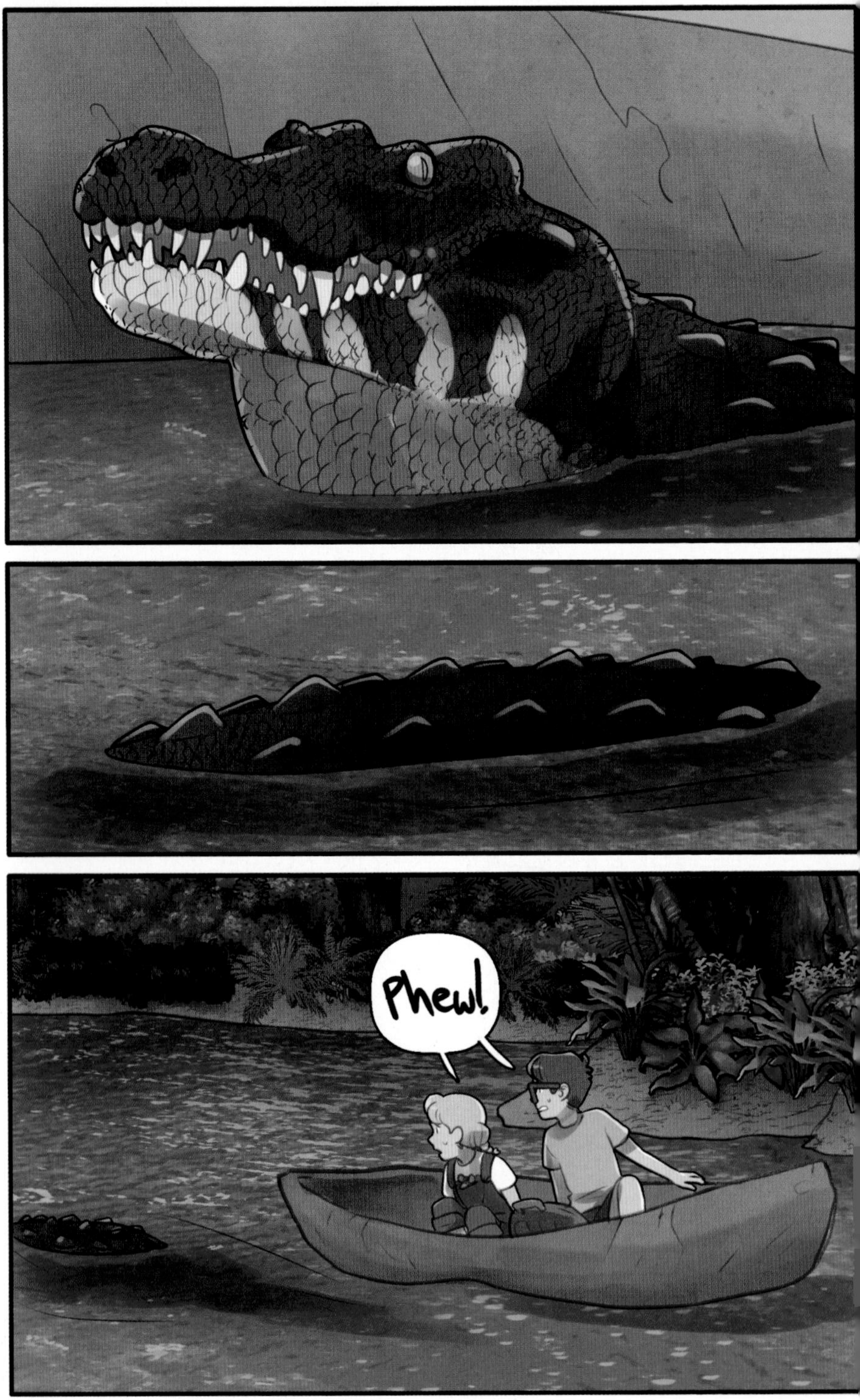
Phew!

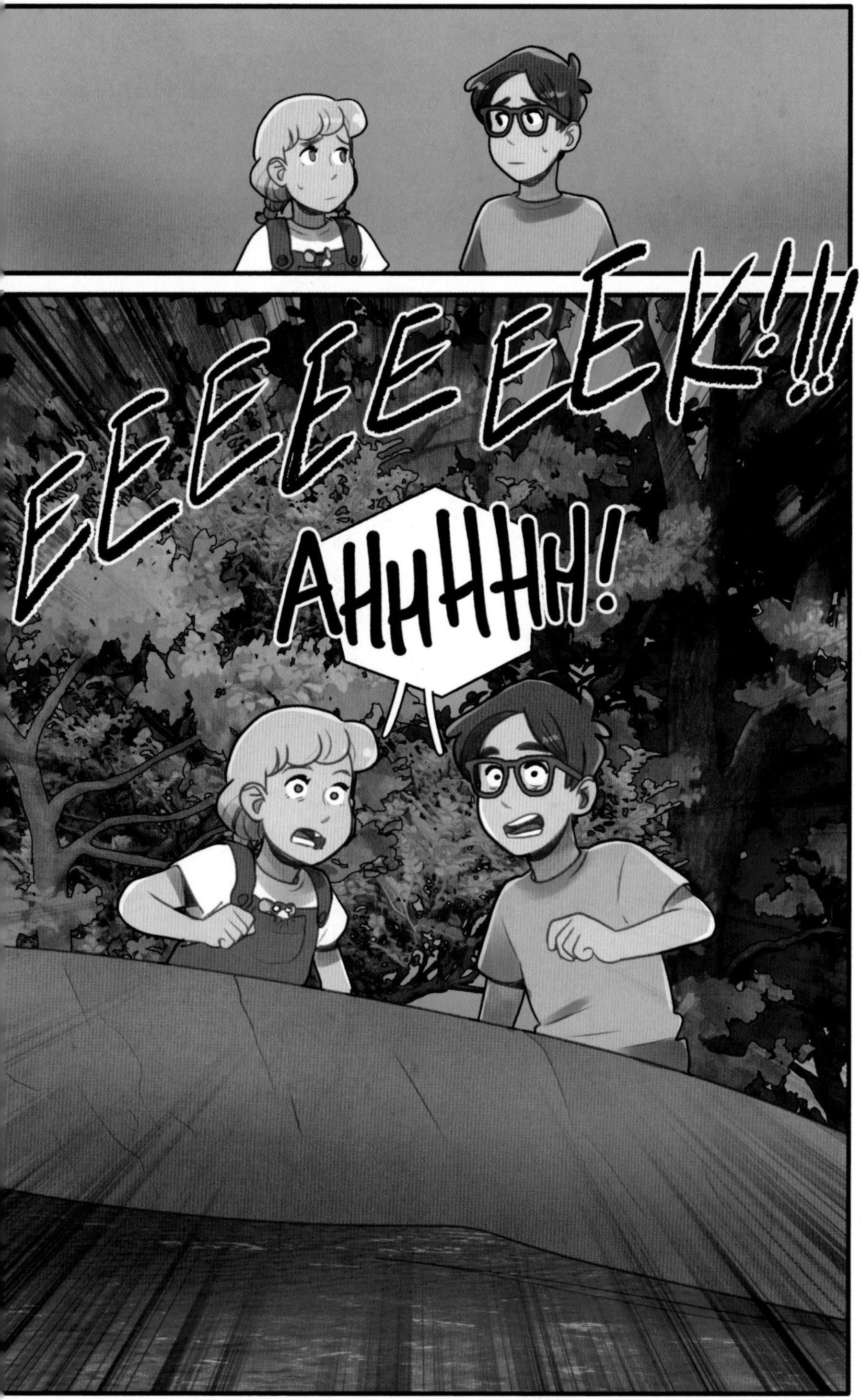
EEEEEEEK!!!
AHHHHH!

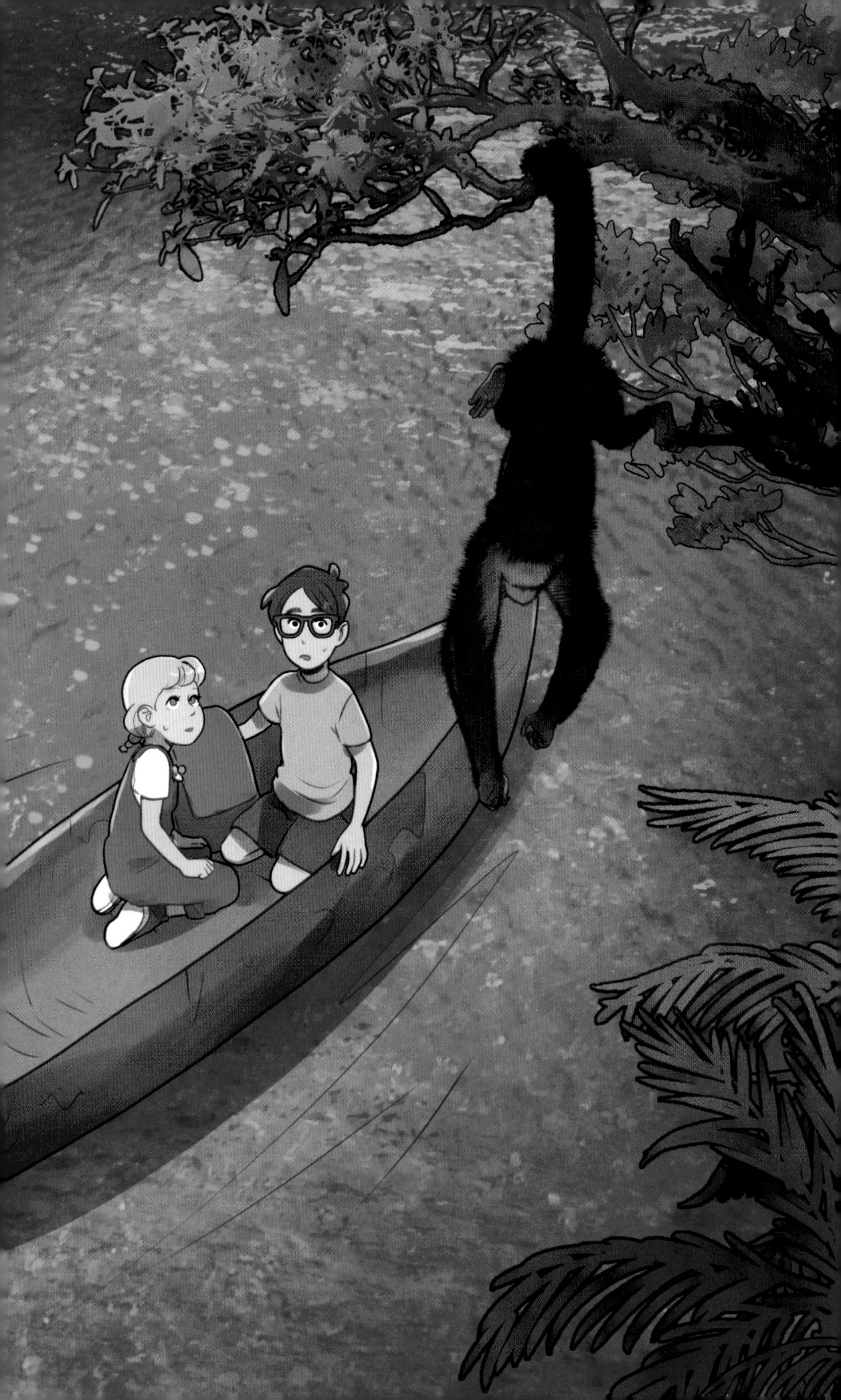

CHAPTER FIVE
Monkey Trouble

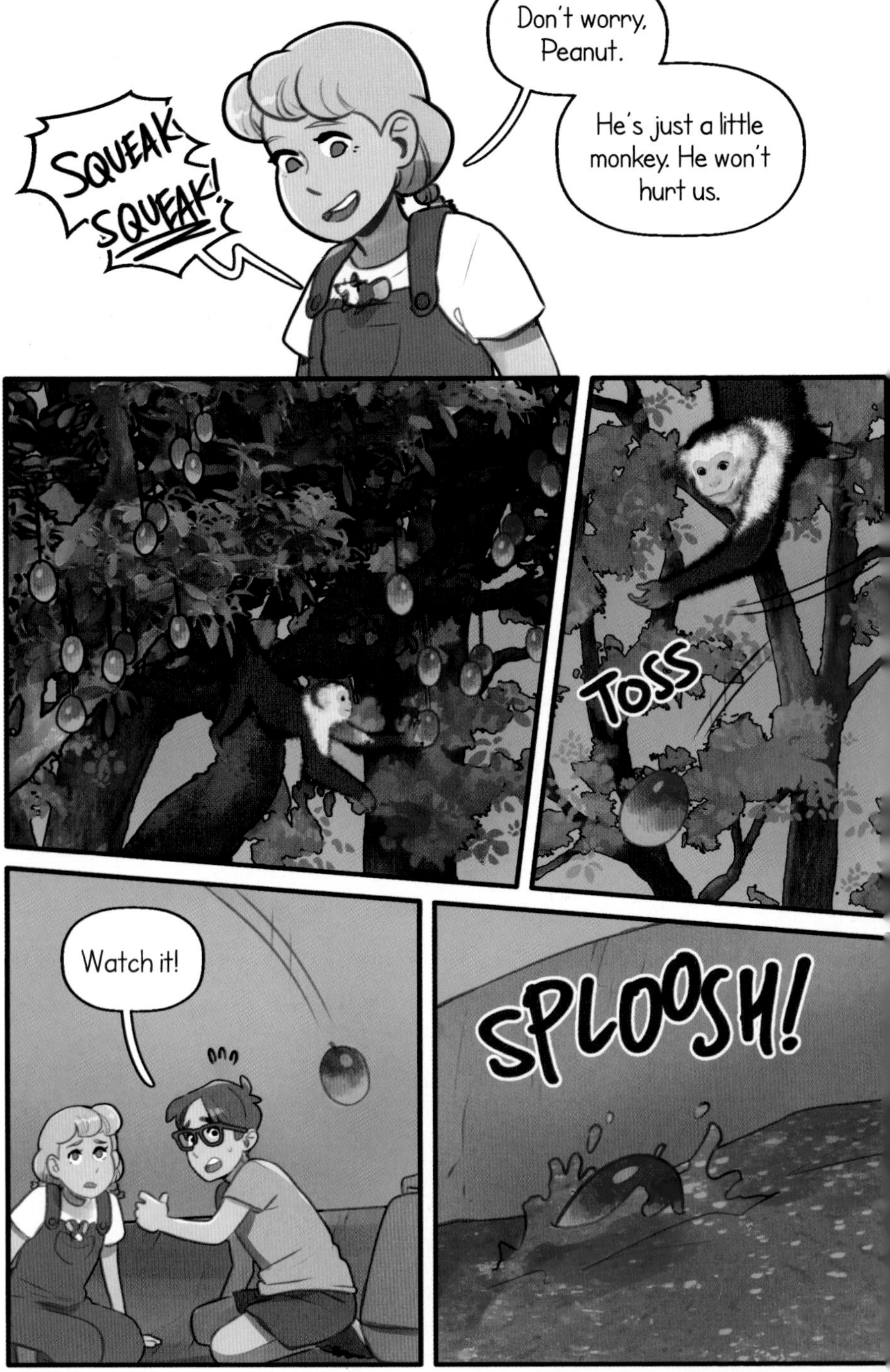
SQUEAK SQUEAK!
Don't worry, Peanut.
He's just a little monkey. He won't hurt us.
TOSS
Watch it!
SPLOOSH!

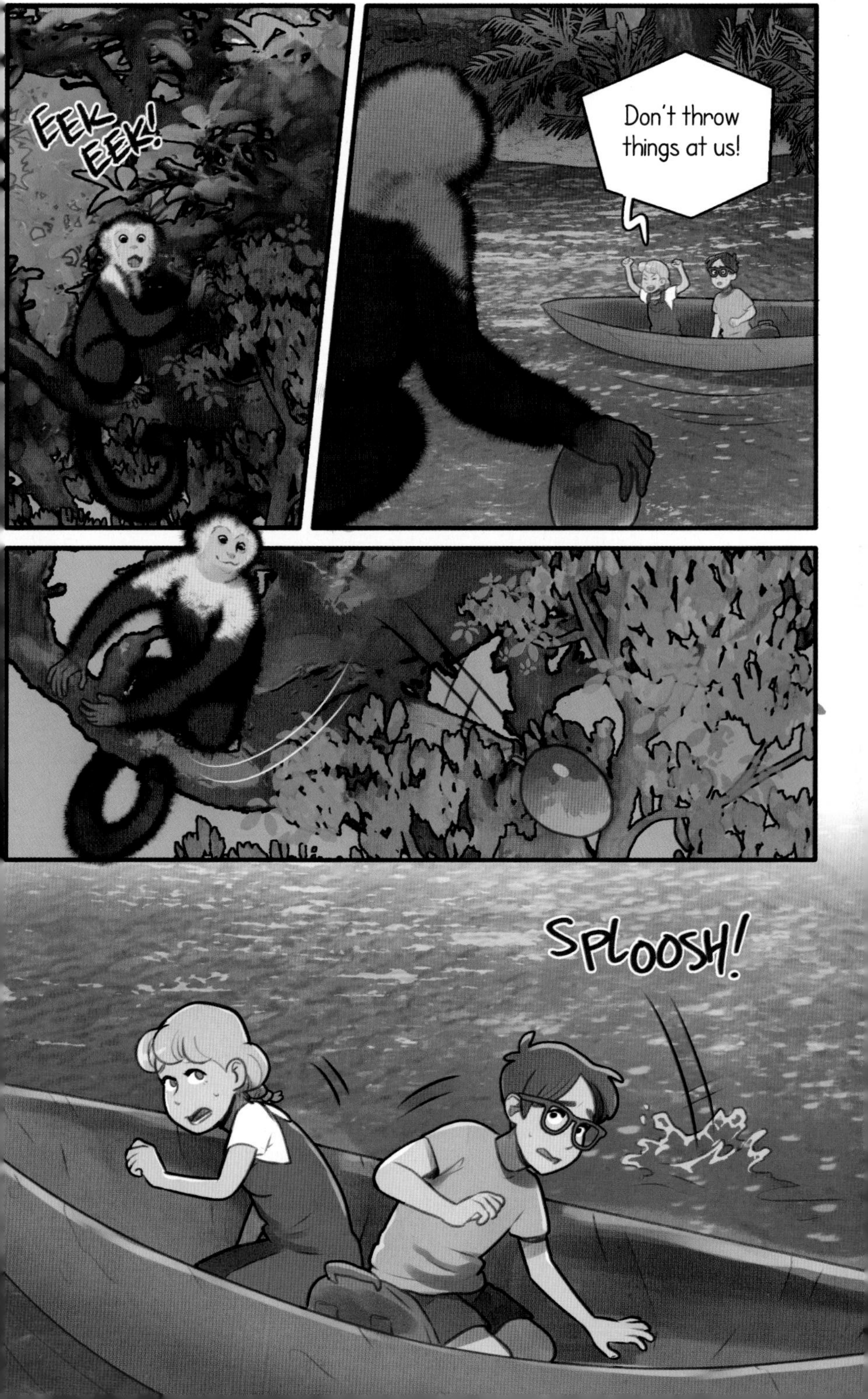
EEK EEK!
Don't throw things at us!
SPLOOSH!

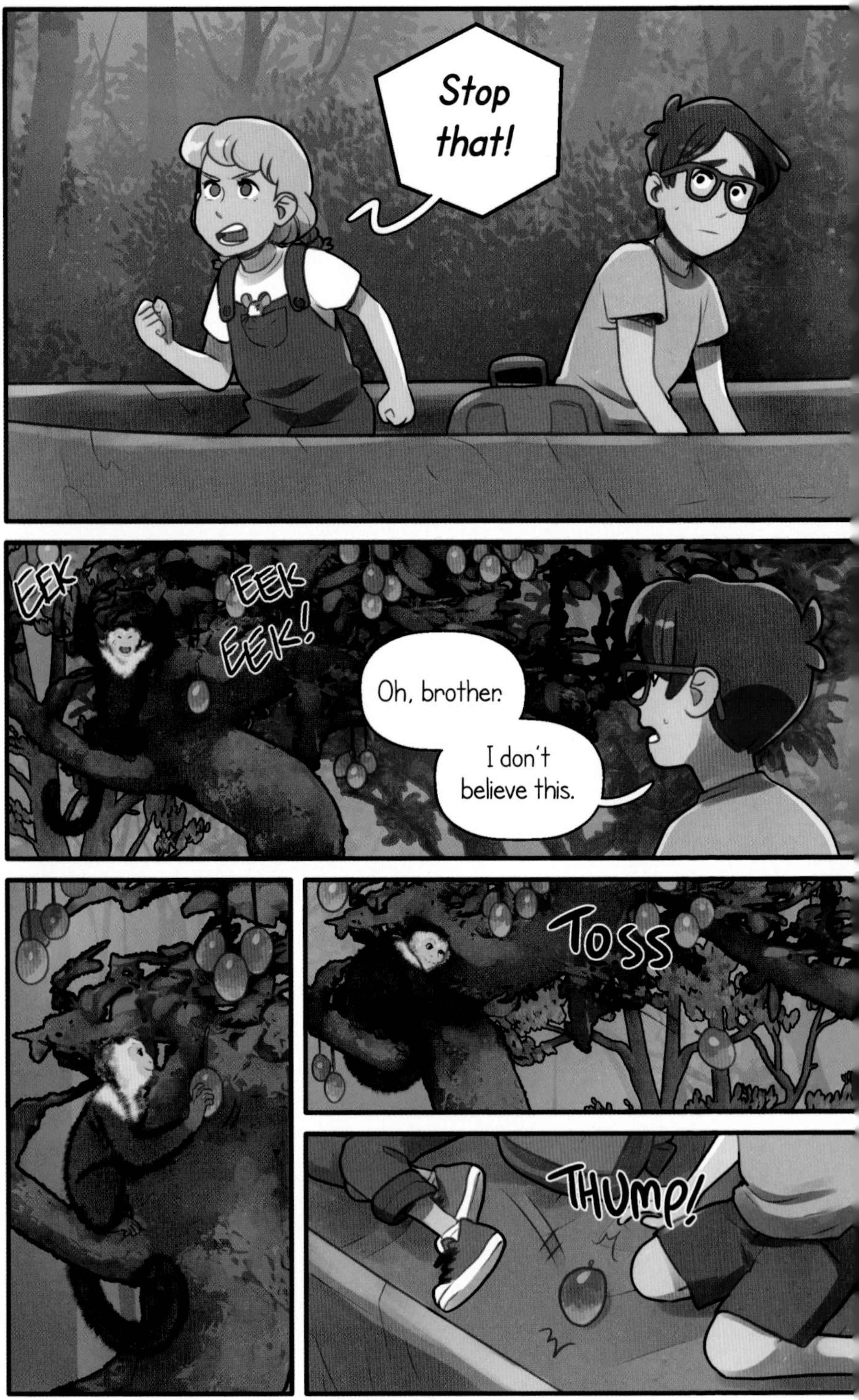
Stop that!
EEK
EEK
EEK!
Oh, brother.
I don't believe this.
TOSS
THUMP!

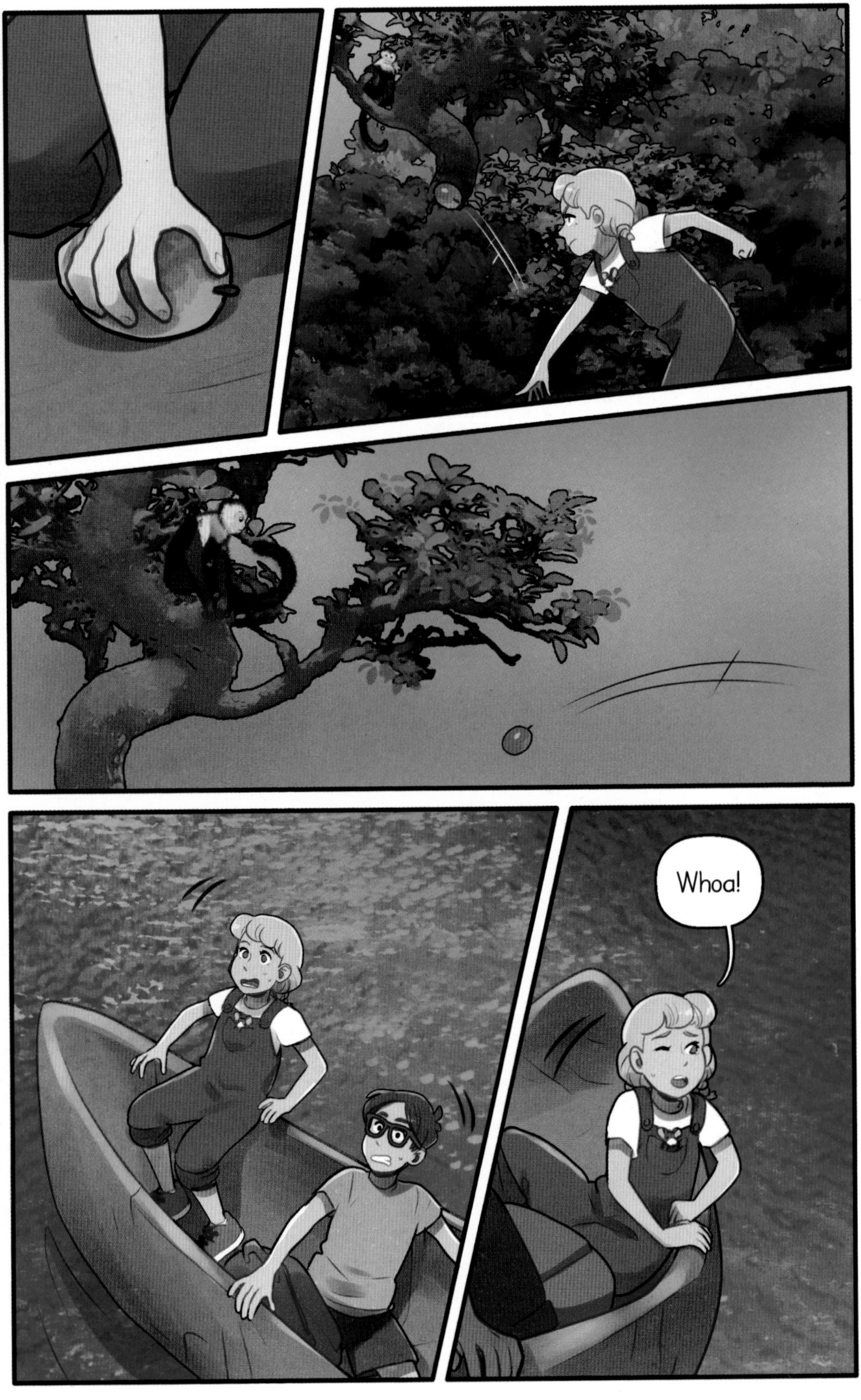
Whoa!

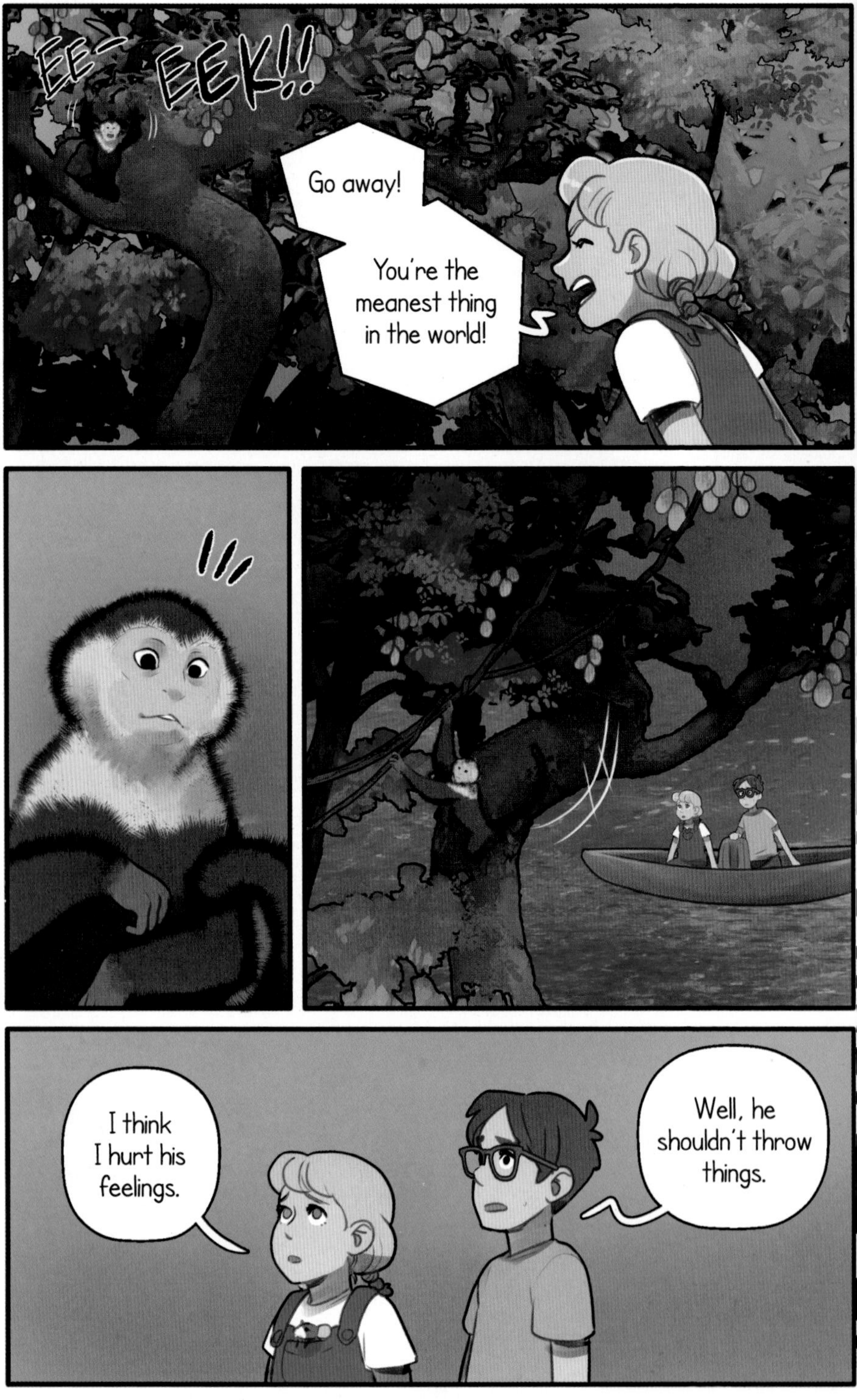
EE— EEK!!
Go away!
You're the meanest thing in the world!
I think I hurt his feelings.
Well, he shouldn't throw things.

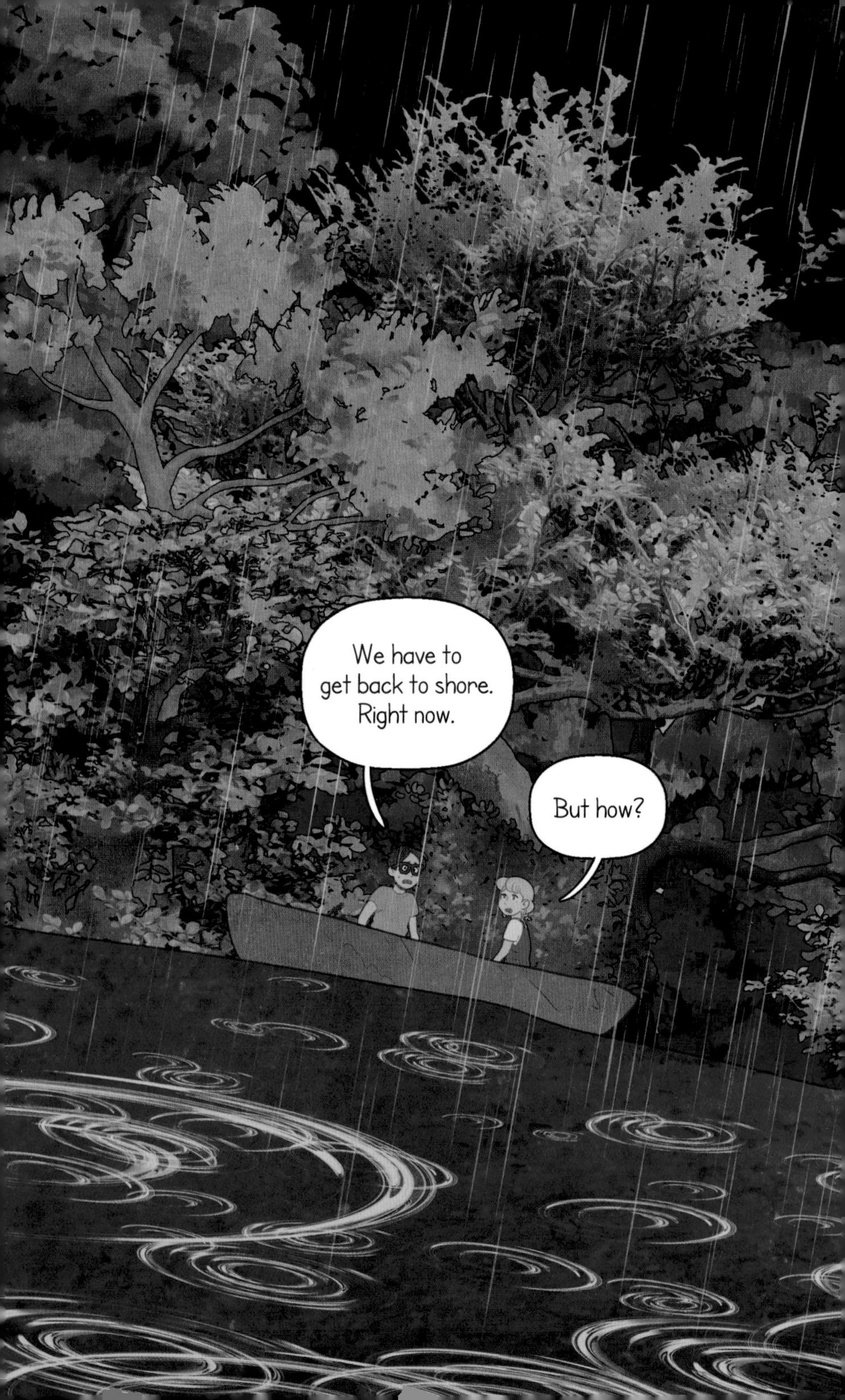
We have to get back to shore. Right now.
But how?

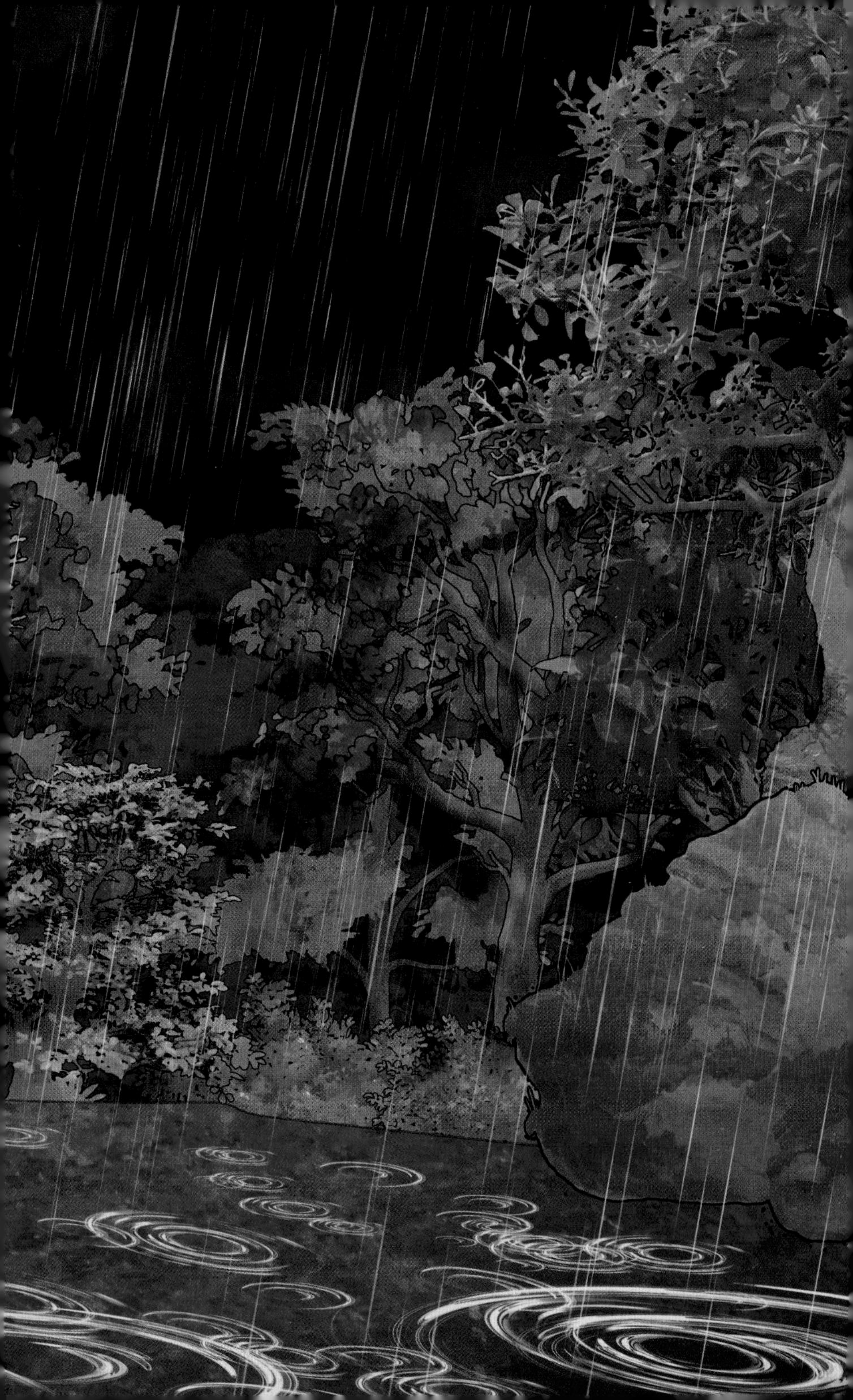

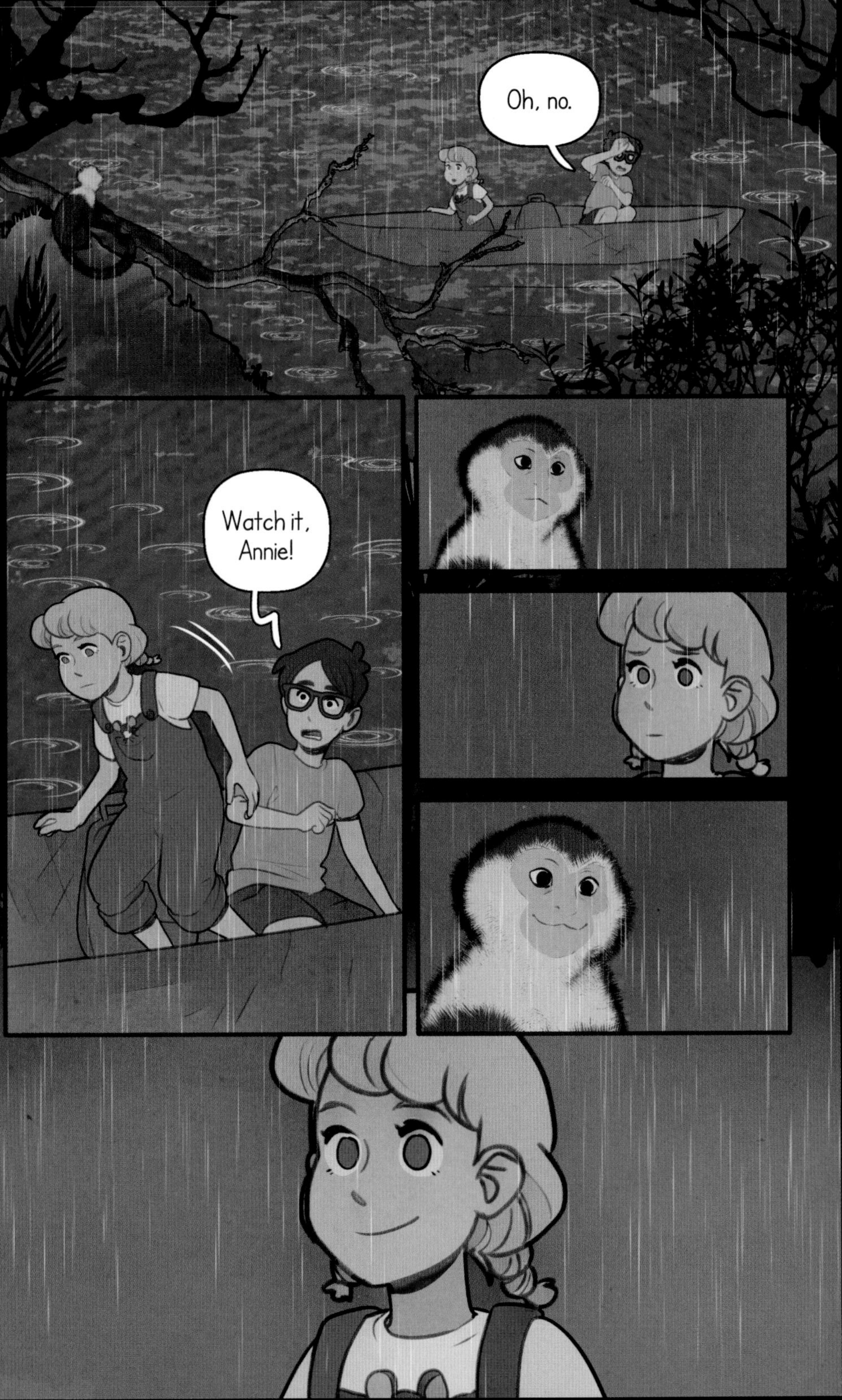
Oh, no.
Watch it, Annie!

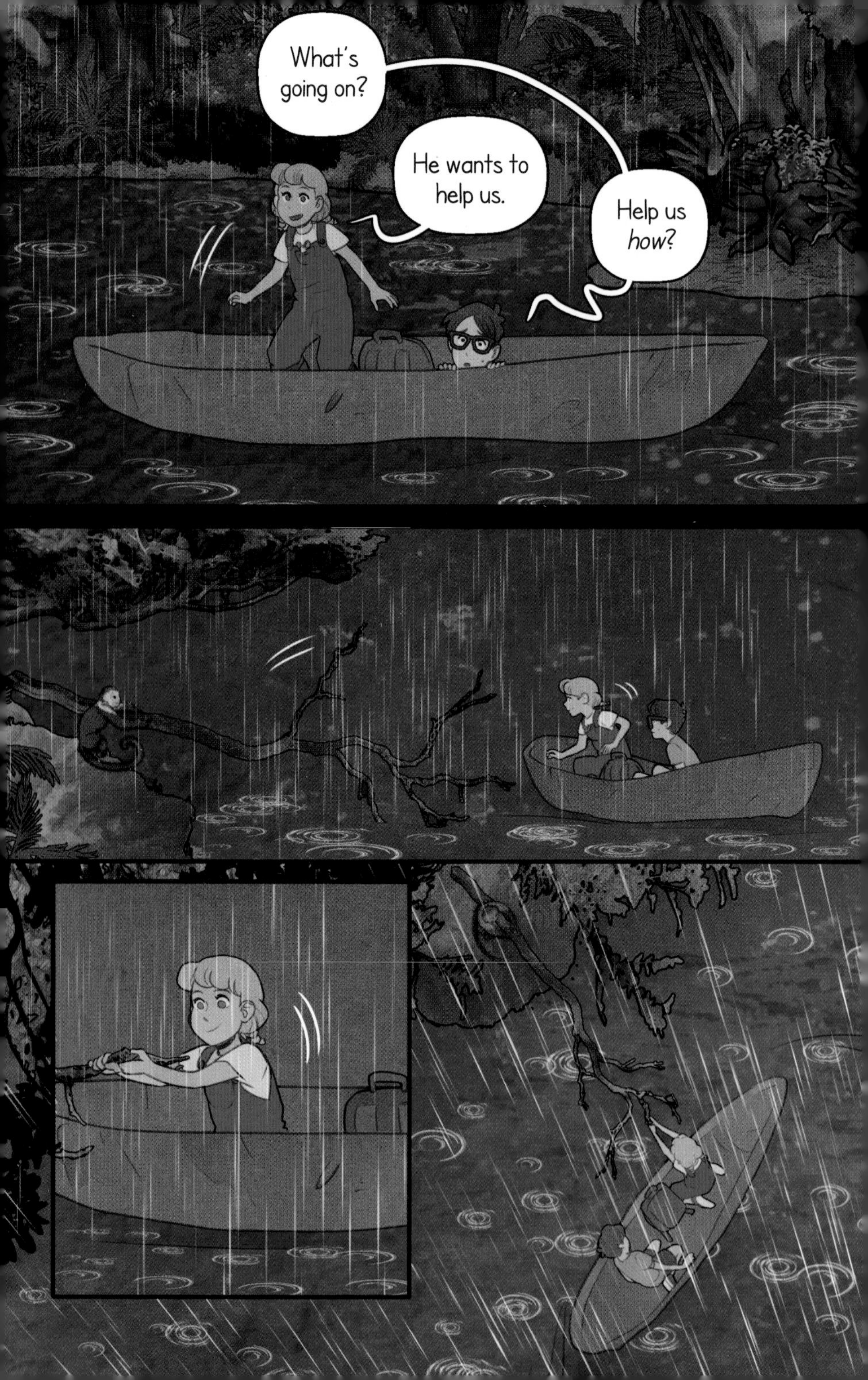
What's going on?
He wants to help us.
Help us *how?*

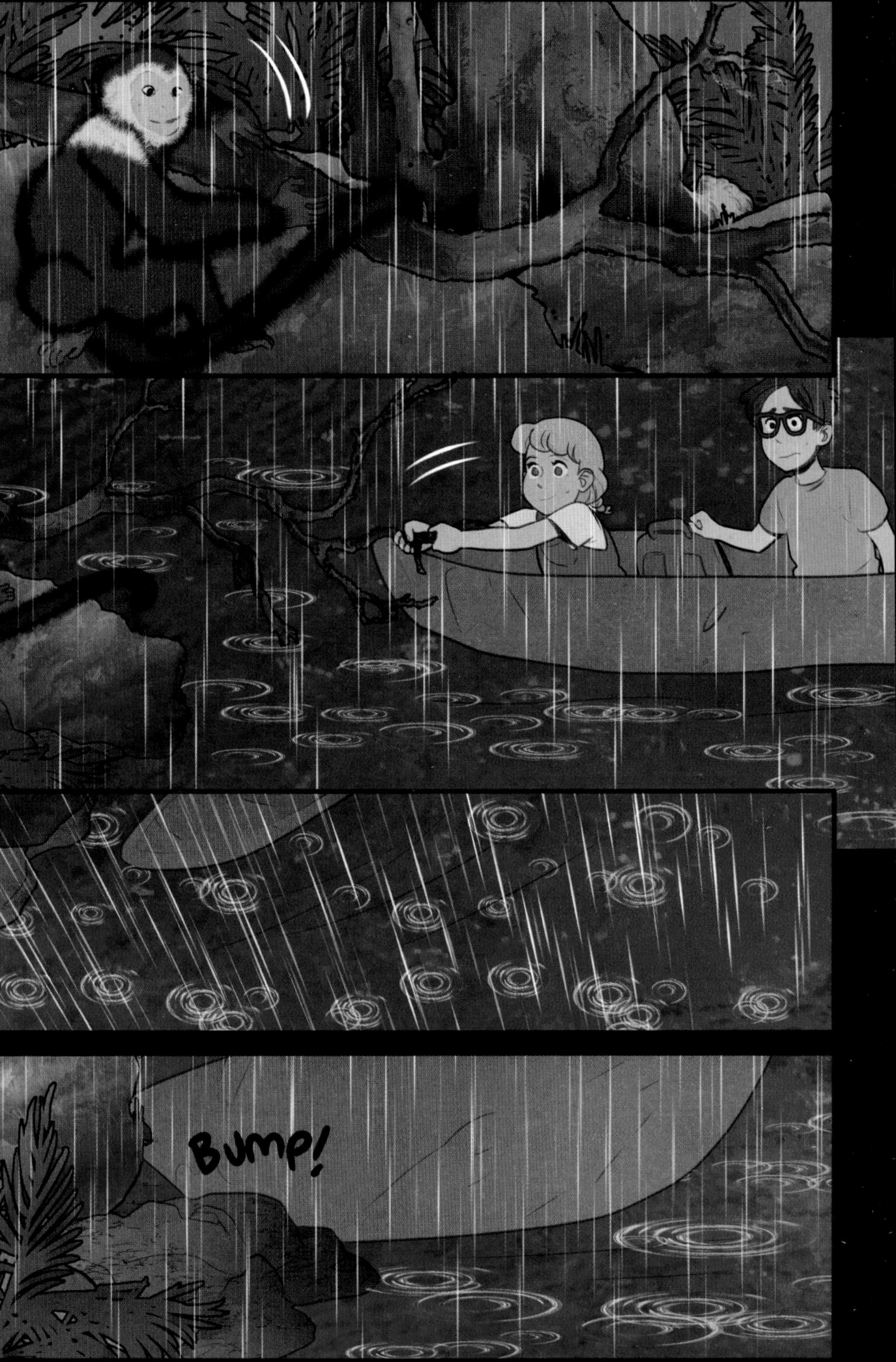
BUMP!

CHAPTER SIX
Freeze!

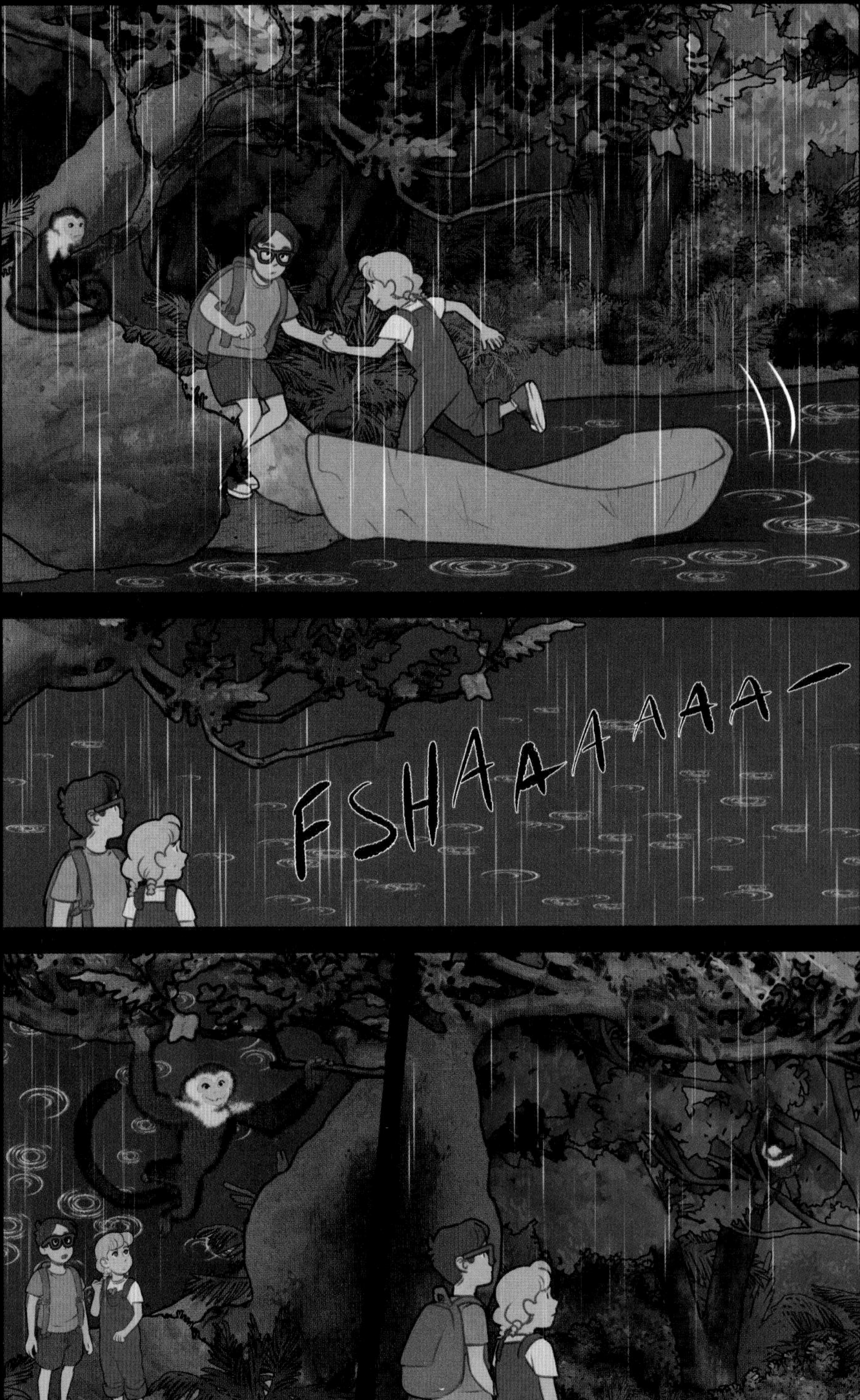
FSHAAAAAA-

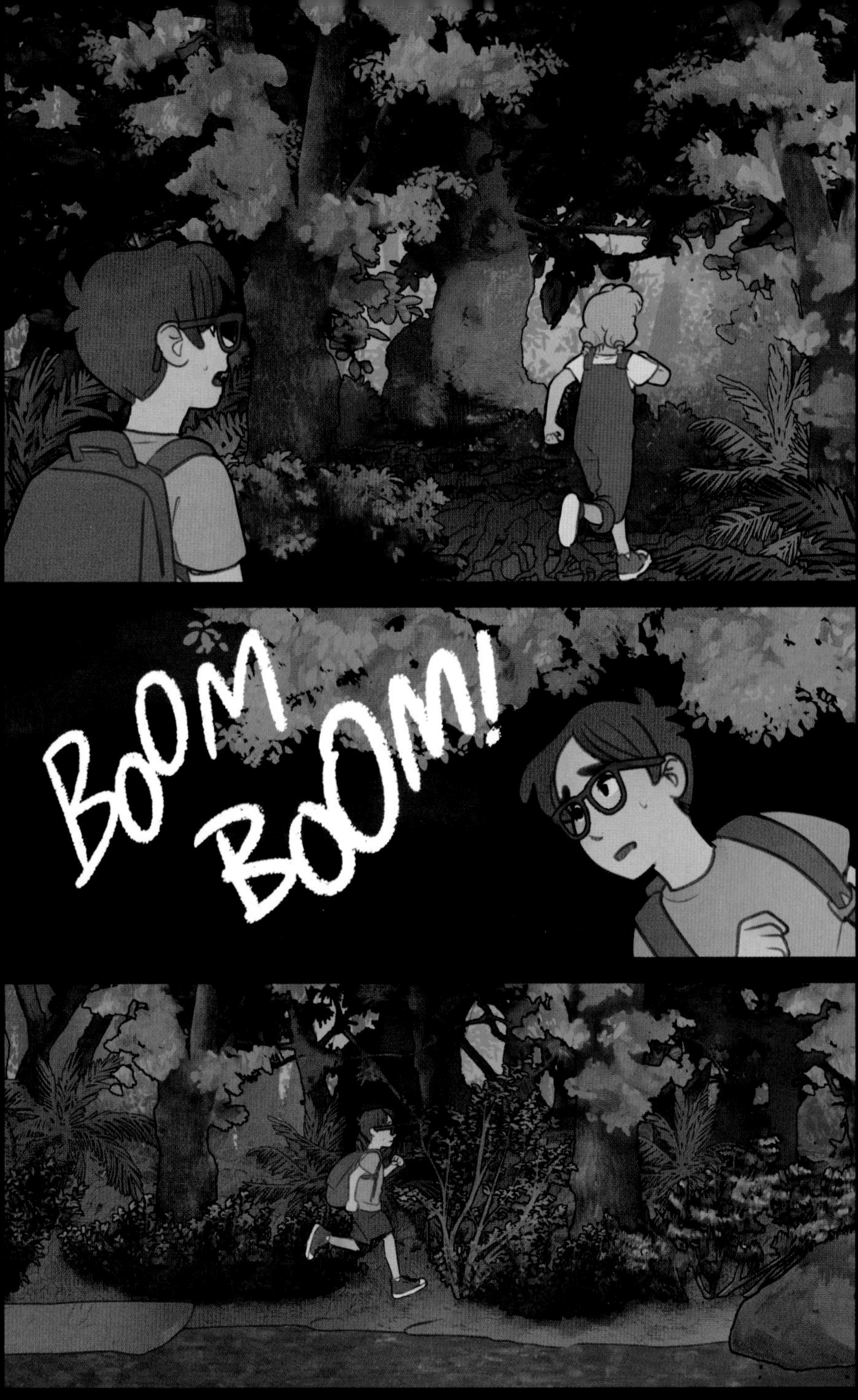
BOOM BOOM!

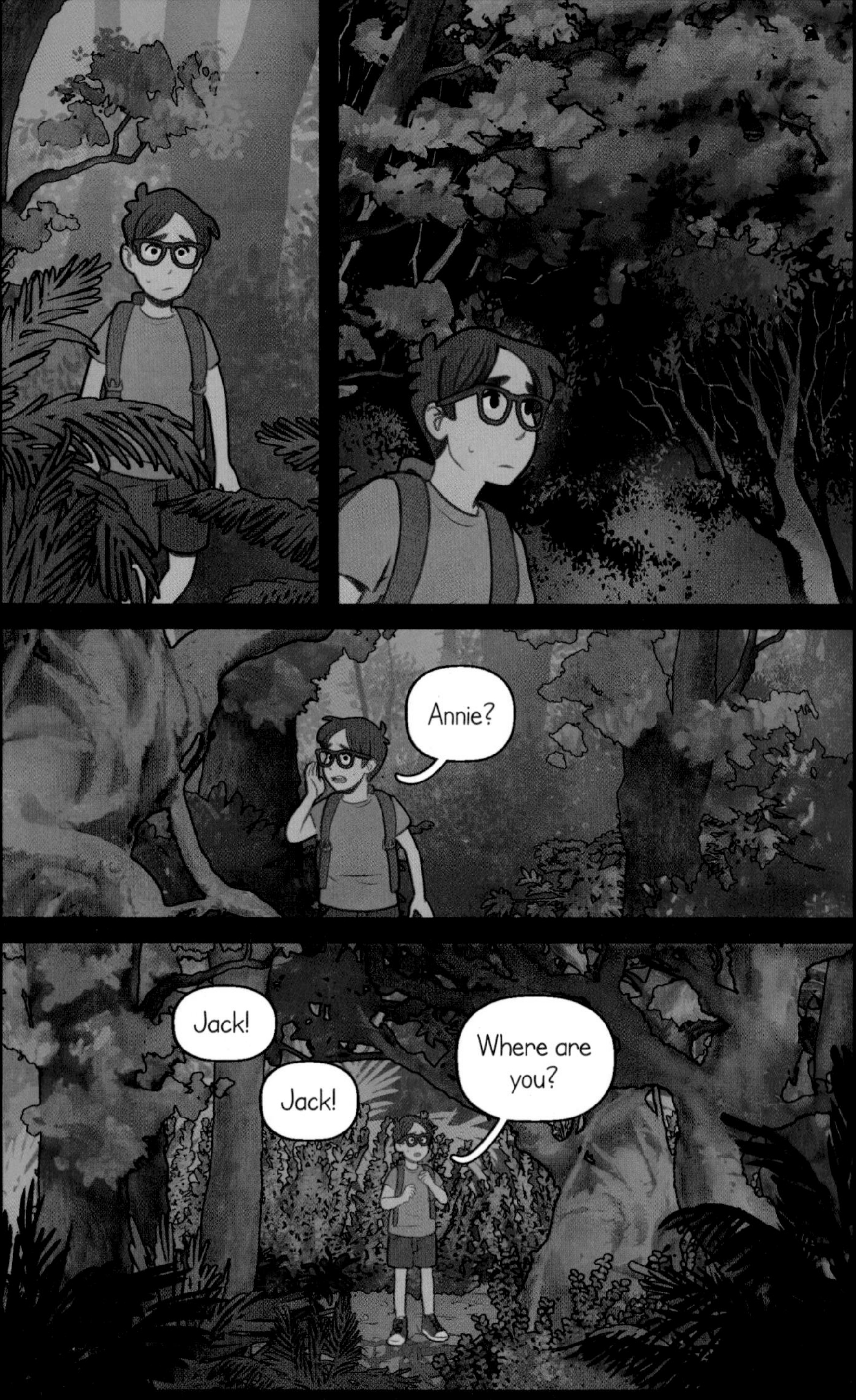
Annie?
Jack!
Jack!
Where are you?

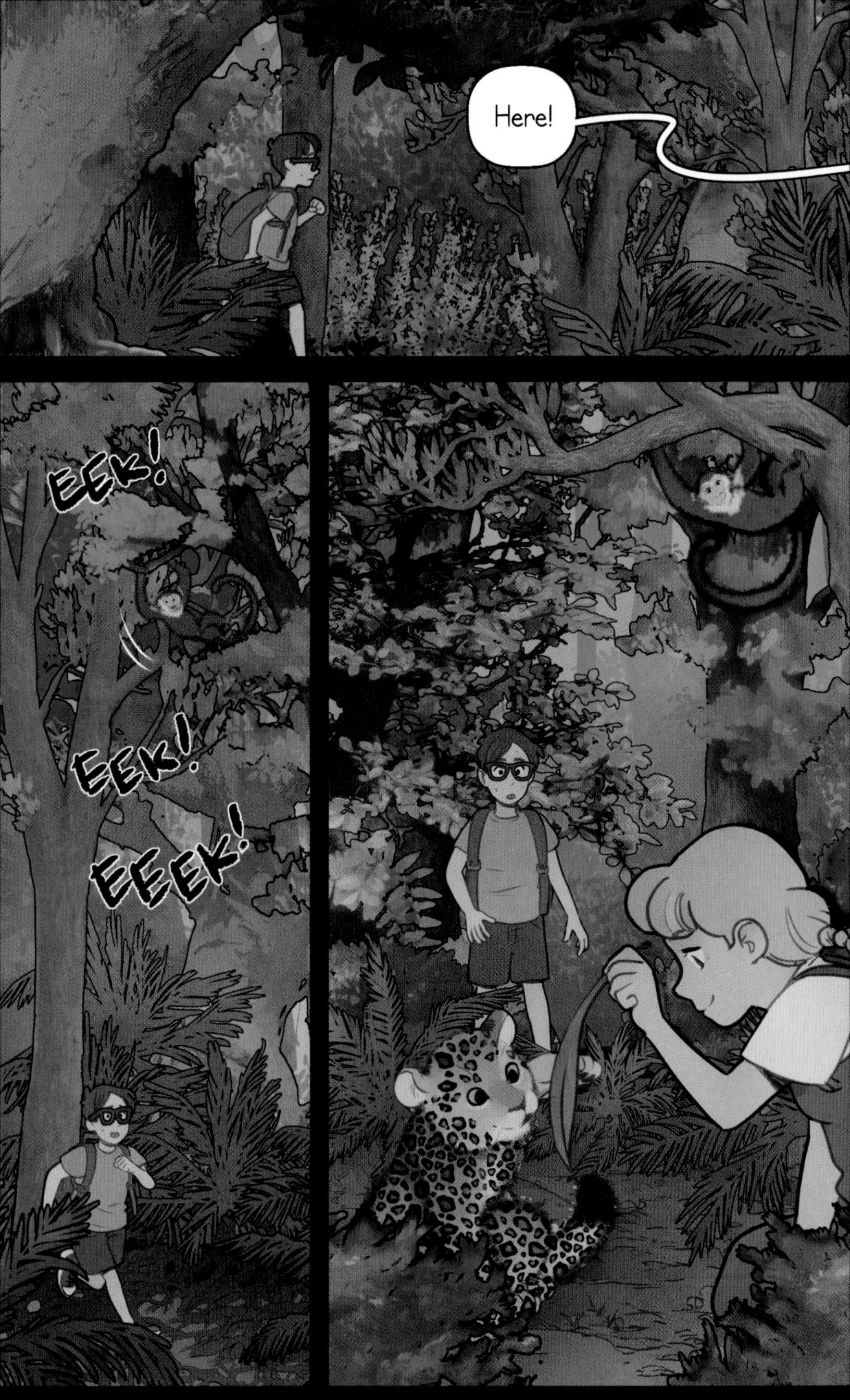
Here!
EEK!
EEK!
EEEK!

What's that?

I don't know, but I love it!

I'd better find out what it is.

Oh, it's so cute.

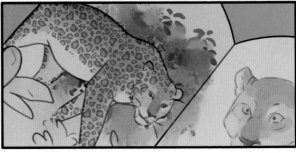

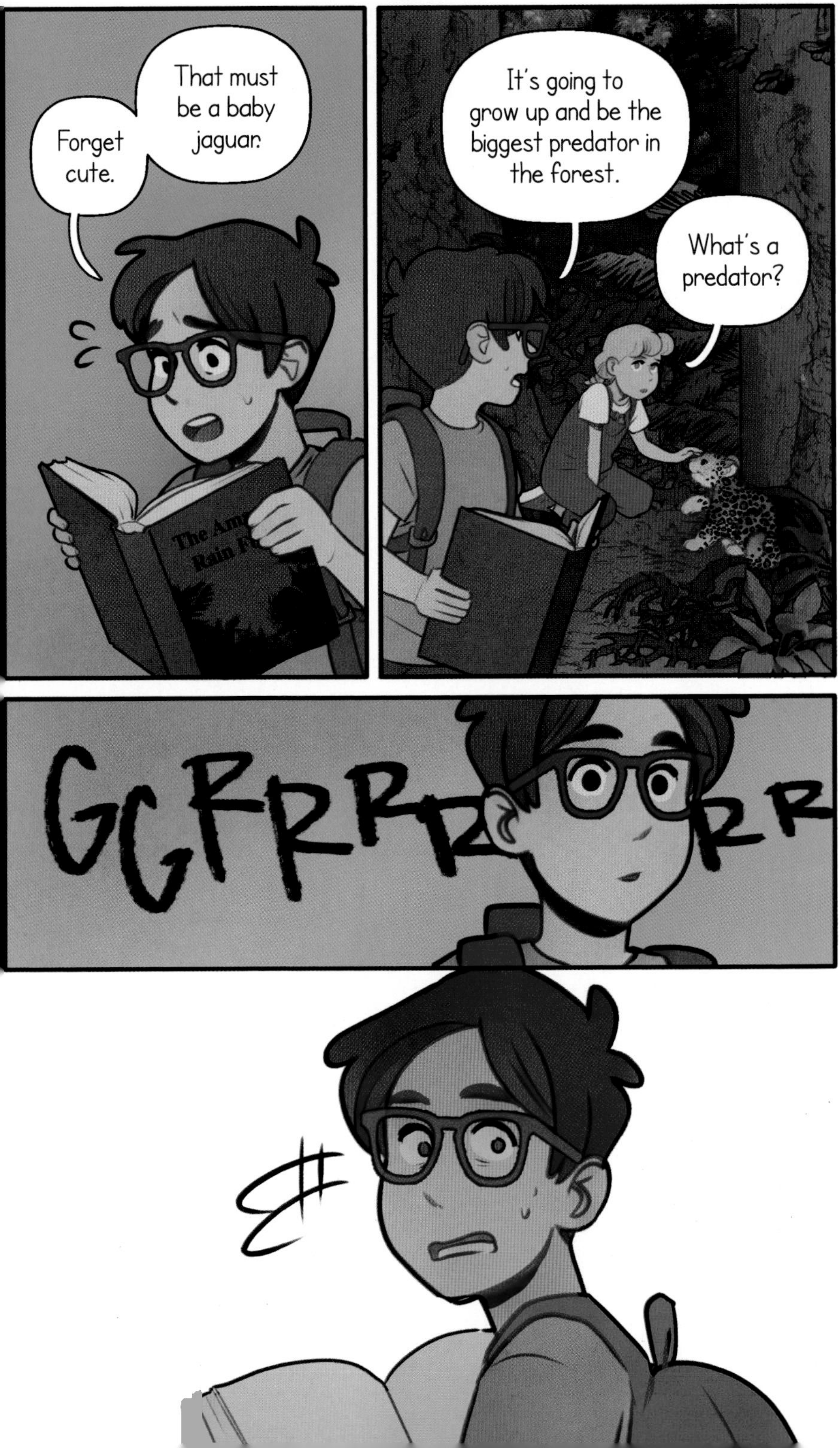

Forget cute.
That must be a baby jaguar.
It's going to grow up and be the biggest predator in the forest.
What's a predator?
GGRRRRRR

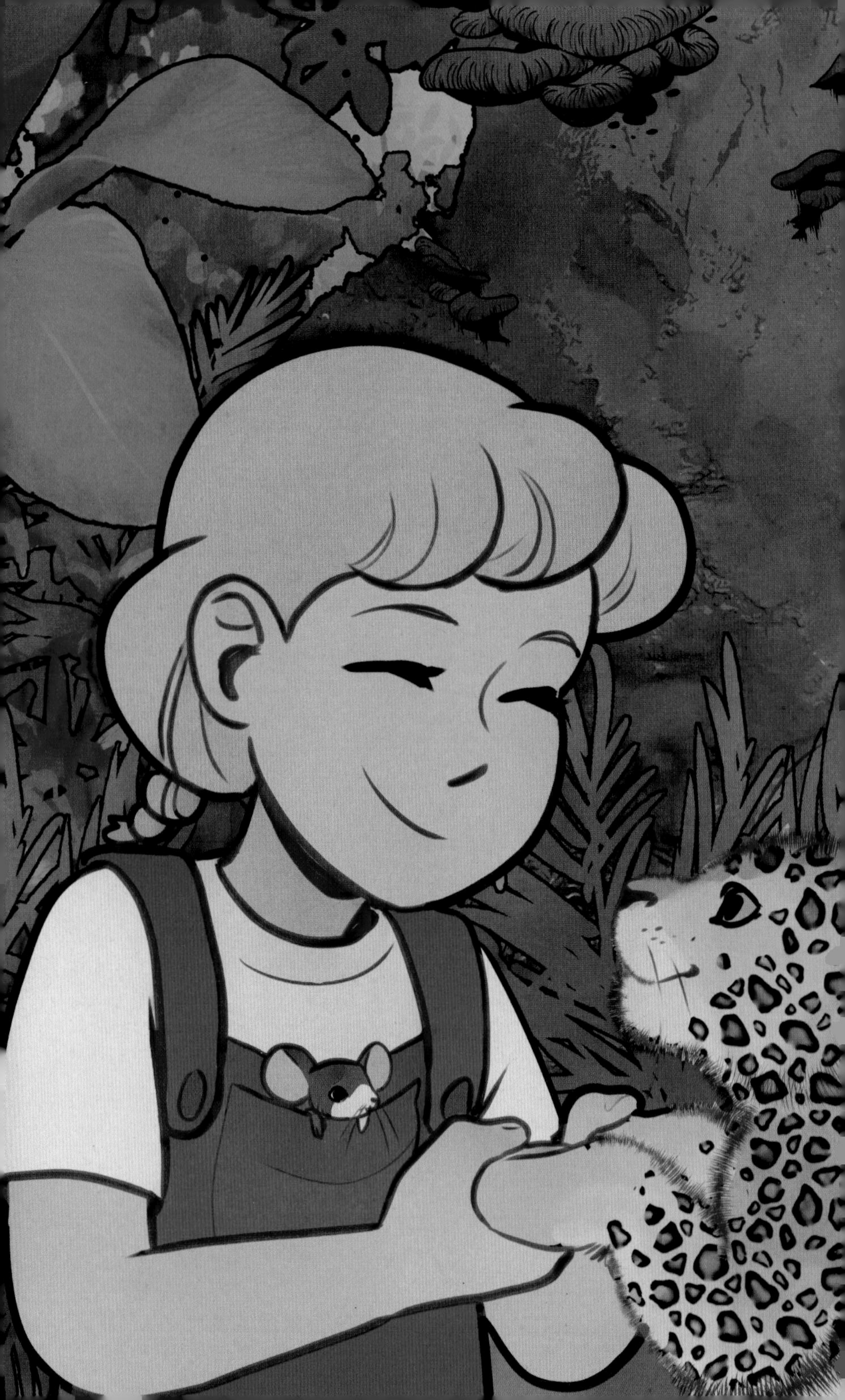

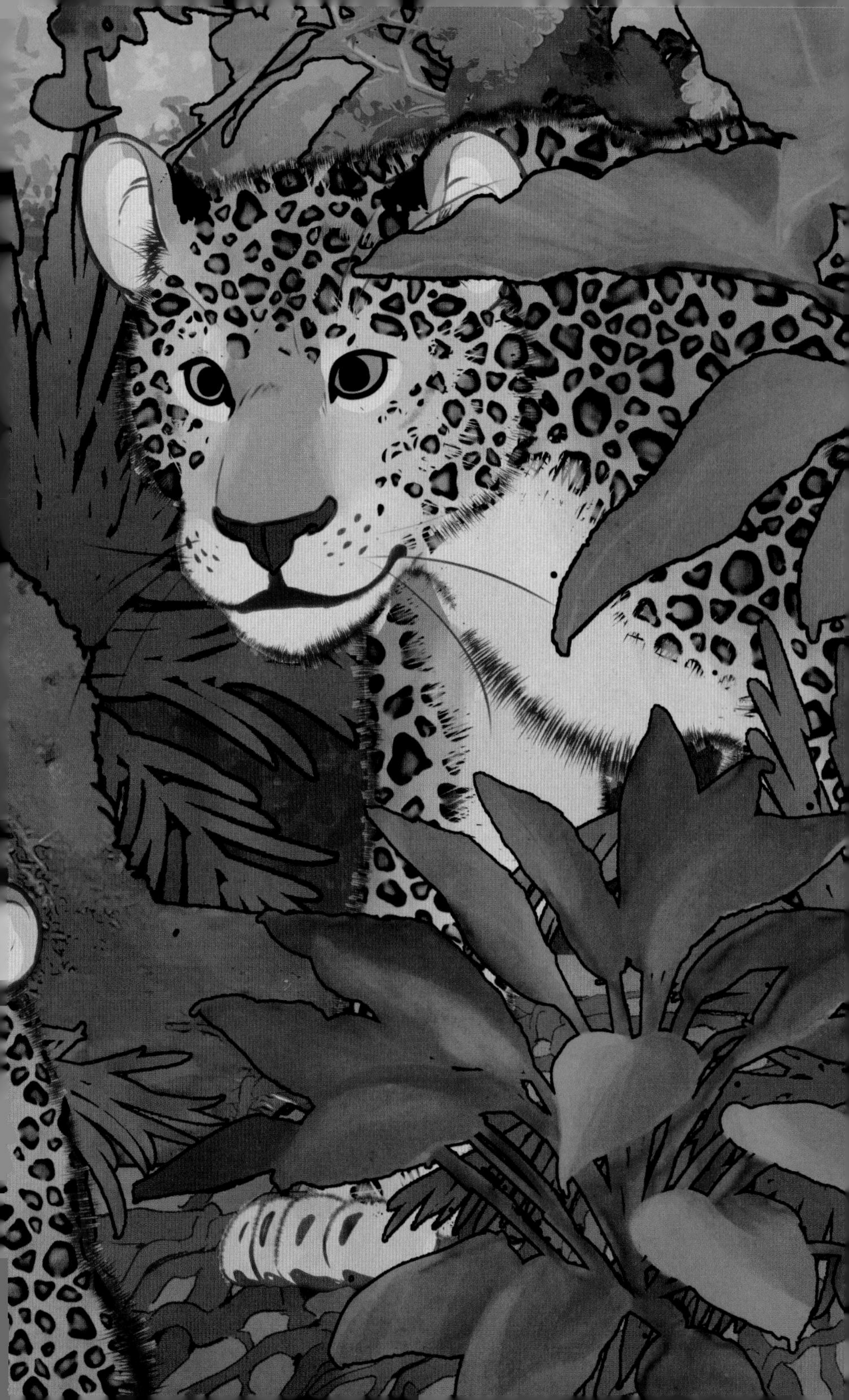

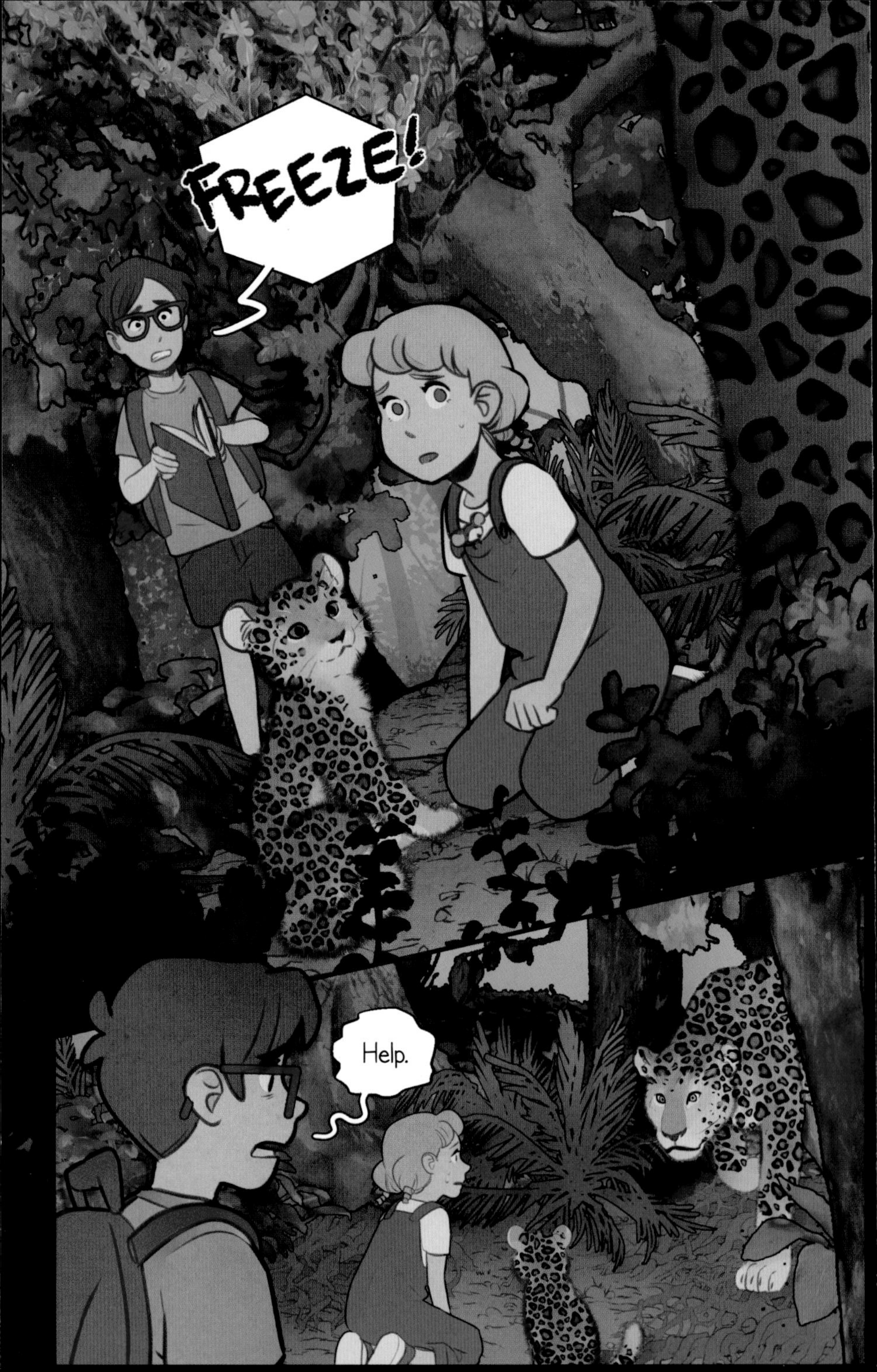
FREEZE!
Help.

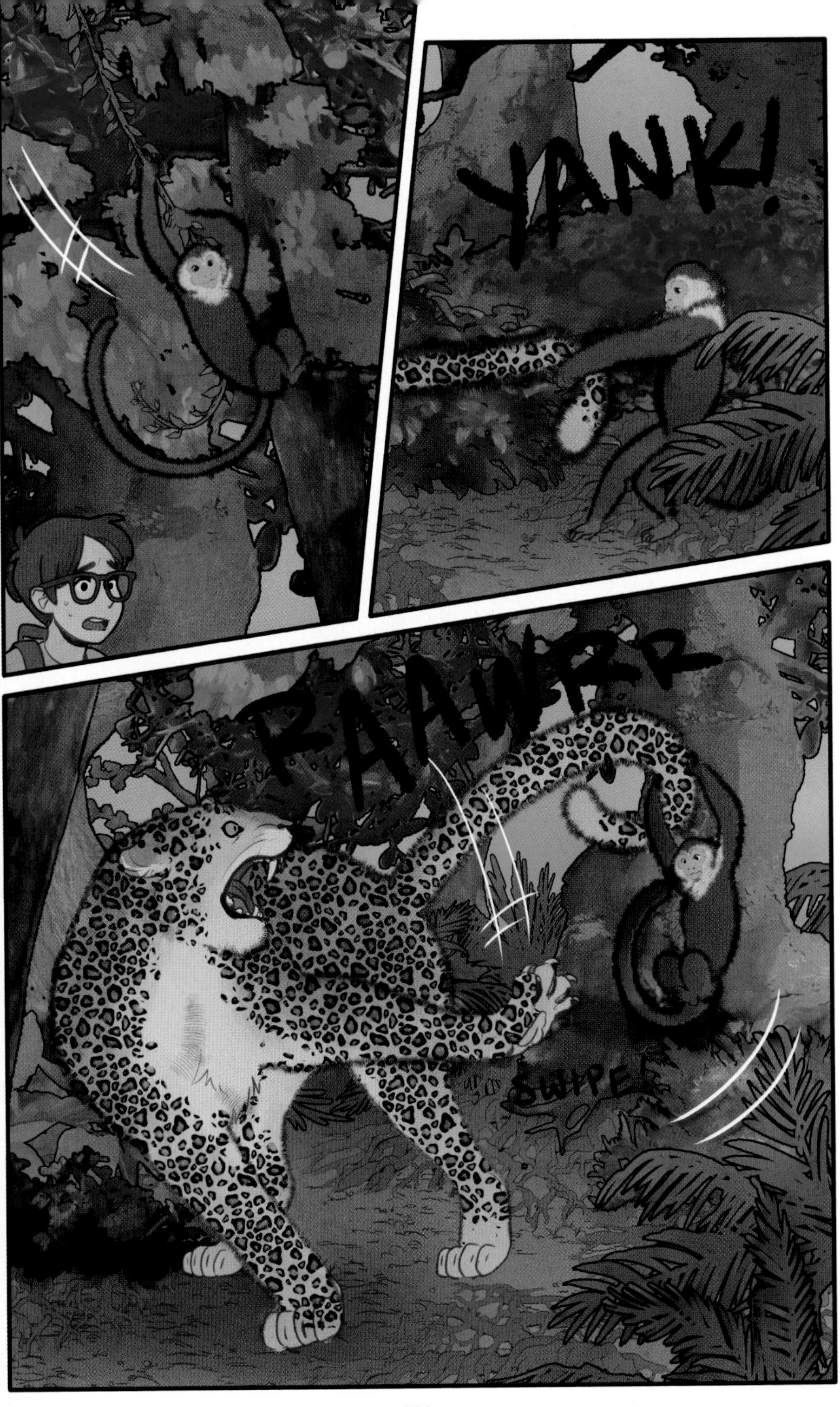
YANK!
RAAWRR
SWIPE!

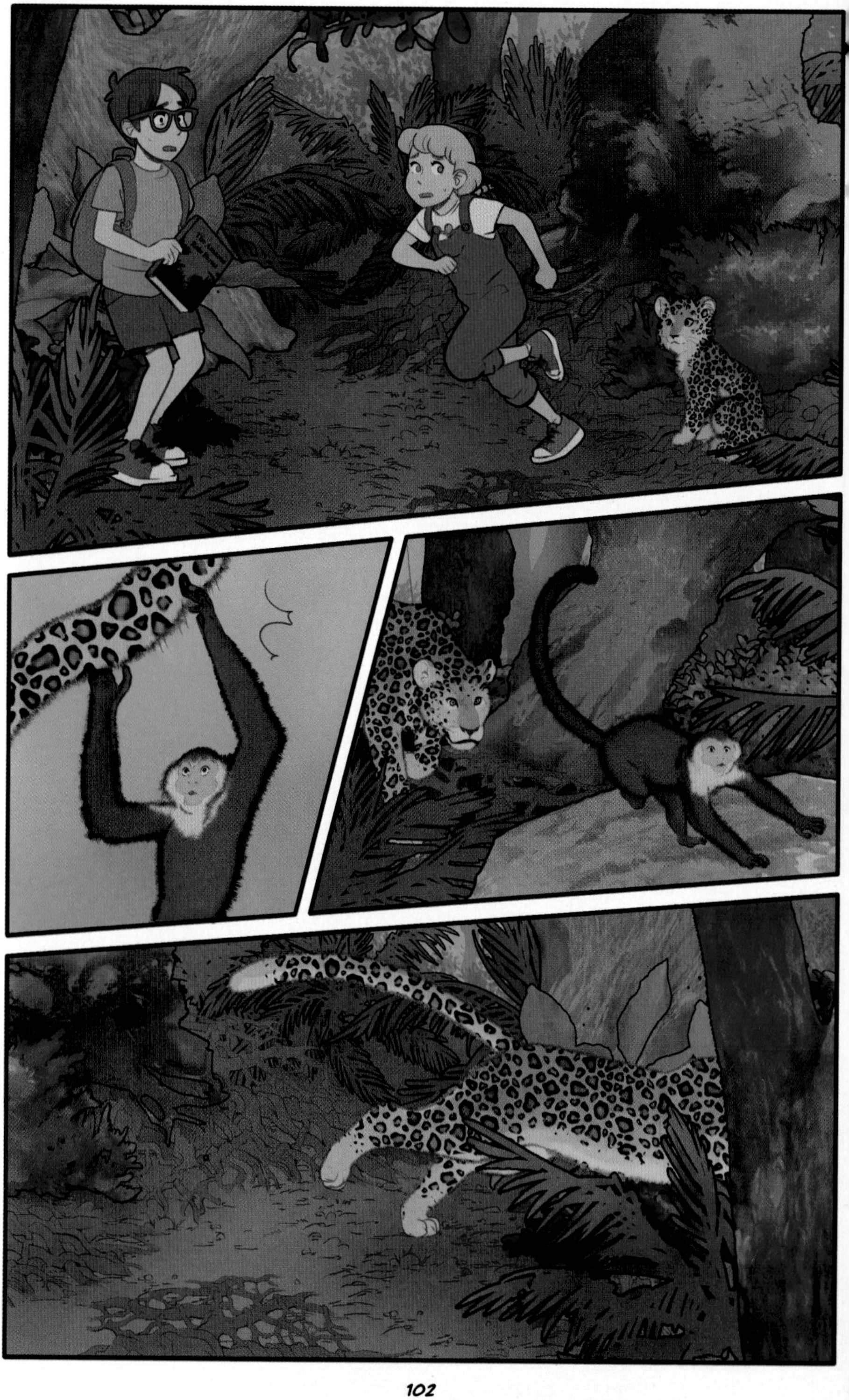

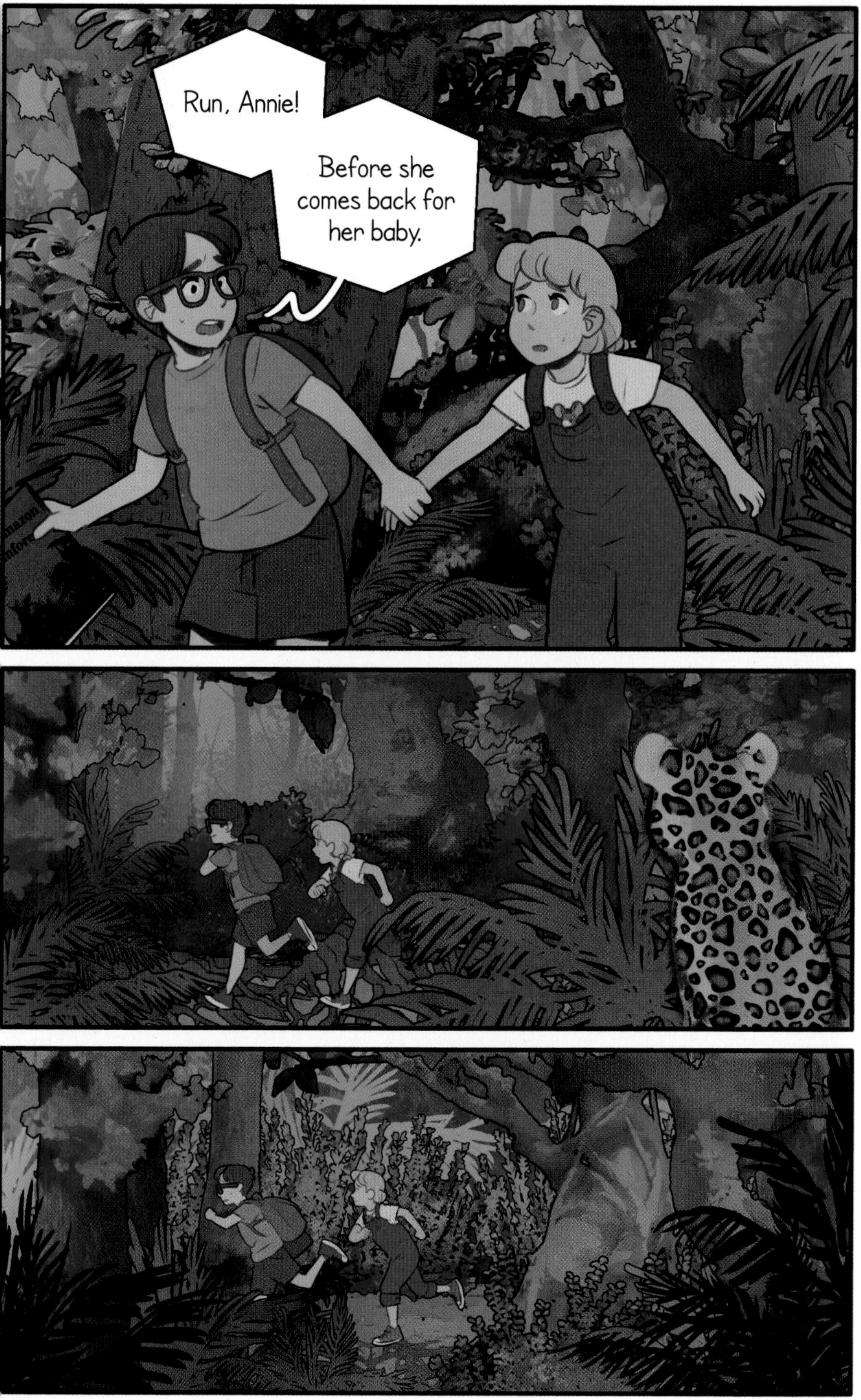
Run, Annie!
Before she comes back for her baby.

CHAPTER SEVEN
Vampire Bats?

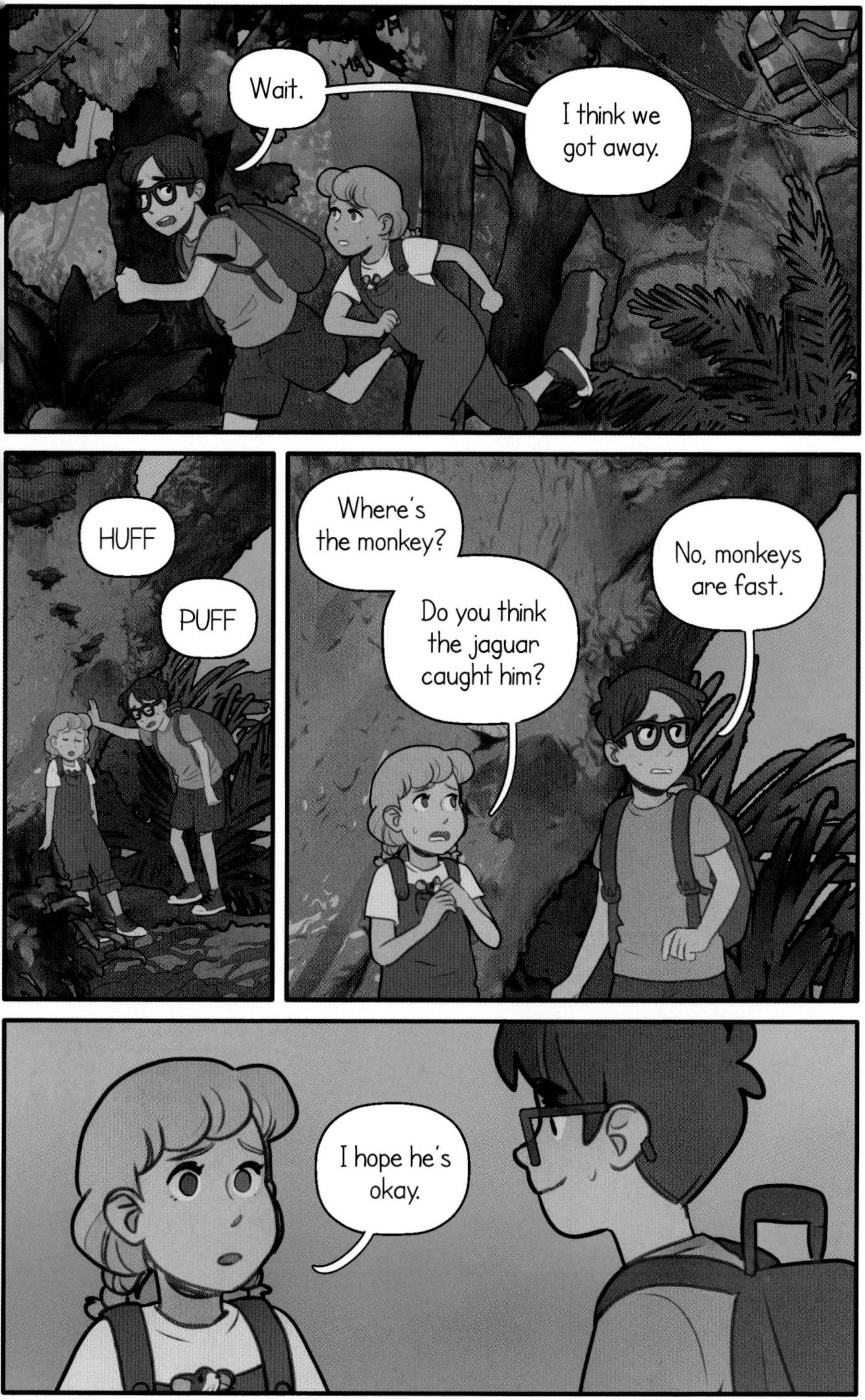
Wait.
I think we got away.
HUFF
PUFF
Where's the monkey?
Do you think the jaguar caught him?
No, monkeys are fast.
I hope he's okay.

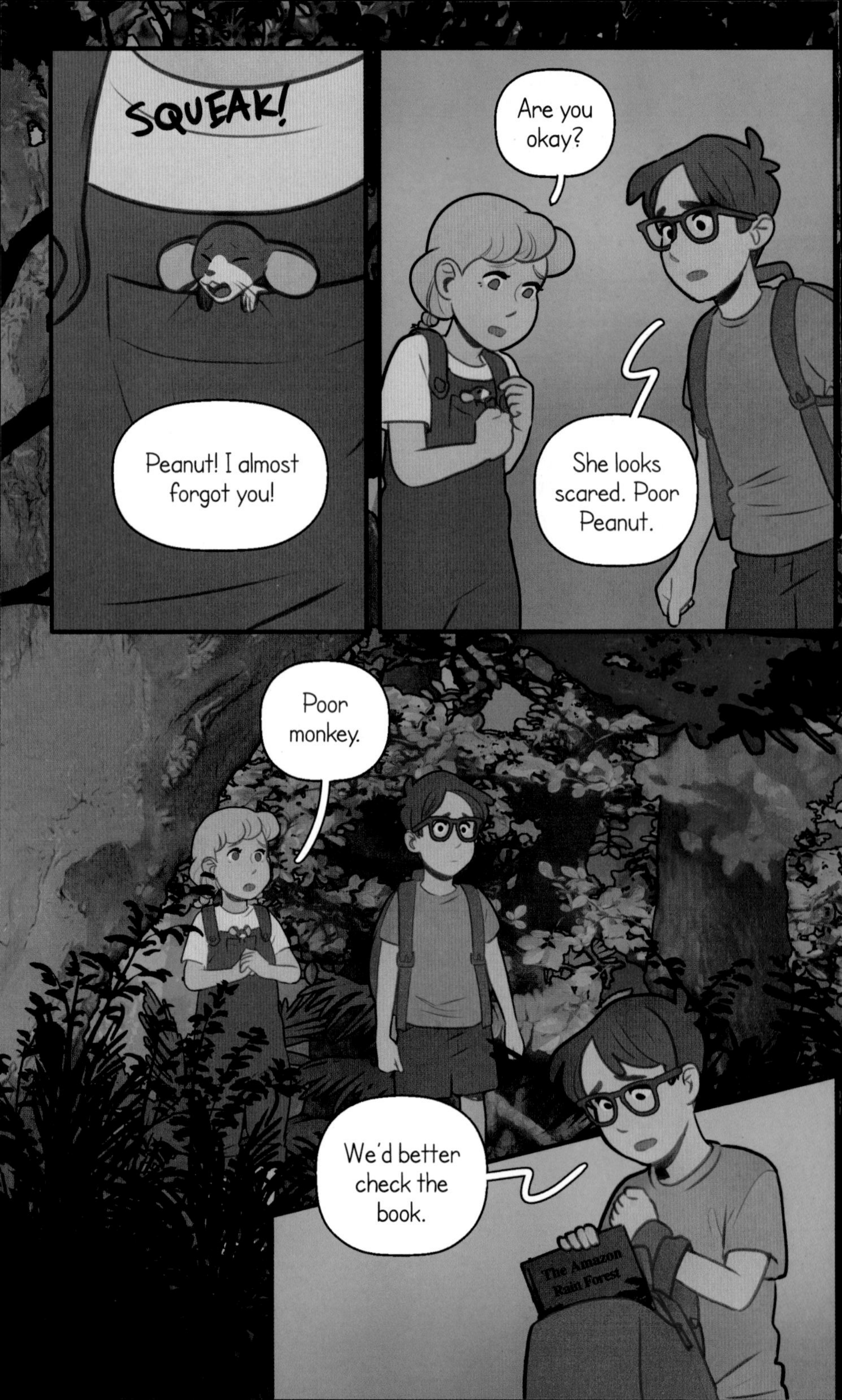
SQUEAK!
Peanut! I almost forgot you!
Are you okay?
She looks scared. Poor Peanut.
Poor monkey.
We'd better check the book.
The Amazon Rain Forest

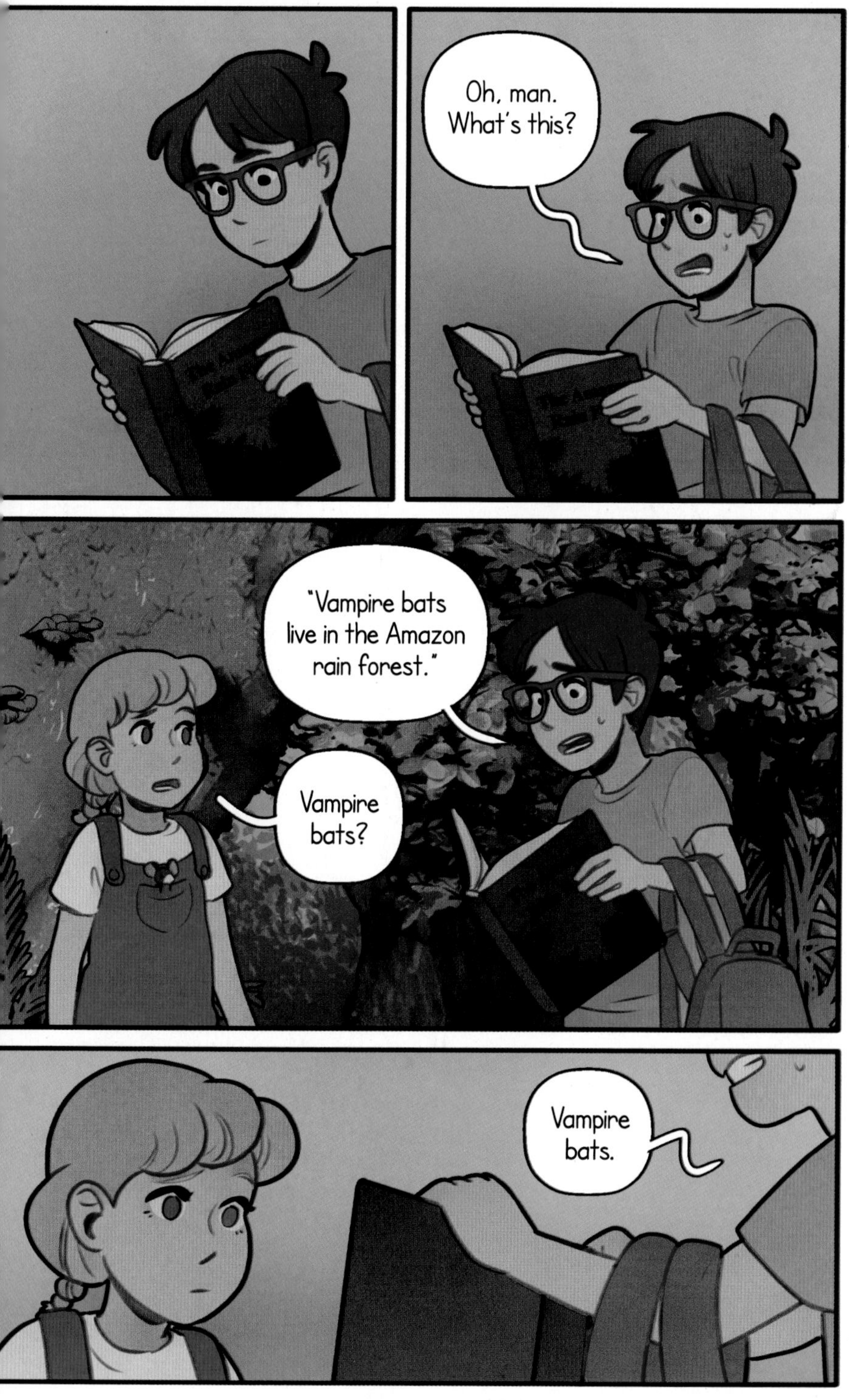
Oh, man.
What's this?
"Vampire bats
live in the Amazon
rain forest."
Vampire
bats?
Vampire
bats.

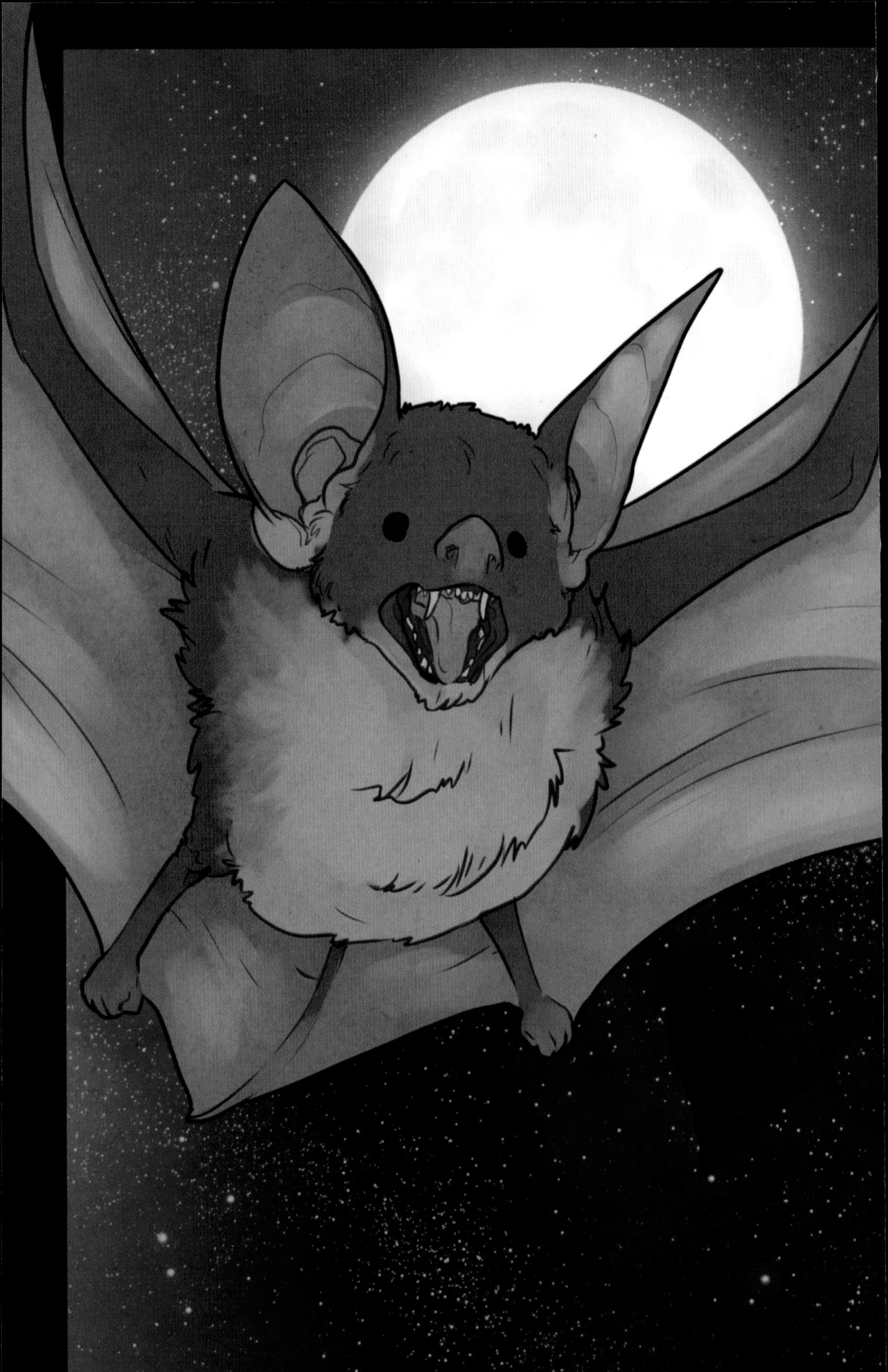

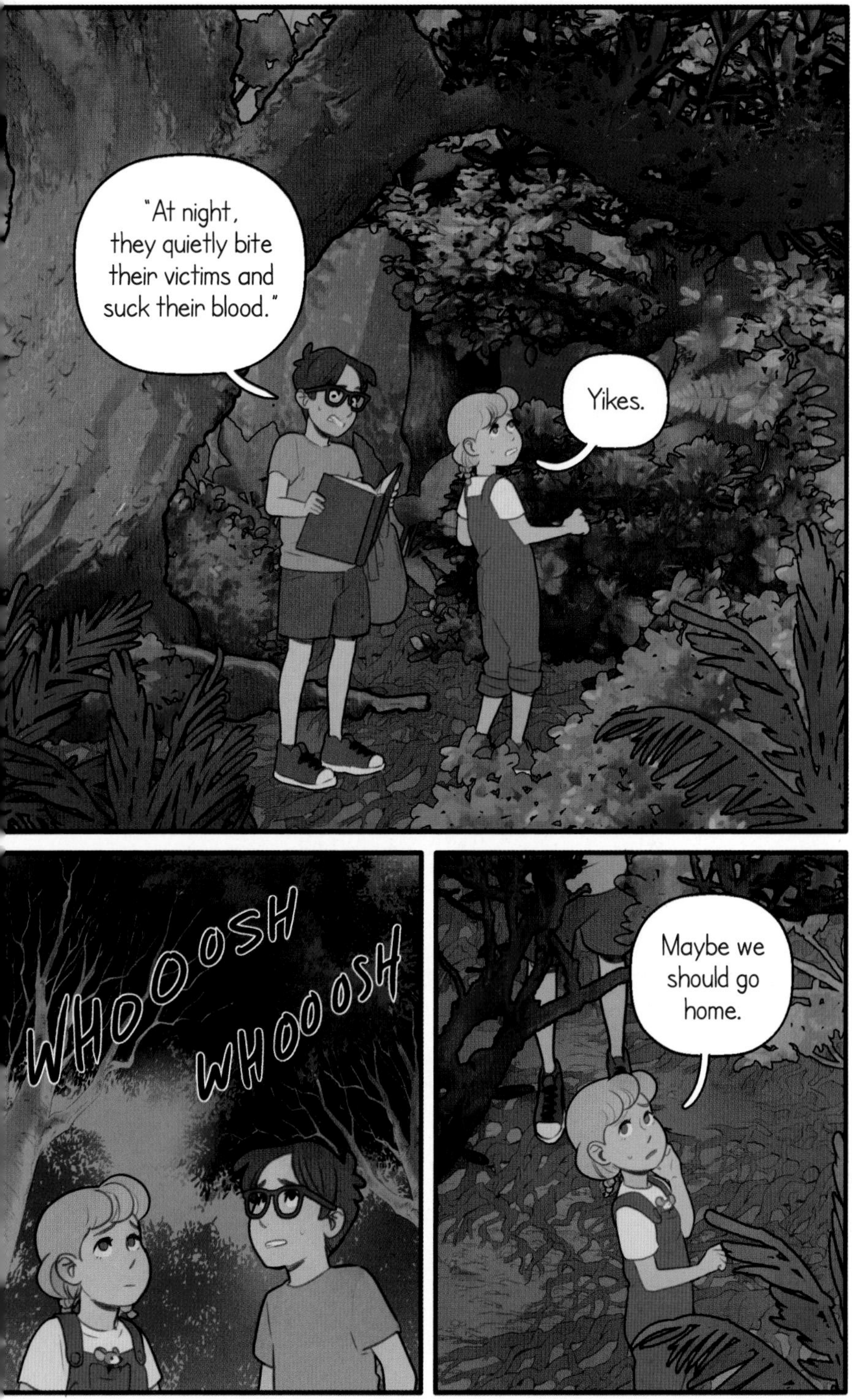
"At night, they quietly bite their victims and suck their blood."
Yikes.
WHOOOSH
WHOOOSH
Maybe we should go home.

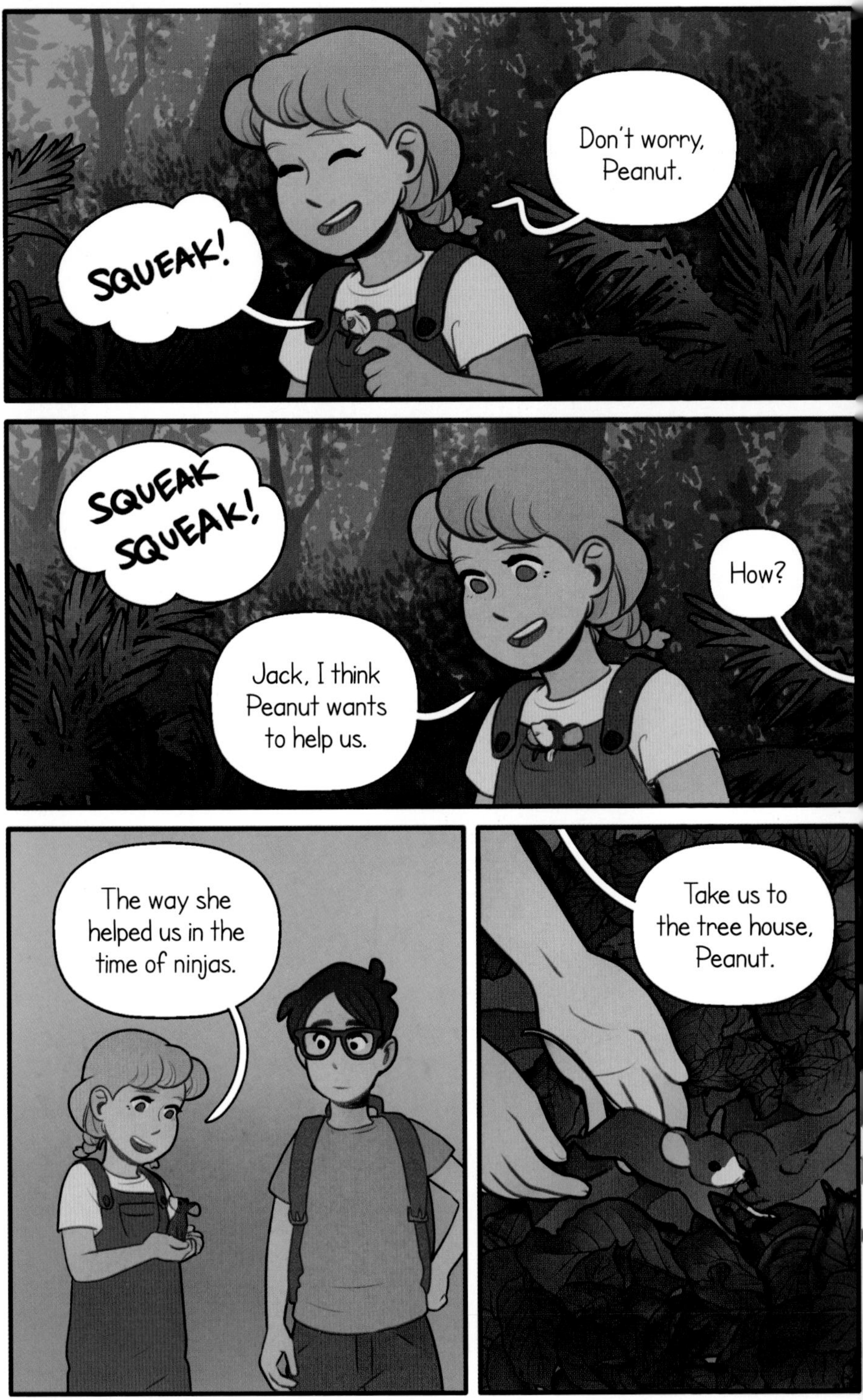
Don't worry, Peanut.
SQUEAK!
SQUEAK SQUEAK!
Jack, I think Peanut wants to help us.
How?
The way she helped us in the time of ninjas.
Take us to the tree house, Peanut.

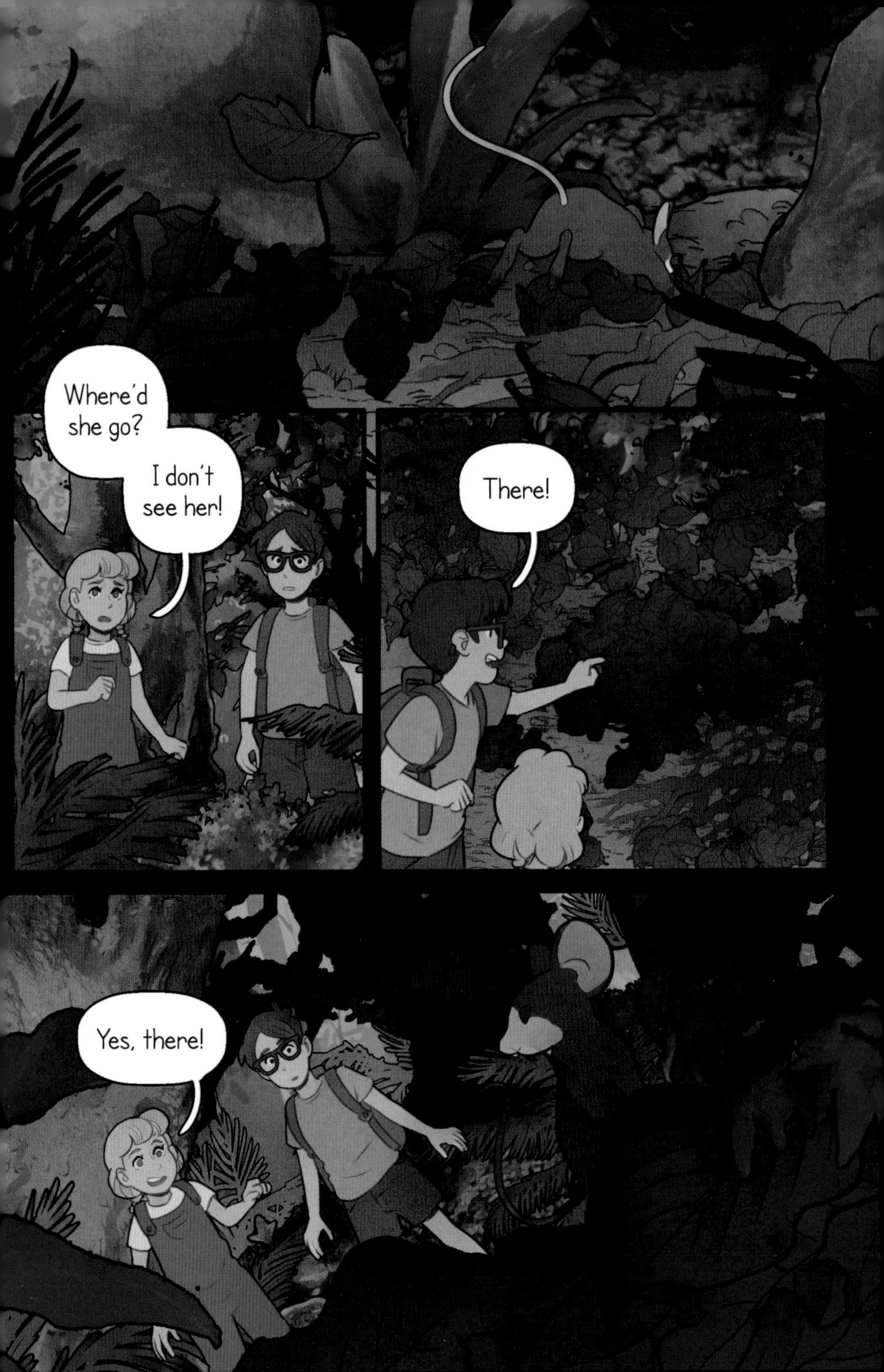
Where'd she go?
I don't see her!
There!
Yes, there!

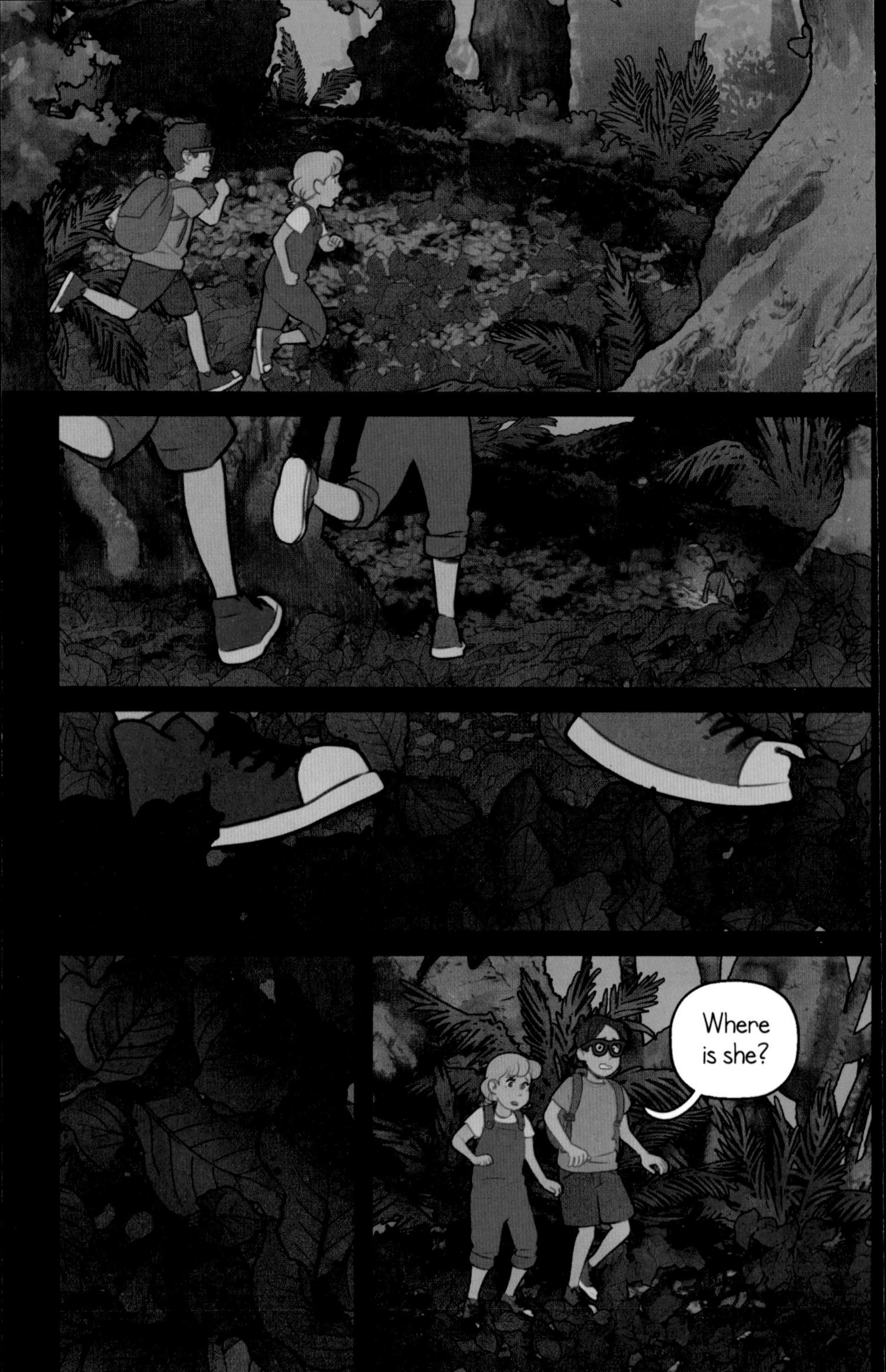
Where is she?

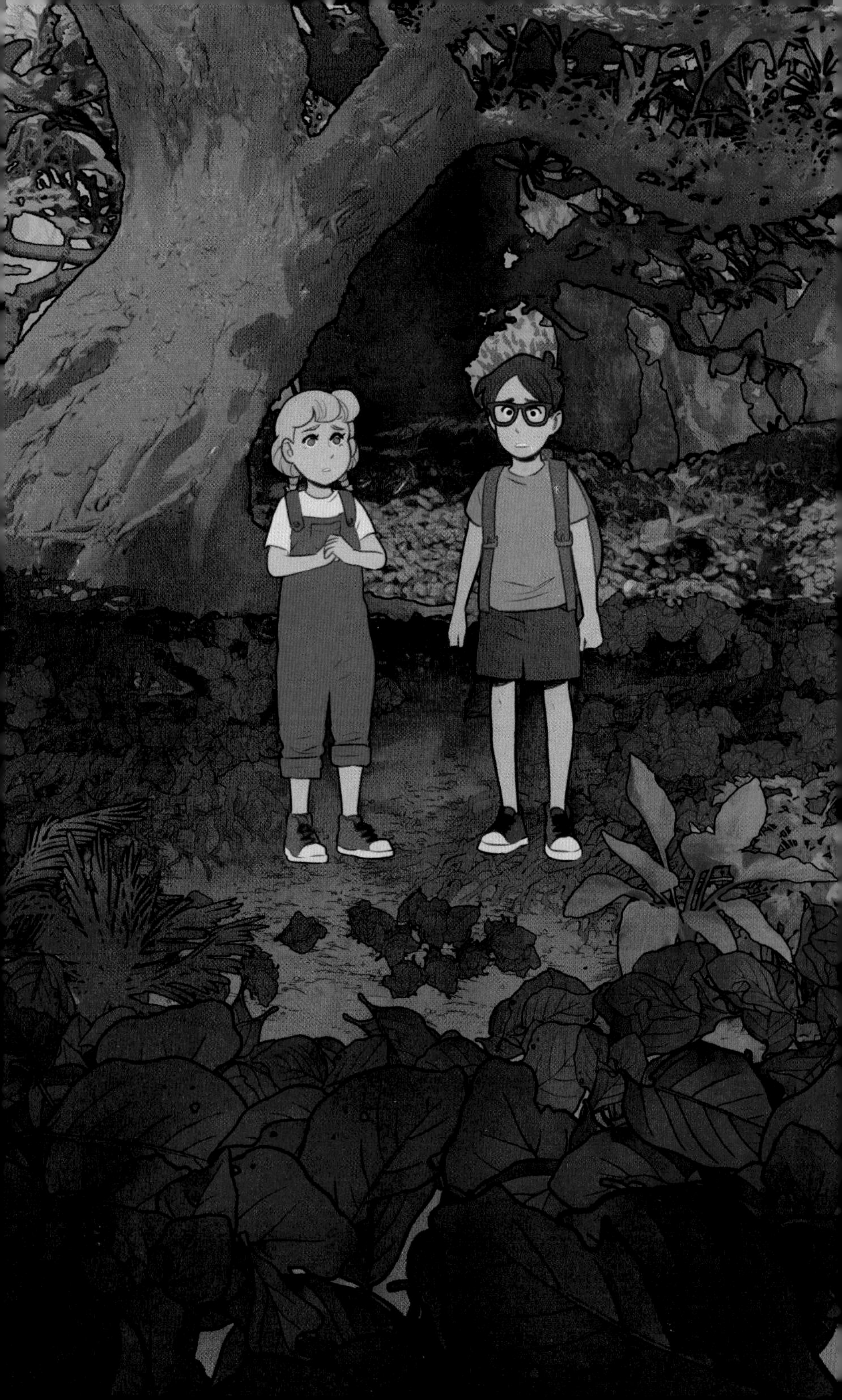

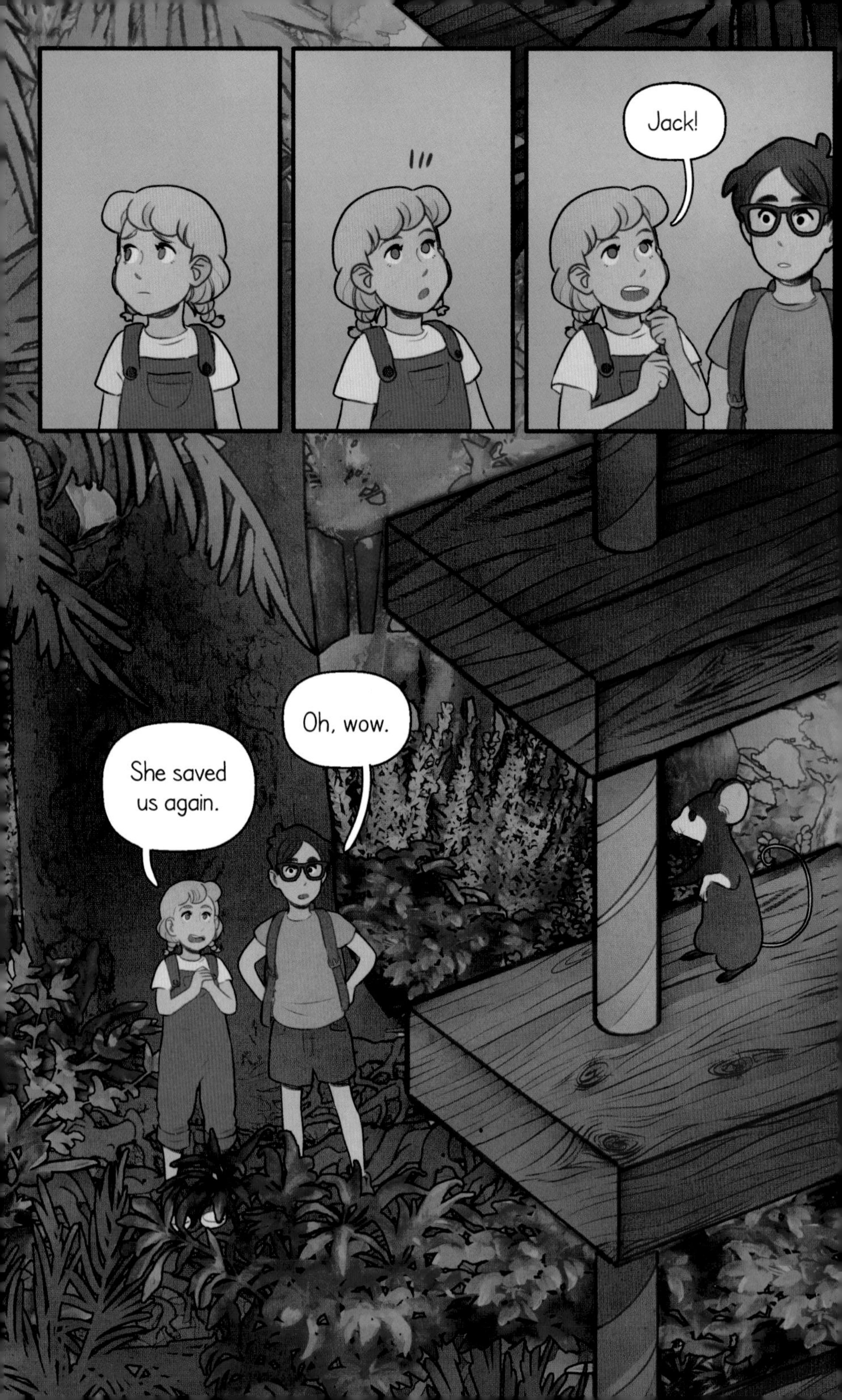
Jack!
She saved us again.
Oh, wow.

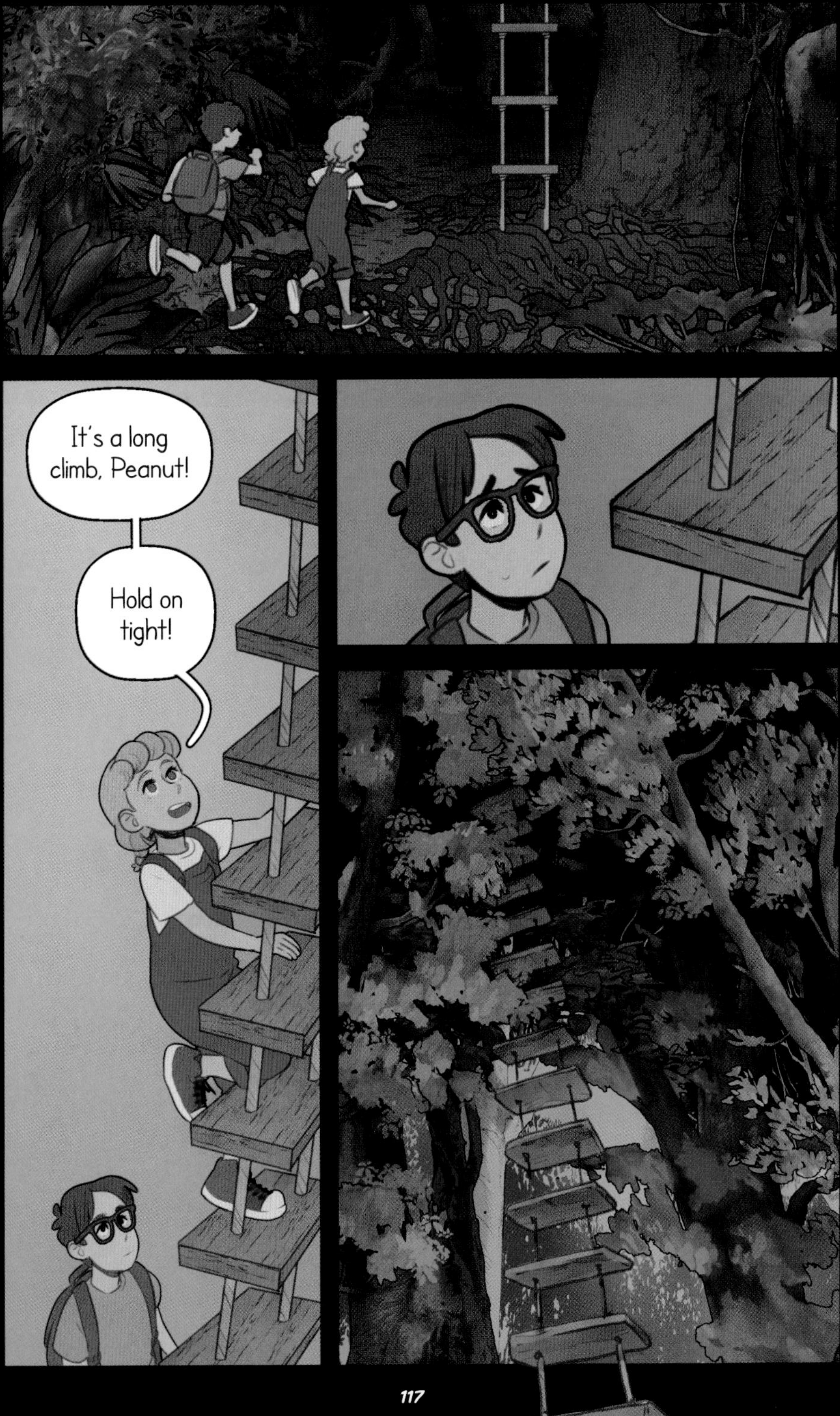
It's a long climb, Peanut!
Hold on tight!

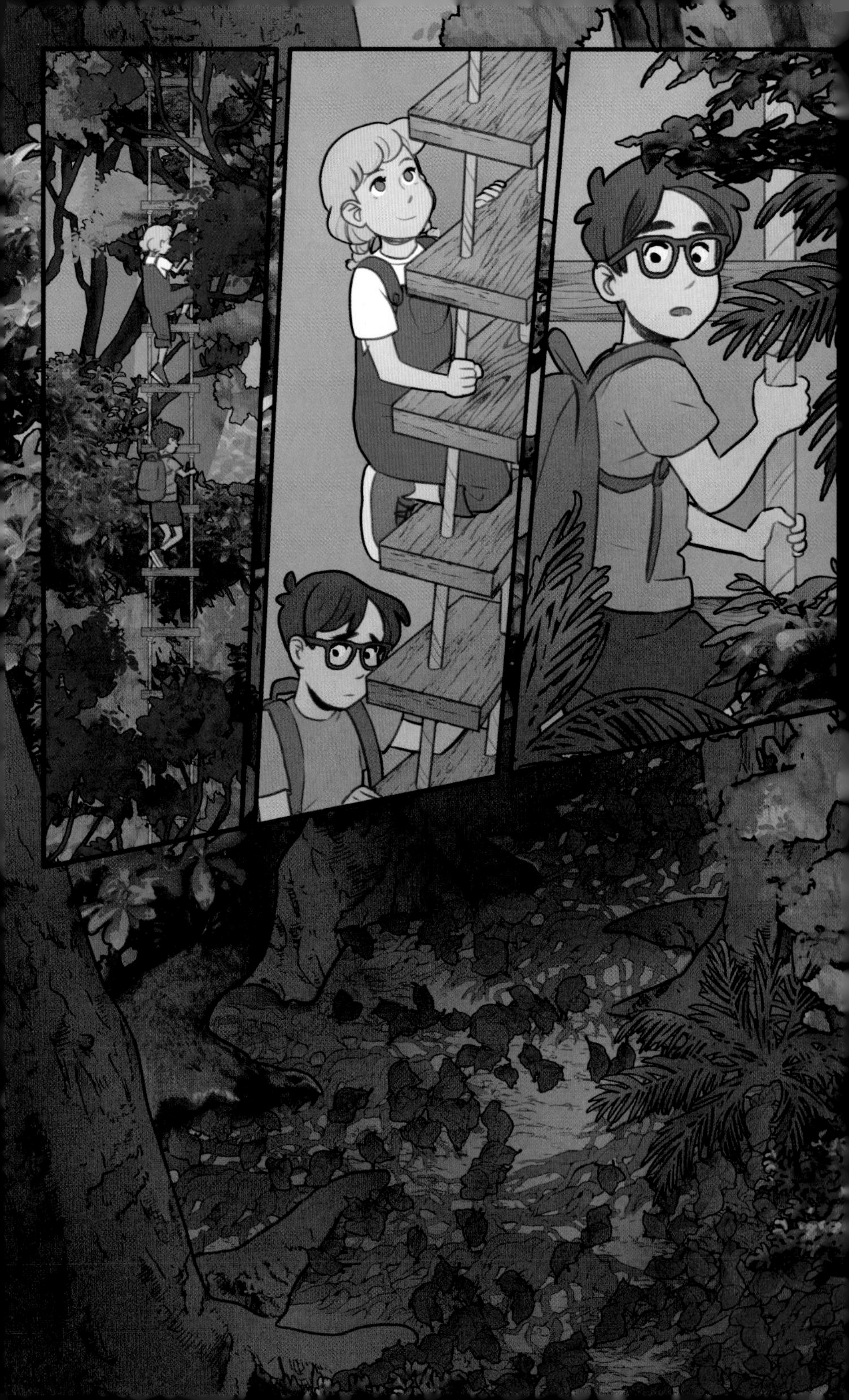

CHAPTER EIGHT

The Thing

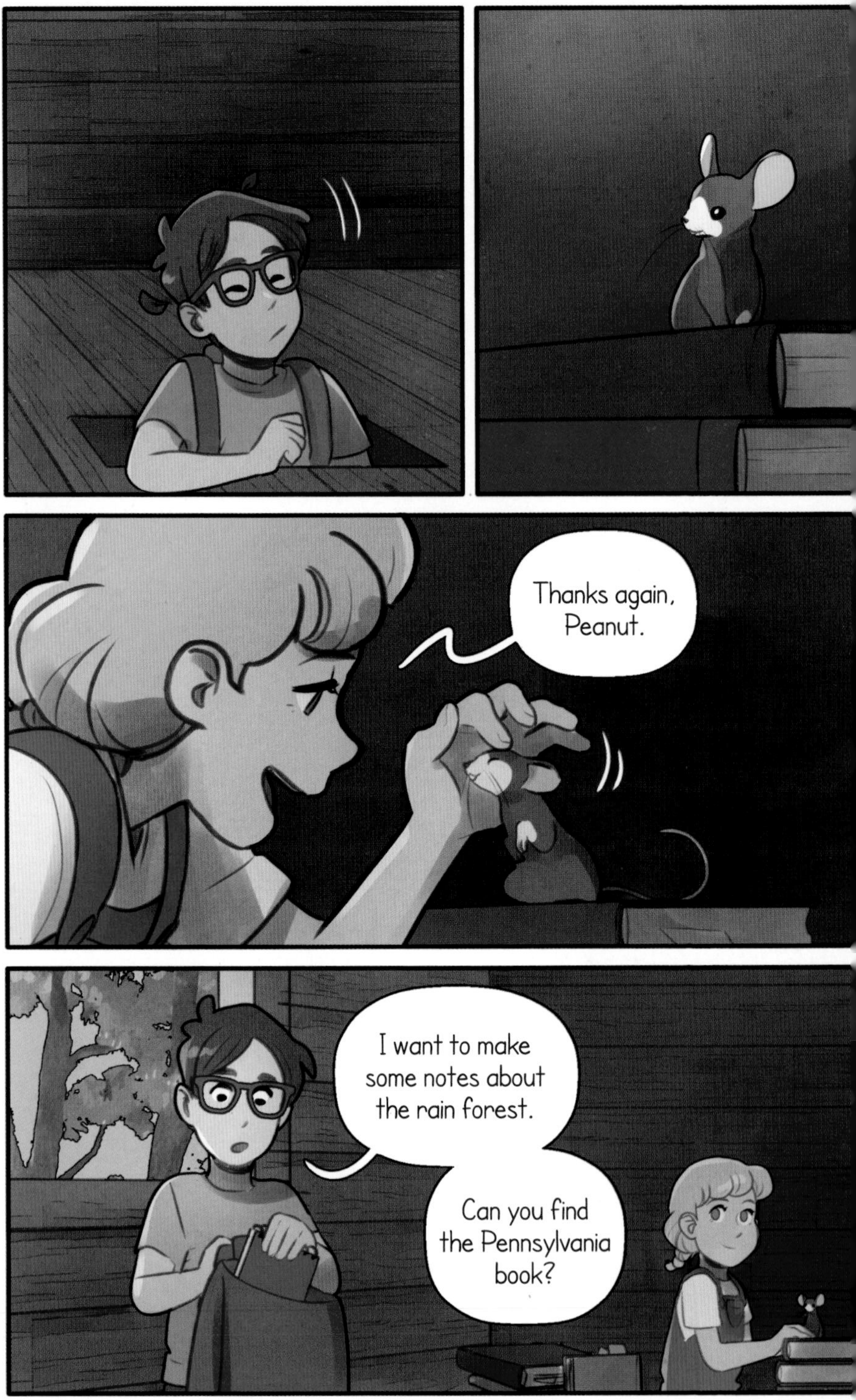
Thanks again, Peanut.
I want to make some notes about the rain forest.
Can you find the Pennsylvania book?

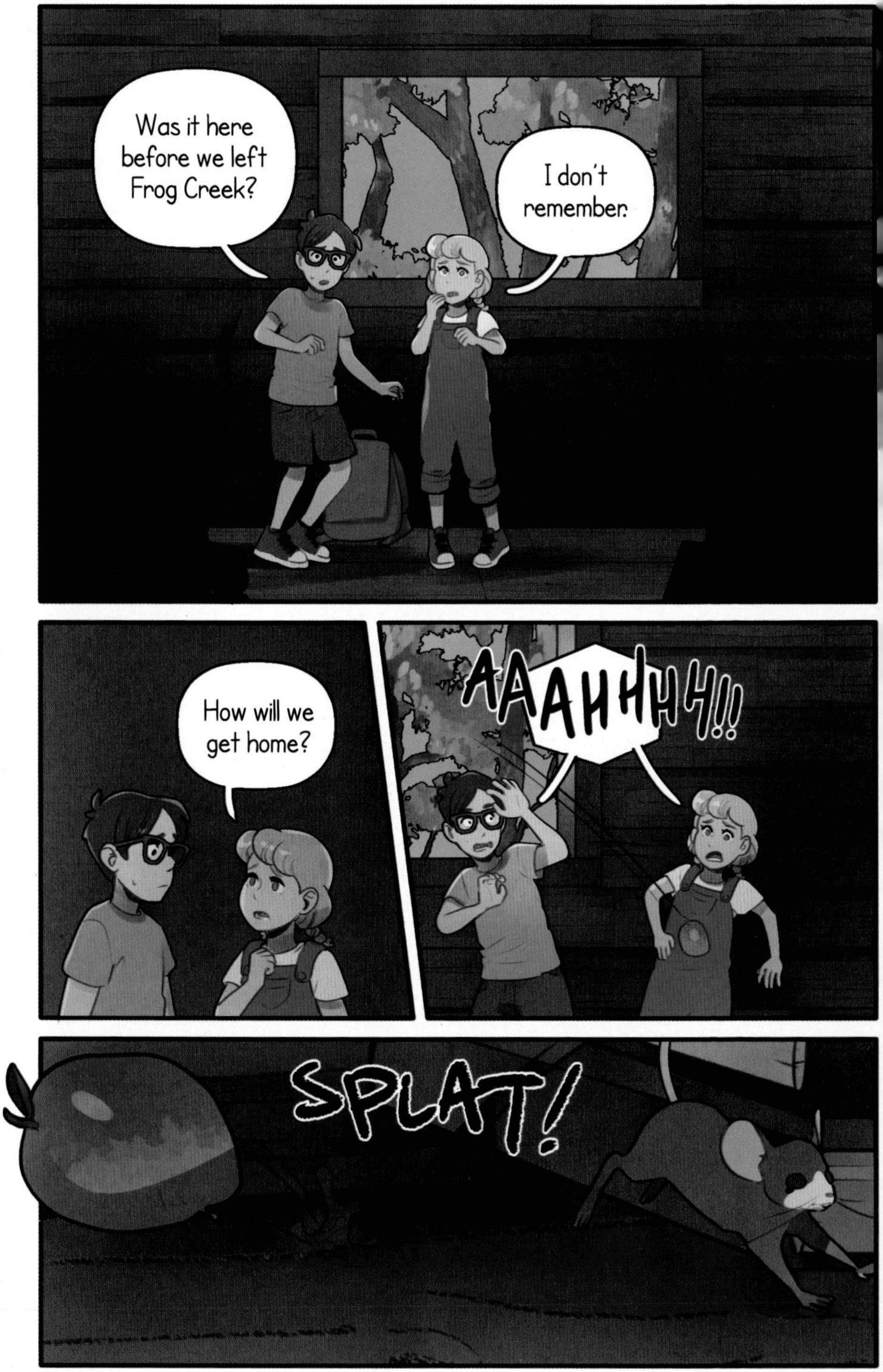
Was it here before we left Frog Creek?
I don't remember.
How will we get home?
AAAHHHH!!
SPLAT!

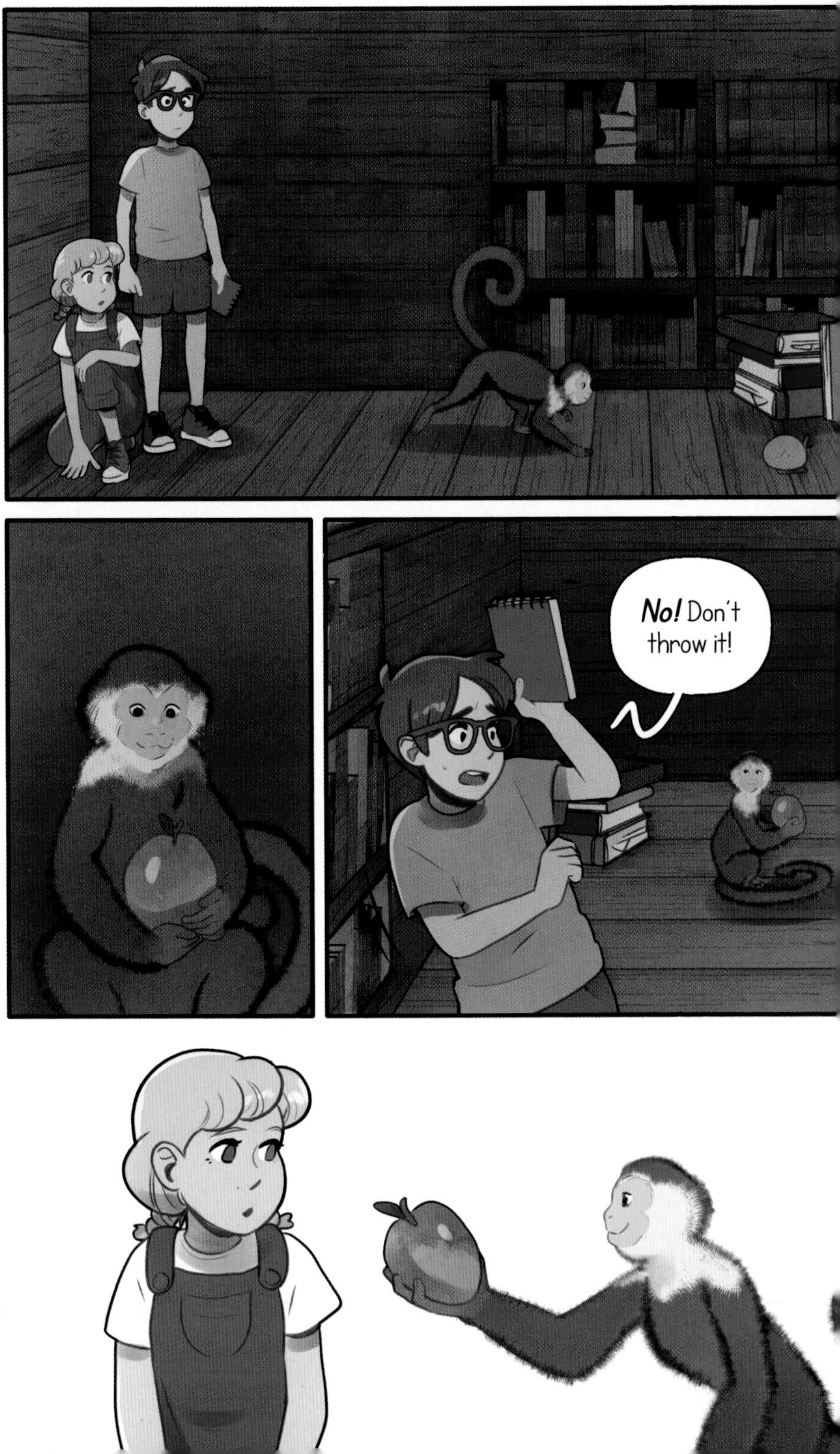
No! Don't throw it!

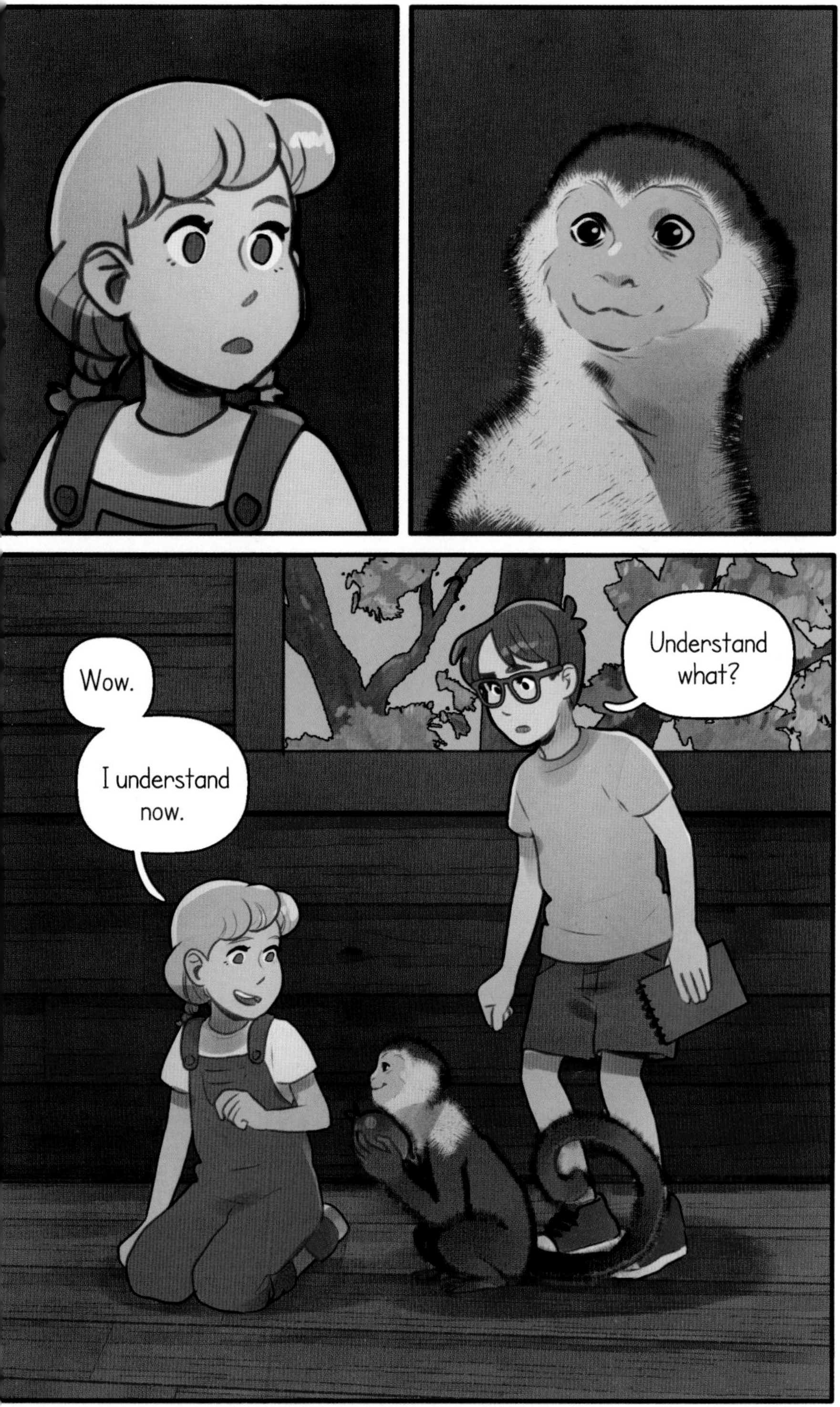
Wow.
I understand now.
Understand what?

This is the thing we need.

What thing?

One of the special things we're supposed to find for Morgan.

Are you sure?

To free her from the spell.

Look! The Pennsylvania book!

PENNSYLV

WASHINGT

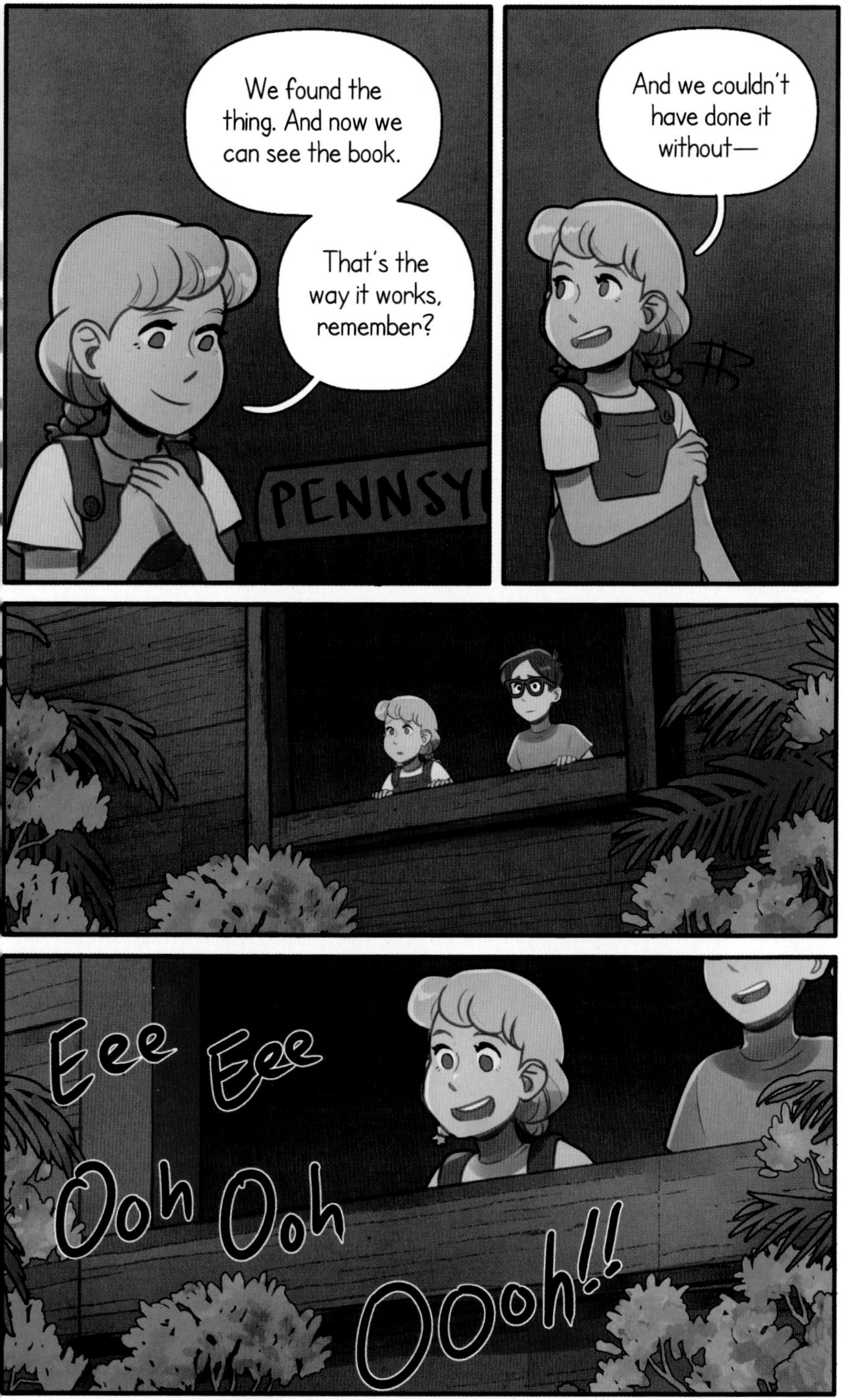
We found the thing. And now we can see the book.
That's the way it works, remember?
PENNSY
And we couldn't have done it without—
Eee Eee
Ooh Ooh
Oooh!!

CHAPTER NINE
Halfway There

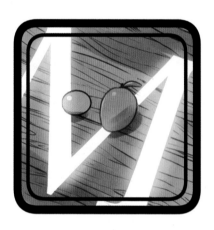

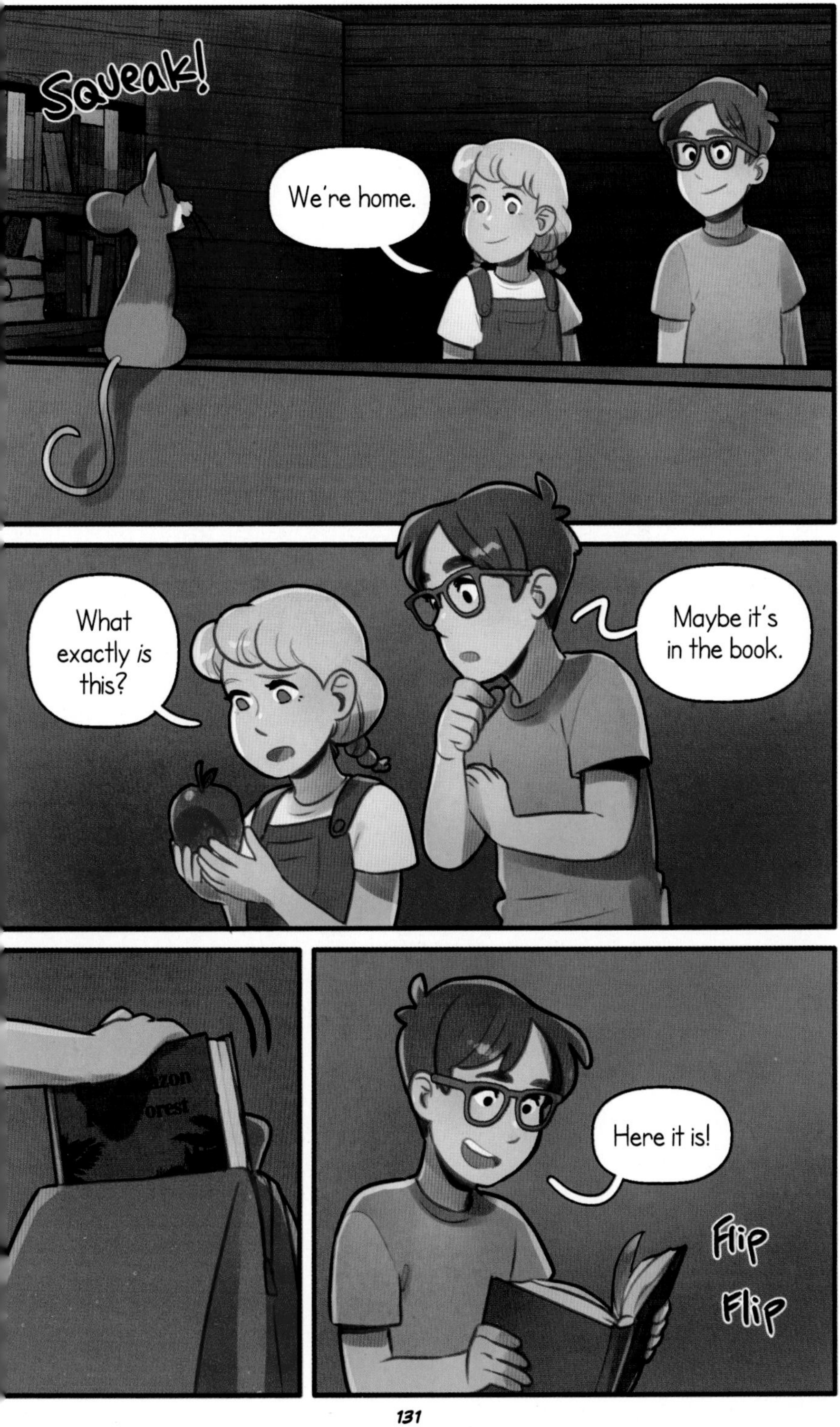

Squeak!
We're home.
What exactly *is* this?
Maybe it's in the book.
Here it is!
Flip
Flip

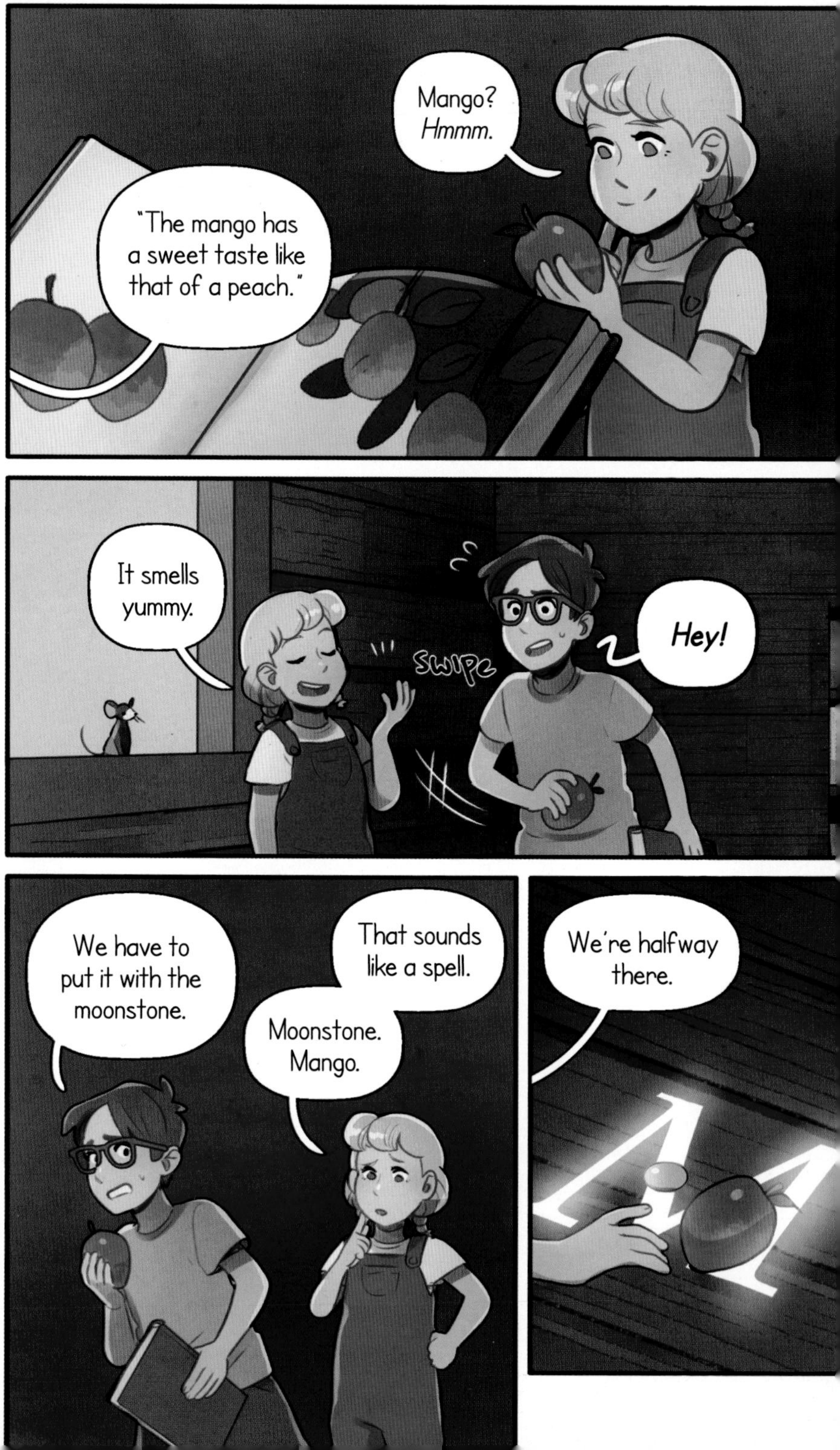
Mango?
Hmmm.
"The mango has a sweet taste like that of a peach."
It smells yummy.
SWIPE
Hey!
We have to put it with the moonstone.
That sounds like a spell.
Moonstone. Mango.
We're halfway there.

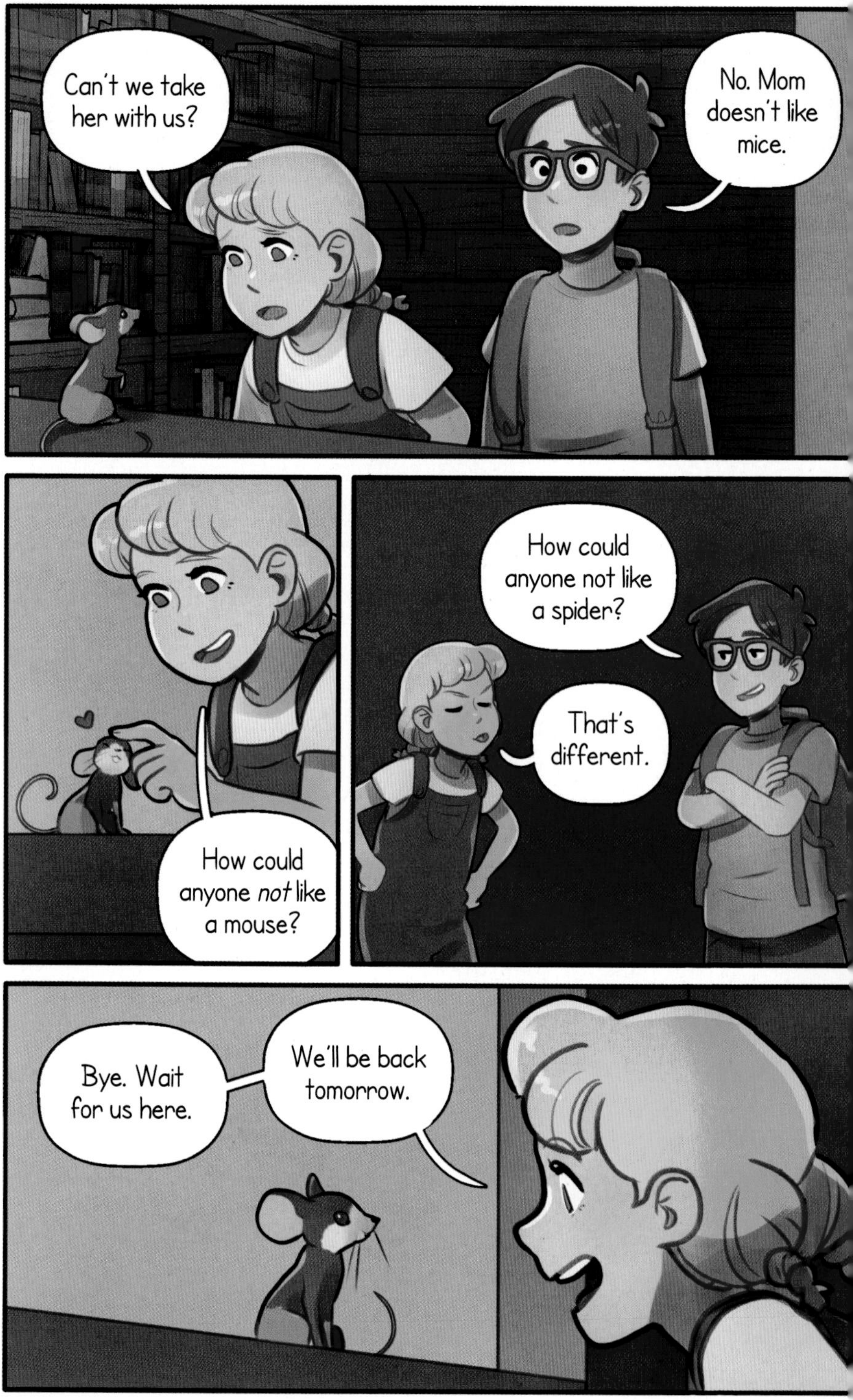
Can't we take her with us?
No. Mom doesn't like mice.
How could anyone *not* like a mouse?
How could anyone not like a spider?
That's different.
Bye. Wait for us here.
We'll be back tomorrow.

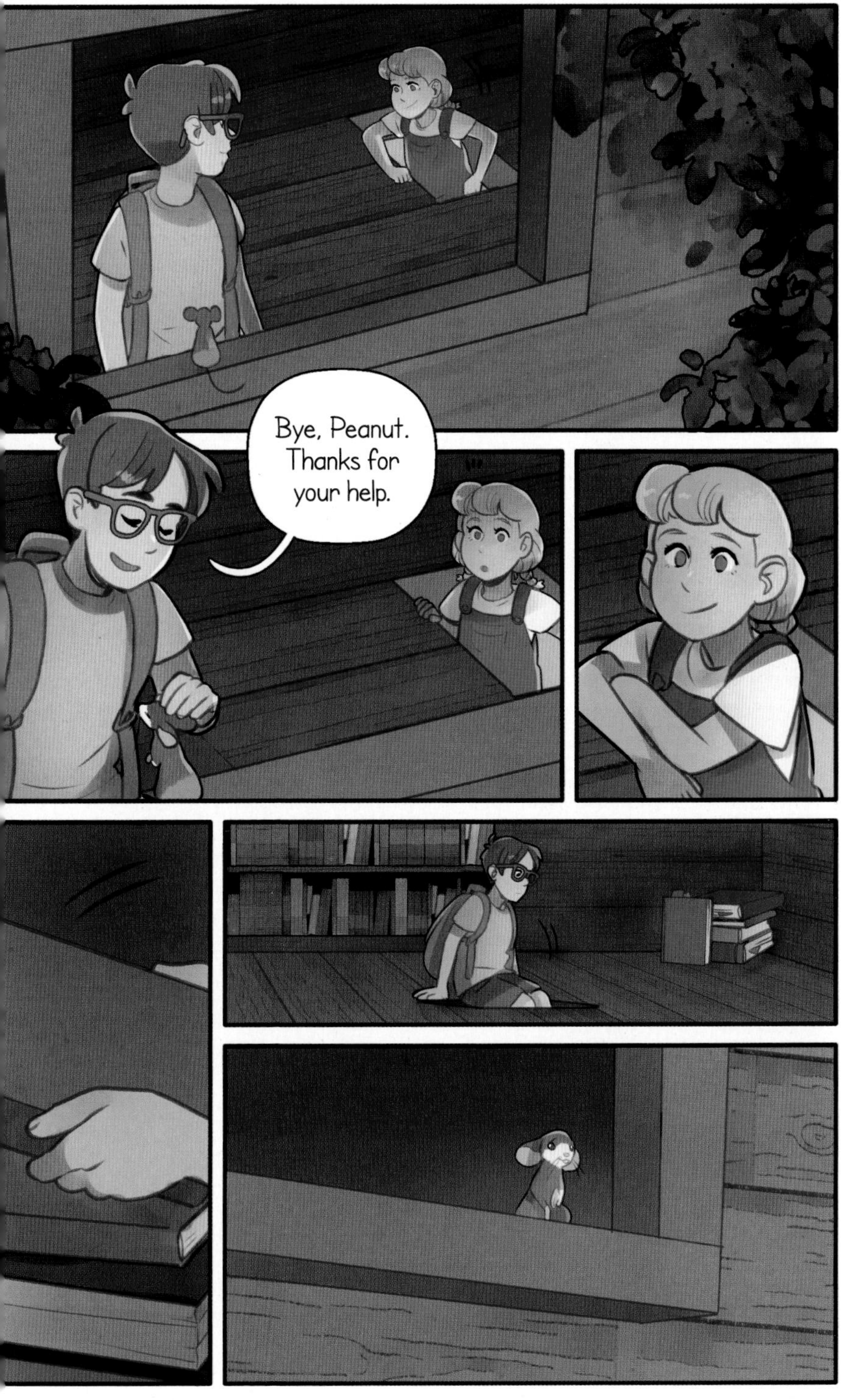
Bye, Peanut. Thanks for your help.

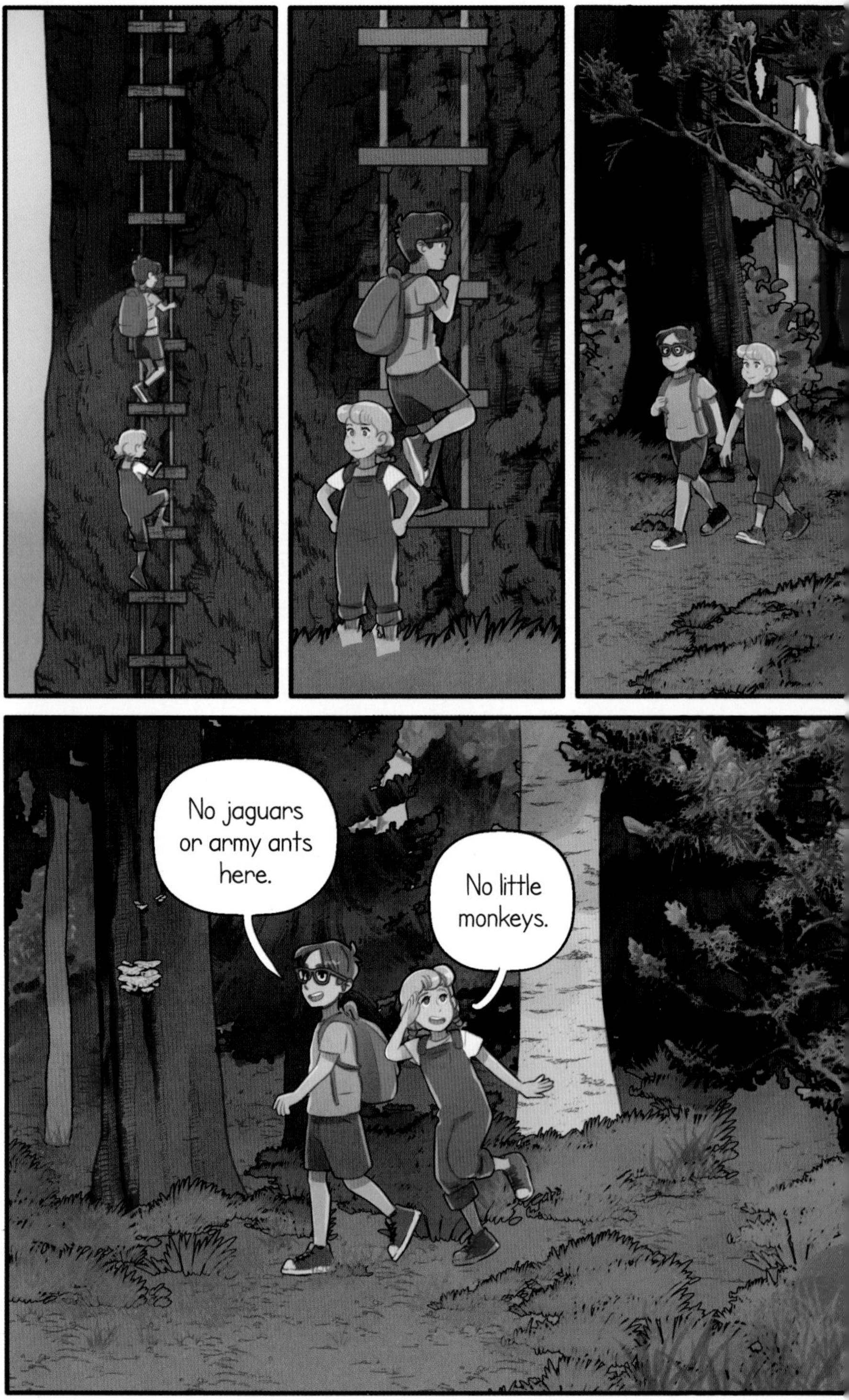
No jaguars or army ants here.
No little monkeys.

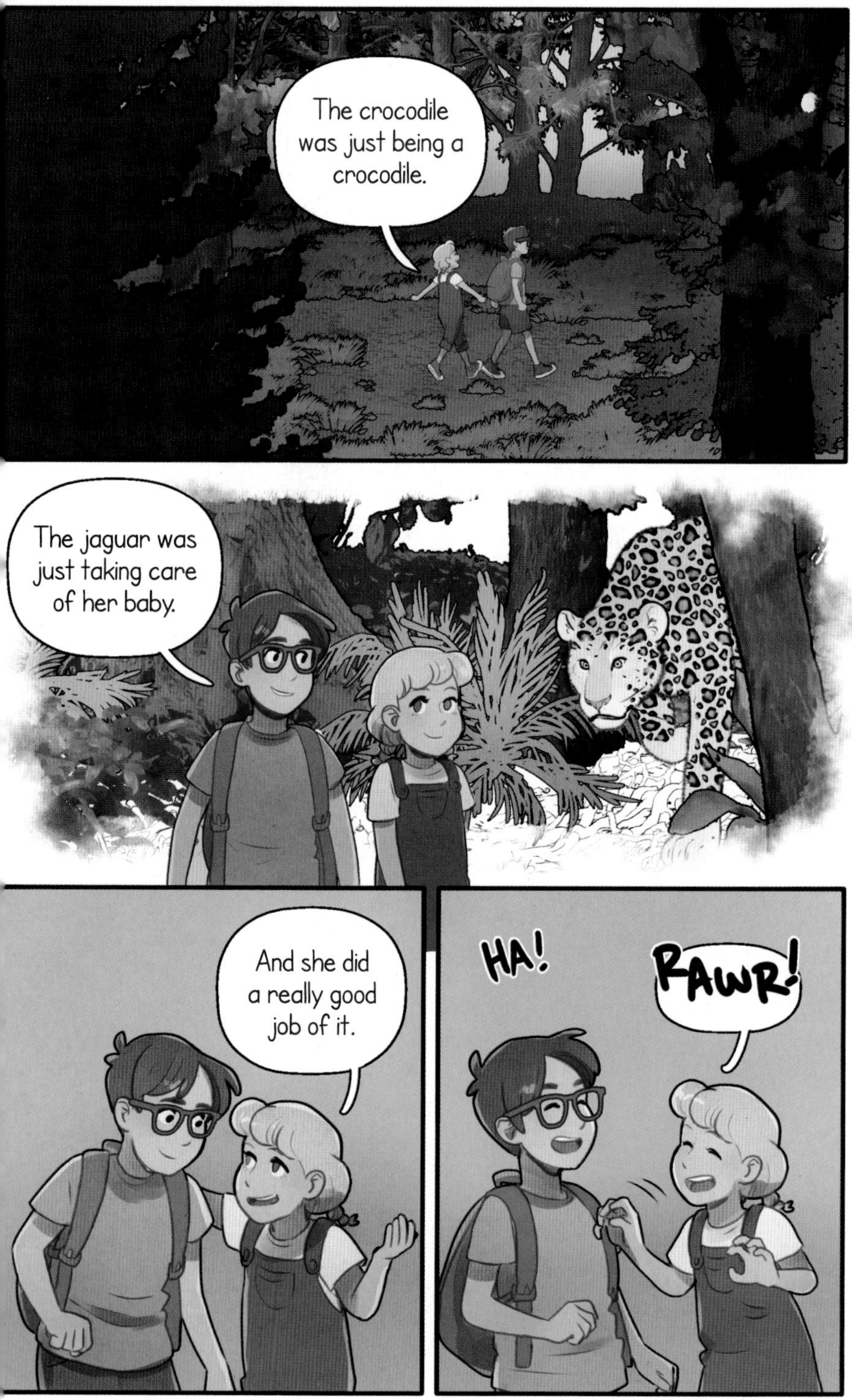
The crocodile was just being a crocodile.
The jaguar was just taking care of her baby.
And she did a really good job of it.
HA!
RAWR!

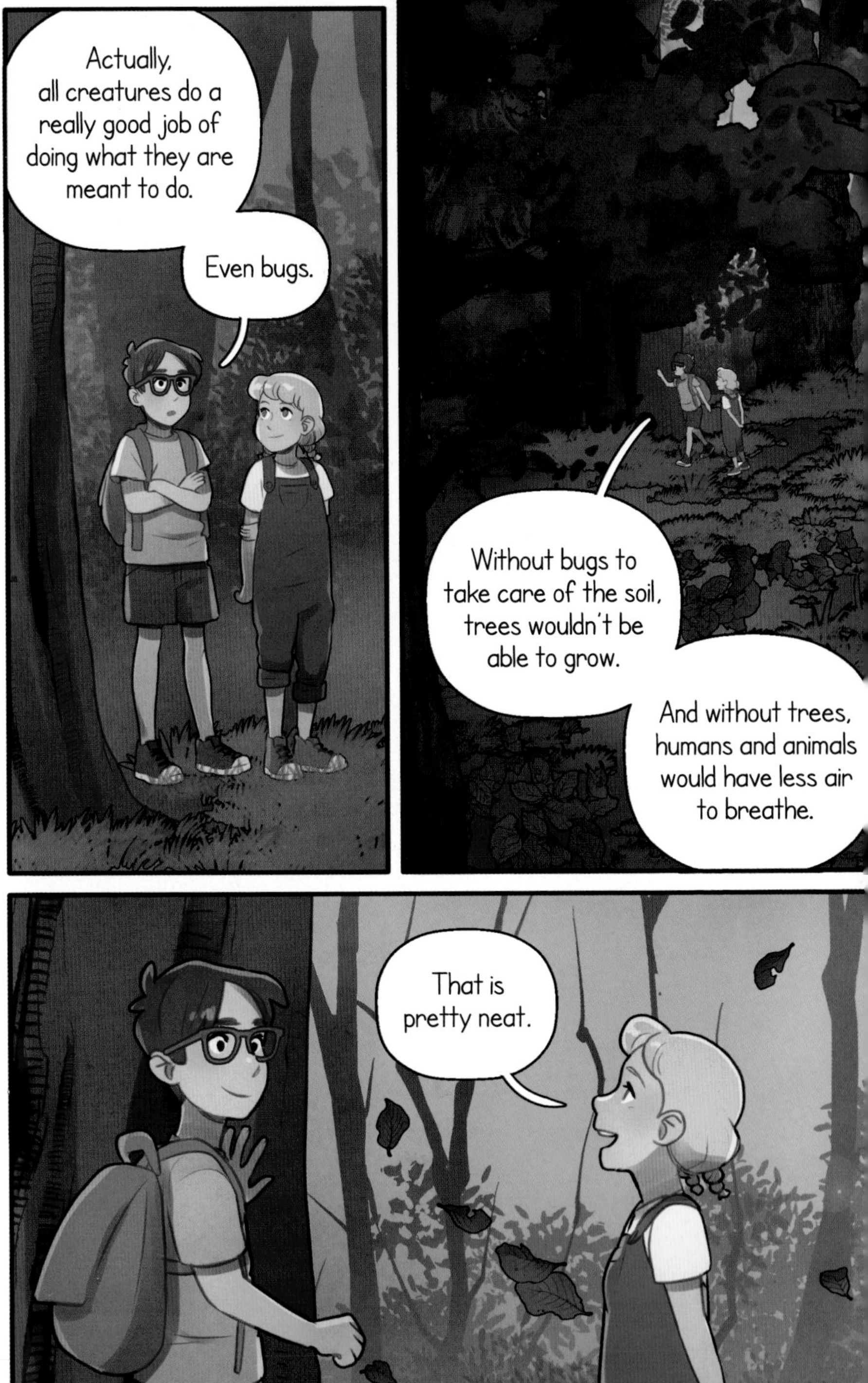
Actually, all creatures do a really good job of doing what they are meant to do.
Even bugs.
Without bugs to take care of the soil, trees wouldn't be able to grow.
And without trees, humans and animals would have less air to breathe.
That is pretty neat.

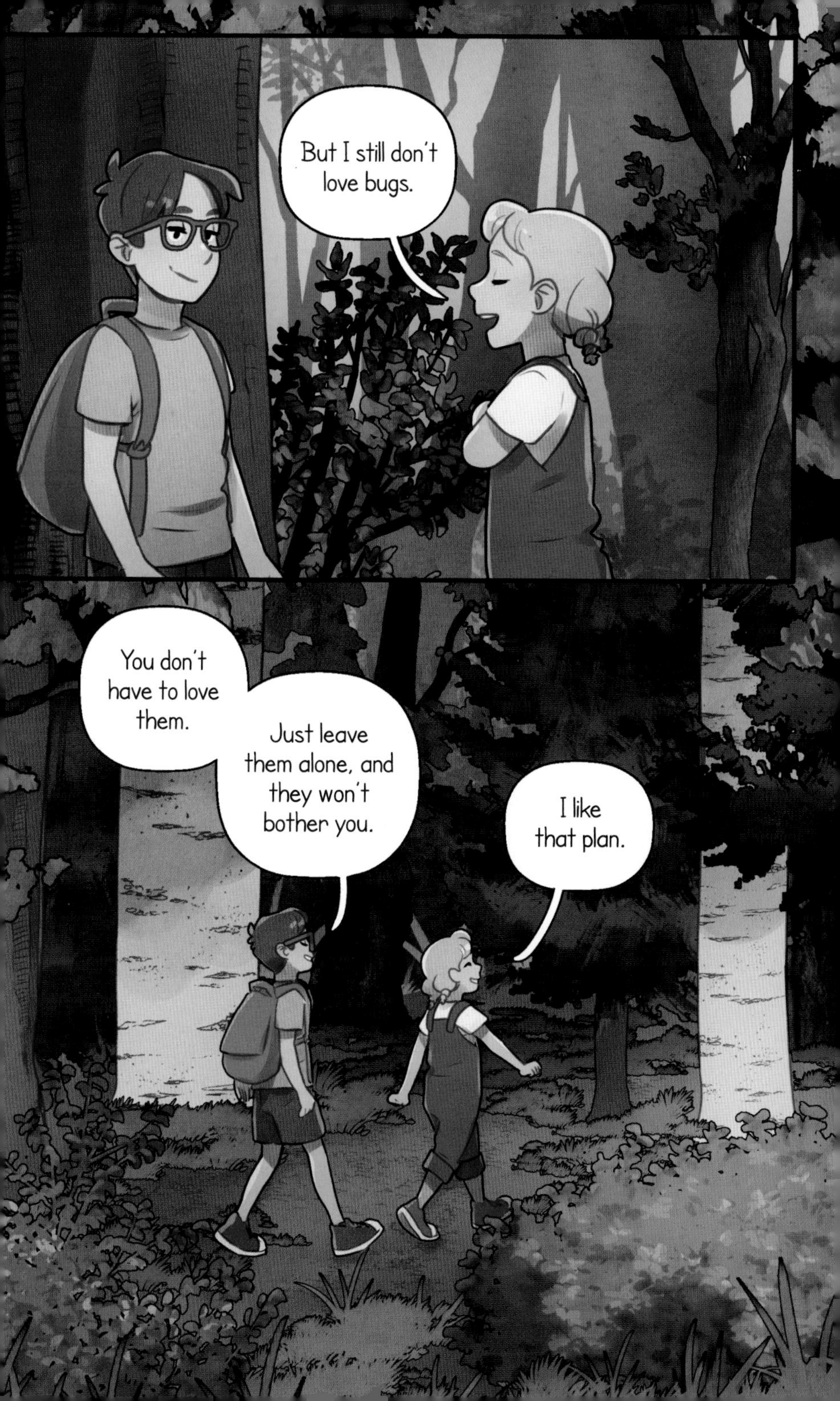
But I still don't love bugs.
You don't have to love them.
Just leave them alone, and they won't bother you.
I like that plan.

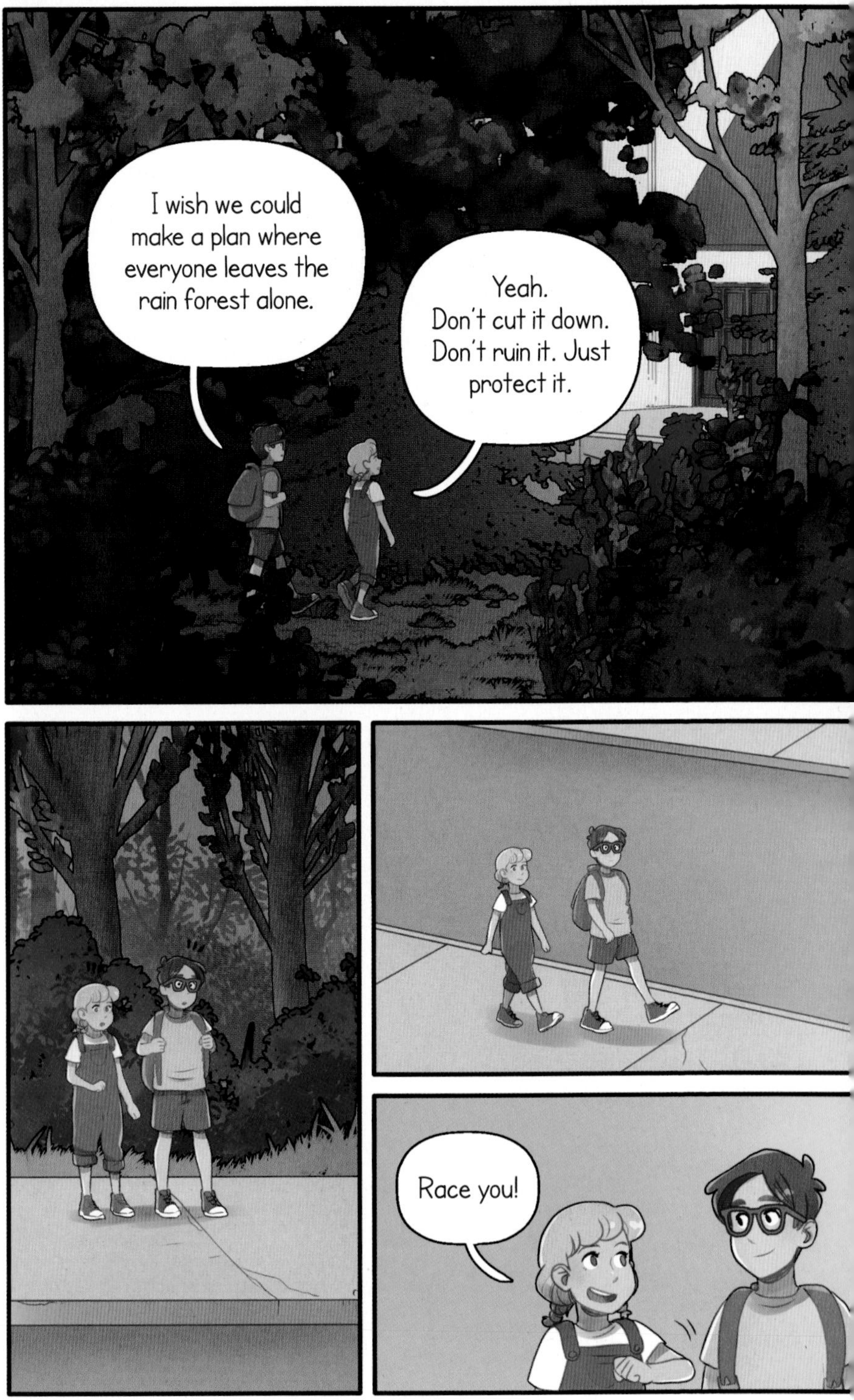

I wish we could make a plan where everyone leaves the rain forest alone.
Yeah. Don't cut it down. Don't ruin it. Just protect it.
Race you!

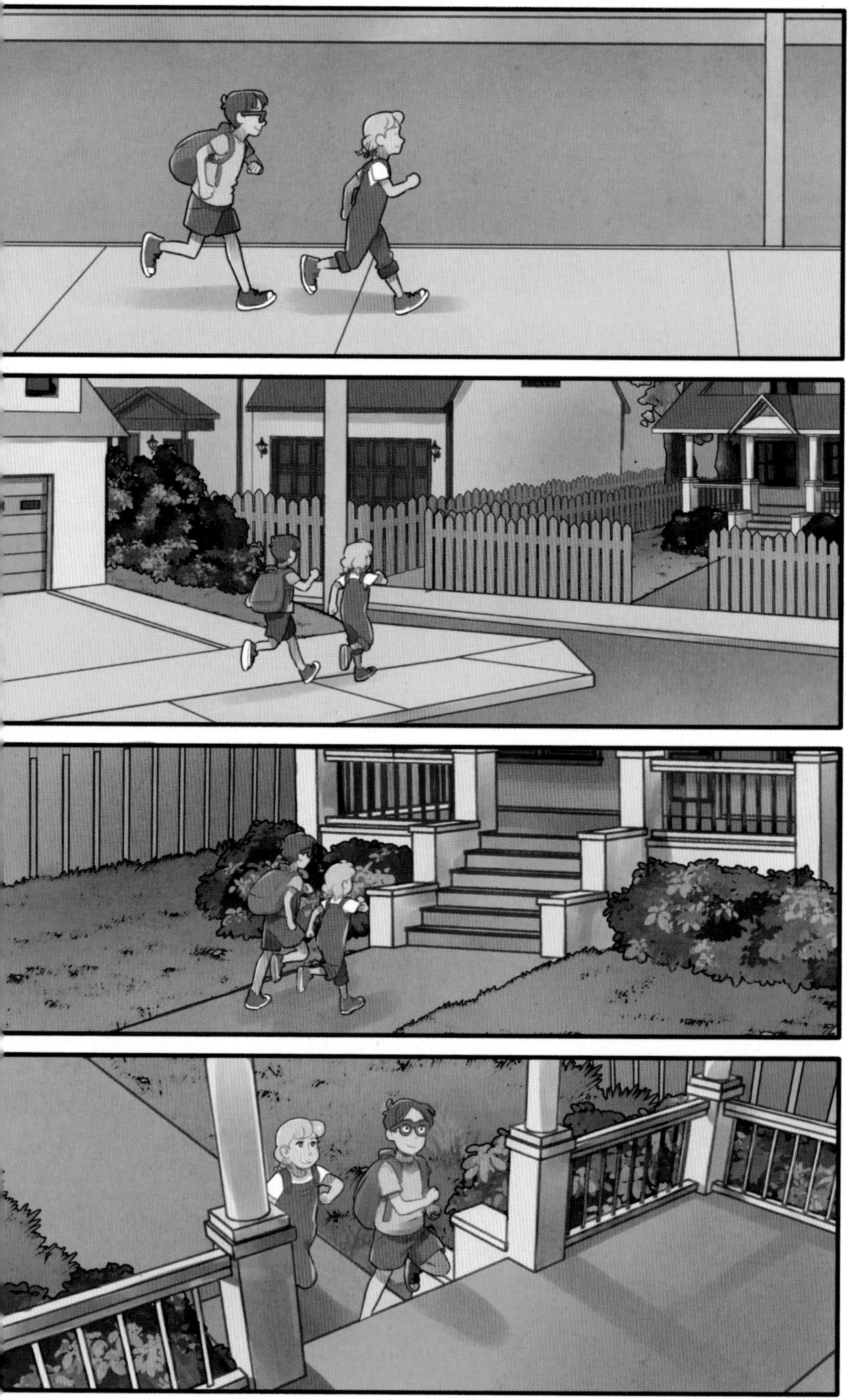

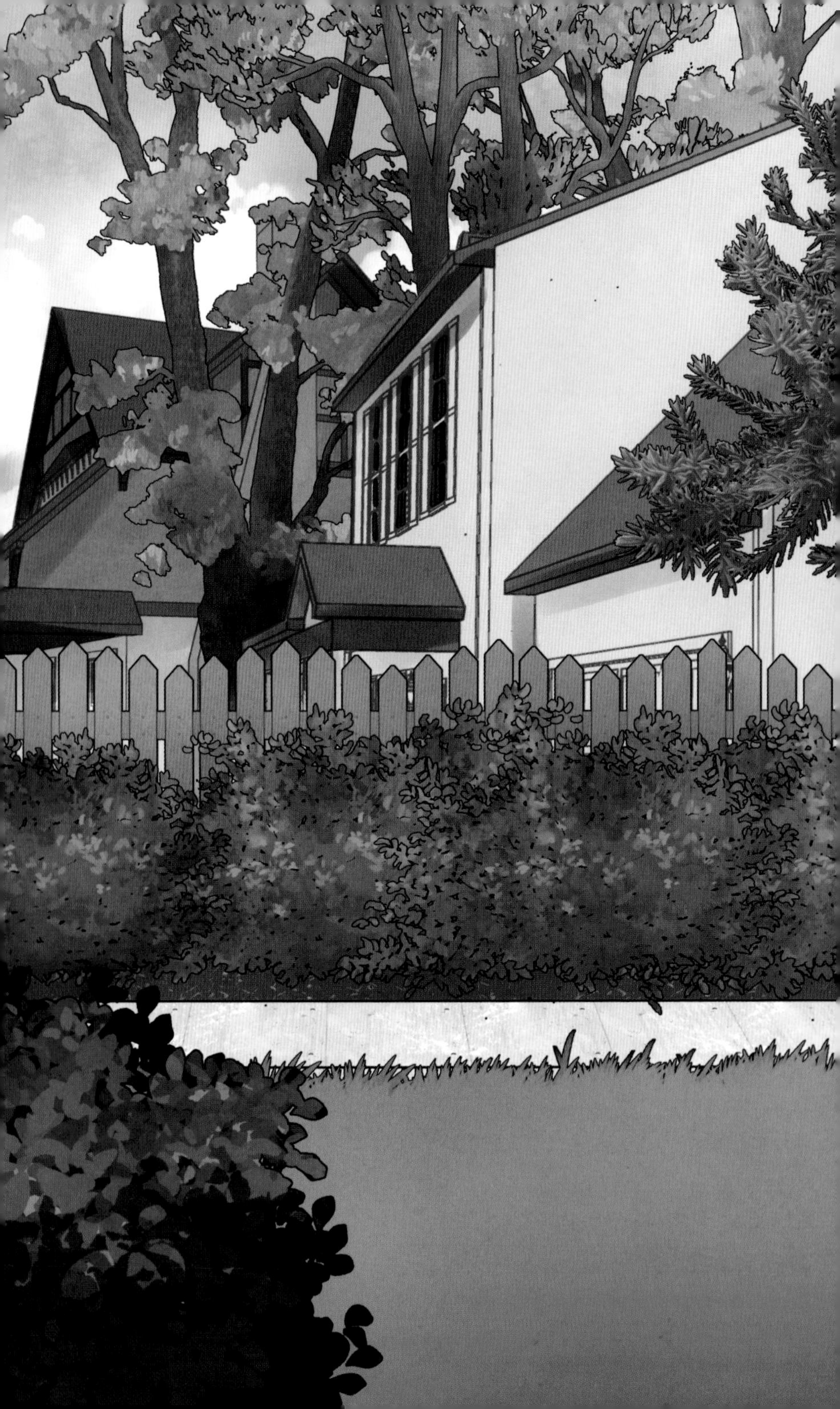

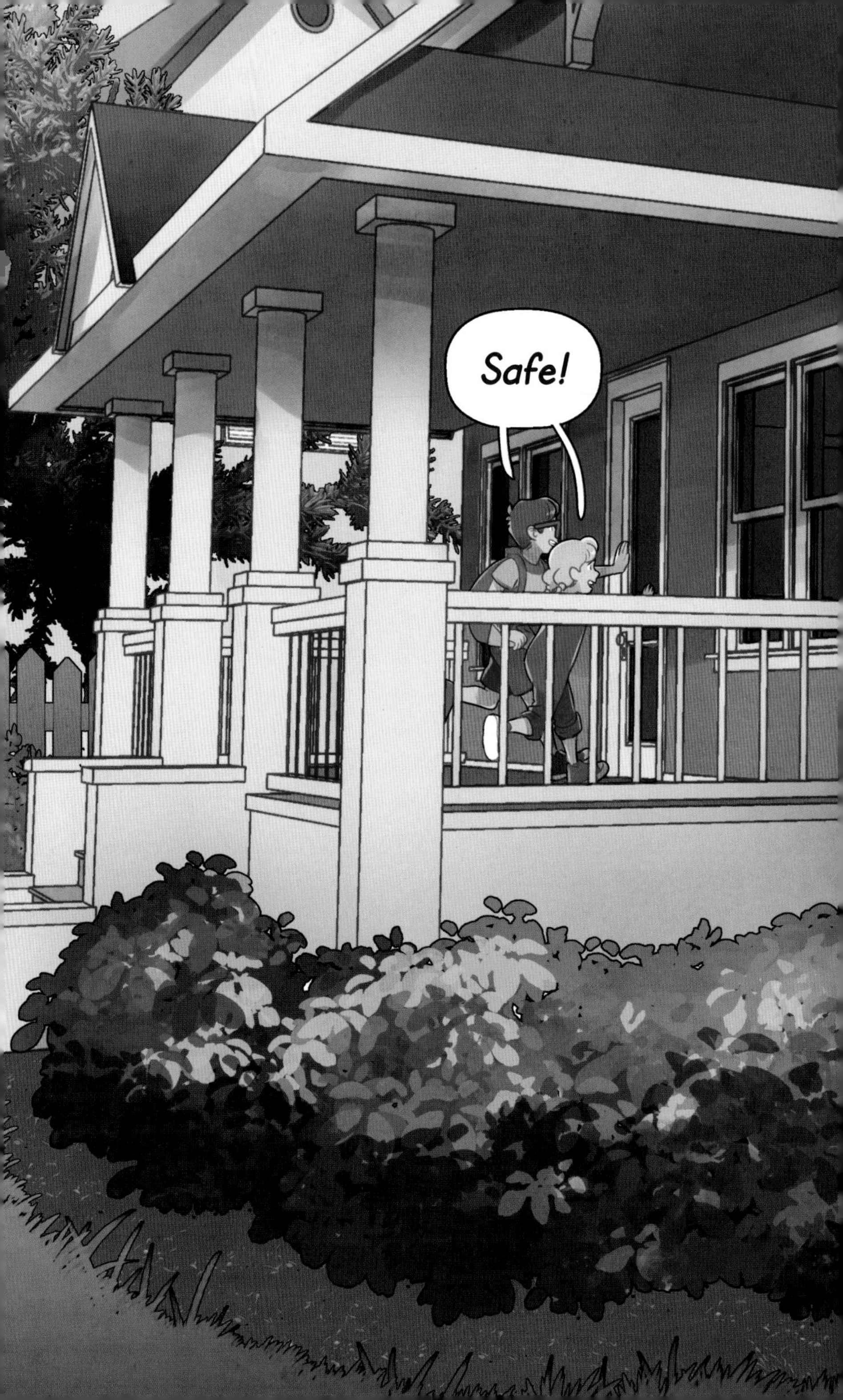
Safe!

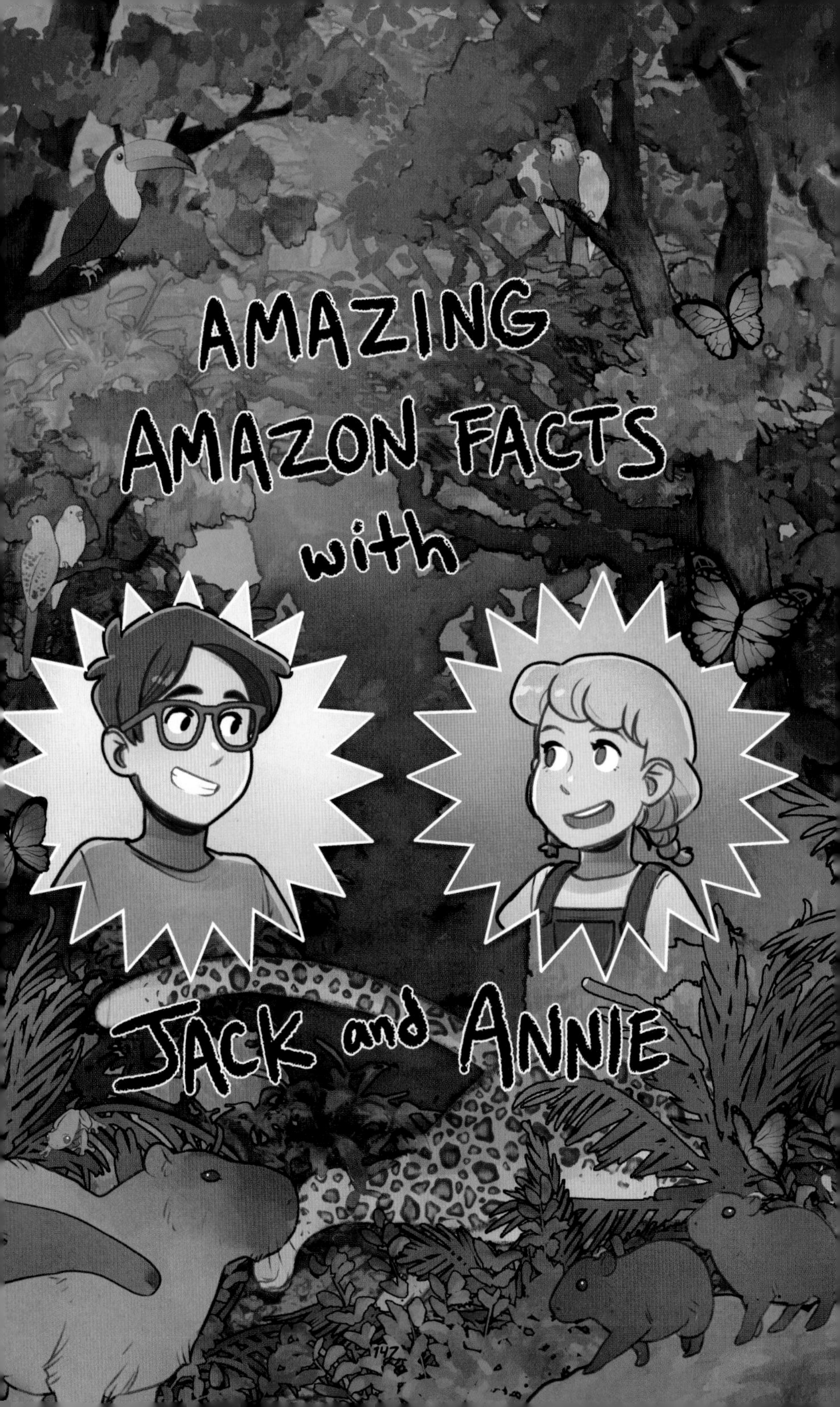
AMAZING
AMAZON FACTS
with
JACK and ANNIE

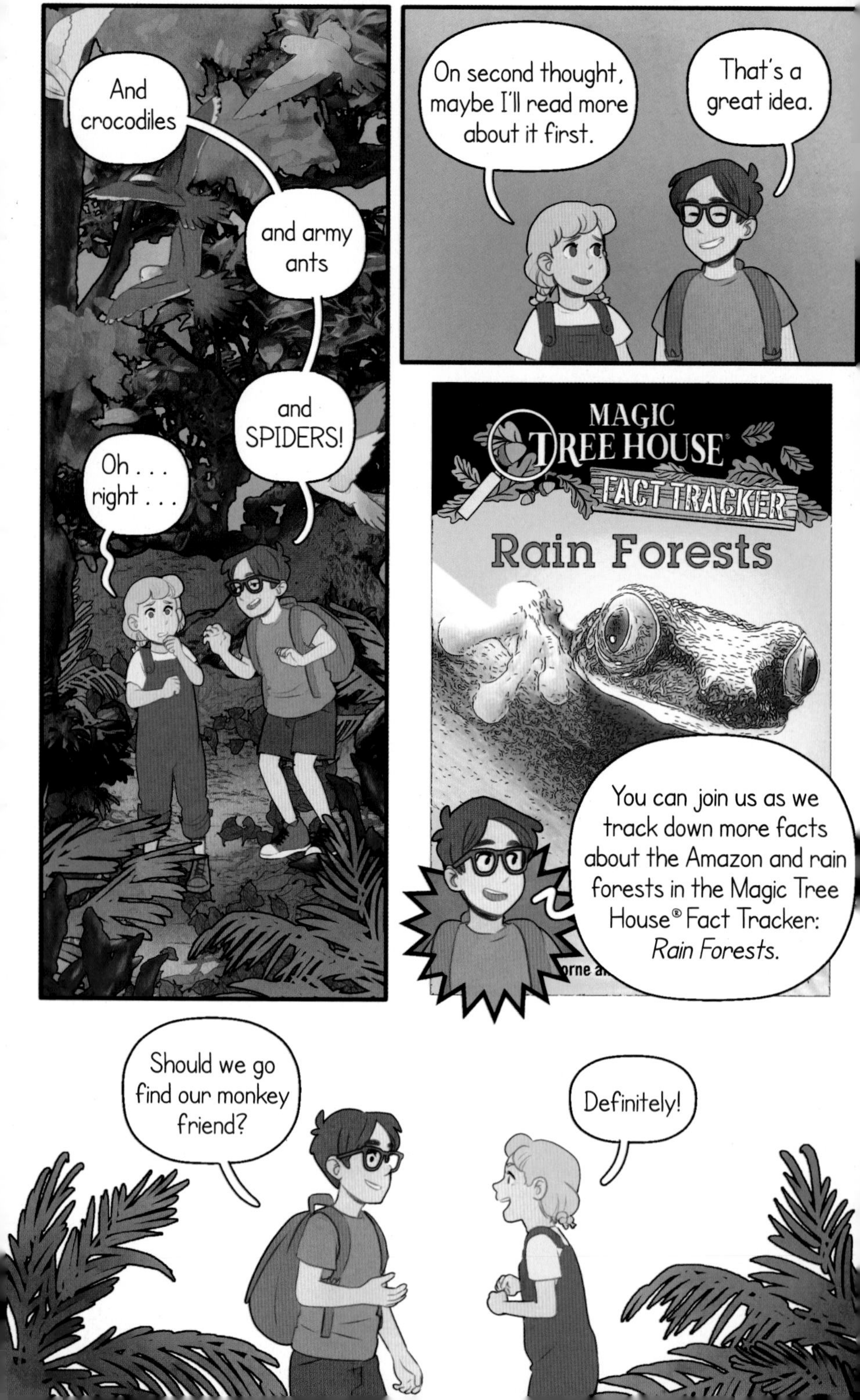
And crocodiles
and army ants
and SPIDERS!
Oh . . . right . . .
On second thought, maybe I'll read more about it first.
That's a great idea.
MAGIC TREE HOUSE®
FACT TRACKER
Rain Forests
You can join us as we track down more facts about the Amazon and rain forests in the Magic Tree House® Fact Tracker: *Rain Forests*.
Should we go find our monkey friend?
Definitely!

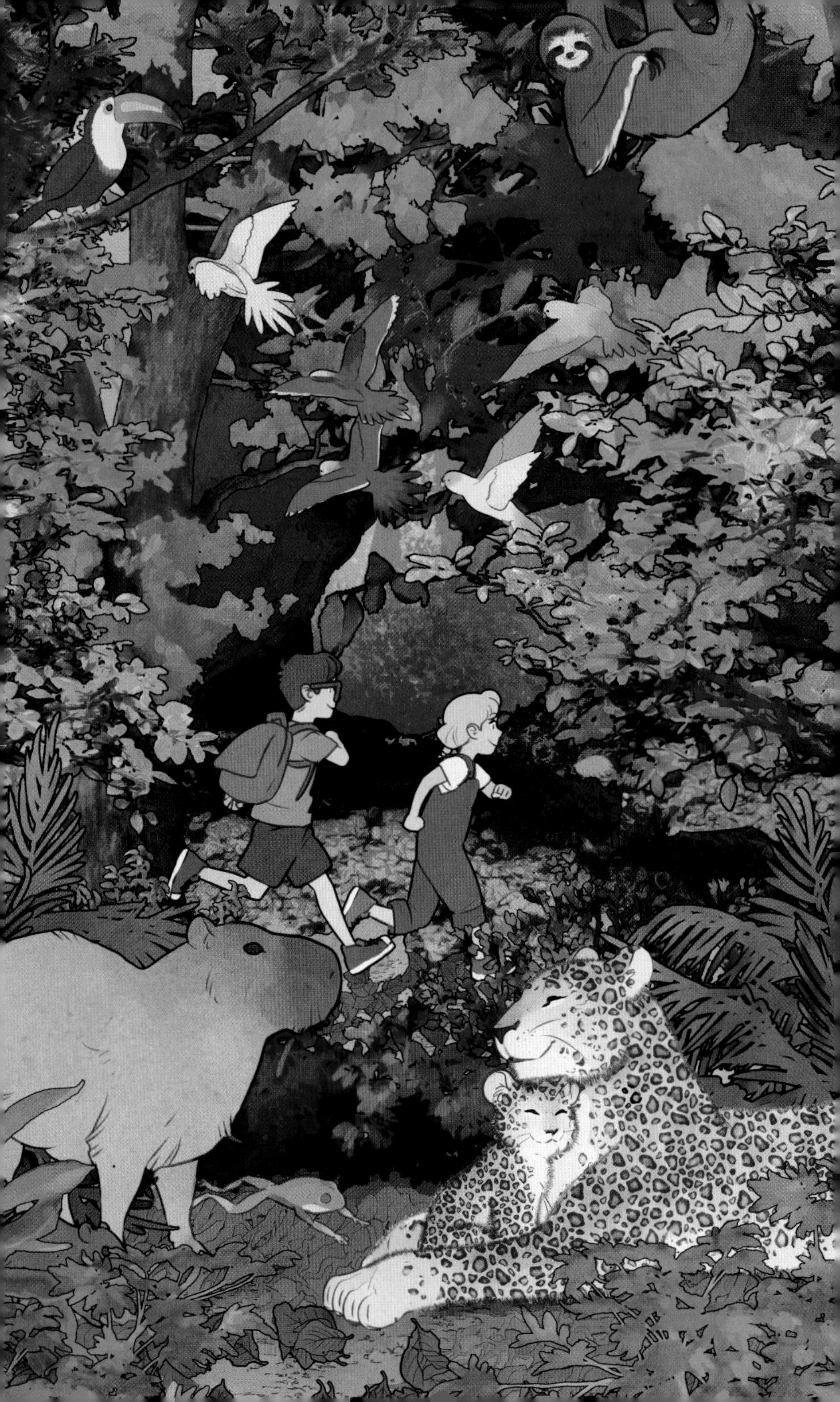

Don't miss another adventure in the Magic Tree House where Jack and Annie get whisked away to ancient Japan!

MARY POPE OSBORNE'S
MAGIC TREE HOUSE
THE GRAPHIC NOVEL
NIGHT OF THE NINJAS
ADAPTED BY JENNY LAIRD
ILLUSTRATED BY KELLY & NICHOLE MATTHEWS

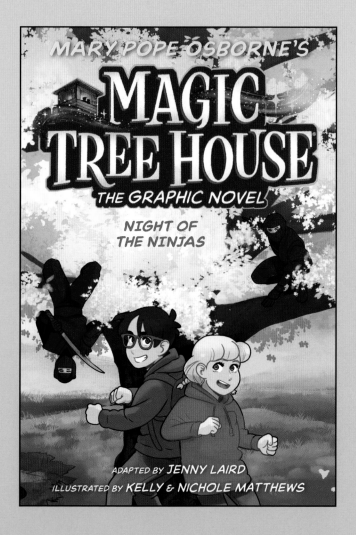

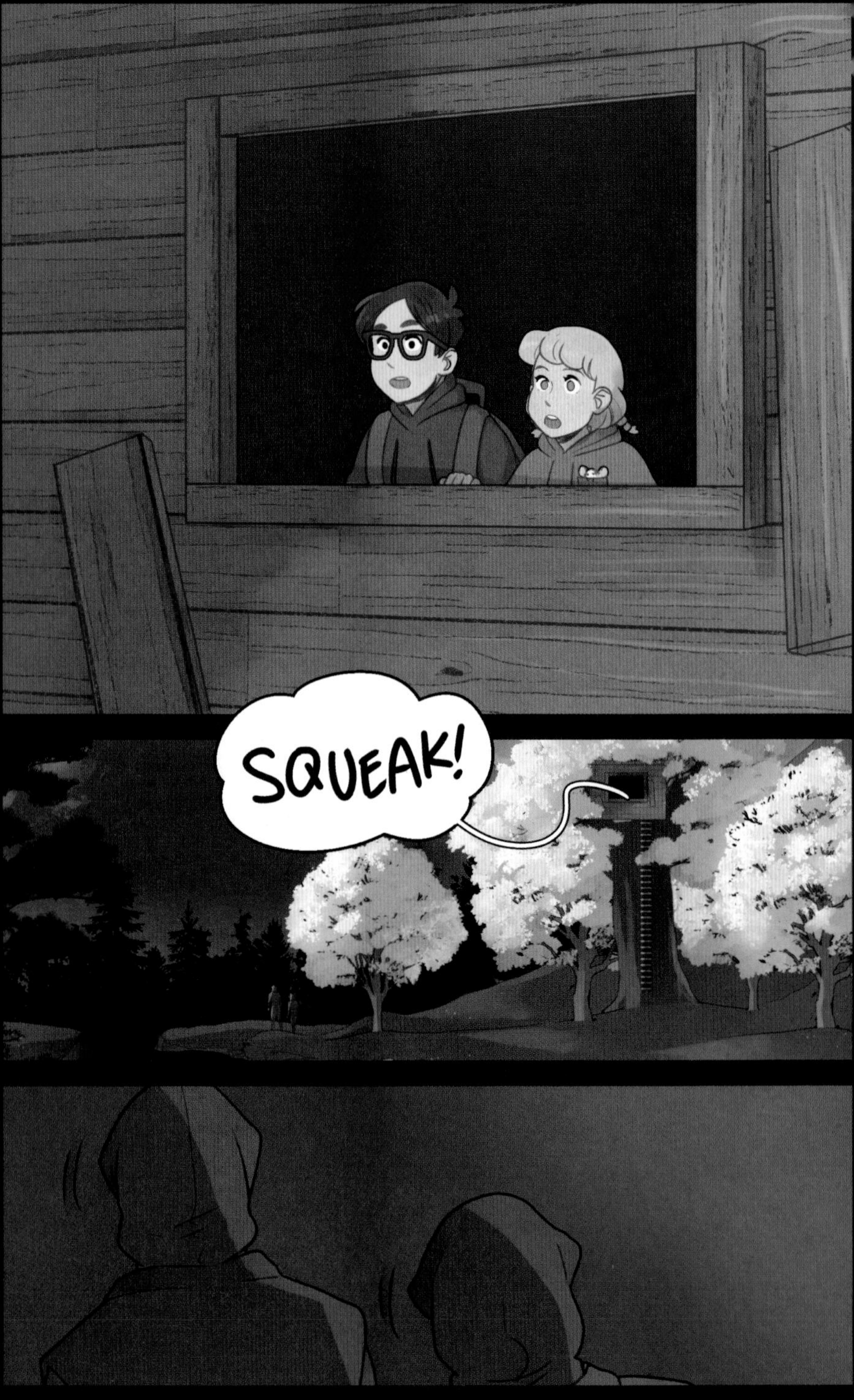
SQUEAK!

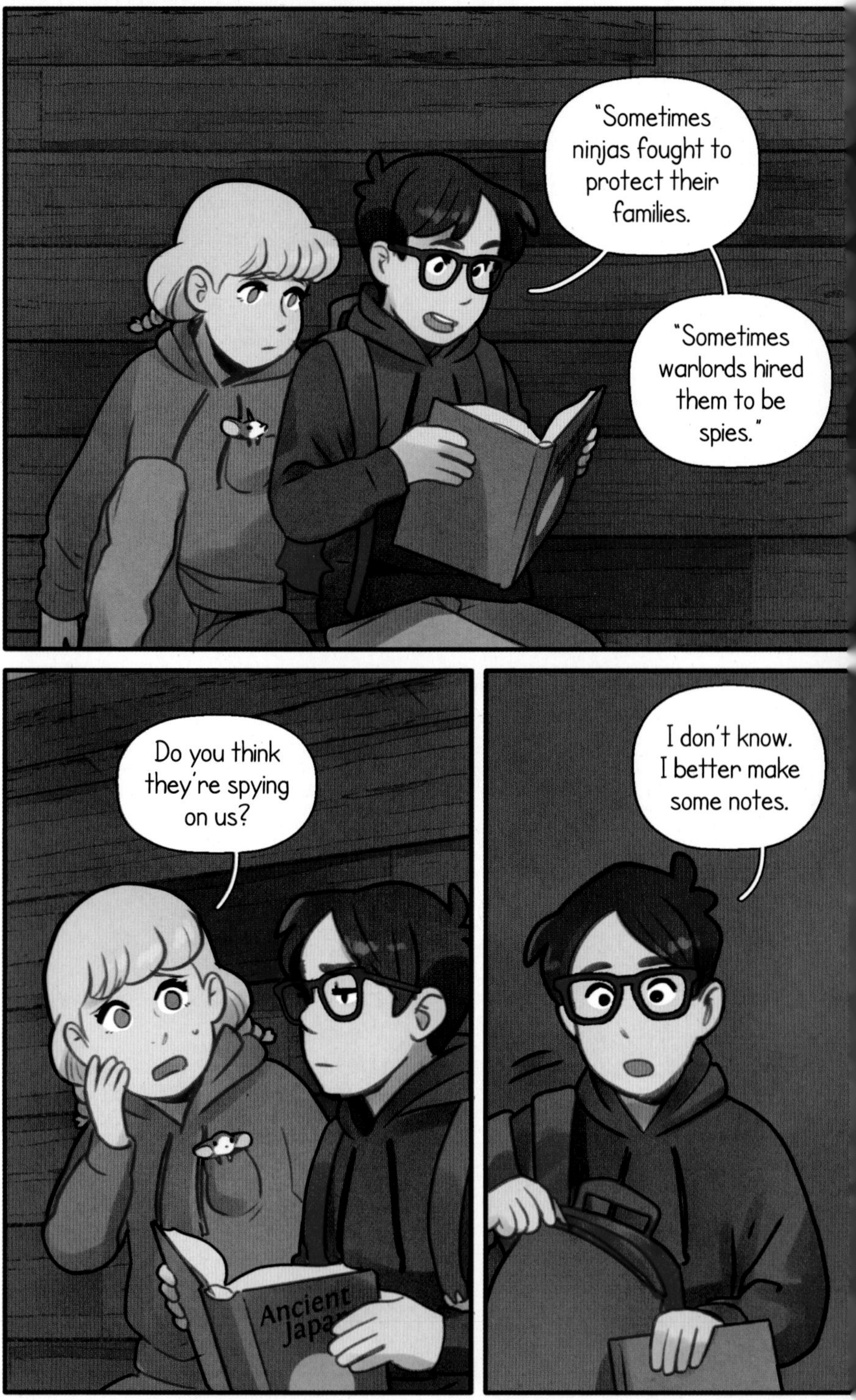
"Sometimes ninjas fought to protect their families.
"Sometimes warlords hired them to be spies."
Do you think they're spying on us?
I don't know. I better make some notes.
Ancient Japan

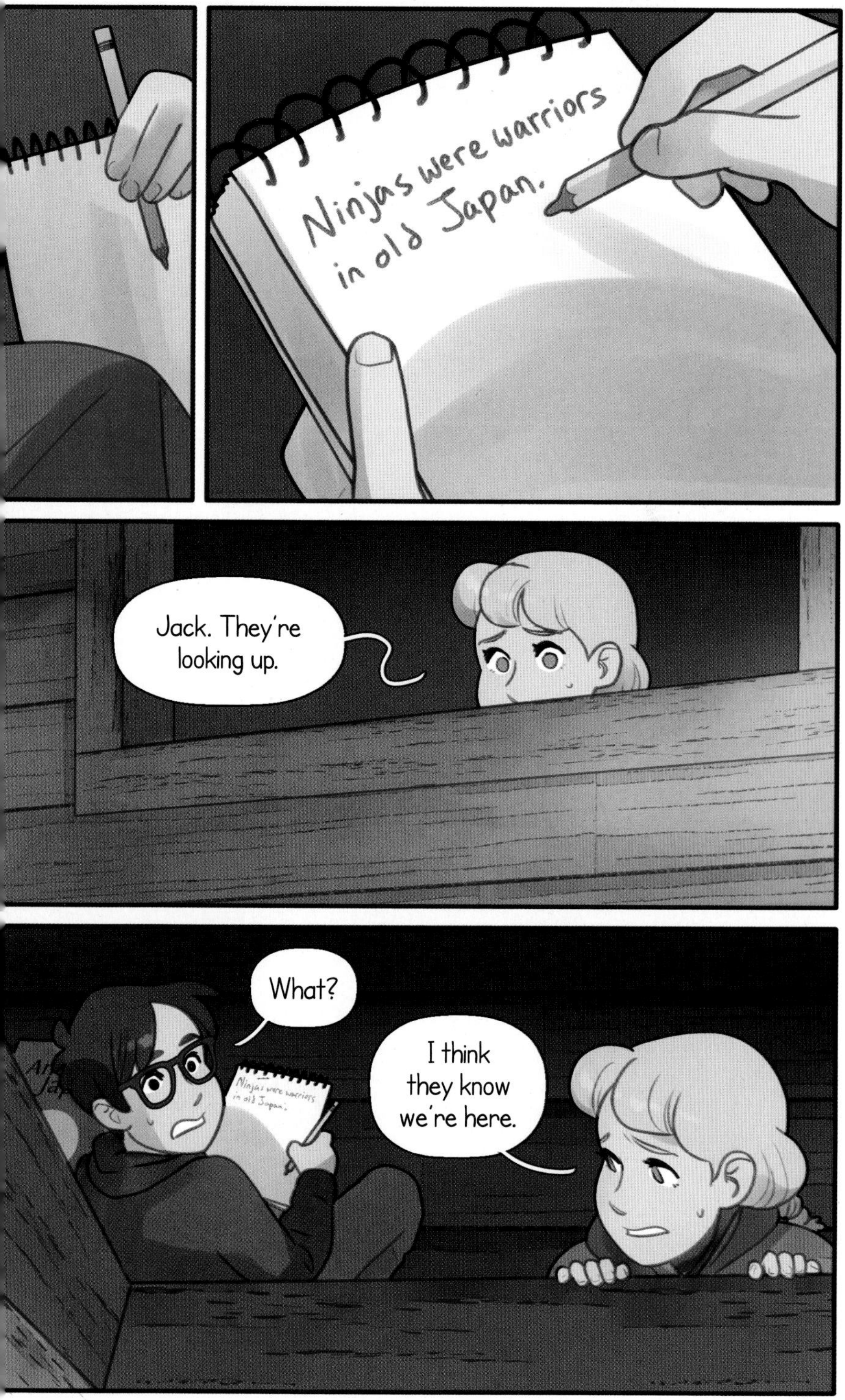
Ninjas were warriors in old Japan.
Jack. They're looking up.
What?
Ninjas were warriors in old Japan.
I think they know we're here.

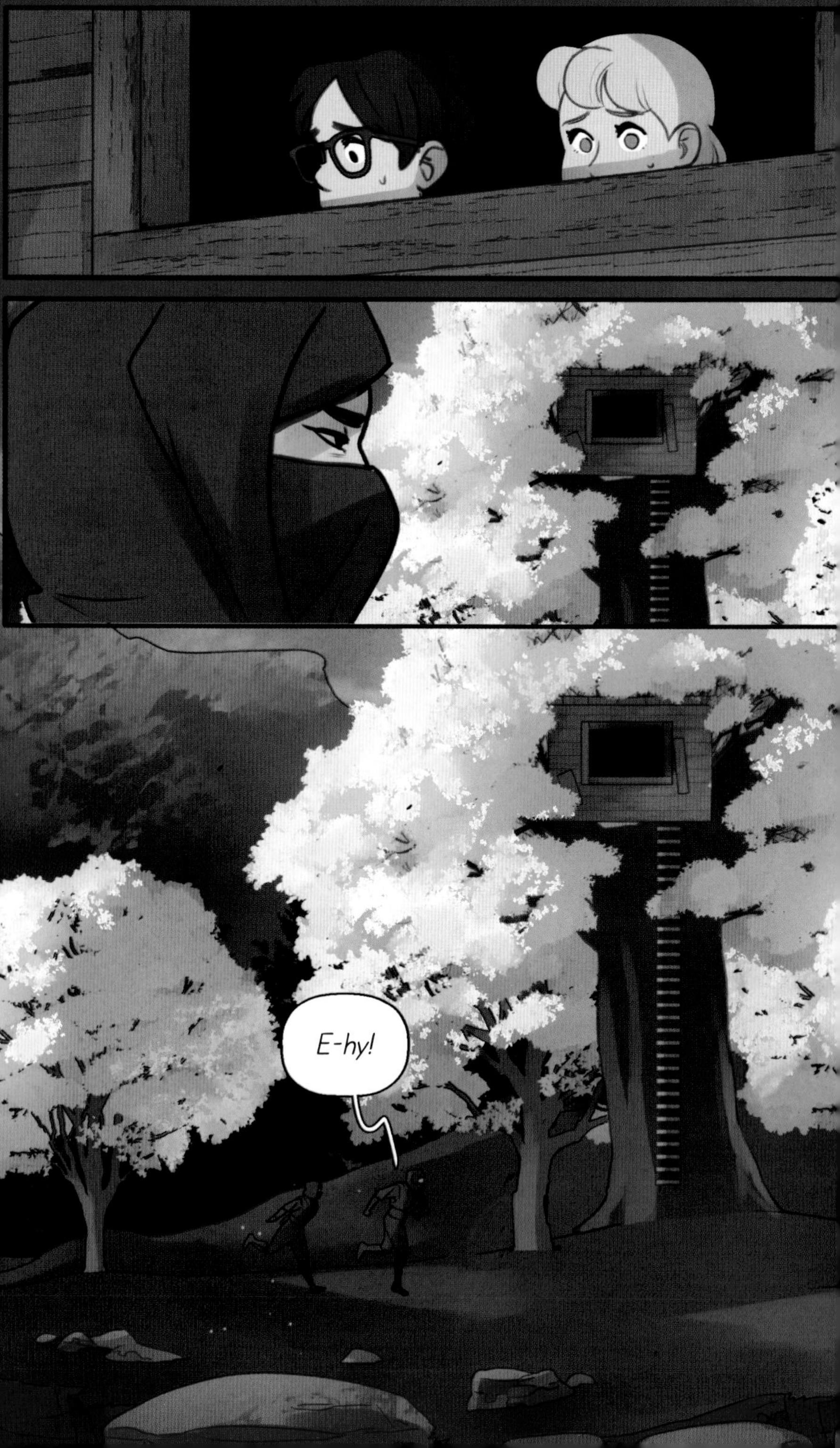
E-hy!

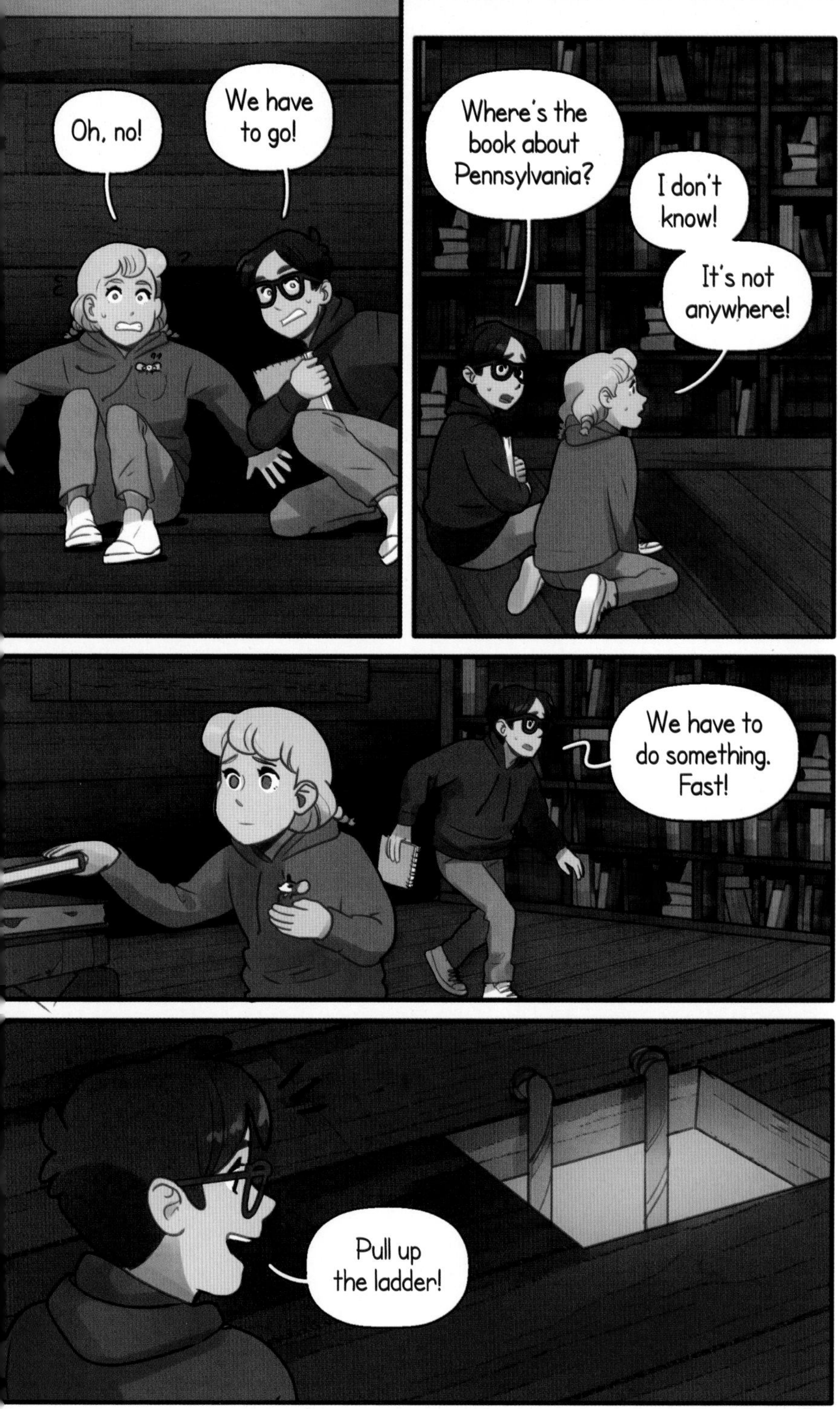
Oh, no!
We have to go!
Where's the book about Pennsylvania?
I don't know!
It's not anywhere!
We have to do something. Fast!
Pull up the ladder!

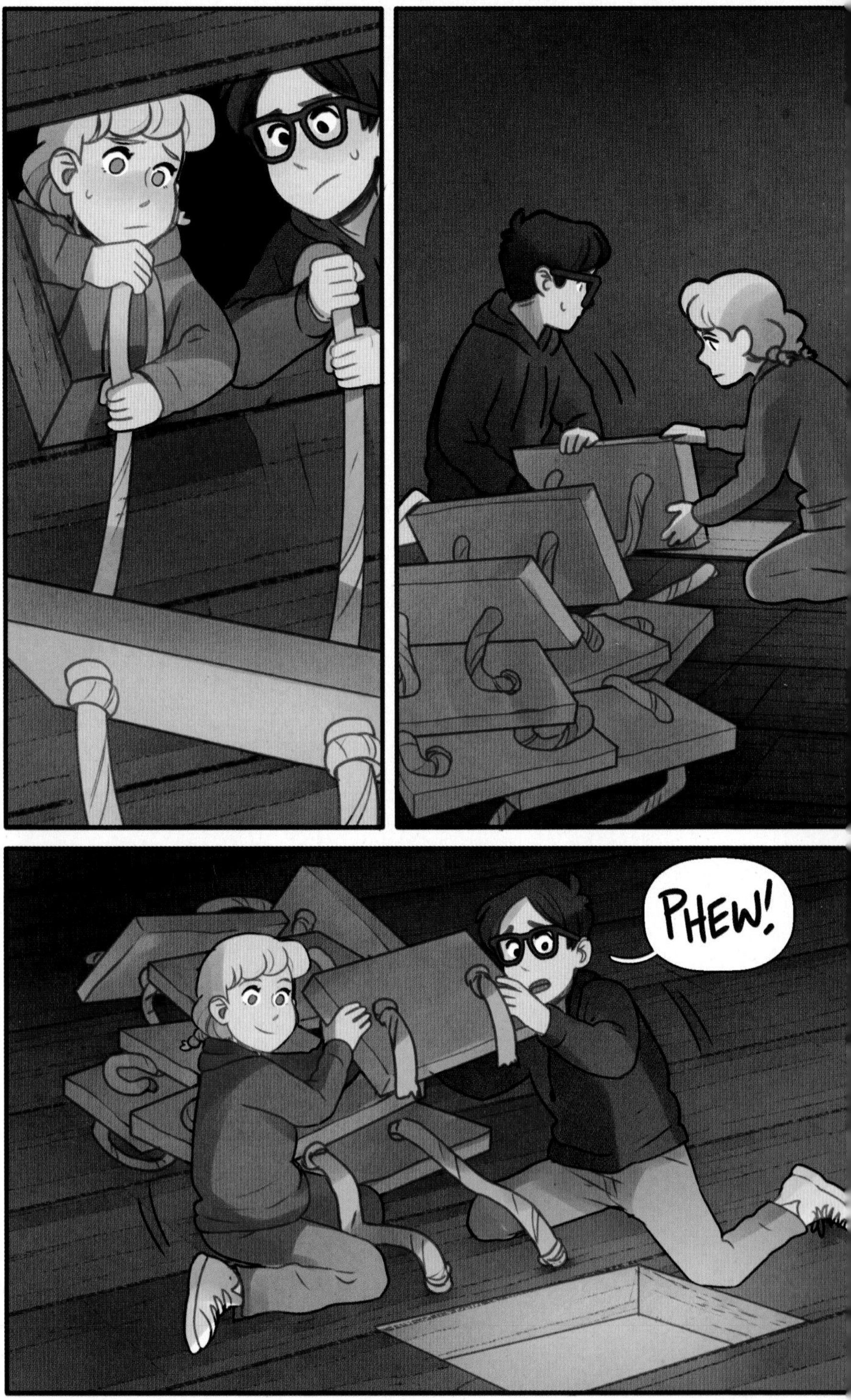
PHEW!

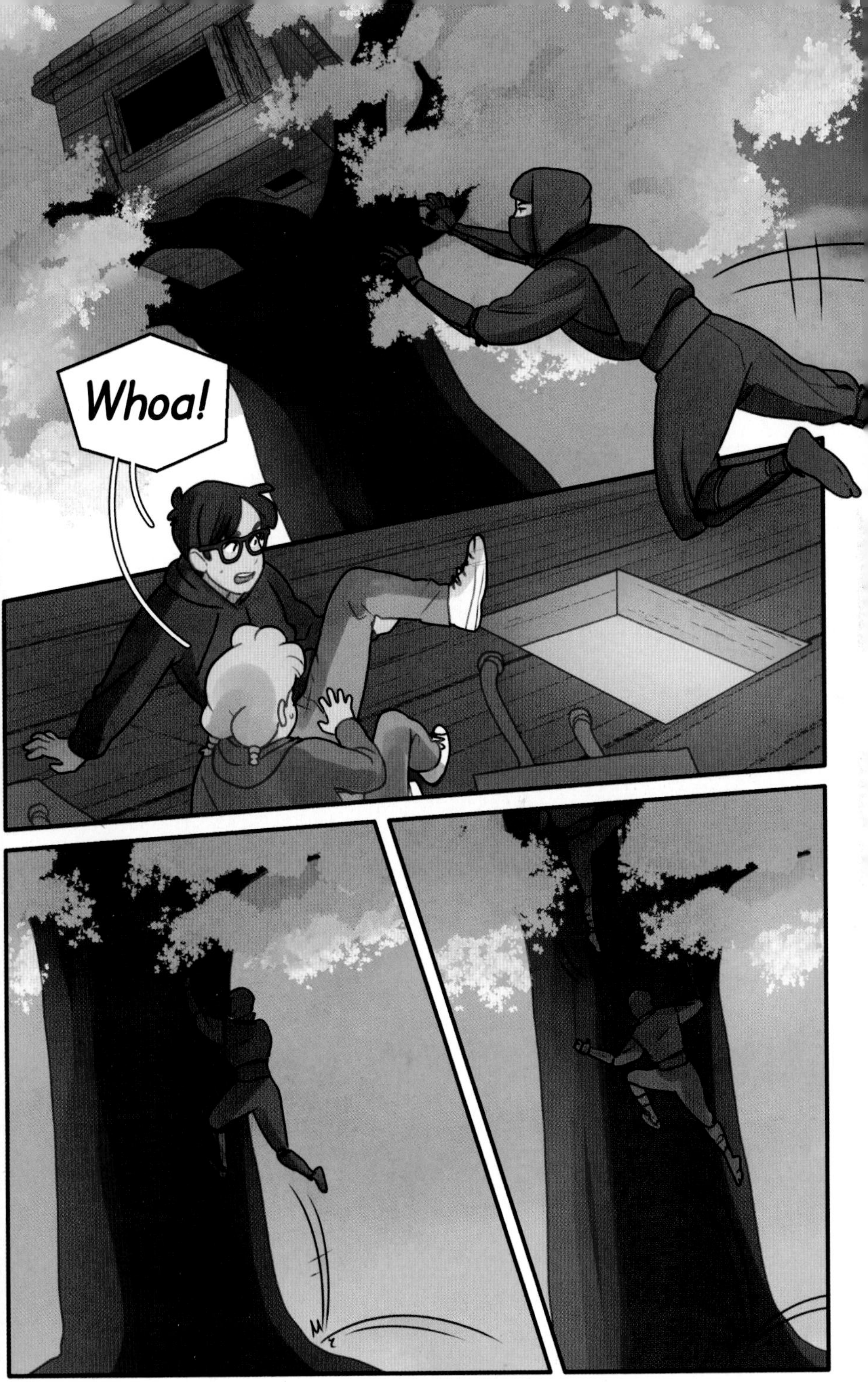
Whoa!

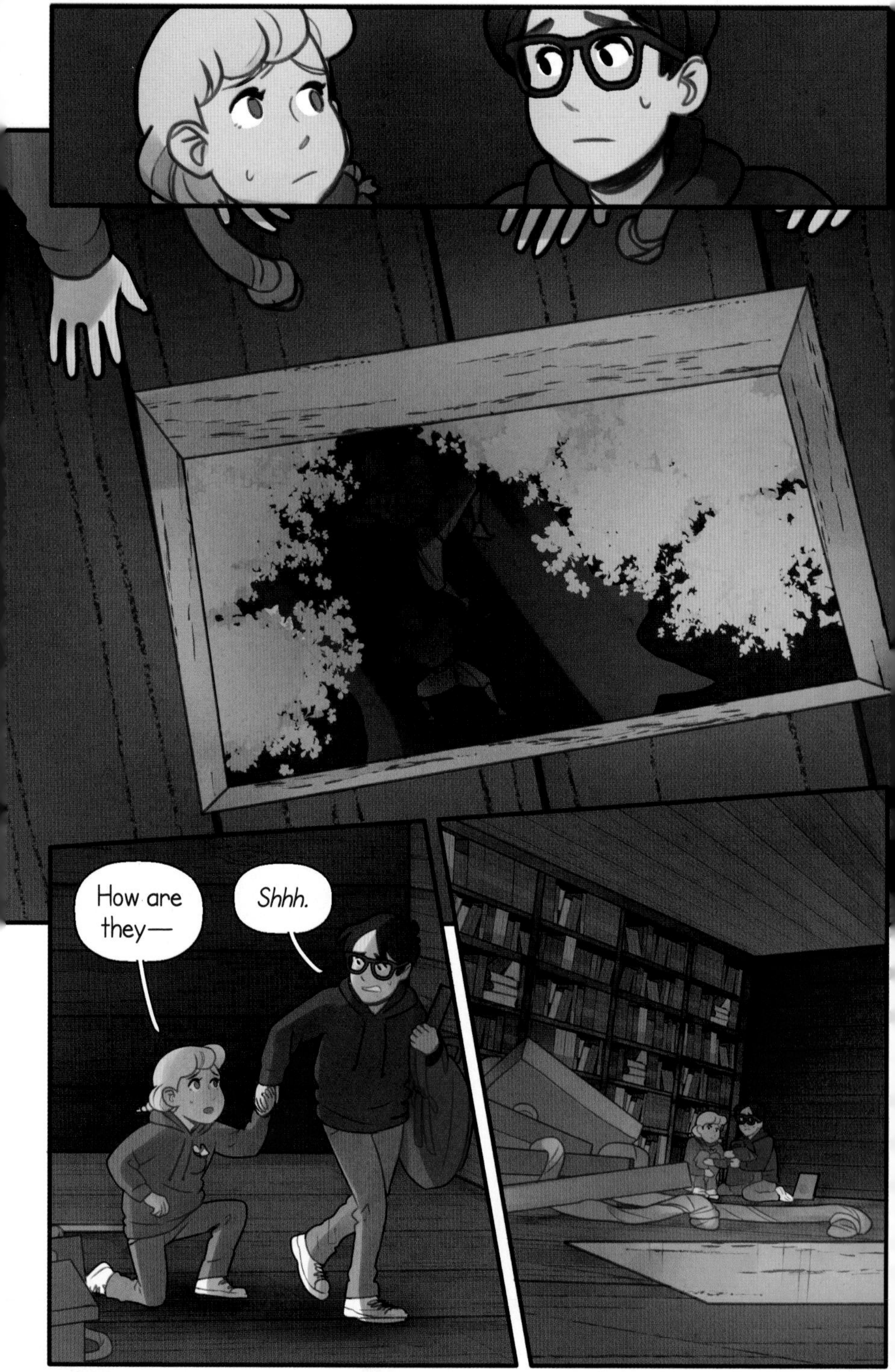
How are they—
Shhh.

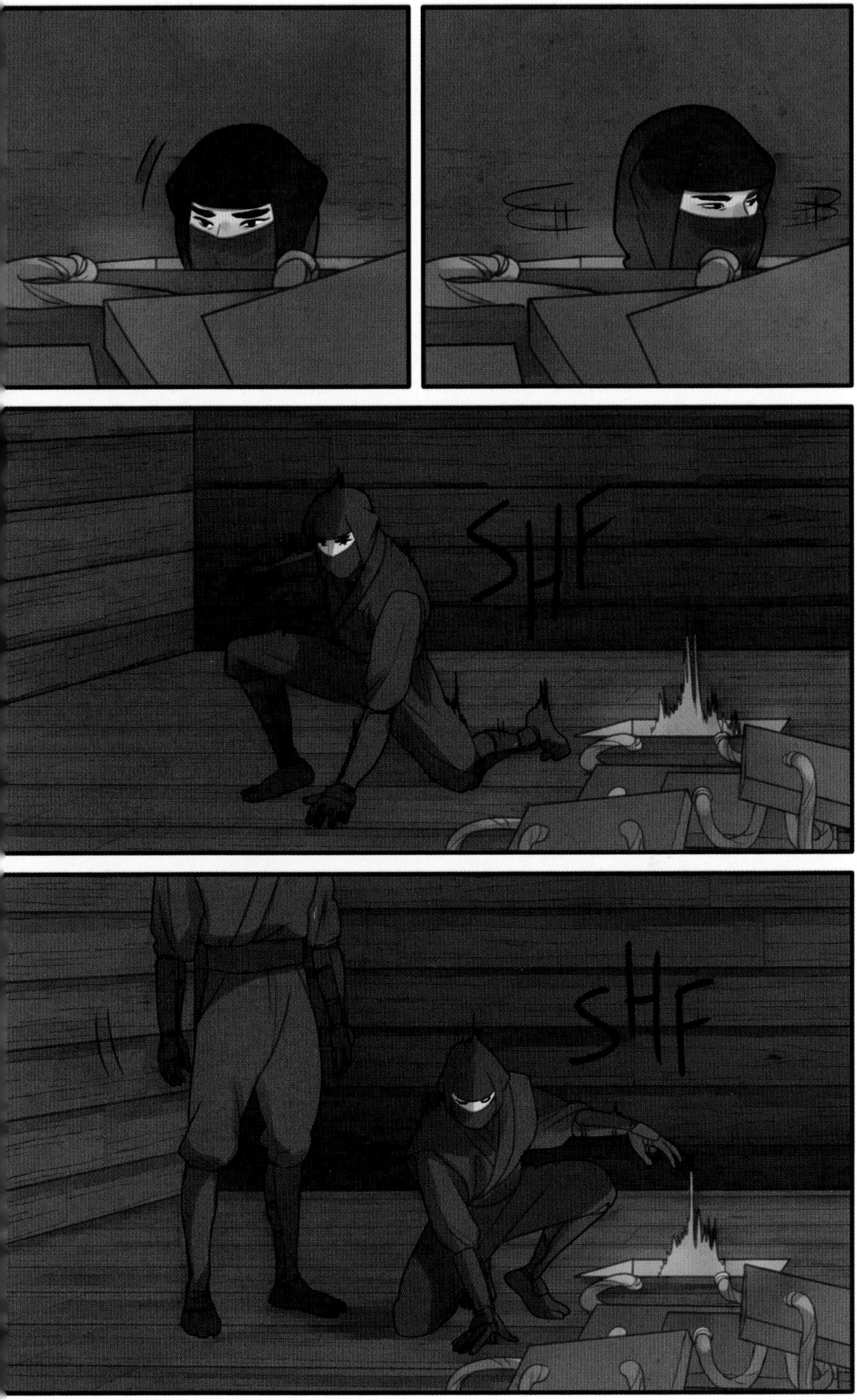
SHF
SHF

LET THE MAGIC TREE HOUSE® WHISK YOU AWAY!

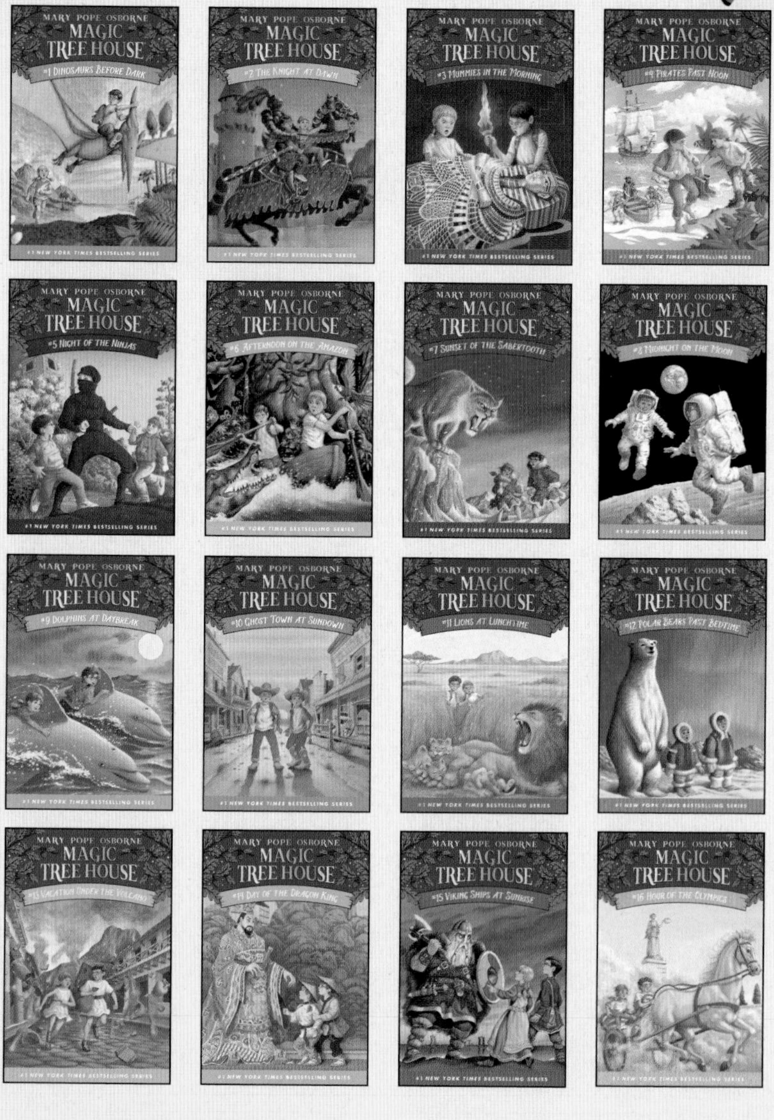
MARY POPE OSBORNE
MAGIC TREE HOUSE
#1 Dinosaurs Before Dark
#1 NEW YORK TIMES BESTSELLING SERIES
MARY POPE OSBORNE
MAGIC TREE HOUSE
#2 The Knight at Dawn
#1 NEW YORK TIMES BESTSELLING SERIES
MARY POPE OSBORNE
MAGIC TREE HOUSE
#3 Mummies in the Morning
#1 NEW YORK TIMES BESTSELLING SERIES
MARY POPE OSBORNE
MAGIC TREE HOUSE
#4 Pirates Past Noon
#1 NEW YORK TIMES BESTSELLING SERIES
MARY POPE OSBORNE
MAGIC TREE HOUSE
#5 Night of the Ninjas
#1 NEW YORK TIMES BESTSELLING SERIES
MARY POPE OSBORNE
MAGIC TREE HOUSE
#6 Afternoon on the Amazon
#1 NEW YORK TIMES BESTSELLING SERIES
MARY POPE OSBORNE
MAGIC TREE HOUSE
#7 Sunset of the Sabertooth
#1 NEW YORK TIMES BESTSELLING SERIES
MARY POPE OSBORNE
MAGIC TREE HOUSE
#8 Midnight on the Moon
#1 NEW YORK TIMES BESTSELLING SERIES
MARY POPE OSBORNE
MAGIC TREE HOUSE
#9 Dolphins at Daybreak
#1 NEW YORK TIMES BESTSELLING SERIES
MARY POPE OSBORNE
MAGIC TREE HOUSE
#10 Ghost Town at Sundown
#1 NEW YORK TIMES BESTSELLING SERIES
MARY POPE OSBORNE
MAGIC TREE HOUSE
#11 Lions at Lunchtime
#1 NEW YORK TIMES BESTSELLING SERIES
MARY POPE OSBORNE
MAGIC TREE HOUSE
#12 Polar Bears Past Bedtime
#1 NEW YORK TIMES BESTSELLING SERIES
MARY POPE OSBORNE
MAGIC TREE HOUSE
#13 Vacation Under the Volcano
#1 NEW YORK TIMES BESTSELLING SERIES
MARY POPE OSBORNE
MAGIC TREE HOUSE
#14 Day of the Dragon King
#1 NEW YORK TIMES BESTSELLING SERIES
MARY POPE OSBORNE
MAGIC TREE HOUSE
#15 Viking Ships at Sunrise
#1 NEW YORK TIMES BESTSELLING SERIES
MARY POPE OSBORNE
MAGIC TREE HOUSE
#16 Hour of the Olympics
#1 NEW YORK TIMES BESTSELLING SERIES

Read all the novels in the #1 bestselling chapter book series of all time!

TRACK THE FACTS WITH JACK & ANNIE!

MAGIC TREE HOUSE FACT TRACKER
Dinosaurs

MAGIC TREE HOUSE FACT TRACKER
Knights and Castles

MAGIC TREE HOUSE FACT TRACKER
Mummies and Pyramids

MAGIC TREE HOUSE FACT TRACKER
Pirates

MAGIC TREE HOUSE FACT TRACKER
Rain Forests

MAGIC TREE HOUSE FACT TRACKER
Space

MAGIC TREE HOUSE FACT TRACKER
Titanic

MAGIC TREE HOUSE FACT TRACKER
Twisters and Other Terrible Storms

MAGIC TREE HOUSE FACT TRACKER
Dolphins and Sharks

MAGIC TREE HOUSE FACT TRACKER
Ancient Greece and the Olympics

MAGIC TREE HOUSE FACT TRACKER
American Revolution

MAGIC TREE HOUSE FACT TRACKER
Sabertooths and the Ice Age

MAGIC TREE HOUSE FACT TRACKER
Pilgrims

MAGIC TREE HOUSE FACT TRACKER
Ancient Rome and Pompeii

MAGIC TREE HOUSE FACT TRACKER
Tsunamis and Other Natural Disasters

MAGIC TREE HOUSE FACT TRACKER
Polar Bears and the Arctic

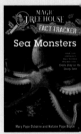
MAGIC TREE HOUSE FACT TRACKER
Sea Monsters

MAGIC TREE HOUSE FACT TRACKER
Penguins and Antarctica
Mary Pope Osborne and Natalie Pope Boyce
Leonardo da Vinci
Monday with a Mad Genius
Ghosts
A Good Night for Ghosts
Leprechauns and Irish Folklore
Rags and Riches
Kids in the Time of Charles Dickens
Snakes and Other Reptiles
Crazy Day with Cobras
Dog Heroes
Dogs in the Dead of Night
Abraham Lincoln
Abe Lincoln at Last!
Pandas and Other Endangered Species
A Perfect Time for Pandas
Horse Heroes
Stallion by Starlight
Heroes for All Times
High Time for Heroes
Soccer
Soccer on Sunday
Ninjas and Samurai
Night of the Ninjas
China
Land of the Emperor's Great Wall
Day of the Dragon King
Sharks and Other Predators
Vikings
Dogsledding and Extreme Sports
Balto of the Blue Dawn
Dragons and Mythical Creatures
Night of the Ninth Dragon
World War II
Super Edition for Readers 9-12
World at War, 1944
Baseball
A Big Day for Baseball
Wild West
Texas
Hurricane Heroes in Texas
Warriors
Warriors in Winter
Benjamin Franklin
To the Future, Ben Franklin!
Narwhals and Other Whales

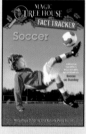

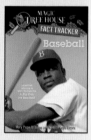

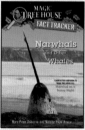

MARY POPE OSBORNE is the author of many novels, picture books, story collections, and nonfiction books. Her #1 *New York Times* bestselling Magic Tree House® series has been translated into numerous languages around the world. Highly recommended by parents and educators everywhere, the series introduces young readers to different cultures and times, as well as to the world's legacy of ancient myth and storytelling.

JENNY LAIRD is an award-winning playwright. She collaborates with Will Osborne and Randy Courts on creating musical theater adaptations of the Magic Tree House® series for both national and international audiences. Their work also includes shows for young performers, available through Music Theatre International's Broadway Junior® Collection.

KELLY & NICHOLE MATTHEWS are twin sisters and a comic-art team. They get to do their dream job every day, drawing comics for a living. They've worked with Boom Studios!, Archaia, the Jim Henson Company, Hiveworks, and now Random House!